Again The Magic

LISA KLEYPAS

Again The Magic

AVON BOOKS
An Imprint of HarperCollins*Publishers*

This is a work of fiction. Names, characters, places, and incidents are products of the author's imagination or are used fictitiously and are not to be construed as real. Any resemblance to actual events, locales, organizations, or persons, living or dead, is entirely coincidental.

AVON BOOKS
An Imprint of HarperCollins*Publishers*
10 East 53rd Street
New York, New York 10022-5299

To Mel Berger,

for being a true friend,
and for giving me the benefits of your strength,
wisdom, and talent for so many years.
Without a doubt,
getting to be one of your authors
is the luckiest thing that ever happened to me.

With love and thanks,
L.K.

One

Hampshire, 1832

A stable boy wasn't supposed to *speak* to an earl's daughter, much less climb up to her bedroom window. God knew what would happen to him if he was caught. He would probably be whipped before being booted off the estate.

McKenna climbed up a support column, curled his long fingers around the ironwork of the second-floor balcony, and hung suspended for a moment before swinging his legs up with a grunt of effort. Catching the edge of the balcony with one heel, he pulled himself onto the balcony and eased over the railing.

He crouched in front of the French doors and cupped his hands on either side of his eyes as he peered into the bedroom, where a single lamp was burning. A girl stood before the dressing table, pulling a brush through her long dark hair. The sight filled McKenna with a rush of pleasure.

Lady Aline Marsden . . . the older daughter of the Earl of Westcliff. She was warm, high-spirited, and beautiful in all ways. Having been allowed too much freedom by her inattentive parents, Aline had spent most of her short life roaming about her family's lavish Hampshire estate. Lord and Lady Westcliff were too caught up in their own social affairs to give any real consideration to the supervision of their three children. The situation was not uncommon for families who inhabited country houses like the one at Stony Cross Park. Their lives were stratified by the sheer size of the estate, as children ate, slept, and played far away from their parents. Moreover, the notion of parental responsibility did not constitute any kind of bond between the earl and countess. Neither of them was particularly inclined to worry over a child who was the product of a practical and loveless union.

Since the day that McKenna had been brought to the estate at the age of eight, he and Aline had been constant companions for ten years, climbing trees, swimming in the river, and running about barefoot. Their friendship had been overlooked because they were children. But eventually things had begun to change between them. No healthy young man could fail to be stirred and set off-kilter by Aline, who, at the age of seventeen, had become the loveliest girl on God's green earth.

At the moment Aline was already dressed for bed, wearing a nightgown made of intricately tucked and ruffled white cotton. As she moved across the room, the lamplight silhouetted the generous curves of her breasts and hips through the thin fabric, and slid over the shining sable locks of her hair. Aline's looks were the kind that caused the heart to stop and the breath to catch. Her coloring alone would have given even a homely woman the appearance of great beauty. But her features were fine and perfect, and perpetually lit with the radiance of unchecked emotion. And as if all that hadn't been quite enough, nature had added one last flourish, a tiny black mark that flirted with the corner of her mouth. McKenna had fantasized endlessly about kissing that tantalizing spot, and following it to the lush curves of her lips. Kissing and kissing her, until she was weak and shivering in his arms.

On more than one occasion McKenna had pondered the question of how a man of the earl's unremarkable looks, paired with a woman of the countess's average attractiveness, could have produced a daughter like Aline. By some quirk of fate, she had inherited just the right combination of features from each. Their son, Marcus, had been somewhat less fortunate, resembling the earl with his broad and harsh-planed face, and his bull-like physical build. Little Livia—rumored to be the result of one of the countess's extramarital affairs—was pretty but not extraordinarily so, lacking her sister's radiant dark magic.

As he watched Aline, McKenna reflected that the time was fast approaching when they could have nothing more to do with each other. The familiarity between them would soon become dangerous, if it had not already. Collecting himself, McKenna tapped gently on a glass pane of the French doors. Aline turned toward the sound and saw him without apparent surprise. McKenna rose to his feet, watching her intently.

Folding her arms across her chest, Aline regarded him with a scowl. *Go away,* she mouthed silently through the window.

McKenna was both amused and consternated as he wondered what the hell he had done now. To his knowledge, he hadn't been involved in any pranks or mischief making, and he hadn't picked any arguments with her. And as a reward, he had been left waiting alone by the river for two hours this afternoon.

Shaking his head stubbornly, McKenna remained where he was. He reached down to rattle the door handle in subtle warning. They both knew that if he was discovered on her balcony, he would bear the brunt of the consequences, not she. And it was for that reason—to preserve his hide— that she reluctantly unlocked the door and opened it. He couldn't help grinning at the success of his ploy, even as she continued to frown.

"Did you forget that we were to meet this afternoon?" McKenna asked without preamble, grasping the edge of the door in one hand. He leaned his shoulder against the narrow wood frame and smiled into her dark brown eyes. Even when he slouched, Aline was forced to crane her neck upward to meet his gaze.

"No, I didn't forget." Her voice, usually so light and sweet, was edged with surliness.

"Then where were you?"

"Does it really matter?"

McKenna tilted his head as he briefly pondered why girls liked to put a fellow through a guessing game when he was in trouble. Arriving at no reasonable answer, he resolutely picked up the gauntlet. "I asked you to meet me at the river because I wanted to see you."

"I assumed that you had changed your plans—since you seem to pre-fer someone else's company to mine." As Aline read the confusion in his expression, her mouth twisted impatiently. "I saw you in the village this morning, when my sister and I went to the milliner's."

McKenna responded with a cautious nod, recalling that he had been sent to the cobbler's by the stable master, to deliver some boots that needed repair. But why the hell would that have offended Aline so?

"Oh, don't be such a dunderhead," Aline exclaimed. "I saw you with one of the village girls, McKenna. You *kissed* her. Right there in the street, for the whole world to see!"

His brow cleared instantly. So he had. His companion had been Mary, the butcher's daughter. McKenna had flirted with her this morning, as he did with most of the girls he knew, and Mary had teased him about some-thing or another until he had laughed and stolen a kiss from her. It had meant nothing to him or to Mary, and he had promptly put the whole in-cident out of his mind.

So that was the source of Aline's irritation—jealousy. McKenna tried to hold back his pleasure at the discovery, but it gathered in a sweet, heavy mass in his chest. Hell. He shook his head ruefully, wondering how to remind her of what she already knew—that a daughter of the peerage shouldn't give a damn about what he did.

"Aline," he protested, half lifting his hands to touch her, then snatch-ing them back. "What I do with other girls has nothing to do with us. You and I are friends. We would never . . . you're not the kind I . . . damn, there's no need for me to explain the obvious!"

Aline looked at him in a way she never had before, her brown eyes filled with an intensity that caused the hairs on the back of his neck to rise. "What if I were a village girl?" she asked. "Would you do the same thing with me?"

It was the first time that McKenna had ever been tongue-tied. He had a knack for knowing what people wanted to hear, and he usually found it to his advantage to oblige them. His easy charm had stood him in good stead, whether it was to wheedle a cross bun from the baker's wife, or to get himself out of trouble with the stable master. But as for Aline's question . . . there was infinite danger in saying either yes or no.

Silently McKenna groped for some half truth that would pacify her. "I don't think of you that way," he finally said, forcing himself to meet her gaze without blinking.

"Other boys do." At his blank look, Aline continued evenly, "Last week when the Harewoods visited, their son William cornered me by the ironstone wall at the bluff and tried to kiss me."

"That arrogant little snot!" McKenna said in instant fury, recalling the stocky, freckle-faced boy who had made no effort to conceal his fascination with Aline. "I'm going to tear his head off the next time I see him. Why didn't you tell me?"

"He's not the only one who's tried," Aline said, deliberately adding fuel to the flame. "Not long ago my cousin Elliot dared me to play a kissing game with him—"

She broke off with a slight gasp as McKenna reached out and seized her.

"Damn your cousin Elliot," he said roughly. "Damn all of them."

It was a mistake to touch her. The feel of her arms, so supple and warm beneath his fingers, made his insides tighten into knots. He needed to touch more of her, needed to bend closer and fill his nostrils with the smell of her . . . the soapy scent of just-washed skin, the hint of rose water, the intimate waft of her breath. Every instinct clamored for him to pull her closer and set his mouth on the velvety curve where her neck met her shoulder. Instead he forced himself to release her, his hands remaining suspended in midair. It was difficult to move, to breathe, to think clearly.

"I haven't let anyone kiss me," Aline said. "I want you—*only* you." A rueful note entered her voice. "But at this rate, I'll be ninety years old before you ever try."

McKenna was unable to conceal his wretched longing as he stared at her. "No. It would change everything, and I can't let that happen."

Carefully Aline reached up to touch his cheek with the tips of her fingers. Her hand was almost more familiar to McKenna than his own. He knew where every tiny scar and nick had come from. In childhood her hand had been chubby and often grimy. Now her hand was slender and white, the nails neatly manicured. The temptation to turn his mouth into her soft palm was excruciating. Instead McKenna steeled himself to ignore the stroke of her fingers against his jaw.

"I've noticed the way you've looked at me lately," Aline said, a flush rising in her pale face. "I know your thoughts, just as you know mine. And with everything I feel for you, and everything you are to me . . . can't I have at least one moment of . . . of . . ." She struggled to find the right word. "Illusion?"

"No," he said gruffly. "Because soon the illusion would end, and we'd both be worse off than before."

"Would we?" Aline bit her lip and looked away, her fists clenching as if she could physically knock away the unpleasant truth that hung so insistently between them.

"I would die before I ever hurt you," McKenna said grimly. "And if I let myself kiss you once, there would be another time, and another, and soon there would be no stopping place."

"You don't know—" Aline began to argue.

"Yes, I do."

They stared at each other in wordless challenge. McKenna kept his face blank. He knew Aline well enough to be certain that if she detected any vulnerability in his facade, she would pounce without hesitation.

Finally Aline let out a sigh of defeat. "All right, then," she whispered, as if to herself. Her spine seemed to straighten, and her tone flattened with resignation. "Shall we meet at the river tomorrow at sunset, McKenna? We'll throw stones, and talk, and fish a little, as always. Is that what you want?"

It was a long time before McKenna could speak. "Yes," he said warily. It was all he could have of her—and God knew it was better than nothing.

A wry, affectionate smile tugged at Aline's lips as she stared at him.

"You had better go then, before you're caught up here. But first, bend down and let me fix your hair. It's sticking up on top."

Had he not been so distracted, McKenna would have pointed out that there was no need for her to neaten his appearance. He was going to his room over the stables, and the five dozen horses that were lodged there didn't give a damn about his hair. But he bent automatically, indulging Aline's slightest wish from sheer force of habit.

Instead of smoothing his unruly black locks, Aline stood on her toes, slid a hand behind the back of his neck, and brought her mouth to his.

The kiss affected him like a lightning strike. McKenna made an agitated sound in his throat, his entire body suddenly immobilized from a shock of pleasure. Oh God, her lips, so lush and delicate, searching his with awkward determination. As Aline had known, there was no way in hell that he could pull away from her now. His muscles locked, and he stood passively, fighting to contain the flood of sensation that threatened to overwhelm him. He loved her, wanted her, with blind adolescent ferocity. His shaky grasp on his self-control lasted for less than a minute before he groaned in defeat and clamped his arms around her.

Breathing harshly, he kissed her over and over, intoxicated by the softness of her lips. Aline responded eagerly, pressing upward, while her fingers curled into the closely shorn strands of his hair. The pleasure of holding her was too great . . . McKenna couldn't stop himself from increasing the pressure of his kisses until her lips parted innocently. He took immediate advantage, exploring the edge of her teeth, the wet silk of her mouth. That surprised her—he sensed her hesitation, and he crooned in his throat until she relaxed. He slid his hand over the back of her head, his fingers conforming to the curve of her scalp, while he sank his tongue more deeply inside her. Aline gasped and clutched his shoulders tightly, responding with a raw, unselfconscious sensuality that devastated him. McKenna longed to kiss and love every part of her, to give her more pleasure than it was possible to bear. He had known desire before, and although his experience was limited, he was not a virgin. But he had never encountered this agonizing blend of emotion and physical hunger before . . . a searing temptation that he could never surrender to.

Tearing his mouth from hers, McKenna buried his face in the shining midnight veil of her hair. "Why did you do that?" he groaned.

Aline's brief laugh was an audible ache. "You're everything to me. I love you. I've always—"

"Hush." He shook her slightly to silence her. Holding her at arm's length, he glared into her flushed, radiant face. "Don't ever say that again. If you do, I'll leave Stony Cross."

"We'll run away together," she continued recklessly. "We'll go to a place where no one can find us—"

"Holy hell, do you know how insane you sound?"

"Why is it insane?"

"Do you think I would ruin your life that way?"

"I belong with you," she said stubbornly. "I'll do whatever I have to, to be with you."

She believed what she was saying—McKenna saw it in her face. It broke his heart, even as it infuriated him. Damn her, she knew that the differences between them were insurmountable, and she had to accept that. He couldn't stay here and be faced with constant temptation, knowing that to give in would result in both their downfalls.

Cradling her face in his hands, McKenna let his fingers touch the outward tips of her dark brows, and drew his thumbs over the warm velvet of her cheeks. And because he couldn't manage to disguise the reverence of his touch, he spoke with cold bluntness. "You think you want me now. But you'll change. Someday you'll find it damned easy to forget about me. I'm a bastard. A servant, and not even an upper servant at that—"

"You're the other half of me."

Shocked into silence, McKenna closed his eyes. He hated his own instinctive response to the words, the leap of primitive joy. "Bloody hell. You're making it impossible for me to stay at Stony Cross."

Aline backed away from him at once, the color draining from her face. "No. Don't go. I'm sorry. I won't say anything else. Please, McKenna—you'll stay, won't you?"

He had a sudden taste of the inevitable pain that he would experience someday, the lethal wounds that would result from the simple act of leaving her. Aline was nineteen . . . he had another year with her, perhaps not even that long. Then the world would open up to her, and McKenna would become a dangerous liability. Or worse, an embarrassment. She would make herself forget this night. She would not want to remember what she had said to a stable boy on the moonlit balcony outside her bedroom. But until then . . .

"I'll stay for as long as I can," he said gruffly.

Anxiety flashed in the dark depths of her eyes. "And tomorrow?" she reminded him. "You'll meet me tomorrow?"

"The river at sunset," McKenna said, suddenly weary from the endless inner struggle of wanting and never having.

Aline seemed to read his mind. "I'm sorry." Her anguished whisper descended through the air as gently as falling flower petals as he climbed down from the balcony.

After McKenna had disappeared into the shadows, Aline padded back into her room and touched her lips. Her fingertips rubbed the kiss deeper into the tender skin. His mouth had been unexpectedly hot, and his taste was sweet and exquisite, flavored with apples that he must have purloined from the orchard. She had imagined his kiss thousands of times, but nothing could have prepared her for the sensual reality of it.

She had wanted to make McKenna acknowledge her as a woman, and she had finally succeeded. But there was no triumph in the moment, only a despair that was as incisive as a knife blade. She knew that McKenna thought she didn't understand the complexity of the situation, when in truth she knew it better than he.

It had been relentlessly instilled in her since the cradle that people did not venture out of their classes. Young men like McKenna would forever be forbidden to her. Everyone from the top of society to the bottom understood and accepted such stratification—it caused universal discomfort to suggest that it could ever be any other way. She and McKenna might as well have been different species, she thought with black humor.

But somehow Aline could not see McKenna as everyone else did. He was no aristocrat, but neither was he a mere stable boy. Had he been born to a family of noble pedigree, he would have been the pride of the peerage. It was monstrously unfair that he had started life with such disadvantages. He was smart, handsome, hardworking, and yet he could never overcome the social limitations that he had been born with.

She remembered the day he had first come to Stony Cross Park, a small boy with unevenly cropped black hair and eyes that were neither blue nor green, but some magical shade in-between. According to the servants' gossip, the boy was the bastard of a village girl who had run off to London, gotten herself in a predicament, and died in childbirth. The unfortunate baby had been sent back to Stony Cross, where his grandparents had cared for him until they became infirm. When McKenna reached the age of eight, he was sent to Stony Cross Park, where he was employed as a hall boy. His duties had been to clean the upper servants' shoes, help the maids carry heavy cans of hot water up and down the stairs, and wash the silver coins that had come from town, so as to prevent the earl and countess from encountering any traces of dirt that might have come from a tradesman's hands.

His full name was John McKenna, but there had already been three servants on the estate named John. It had been decided that the boy would be referred to by his last name until a new one was chosen for him . . . but somehow that had been forgotten about, and he had been simply McKenna ever since. At first most of the servants had taken little notice of him, except for the housekeeper, Mrs. Faircloth. She was a broad-faced, rosy-cheeked, kindhearted woman who was the closest thing to a parent that McKenna had ever known. In fact, even Aline and her younger sister, Livia, were far more apt to go to Mrs. Faircloth than they were to approach their own mother. No matter how busy the housekeeper was, she always seemed to have a moment to spare for a child, to bandage a hurt finger, to admire an empty bird's nest that had been found outside, or to glue the broken part of a toy back into place.

It had been Mrs. Faircloth who had sometimes dismissed McKenna from his duties so that he could run and play with Aline. Those afternoons had been the boy's only escape from the unnaturally restrained existence of a child servant.

"You must be kind to McKenna," Mrs. Faircloth had admonished Aline, when she had run to her with a tale of how he had broken her doll's painted wicker perambulator. "He has no family at all now, nor does he have nice clothes to wear, nor good things to eat for his supper, as you do. Much of the time while you are playing, he is working for his keep. And if he makes too many mistakes, or he is ever thought to be a bad boy, he may be sent away from here, and we will never see him again."

The words had sunk into Aline's marrow. From then on she had sought to protect McKenna, taking the blame for his occasional acts of mischief, sharing the sweets that her older brother sometimes brought from town, and even making him study the lessons that her governess gave her to read. And in return McKenna had taught her how to swim, how to skip pebbles across a pond, how to ride a horse, and how to make a whistle from a blade of grass stretched between her thumbs.

Contrary to what everyone, even Mrs. Faircloth, believed, Aline had never thought of McKenna as a brother. The familial affection she felt for Marcus bore no resemblance to her relationship to McKenna. McKenna was her counterpart, her compass, her sanctuary.

It had been only natural that as she developed into a young woman, she would become physically attracted to him. Certainly every other female in Hampshire was. McKenna had grown into a tall, big-boned male with striking looks, his features strong if not precisely chiseled, his nose long and bold, his mouth wide. His black hair hung over his forehead in a perpetual spill, while those singular turquoise eyes were shadowed by extravagant dark lashes. To compound his appeal, he possessed a relaxed charm and a sly sense of humor that had made him a favorite on the estate and in the village beyond.

Aline's love for McKenna made her want the impossible; to be with him always, to become the family he had never had. Instead she would have to accept the life her parents chose for her. Although love matches among the upper classes were no longer as objectionable as they once had been, the Marsdens still insisted on the tradition of arranged marriage.

Aline knew exactly what was in store for her. She would have an indolent aristocratic husband, who would use her to breed his children and turn a blind eye when she took a lover to amuse herself in his absence. Every year she would spend the season in London, followed by the country house visits in summer, and then the autumn hunts. Year after year she would see the same faces, hear the same gossip. Even the pleasures of motherhood would be denied her. Servants would care for her children, and when they were older, they would be sent away to boarding school as Marcus had been.

Decades of emptiness, Aline thought gloomily. And worst of all would be knowing that McKenna was out there somewhere, entrusting another woman with all his thoughts and dreams.

"God, what am I to do?" Aline whispered in agitation, flinging herself onto her brocade-covered bed. She clutched a pillow in her arms and dug her chin into the downy plumpness of its surface, while reckless thoughts clattered through her mind. She couldn't lose him. The thought made her shaky, filled her with wildness, made her want to scream.

Flinging aside the pillow, Aline lay on her back and stared blindly into the dark folds of the overhead canopy. How could she keep McKenna in her life? She tried to imagine taking him as her lover after she was married. Her mother had affairs . . . many aristocratic ladies did, and as long as they were discreet, no one objected. But Aline knew that McKenna would never accept such an arrangement. Nothing was half measure for him—he would not consent to share her. A servant he might have been, but he had as much pride and possessiveness as any man on earth.

Aline did not know what to do. It seemed the only choice was to steal every moment she could with him, until fate pulled them apart.

Two

After his eighteenth birthday, McKenna had begun to change with astonishing speed. He grew so quickly that he made Mrs. Faircloth exclaim in fond exasperation that it was no use in letting his trousers out, as it would just have to be done again the next week. He was ravenously hungry all the time, but no amount of food served to satisfy either his appetite or fill out his lanky, big-boned frame.

"The lad's size bodes well for his future," Mrs. Faircloth said proudly as she discussed McKenna with the butler, Salter. Their voices carried clearly from the stone-flagged hall to the second-floor balcony where Aline happened to be passing. Alert to any mention of McKenna, she stopped and listened intently.

"Indisputably," Salter said. "Nearly six feet tall already . . . I should say he'll easily attain the proportions of a footman someday."

"Perhaps he should be brought in from the stables and begin an apprenticeship as a footboy," Mrs. Faircloth suggested in a diffident tone that made Aline grin. She knew that behind Mrs. Faircloth's casual manner was a keen desire to bring him up from the lowly position of stable boy to something more prestigious.

"Heaven knows," the housekeeper continued, "we could use another pair of hands to carry coal and clean the silverplate, and polish the looking glasses."

"Hmm." There came a long pause. "I believe you're right, Mrs. Faircloth. I shall recommend to the earl that McKenna be made a footboy. If he concurs, I will order a livery to be made."

Regardless of the increase in pay and the privilege of sleeping in the house, McKenna was somewhat less than grateful for his new status. He had enjoyed working with the horses and living in the relative privacy of the stables, and now he spent at least half his time in the manor wearing a conventional full dress livery of black plush breeches, a mustard-colored waistcoat, and a blue pigeon-tailed coat. More aggravating yet was the time every Sunday when he was required to accompany the family to church, open the pew for them, dust the bench, and set out their prayer books.

Aline couldn't help but be amused by the amicable teasing that McKenna had endured from the village boys and girls who waited outside the church. The sight of their friend clad in the detested livery was an irresistible opportunity for them to comment on the sight of his legs in white stockings. They speculated loudly on whether the bulge of his calves was truly made of muscle or perhaps the "falsies" that footmen sometimes used to make their legs more shapely. McKenna maintained a suitably impassive facade, but he flashed them a glance promising vengeance, causing them to howl in delight.

Mercifully, the rest of McKenna's time was occupied with gardening and cleaning the carriages, which allowed him to wear his regular disreputable trousers and loose white shirt. He became deeply sun-browned, and although the bronze hue of his skin clearly proclaimed him to be of the working classes, it enhanced the vivid blue-green of his eyes and made his teeth look even whiter than usual. Not surprisingly, McKenna began to attract the notice of female guests at the estate, one of whom even attempted to hire him away from Stony Cross Park.

Despite the lady's best efforts to entice him, McKenna declined the offer of employment with bashful discretion. Unfortunately, that sense of tactful restraint was not shared by the other servants, who teased McKenna until he turned red beneath his tan. Aline questioned him about the lady's offer, as soon as she found an opportunity to be alone with him. It was midday, right after McKenna had finished his outdoor chores, and he had a few precious minutes of leisure before he would dress in his livery to work in the manor.

They lounged together at their favorite spot by the river, where a meadow sloped down to the banks. Tall grasses camouflaged them from view as they sat on flat rocks that had been worn smooth by the quietly persistent flow of water. The air was thick with the scents of bog myrtle and sun-warmed heather, a mixture that soothed Aline's senses.

"Why didn't you go with her?" Aline asked, drawing her knees up beneath her skirts and locking her arms around them.

Stretching out his long, lanky body, McKenna propped himself up on one elbow. "With whom?"

She rolled her eyes at his pretended ignorance. "Lady Brading—the woman who wanted to hire you. Why did you refuse her?"

His slow smile nearly blinded her. "Because I belong here."

"With me?"

McKenna was silent, his smile lingering as he stared into her eyes. Unspoken words drifted between them . . . words as tangible as the very air they breathed.

Aline wanted to curl up beside him like a drowsing cat, relaxing in the sunshine and the shelter of his body. Instead she forced herself to remain still. "I overheard one of the footmen saying that you could have gotten double the salary you earn now—only you would have to provide her with a different kind of service than you're used to."

"That must have been James talking," McKenna muttered. "Damn his loose tongue. How would he know, anyway?"

Aline was fascinated to see a blush crossing the crests of his cheeks and the heavy bridge of his nose. Then she understood. The woman had wanted to hire McKenna to come to her bed. A woman at least twice his age. Aline felt her own face begin to heat, and she let her gaze slip over the broad slope of his shoulder, down to the large hand that rested on a green-black berth of moss.

"She wanted you to sleep with her," Aline said rather than asked, breaking a silence that had become painfully intimate.

McKenna's shoulders twitched in the barest hint of a shrug. "I doubt that sleeping was her intention."

Her heart was spurred into a violent cadence as she realized that this had not been the first time that such a thing had happened to McKenna. She had never allowed herself to dwell fully on McKenna's sexual experience—the prospect was too disturbing to contemplate. He was *hers,* and it was unbearable to think of him turning to someone else for needs that she longed to fulfill. *If only, if only . . .*

Smothering beneath the weight of jealousy, Aline fixed her gaze on McKenna's big, callused hand. Some other woman knew more of McKenna than she did, than she ever would. Someone had taken his body over hers, inside hers, and had known the warm sweetness of his mouth, and the glide of his hand on her skin.

Carefully she pushed back a lock of hair that had blown across her eyes. "When . . . when was the first time you—" She was forced to stop as the words stuck in her throat. It was the first time she had ever asked about his sexual pursuits—a subject that he had always taken scrupulous care to avoid.

McKenna did not reply. Glancing up at him, Aline saw that he appeared to be lost in deep contemplation of a beetle as it climbed up a long blade of grass. "I don't think we should talk about that," he said eventually, his voice very soft.

"I don't blame you for sleeping with other girls. I expected it, actually . . . I just . . ." Aline shook her head slightly, pained and bemused as she forced herself to admit the truth. "I just wish that it could be me," she managed, while the lump in her throat expanded.

McKenna's head bent, the sunlight slipping over his dark hair. He sighed and reached out to her face, stroking back the lock of hair as it fell over her cheek once more. The tip of his thumb brushed the beauty mark near her mouth, the little black fleck that had always seemed to fascinate him so. "It can't ever be you," he murmured.

Aline nodded, while raw emotion made her mouth pucker and her eyes squint against the threat of tears. "McKenna—"

"Don't," he warned roughly, snatching his hand back, his fingers closing tightly around a pocket of empty air. "Don't say it, Aline."

"It doesn't change anything, whether I say it or not. I need you. I need to be with you."

"No—"

"Imagine how you would feel if I slept with some other man," she said in reckless misery, "knowing he was giving me the pleasure that you can't, that he was holding me in his arms at night and—"

McKenna made a growling sound and rolled over her swiftly, spreading her beneath him on the hard ground. His body was heavy and powerful, settling deeper as Aline's legs opened instinctively beneath her skirts. "I would kill him," McKenna said harshly. "I couldn't bear it." He glared into her tear-blotched face, and then his gaze moved to her flushed throat and the rapid movements of her uplifted breasts. An odd mixture of triumph and alarm filled Aline as she saw the sexual heat in his gaze, and felt the aggressive male energy of his body. He was aroused—she could feel the hard, insistent prodding between her thighs. McKenna closed his eyes, struggling to control himself. "I have to let go of you," he said tightly.

"Not yet," Aline whispered. She wriggled a little, her hips lifting against his, and the movement caused a ripple of sensation deep in her abdomen.

McKenna groaned, hanging over her, while his fingers dug into the dense layer of moss that covered the ground. *"Don't."* His voice was ragged with anger and strain and . . . something else . . . something that sounded like excitement.

Aline moved again, flooded with a peculiar feeling of urgency, wanting things she couldn't find words for. Wanting his mouth . . . hands . . . body . . . wanting to possess him and be possessed. Her body felt swollen, the tender place between her legs aching deliciously with each slow rub against the ridge of his arousal. "I love you," she said, fumbling for a way to convince him of the enormity of her need. "I'll love you until the day I die. You're the only man I'll ever want, McKenna, the only—"

Her words were smothered as he seized her mouth in a soft, open kiss. She moaned in satisfaction, welcoming the tender exploration, the tip of his tongue searching the delicate insides of her lips. He kissed her as if he were stealing secrets from her mouth, ravaging her with exquisite gentleness. Hungrily she slid her hands under his shirt and over his back, savoring the feel of flexing muscle and the sleekness of his skin. His body was so hard, sculpted muscle overlaying steel—a body so faultless and hale that she was awed by him.

His tongue entered her mouth more deeply, causing her to whimper at the subtle gradations of ever-increasing pleasure. His arms curved around her protectively, and he shifted his weight to keep from crushing her, even as he continued to devour her with sweet, soul-stealing kisses. His breath was unsettled and much too fast, as if he had run for miles without stopping. Aline pressed her lips against his throat, discovering that the driving pace of his heart matched her own. He knew, as she did, that every moment of forbidden intimacy came with a price that neither of them could afford. Inflamed beyond the point of caution, McKenna reached for the buttons at the front of her gown, then hesitated as he struggled once more with his conscience.

"Go on," Aline said thickly, her heart thundering in her chest. She kissed the hard line of his jaw, his cheeks, every part of his face that she could reach. Finding a sensitive spot on the side of his neck, she concentrated on the vulnerable place until his entire body quivered. "Don't stop," she whispered feverishly. "Don't stop yet. No one can see. McKenna, please love me . . . love me . . ."

The words seemed to erode his will to resist, and he made a rough sound as his fingers worked quickly at the row of buttons. She wore no corset, nothing but a thin lawn chemise that clung to the round curves of her breasts. After spreading her bodice open, McKenna tugged the chemise down, exposing the soft pink tips of her nipples. Aline stared up into his tense face, relishing his absorbed expression, the way his eyes had narrowed in passion. He touched her breast, his fingers curving beneath the pale weight, his thumb passing delicately over the peak until it contracted. He bent over her, circled the aroused nipple with lazy strokes of his tongue. Aline gasped in pleasure, her thoughts catching fire and burning to ashes as he drew her fully into his mouth. He tugged and licked steadily, until heat gathered in every part of her, and the place between her thighs had begun to throb in fervid demand. Letting out a shivering breath, McKenna pressed his cheek against the naked curve of her breast.

Unable to stop herself, Aline slipped her fingers into the waist of his trousers, past the fasteners of his braces. The surface of his stomach was tightly muscled, the skin satin-smooth except for the sprinkling of coarse hair beneath the hollow of his navel. Her hand shook as she searched for the first button of the trousers. "I want to touch you," she whispered. "I want to feel you there—"

"Hell, *no,*" McKenna muttered, catching her wrists in his hands and dragging them over her head. His turquoise eyes were brilliant as his hot gaze traveled from her mouth to her breasts. "For God's sake, I can barely control myself as it is. If you touch me, I won't be able to stop myself from finishing this."

She writhed helplessly beneath him. "I want you to."

"I know that," McKenna muttered, bending to blot his gleaming forehead on his sleeve, while maintaining his careful hold on her wrists. "But I'm not going to. You have to stay a virgin."

Aline tugged almost angrily at her imprisoned arms. "I'll do as I please, and be damned to everyone!"

"Brave words," he mocked gently. "But I'd like to hear what you'd tell your husband on your wedding night, when he discovered your maidenhood had already been taken."

The quaint sound of the word "maidenhood" made Aline smile grimly despite her misery. Virginity . . . the only thing the world seemed to expect of her. Relaxing beneath him, she let her wrists go lax in his grip. She stared into his eyes, feeling as if the entire world was covered in shadow, and he was the only source of light. "I'll marry no one but you, McKenna," she whispered. "And if you ever leave me, I'll be alone for the rest of my life."

His dark head lowered over hers. "Aline," he said in the hushed voice that he might have used in prayer. "I would never leave unless you told me to go."

His mouth descended to her bare breasts. Aline pushed upward impulsively, offering herself without reservation, crying out as he took a hard, budded nipple into his mouth. He wet the rosy flesh with his tongue, swirling and flicking until she moaned in frustration. "McKenna," she said fitfully, tugging in vain at her trapped arms, "I need you . . . please do something, I'm aching so . . ."

He shifted his long body so that he could pull up the front of her skirts. The thickness of his erection strained behind his trousers as it pressed against her hip. Aline longed to touch him, to explore his body with the same tenderness he showed her, but he wouldn't let her. He reached beneath the layers of muslin and lace-trimmed lawn, and found the waist of her drawers. Deftly he untied the tapes that fastened the garment, then paused to stare into her half-closed eyes.

"I should stop." His warm hand settled on her stomach, over the drawers. "This is too dangerous, Aline." He pressed his forehead to hers, until their perspiration mingled and their breath filled each other's mouths in warm, tender puffs. "Oh God, how I love you," he said huskily.

The weight of his hand made her shiver. Instinctively she spread her thighs and nudged upward strongly, trying to bring his fingers where she needed them most. With great care he reached beneath the veil of thin cotton, touching between her wide-open legs. He fondled the patch of springy curls, his fingertips tenderly burrowing to find the plump mound beneath. Aline gasped against his mouth as he parted her swollen flesh, spreading the soft folds to find the opening of her body. She burned with equal parts of embarrassment and excitement, turning her face to the side as his gentle exploration continued. He was familiar with the intricacies of a woman's flesh, knowing exactly where she was most sensitive, his fingertips skating over the aching peak of her sex with incredible lightness. His calluses rasped the wet skin, the sensation so sweet and delicately maddening that she let out another shaking cry.

"Hush," McKenna murmured, caressing all around the aroused bud, while his head lifted as he surveyed the meadow beyond the tall grasses. "Someone might hear."

Aline bit her lip as she fought to obey, though small whimpers kept slipping from her throat. McKenna continued to watch for uninvited company, his alert gaze skimming the estate grounds at the edge of the meadow. His middle finger found the barrier of her virginity and kneaded the fragile impediment until it softened. Aline closed her eyes against the glare of sunlight, offering no resistance as McKenna used his knees to push her legs wider, until the insides of her thighs were stretched and taut. He entered her with his finger, pausing as he felt her jerk with surprise. His mouth touched her forehead, and he whispered against her damp silken skin. "Sweetheart . . . I won't hurt you."

"I know, it's just . . ." She forced herself to lie passively beneath him as she felt his finger glide further inside. Her voice caught with a low throb. "It feels so str-strange . . ."

McKenna pushed it all the way to the second knuckle, and stroked the sleek inner walls, while her body automatically grasped and clung to the gentle invasion. Groaning as he felt the frantic throbbing of her flesh, McKenna fitted the heel of his hand against the tingling peak of her sex. He began a slow, rocking motion, his finger thrusting deeper, his hand nudging her rhythmically.

"Oh . . ." Aline couldn't stop from hitching upward in slavish obedience to the provocations of his hand. "Oh, McKenna . . ."

He slid his free arm beneath her back, lifting her breasts as he kissed her breasts again, his tongue playing over the stiff tips. A swell of sensation rose, then retreated to leave her moaning with excitement. McKenna didn't falter, caressing her steadily, his teeth catching at her nipples until they turned redder, harder. Aline concentrated on the deep slide of his finger, the coiling, clenching pleasure that went through her loins and spine, until she lost awareness of everything but his hands, his mouth, his heavy body poised over hers. She imagined his sex plunging into her, rending and stretching and filling her . . . and suddenly she couldn't move as voluptuous spasms began to roll through her . . . waves of relief so intense that she wailed from it, while his mouth hastily covered hers to muffle all sound. Shuddering and sobbing, she rode the pleasure to its dizzying summit, then drifted downward while his slick fingers eased her into tranquillity.

Murmuring quietly, McKenna held and stroked her until she went limp beneath him, her limbs turning heavy and warm. His hand began to withdraw from her drenched sex, but she reached down and covered his fingers with her own. "Come inside me," she whispered. "I want you so, McKenna. Come in me, come—"

"No," he said through clenched teeth. He rolled away with a groan, his fingers biting into the damp earth and dislodging great fistfuls of moss. "Cover yourself. I can't touch you anymore, or I won't be able to stop myself from—" He broke off with a shuddering sound that betrayed how very close he was to taking her. "Pull down your skirts. Please."

"I want you," she said breathlessly.

"Now. I mean it, Aline."

She didn't dare disobey, not when she could hear that biting note in his voice. Heaving a sigh, she struggled to restore her clothing. After a while McKenna rested on his side to watch her. He seemed to have regained control over himself, though his eyes were still bright with unspent passion.

Aline shook her head with a wistful smile. "No one will ever look at me the way you do. As if you love me with every part of yourself."

Slowly he reached out and tucked a lock of hair behind her ear. "That's how you look at me too."

She caught at his hand and kissed the rough surface of his knuckles. "Promise me that we'll be together always."

But he remained silent, for they both knew it was a promise that he couldn't make.

Aline knew that the safest thing would be to pretend those passion-filled minutes by the river had never existed. It was impossible, however. Whenever McKenna was nearby, she felt her entire body thrilling to his presence. Emotions seemed to spill from her, charging the atmosphere until she was certain that anyone could sense them. She didn't dare meet McKenna's gaze in front of others, afraid that her expression might give her away. McKenna did far better than she in maintaining an impassive facade, but some of the servants, including Mrs. Faircloth, remarked on how unusually quiet he had been for the past week. It was clear to those who knew him well that something was troubling him.

"It's his age, I suppose," Mrs. Faircloth told Salter, the butler. "Young men are all high spirits and mischief one day, all gloom and rebellion the next."

"No matter what his temperament, McKenna had better do his work well," Salter said dourly. "Or it's back to the stables for good, and he'll be a lower servant for the rest of his days."

When Aline repeated the comment to McKenna one afternoon, he pulled a face and laughed. He was busy polishing the lacquered panels of a carriage, while Aline sat on an overturned bucket and watched him. The covered carriage room was empty and silent, save for the whickering and shifting of the horses in the stalls beyond the court.

McKenna's exertions had caused him to sweat until his white shirt clung limply to the muscular surface of his back. His shoulders bunched and flexed as he applied a film of wax to the black lacquer, and rubbed it until it shone like glass. Aline had offered to help him, but he had adamantly refused and taken the cloth from her. "It's my job," he had told her brusquely. "You sit over there and watch."

Aline had obeyed with pleasure, enjoying the masculine grace of his movements. As in everything else he did, McKenna performed the task meticulously. He had been taught since childhood that good work was its own reward—and that, coupled with a complete lack of ambition, made him a perfect servant. It was the only fault that Aline could find with him— his automatic acceptance of his lot in life, a resignation so intrinsic that it seemed nothing could ever change it. In fact, she mused guiltily, if it wasn't for her, McKenna would have been perfectly happy with his fate. She was the only thing he had ever wanted that he couldn't have. And she knew how selfish it was of her to keep him so firmly tied to her, but she couldn't make herself let him go. He was as necessary to her as food and water and air.

"You don't want to be a lower servant forever, do you?" she pressed, bringing her thoughts back to their conversation.

"I'd like it better than working in the house and wearing livery," he retorted.

"Mrs. Faircloth thinks that you could make it to first footman some-day, or even valet." Aline neglected to mention the housekeeper's regret-ful observation that although McKenna would make a wonderful valet, his chances of that were greatly diminished by his handsomeness. No master wanted to have a valet whose looks and bearing outshone his own. Far better to keep someone like McKenna in livery that clearly marked him as a servant. "And then you would be better paid."

"I don't care about that," he muttered, applying more wax to the door of the extension-front carriage. "What do I need more money for?"

Aline frowned thoughtfully. "To buy a little cottage someday, and farm your own plot of land."

McKenna paused in the midst of his polishing and glanced over his shoulder with a sudden devilish spark in his blue-green eyes. "And who would live with me, in my cottage?"

Aline met his gaze and smiled, while a fantasy took hold of her and suffused her with warmth. "Me, of course."

Considering that, McKenna hung the waxing cloth on the hook of the carriage lamp before approaching her slowly. Aline's stomach quivered at the look on his face. "I'd need to earn a fair coin for that," he murmured. "Keeping you would be an expensive proposition."

"I wouldn't cost so much," she protested indignantly.

He gave her a skeptical glance. "The price of your hair ribbons alone would beggar me, wife."

The word "wife," uttered in that low tone, made her feel as if she had swallowed a spoonful of sugar syrup. "I'll make up for it in other ways," she replied.

Smiling, McKenna reached down and pulled her to her feet. His hands ran lightly over her sides, lingering just beneath her arms, the heels of his hands brushing against her breasts. The musky male scent of him and the gleam of his sweat-dampened skin made her swallow hard. She drew a little rose-embroidered handkerchief from her sleeve and blotted his forehead.

Taking the dainty cloth from her, McKenna regarded the handiwork of green and pink silk threads with a smile. "Did you do this?" His thumb stroked over the embroidered flowers. "It's beautiful."

She colored in pleasure at the compliment. "Yes, I worked on it in the evenings. A lady should never sit with idle hands."

McKenna tucked the handkerchief into the waist of his trousers and glanced swiftly at their surroundings. Ascertaining that they were completely alone, he slid his arms around her. His hands skimmed over her back and hips to exert delicious pressure in just the right places, adjusting their closeness with sensuous precision. "Will you be there waiting for me every night, in our cottage?" he murmured.

She nodded, leaning against him.

McKenna's bristly black lashes lowered until they cast shadows on his cheeks. "And you'll scrub my back when I'm tired and dusty from the field?"

Aline pictured his large, powerful body lowering into a wooden tub . . . his pleasured sigh at the heat of the water . . . his bronzed back shining in the firelight. "Yes," she breathed. "And then you can soak while I hang the stew pot over the fire, and I'll tell you about the argument I had with the miller, who didn't give me enough flour because his scale was weighted."

McKenna laughed softly while his fingertip skimmed lightly along her throat. "The cheat," he murmured, his eyes sparkling. "I'll speak with him tomorrow—no one tries to fleece my wife and gets away with it. In the meantime, let's go to bed. I want to hold you all night long."

The thought of being tucked in a cozy bed with him, their naked bodies entwined, made Aline tremble with longing. "You'll probably fall asleep as soon as your head touches the pillow," she said. "Farming is hard work—you're exhausted."

"Never too tired to love you." His arms slid around her, and he hunched over to nuzzle the curve of her cheek. His lips were like hot velvet as he whispered against her skin. "I'm going to kiss you from your head to your toes. And I won't stop until you're crying for me, and then I'll pleasure you until you're weak from my loving."

Aline slid her fingers to the hard back of his neck and guided his mouth to hers. His lips covered hers, molding gently until she opened to admit the exquisite probing of his tongue. She wanted the life he had just described . . . she wanted it infinitely more than the future that awaited her. Yet that life belonged to another woman. The thought of someone else sharing his days and nights, his secrets and dreams, filled her with desperation.

"McKenna," she moaned, turning her mouth from his, "promise me . . ."

He held her tight, stroking her back, rubbing his cheek against her hair. "Anything. Anything."

"If you ever marry someone else, promise that you'll always love me best."

"Sweet, selfish darling," he murmured tenderly. "You'll have my heart always—you've ruined me for life."

Aline wrapped her arms around his neck. "Do you resent me for that?" Her voice was muffled against his shoulder.

"I should. If not for you, I might have been content with ordinary things. With an ordinary girl."

"I'm sorry," she said, hugging him fiercely.

"Are you?"

"No," she admitted, and McKenna laughed, tugging her head back to kiss her.

His mouth was firm and demanding, his tongue sliding deep with ruthless sensuousness. As Aline's knees weakened, she molded herself to him until no inch of space remained between them. McKenna supported her easily, holding her between his thighs, his big hand cradling the back of her neck. The pressure of his lips altered as he licked inside her mouth with an erotic playfulness that drew a ragged sigh from her. Just as she thought she would melt to the floor in a puddle of bliss, Aline was disgruntled as McKenna abruptly took his mouth from hers.

"What is it?" she asked thickly.

McKenna silenced her with a touch of his forefinger on her lips, staring at the doorway of the carriage room with narrowed eyes. "I thought I heard something."

Aline frowned in sudden worry, watching as he strode swiftly across the flagstones to the arched opening. He gazed from one side of the empty courtyard to the other. Detecting no sign of anyone, he shrugged and returned to Aline.

She slipped her arms around his lean waist. "Kiss me again."

"Oh no," he said with a crooked grin. "You're going back to the house—I can't work with you here."

"I'll be quiet," she said, her lower lip pushing out mutinously. "You won't even know I'm here."

"Yes, I will." He glanced down at his own aroused body and then gave her a wry look. "And it's hard for a man to get his work done when he's in this condition."

"I'll make it all better," she purred, her hand stealing down to the fascinating bulge of his erection. "Just tell me what to do."

With a laughing groan, McKenna stole a swift, warm kiss from her lips and pried her away from him. "I've already told you what to do—go back to the house."

"Will you climb up to my room tonight?"

"Maybe."

She gave him a mock-threatening glare, and McKenna grinned, shaking his head as he returned to the carriage.

Although they were both mindful of the need for caution, they took every opportunity to sneak away together. They met in the woods, or at their place by the river, or at night on her balcony. McKenna steadfastly refused to cross the threshold of Aline's room, saying that he could not be responsible for his actions, were he to find himself near a bed with her. His self-restraint was far greater than hers, though Aline was well aware of the effort it cost him, and how badly he wanted her. He pleasured her twice again, kissing and holding and caressing her until she was limp with fulfillment. And then late one afternoon, as they lay together by the river, McKenna finally allowed Aline to bring him to release. It would forever be the most erotic experience of her life, with McKenna panting and groaning her name, his flesh stiff and silky hard as it slipped through the ardent grasp of her fingers, his powerful body helpless at her touch. Aline enjoyed his climax more than her own, loving the fact that she could give him the same ecstasy that he had shown to her.

If these were their halcyon days, however, their time was far too short-lived. Aline knew that her love affair with McKenna, such as it was, could never last. All the same, she did not expect it to end so quickly, nor in such a brutal manner.

Her father summoned Aline to his study after supper one evening—something he had never done before. There had never been any reason for the earl to speak either to her or to her sister Livia, privately. Marcus, his son, was the only offspring that the earl gave any attention to . . . and neither of the girls envied their older brother for that. The earl was especially critical of his heir, demanding perfection at all times, preferring to motivate with fear rather than with praise. And yet for all the harsh treatment Marcus had received, he was essentially a kind and good-natured boy. Aline hoped very much that he wouldn't turn out to be like their father someday, but there were many years of the earl's ruthless molding in store for him.

By the time Aline reached the study, she felt as if her stomach had turned into a block of ice. The coldness spread outward through her limbs until it had reached the tips of her fingers and toes. There was no question in her mind about why she had received this unusual command from her father. The earl must have found out somehow about her involvement with McKenna. If it were anything else, he would have had her mother or Mrs. Faircloth speak to her. But the fact that he was bothering to communicate with her directly conveyed that the matter was one of importance. And her instincts warned that the coming confrontation was going to be ugly indeed. Frantically she tried to think of how to react, how best to protect McKenna. She would do anything, promise anything, to keep him safe from the earl's wrath.

Chilled and sweating, she reached the study, with its dark-paneled interior and the massive mahogany desk where much of the estate business was conducted. The door was open, and a lamp was burning inside. She entered the room and found her father standing by the desk.

The earl was not a handsome man—his features were too broad and harsh, as if fashioned by a sculptor who had been in too much of a hurry to refine the deep strikes of his chisel. Had the earl possessed a measure of warmth or wit, or any increment of kindness, his features might have lent themselves to a certain hard attractiveness. Unfortunately he was an utterly humorless man, who, with all his God-given advantages, had found life to be a bitter disappointment. He took no pleasure in anything, especially in his family, who seemed to be little more than a collective burden to him. The only approval he had ever shown to Aline was a reluctant pride in the physical beauty that friends and strangers had complimented so often. As for her thoughts, her character, her hopes and fears—he knew and cared nothing about such intangibles. He had made it clear that Aline's only purpose in life was to marry well.

As she faced her father, Aline wondered how it was possible to have so little feeling for the man who had sired her. One of the many bonds between her and McKenna was the fact that neither of them had ever known what it was like to be loved by a mother or father. It was only because of Mrs. Faircloth that either of them had any concept of parental affection.

Reading the active hatred in her father's gaze, Aline reflected that this was how he had always looked at Livia. Poor Livia, who through no fault of her own had been sired by one of the countess's lovers.

"You sent for me, Father?" she murmured tonelessly.

The lamplight sent jagged shadows across the Earl of Westcliff's face as he regarded her coldly. "At this moment," he remarked, "I have never been more certain that daughters are a curse from hell."

Aline made her face blank, though she was forced to take a quick breath as her lungs contracted.

"You've been seen with the stable boy," the earl continued. "Kissing, with your hands on each other . . ." He paused, his mouth contorting briefly before he managed to school his features. "It seems your mother's blood has finally risen to the fore. She has a similar taste for the lower order . . . although even she has the discernment to indulge in footmen, whereas you seem to have confined your interest to nothing better than stable offal."

The words filled Aline with a hatred that was almost lethal in its intensity. She wanted to strike at her father's sneering face, vanquish him, hurt him to the bottom of his soul . . . if he had one. Focusing on a small square of paneling, Aline schooled herself into perfect stillness, flinching only a little as her father reached out and seized her jaw in one hand. The clench of his fingers bit cruelly into the small muscles of her face.

"Has he taken your virtue?" he barked.

Aline looked directly into the obsidian surface of his eyes. "No."

She saw that he didn't believe her. The bruising grip on her face tightened. "And if I summon a physician to examine you, he will confirm that?"

Aline did not blink, only stared back at him, silently daring him. "Yes." The word came out like a hiss. "But had it been left to me, my virginity would be long gone. I offered it freely to McKenna—I only wish that he had accepted it."

The earl let go of her with an infuriated sound and struck out swiftly, his palm cracking against her cheek. The force of the slap numbed her face and snapped her head to the side. Stunned, Aline held her palm to her swelling cheek and stared at him with round eyes.

The sight of her astonishment and pain seemed to calm the earl somewhat. Letting out a deep breath, he went to his chair and sat with haughty grace. His glittering black gaze found her. "The boy will be gone from the estate by the morrow. And you will ensure that he never dares to approach you again. Because I will find out if he does—and I will use every means at my disposal to ruin him. You know that I have the power, and the will, to do it. No matter where he goes, I will have him hunted and found. And I will take the greatest pleasure in making certain that his life is brought to a miserable and torturous end. He deserves no less for defiling the daughter of a Marsden."

Aline had never truly understood before that to her father she was a piece of property, that her feelings meant nothing to him. She knew he meant every word—he would crush McKenna like a hapless rodent beneath his foot. That must not happen. McKenna must be shielded from her father's vindictiveness, and provided for. She couldn't allow him to be punished simply because he had dared to love her.

While fear gnawed at her heart, she spoke in a brittle voice that didn't seem to be her own. "McKenna won't come back if he believes that I want him gone."

"Then for his sake, make him believe it."

Aline did not hesitate in her reply. "I want a situation found for him. A decent one—an apprenticeship—something that will allow him to better himself."

Her father actually blinked at the bold demand. "What gives you the temerity to believe that I would do that for him?"

"I am still a virgin," she said softly. "For now."

Their gazes held for a frozen moment.

"I see," the earl murmured. "You will threaten to rut with the first man you can find, be he a pauper or a pig farmer, if I don't grant your request."

"Precisely." It required no acting skill for Aline to convince him. She was sincere. After McKenna had left for good, nothing would hold any value for her. Not even her own body.

Aline's audacity seemed to interest the earl, fully as much as it annoyed him. "It seems you may have some of my blood in you yet," he murmured. "Though that is, as always, very much in question, considering your mother. Very well, I will find a situation for the insolent bastard. And you'll do your part to ensure that Stony Cross is rid of him."

"I have your word on that?" she persisted quietly, her fists clenched at her sides.

"Yes."

"Then you have mine in return."

A contemptuous sneer distorted his features. "I don't require your word, daughter. Not because I trust you—I assure you, I do not. But because I have learned that the honor of a woman is of less value than the sweepings from the floor."

Since no reply was required, Aline stood there stiffly until he snapped at her to leave. Numb and disoriented, she walked to her room, where she would wait for McKenna to come for her. Thoughts clamored frantically in her mind. One thing was certain—no power on earth would ever keep McKenna away from her, as long as he believed that she still loved him.

Three

It had been a long, hard day's work for McKenna, helping the gardener's assistants to construct a stone wall around the fruit orchard. Hours of lifting heavy rock had caused his muscles to tremble with strain. With a rueful grin, he reflected that he wouldn't be of much use to Aline for a day or two—he was almost too sore to move. But perhaps she would let him lay his head in her lap, and allow him to nap for a few minutes, with her perfume and softness surrounding him. Sleeping while her gentle fingers stroked his hair . . . the thought filled him with weary anticipation.

However, before he could go to Aline, he would have to see Mrs. Faircloth, who had bid him to come to her at once. After bathing in the old iron tub that all the menservants made use of, McKenna went to the kitchen with his hair still wet. His skin was scented with the acrid soap that was used to clean floors and wash the laundry, as well as given to the servants for their personal needs.

"The hall boy said you wanted me," McKenna said without preamble. As he glanced at the housekeeper, he was puzzled by the consternated look on her face.

"Lord Westcliff has asked to see you," Mrs. Faircloth said.

Suddenly the large kitchen lost its comforting warmth, and the rich sweetness of a pot of jam simmering on the stove ceased to call to his ever-ravenous appetite. "Why?" McKenna asked cautiously.

Mrs. Faircloth shook her head. The heat of the kitchen had caused wisps of her salt-and-pepper hair to stick to the sides of her cheeks. "I'm sure I don't know, and neither does Salter. Have you gotten into some kind of mischief, McKenna?"

"Mischief, no."

"Well, to my knowledge you have done your work, and you've behaved yourself as well as a boy your age is able." She frowned contemplatively. "Perhaps the master wishes to commend you, or send you about some special task."

However, they both knew that was unlikely. The earl would never summon a lower servant for such a reason. It was the butler's province to offer praise or discipline, or hand down new responsibilities. "Go put on your livery," Mrs. Faircoth bade him. "You can't appear before the master in your ordinary garb. And be quick about it—he won't want to be kept waiting."

"Hell," McKenna muttered, cringing at the idea of dressing in the hated livery.

Pretending to scowl, the housekeeper raised a wooden spoon threateningly. "Another blasphemous word in my presence, and I'll rap your knuckles."

"Yes, ma'am." McKenna lowered his head and attempted a meek expression, which made her laugh.

She patted his cheek with her warm, plump hand. Her eyes were soft pools of brown as she smiled. "Be off with you, and after you've seen the earl, I'll have some fresh bread and jam waiting for you."

As McKenna left to comply, his smile vanished, and he let out a long, taut sigh. Nothing good would come of the earl's request. The only possible reason for the summons was his relationship with Aline. A slightly nauseous feeling came over him. McKenna feared nothing except the possibility of being sent away from her. The thought of days, weeks, months passing without being able to see her was unfathomable . . . like being told that he must try to live under water. He was overwhelmed with the need to find her, *now,* but there was no time. One did not tarry when the earl had sent for him.

Dressing quickly in the livery of gold-braided velvet, pinching black shoes, and white stockings, McKenna went to the study where Lord West-cliff waited. The house seemed peculiarly quiet, filled with the hush that occurred before an execution took place. Using two knuckles as Salter had taught him, McKenna gave the door a cautious rap.

"Enter," came the master's voice.

McKenna's heart pounded so hard that he felt light-headed. Making his face expressionless, he entered the room and waited just inside the door. The room was stark and simple, paneled in gleaming cherrywood and lined on one side with long, rectangular, stained-glass windows. It was furnished sparsely, with bookshelves, hard-seated chairs, and a large desk where Lord Westcliff sat.

Obeying the earl's brief gesture, McKenna ventured into the room and stopped before the desk. "My lord," he said humbly, waiting for the ax to fall.

The earl regarded him with a narrow-eyed stare. "I've been consider-ing what is to be done with you."

"Sir?" McKenna questioned, his stomach dropping with sickening abruptness. He glanced into Westcliff's hard eyes and then looked away instinctively. No servant ever dared to hold the master's gaze. It was an untenable sign of insolence.

"Your service is no longer required at Stony Cross Park." The earl's voice was a quiet lash of sound. "You will be dismissed forthwith. I have undertaken to secure another situation for you."

McKenna nodded dumbly.

"I am acquainted with a shipbuilder in Bristol," Westcliff continued, "a Mr. Ilbery, who has condescended to hire you as an apprentice. I know him to be an honorable man, and I expect that he will be a fair, if de-manding, taskmaster . . ."

Westcliff said something else, but McKenna only half heard him. Bristol . . . he knew nothing about it, save that it was a major trading port, and that it was hilly and rich with coal and metal. At least it was not too far away—it was in a neighboring county—

"You will have no opportunity to return to Stony Cross," the earl said, recapturing his attention. "You are no longer welcome here, for reasons that I have no wish to discuss. And if you do attempt to return, you will regret it bitterly."

McKenna understood what he was being told. He had never felt so much at someone else's mercy. It was a feeling that a servant should be well accustomed to, but for the first time in his life, he resented it. He tried to swallow back the seething hostility, but it remained sharp and stinging in the back of his throat. *Aline* . . .

"I've arranged for you to be transported tonight," Westcliff said coolly. "The Farnham family is conveying goods to be sold at Bristol market. They will allow you to ride in the back of their cart. Collect your belongings at once, and take them to the Farnhams' home in the village, from whence you will depart." Reaching into his desk drawer, he extracted a coin and flicked it to McKenna, who caught it reflexively. It was a crown, the equivalent of five shillings.

"Your month's pay, though you are a few days short of the full four weeks," Westcliff commented. "Never let it be said that I am ungenerous."

"No, my lord," McKenna half whispered. This coin, along with the meager hoard of savings in his room, would amount to approximately two pounds. He would have to make it last, since his apprenticeship would probably begin as unpaid labor.

"You may leave now. You will leave your livery behind, as you have no further need of it." The earl turned his attention to some papers on his desk, ignoring McKenna completely.

"Yes, my lord." McKenna's mind was a welter of confusion as he left the study. Why had the earl not asked any questions, why had he not demanded to know precisely how far their short-lived affair had gone? Perhaps the earl had not wanted to know. Perhaps Westcliff was assuming the worst, that Aline had indeed taken McKenna as her lover. Would Aline be punished for it?

He would not be here to find out. He would not be able to protect or comfort her . . . he was being removed from her life with surgical precision. But he was damned if he wouldn't see her again. The stupor faded, and suddenly his breath seemed to burn in his throat and chest, as if he had inhaled lungfuls of fire.

Aline nearly doubled over with agony as she heard the sounds she had been expecting . . . the quiet scrape of McKenna climbing up to her balcony. Her stomach roiled, and she clenched her fist against her abdomen. She knew what she had to do. And she knew that even without her father's manipulations, her involvement in McKenna's life could only have resulted in unhappiness for them both. McKenna would be better off to make a new start, unfettered by anything or anyone from his past. He would find someone else, someone who was at liberty to love him as she would never be. And no doubt many female hearts would be offered to a man like him.

Aline only wished that there was another way to set him free—a way that wouldn't cause them both so much pain.

She saw McKenna on her balcony, a big shadow behind the web of the lace curtain. The door had been left slightly open . . . he nudged it with his foot, but as always, he did not dare to cross the threshold. Carefully Aline lit a candle by her bedside, and watched as her own reflection flickered to life in the panes of glass, superimposed on McKenna's dark form before the door opened further and the image slid away.

Aline sat on the corner of the bed nearest the balcony, not trusting herself to come any closer to him. "You talked with the earl," she said without inflection, as a trickle of sweat eased down her tense back.

McKenna was very still, reading the stiffness of her posture, the way she withheld herself from him. She should have already been in his arms by now. "He told me—"

"Yes, I know what he told you," Aline interrupted softly. "You're leaving Stony Cross Park. And it's for the best, really."

McKenna gave a slow, confused shake of his head. "I need to hold you," he whispered, and for the first time ever he stepped into her room. He was stayed, however, as Aline raised her hand in a gesture of restraint.

"Don't," she said, and her breath caught before she could continue. "It's all over, McKenna. The only thing to do now is say your goodbyes and disappear."

"I'll find a way to come back," he said thickly, his gaze haunted. "I'll do whatever you ask—"

"That wouldn't be wise. I . . ." Self-loathing twisted through her as she forced herself to go on. "I don't want you to come back. I don't want to see you ever again."

Staring at her blankly, McKenna took a step back from her. "Don't say that," he murmured huskily. "No matter where I go, I'll never stop loving you. Tell me you feel the same, Aline. God . . . I can't live without some shred of hope."

It was precisely that hope that would prove his eventual ruin. If he had hope, he would come back to her, and then her father would destroy him. The only way to save McKenna was to drive him away for good . . . to extinguish all faith in her love. If she didn't accomplish that, then no power on earth would be enough to keep him from her.

"I apologized to my father, of course," Aline said in a light, brittle voice. "I asked him to get rid of you, to spare me the embarrassment. He was angry, of course—he said that I should have at least looked somewhere higher than the stables. He was right. Next time I'll choose with more discrimination."

"Next time?" McKenna looked as if he had been struck.

"You've amused me for a while, but I'm bored with you now. I suppose we should try to part as friends, only . . . you are just a servant, after all. So let us end it cleanly. It's best for both of us if you go before I am forced to say things that will make us both even more uncomfortable. Go, McKenna. I don't want you anymore."

"Aline . . . you love me . . ."

"I was playing with you. I've learned all I can from you. Now I need to find a *gentleman* to practice with."

McKenna was silent, staring at her with the gaze of a fatally wounded animal. Desperately Aline wondered how long she could continue before she broke.

"How could I love someone like you?" she asked, each mocking word causing a stab of agony in her throat. "You're a bastard, McKenna . . . you have no family, no blood, no means . . . what could you offer me that I couldn't get from any man of low breed? Go, please." Her nails left bloody crescents in her own palms. *"Go."*

As the silence unraveled, Aline lowered her head and waited, trembling, praying to a merciless God that McKenna would not come to her. If he touched her, spoke to her once more, she would crumble in anguish. She made herself breathe in and out, forcing her lungs to work, willing her heart to keep beating. After a long time she opened her eyes and looked at the empty doorway.

He was gone.

Rising from the bed, she managed to reach the washstand, and she clutched her arms around the porcelain bowl. Nausea erupted in punishing spasms, and she gave in to it with a wretched gasp, until her stomach was empty and her knees had lost all ability to function. Stumbling and crawling to the balcony, she huddled against the railing and gripped the iron bars.

She saw McKenna's distant figure walking along the drive that led from the manor house . . . the drive that connected to the village road. His head was bowed as he left without a backward glance.

Aline watched him hungrily through the painted bars, knowing that she would never see him again. "McKenna," she whispered. She watched through the painted bars until he disappeared, following a bend in the road that would lead him far away from her. And then she pressed her icy, sweating face to the sleeve of her gown, and wept.

Four

Mrs. Faircloth came to the doorway of Aline's cabinet, a small antechamber of her bedroom. The tiny room had originally come from a chateau built in the early seventeenth century. Years ago the earl and countess had bought the vaulted cabinet while traveling abroad. It had been packed into crates—paneling, painting, ceiling, and floor—and completely reconstructed at Stony Cross Park. Such rooms were rare in England but common in France, where the upper class used such places daydreaming, studying and writing, and conversing intimately with a friend.

Aline huddled in the corner of a chaise that had been lodged against the age-rippled glass window, staring at nothing. The narrow sill beneath the windowpanes was lined with small objects . . . a tiny painted-metal horse . . . a pair of tin soldiers, one of them missing an arm . . . a cheap wooden button from a man's shirt . . . a small folding knife with a handle carved from a stag's horn. All the items were bits and pieces of McKenna's past that Aline had collected. Her fingers were curled around the spine of a pocket-sized book of verse, the nonsensical kind used to teach children the rules of grammar and spelling. Mrs. Faircloth remembered more than one occasion on which she had seen Aline and McKenna reading the primer together as children, their heads close together as Aline doggedly tried to teach him his lessons. And McKenna had listened reluctantly, though it had been clear that he would have much preferred to be running through the woods like an uncivilized creature.

Frowning, Mrs. Faircloth set a tray of soup and toast on Aline's lap. "It's time for you to eat something," she said, masking her concern with a stern voice.

In the month since McKenna had left, Aline had been unable to eat or sleep. Broken and dispirited, she spent most of her time alone. When she was commanded to join the family for supper, she sat without touching her food and remained unnaturally silent. The earl and countess chose to regard Aline's decline as childish pouting. However, Mrs. Faircloth did not share their opinion, wondering how they could so easily discount the profound attachment between Aline and McKenna. The housekeeper had tried to reason herself out of her worry, reminding herself that they were mere children, and as such, they were resilient creatures. Still . . . losing McKenna seemed likely to unhinge Aline.

"I miss him too," the housekeeper had said, her throat tight with shared grief. "But you must think of what is best for McKenna, and not for you. You wouldn't want him to stay here and be tormented by all the things he could never have. And it serves no one to let yourself go to pieces this way. You're pale and thin, and your hair is as rough as a horse's tail. What would McKenna think if he saw you right now?"

Aline lifted a dull gaze to hers. "He would think it was what I deserved, for being so cruel."

"He will understand someday. He'll reflect on it and realize that you could only have done it for his own good."

"Do you think so?" Aline asked without apparent interest.

"Of course," Mrs. Faircloth asserted stoutly.

"I don't." Aline picked up the metal horse from the window and regarded it without emotion. "I think that McKenna will hate me for the rest of his life."

The housekeeper meditated on the words, becoming more and more convinced that if something were not done soon to jolt the girl from her grief, it might cause permanent damage to her health.

"Perhaps I should tell you . . . I've received a letter from him," Mrs.

Faircloth said, although she had meant to keep the information to herself. There was no predicting how Aline would react to the news. And if the earl learned that Mrs. Faircloth had allowed Aline to see such a letter, there would be yet another position at Stony Cross Park to be filled—her own.

The girl's dark eyes were suddenly alive, filled with a frantic blaze. "When?"

"This very morning."

"What did he write? How is he?"

"I haven't read the letter yet—you know how my eyes are. I need the proper light . . . and I've misplaced my spectacles . . ."

Aline shoved the tray aside and struggled out of the chaise. "Where is it? Let me see it at once—oh, why did you wait so long to tell me?"

Troubled by the feverish color that had swept over the girl's face, Mrs. Faircloth tried to settle her. "The letter is in my room, and you will not have it until you finish every morsel on that tray," she said firmly. "To my knowledge, nothing has passed your lips since yesterday—you'll likely faint before you even reach the stairs."

"God in heaven, how can you talk about food?" Aline demanded wildly.

Mrs. Faircloth stood her ground, holding Aline's challenging gaze without blinking, until the girl threw up her hands with a wrathful sound. Reaching down to the tray, she grabbed a piece of bread and tore it angrily with her teeth.

The housekeeper viewed her with satisfaction. "All right, then. Come to find me when you're done—I'll be in the kitchen. And then we'll go to my room to fetch the letter."

Aline ate so quickly that she nearly choked on the bread. She fared little better with the soup, the spoon shaking too violently in her hand to deliver more than a few drops to her mouth. She couldn't seem to focus on one thought, her mind jumbled and spinning. She knew that there would be no words of forgiveness or understanding in McKenna's letter—there would be no mention of her. That didn't matter. All she wanted was some reassurance that he was alive and well. Oh God, she was starved for news of him!

Fumbling with the spoon, she threw it impatiently into the corner and shoved her feet into her shoes. It was a sign of how stupidly self-absorbed she had been that she hadn't already thought to ask Mrs. Faircloth to begin a correspondence with McKenna. Although it was impossible for Aline to communicate with him, she could at least maintain a fragile link through the housekeeper. The thought caused a warm ache of relief inside her, thawing the detachment that had encased her for weeks. Ravenous for the letter, craving the sight of the marks that McKenna's hand had made on parchment, Aline hurried from the room.

When she reached the kitchen, her appearance earned a few odd glances from the scullery maid and the pair of cook maids, and she realized that her face must be very red. Excitement burned through her, making it difficult to stay calm as she moved around the huge wooden table to the side where Mrs. Faircloth and the cook stood, close to the brick-built oven range over the hearth. The air was laden with the smell of fish frying, the rich, fatty aroma seeming to curdle the contents of Aline's stomach. Fighting a surge of nausea, she swallowed repeatedly and went to the housekeeper, who was making a list with the cook.

"The letter," Aline whispered in her ear, and Mrs. Faircloth smiled.

"Yes. Just a moment more, my lady."

Aline nodded with an impatient sigh. She turned to face the stove, where a cook maid was clumsily attempting to turn the fish. Oil splashed from the pan repeatedly as each piece was flipped, the liquid spilling into the basket grate filled with unused coal. Raising her brows at the girl's ineptitude, Aline nudged her elbow into the housekeeper's plump side. "Mrs. Faircloth—"

"Yes, we're almost finished," the housekeeper murmured.

"I know, but the stove—"

"One more word with Cook, my lady."

"Mrs. Faircloth, I don't think the cook maid should—"

Aline was interrupted by a shocking blast of heat accompanied by an explosive roar as the oil-soaked basket grate caught fire. Flames shot up to the ceiling and spread to the pan of fish, turning the range into an inferno. Stunned, Aline felt the cook maid stumble against her, and the breath was knocked from her lungs as her back struck the edge of the heavy table.

Hiccupping for air, Aline was dimly aware of the kitchen maids' frightened screams, overlaid by Mrs. Faircloth's sharp cries for someone to fetch a sack of bicarbonate salts from the larder, to smother the blaze. Aline turned to escape the heat and the smoke, but it seemed she was surrounded by it. Suddenly her body was encompassed with a pain more searing than anything she had ever imagined possible. Panicking at the realization that her clothes were on fire, she ran instinctively, but there was no escape from the flames that ate her alive. She had a blurred flash of Mrs. Faircloth's horrified face, and then someone knocked her violently to the ground . . . a man's voice cursing . . . there were punishing blows to her legs and body as he beat at her burning clothes. Aline cried out and fought him, but she could no longer breathe or think or see as she sank into the darkness.

Five

Twelve years later

"It seems that the Americans have arrived," Aline said dryly, as she and her sister, Livia, returned to the manor house after an early-morning walk. She paused beside the honey-colored stone facade to have a good look at the four ornate vehicles that were stopped in front of the manor house. Servants dashed across the large courtyard that fronted the manor house, from the stables located on one side, to the servants' quarters on the other. The guests had come with a great quantity of trunks and baggage for their month-long stay at Stony Cross Park.

Livia came to stand by Aline. She was a winsome young woman of twenty-four, with light brown hair and hazel-green eyes and a slim, small figure. From her blithe manner, one would think she hadn't a care in the world. But it became evident to anyone who looked into her eyes that she had paid a high price for the rare moments of happiness she had known.

"Silly things," Livia said lightly, referring to their guests, "haven't they been told that it isn't done to arrive so early in the day?"

"It would seem not."

"Rather ostentatious, aren't they," Livia murmured, observing the gilded moldings and painted panels on the sides of the carriages.

Aline grinned. "When Americans spend their money, they like for it to show."

They laughed and exchanged impish glances. This wasn't the first time that their brother, Marcus, now Lord Westcliff, had hosted Americans at his renowned hunting and shooting parties. It seemed that in Hampshire, it was always the season for something . . . grouse in August, partridge in September, pheasant in October, rooks in spring and summer, and rabbits all year round. The traditional chase took place twice a week, with ladies occasionally riding to the hounds as well. All manner of business was conducted at these parties, which often lasted weeks and included influential political figures or rich professional men. During these visits, Marcus cleverly persuaded certain guests to side with him on one issue or another, or to agree to some business matter that would serve his interests.

The Americans who came to Stony Cross were usually nouveaux riches . . . their fortunes made from shipping and real estate, or factories that produced things like soap flakes or paper rolls. Aline had always found Americans rather engaging. She liked their high spirits, and she was touched by their eagerness to be accepted. Out of fear of seeming too modish, they wore clothes that were a season or two behind the current fashion. At dinner they were terribly anxious about whether they either had been seated below the salt or had been given the more prestigious locations near the host. And generally they were concerned about quality, making it clear that they preferred Sèvres china, Italian sculpture, French wine . . . and English peers. Americans were notoriously eager to make transatlantic marriages, using Yankee fortunes to catch impoverished British blue bloods. And no blood was more exalted than that of the Marsdens, who possessed one of the most ancient earldoms of the peerage.

Livia liked to joke about their pedigree, claiming that the renowned Marsden lineage could make even a black sheep like herself seem attractive to an ambitious American. "Since no decent Englishman would have me, perhaps I should marry one of those nice rich Yankees and sail with him across the Atlantic."

.Aline had smiled and hugged her tightly. "You wouldn't dare," she whispered into her sister's hair. "I would miss you too much."

"What a pair we are," Livia responded with a rueful laugh. "You realize that we'll both end up old and unwed, living together with a great
horde of cats."

"God save me," Aline had said with a laughing groan.

Thinking back to that conversation, Aline slid an arm around her sister's shoulders. "Well, dear," she said lightly, "here is an opportunity for
you to land an ambitious American with large pockets. Just what you
were hoping for."

Livia snorted. "I was joking about that, as you well know. Besides,
how can you be certain that there are eligible gentlemen in the party?"

"Marcus told me a bit about the group last evening. Have you ever
heard of the Shaws of New York? They've had money for three generations, which is *forever* in America. The head of the family is Mr. Gideon
Shaw, who is unmarried—and apparently quite fine-looking."

"Good for him," Livia said. "However, I have no interest in husband
hunting, no matter how attractive he may be."

Aline tightened her arm protectively about Livia's narrow shoulders.
Since the death of her fiancé, Lord Amberley, Livia had vowed never to
fall in love again. However, it was clear that Livia needed a family of her
own. Her nature was too affectionate to be squandered on a life of spin-
sterhood. It was a measure of how deeply Livia had loved Amberley, that
she still mourned him two years after his death. And yet surely Amberley,
the most kindhearted of young men, would never have wanted Livia to
spend the rest of her life alone.

"One never knows," Aline said. "It's possible that you will meet a
man whom you will love as much as—if not more than—you did Lord
Amberley."

Livia's shoulders stiffened. "Lord, I hope not. It hurts too much to
love someone that way. You know that as well as I."

"Yes," Aline admitted, struggling to close away the memories that
stirred behind an invisible door in her mind. Memories so incapacitating
that she had to ignore them for the sake of her own sanity.

They stood together in silence, each understanding the other's unspoken sorrows. How strange, Aline thought, that the younger sister she had

always thought of as something of a nuisance would turn out to be her dearest friend and companion. Sighing, Aline turned toward one of the four towers that cornered the main body of the manor house. "Come," she said briskly, "let's go in through the servants' entrance. I don't wish to meet our guests while I'm dusty from our walk."

"Neither do I." Livia fell into step beside her. "Aline, don't you ever tire of acting as hostess for Marcus's guests?"

"No, I don't mind it, actually. I like to entertain, and it's always pleasant to hear the news from London."

"Last week old Lord Torrington said that you have a way of making others feel more clever and interesting than they really are. He said that you are the most accomplished hostess he has ever known."

"Did he? For those kind words, I will put extra brandy in his tea the next time he visits." Smiling, Aline paused at the tower entrance and glanced over her shoulder at the entourage of guests and their servants, who milled in the courtyard as various trunks were carried this way and that. It seemed to be a boisterous group, this entourage of Mr. Gideon Shaw's.

As Aline surveyed the courtyard, her gaze was drawn by a man who was taller than the rest, his height exceeding even that of the footmen. He was big and black-haired, with broad shoulders and a confident, masculine way of walking that was very nearly a strut. Like the other Americans, he was dressed in a suit that was well tailored but scrupulously conservative. He stopped to chat easily with another guest, his hard profile partially averted.

The sight of him made Aline feel uneasy, as if her usual self-possession had suddenly been stripped away. At this distance she could not see his features clearly, but she sensed his power. It was in his movements, the innate authority of his stance, the arrogant tilt of his head. No one could doubt that he was a man of consequence . . . perhaps he was Mr. Shaw?

Livia preceded her inside the house. "Are you coming, Aline?" she said over her shoulder.

"Yes, I . . ." Aline's voice drifted into silence as she continued to stare at the distant figure, whose barely contained vitality made every other man in the vicinity seem pallid by comparison. Finishing his brief conversation, he strode toward the entrance of the manor. As he set foot on the first step, however, he stopped . . . as if someone had called out his name. His shoulders seemed to tauten beneath his black coat. Aline watched him, mesmerized by his sudden stillness. Slowly he turned and looked right at her. Her heart gave a hard, hurtful extra thump, and she retreated quickly into the tower before their gazes met.

"What is it?" Livia asked with a touch of concern. "You're flushed all of a sudden." She came forward and took Aline's hand, tugging impatiently. "Come, we'll bathe your face and wrists with cool water."

"Oh, I'm perfectly all right," Aline replied, but the pit of her stomach felt queer and fluttery. "It's just that I saw a gentleman in the courtyard . . ."

"The black-haired one? Yes, I noticed him too. Why is it that Americans are always so tall? Perhaps it's something in the climate—it makes them grow like weeds."

"In that case, you and I should go for an extended stay," Aline said with a smile, for both she and Livia were small of stature. Their brother, Marcus, was also no more than average in height, but his build was so muscular and bull-like that he posed a perilous physical threat to any man foolish enough to challenge him.

Chatting comfortably, the sisters made their way to their private apartments in the east wing. Aline knew that she would have to be quick about changing her gown and freshening her appearance, as the Americans' early arrival had undoubtedly set the household in a commotion. The guests would want refreshments of some kind, but there was no time to prepare a full-blown breakfast. The Americans would have to be content with beverages until a midmorning "nuncheon" could be assembled.

Rapidly Aline went through a mental list of the contents of the pantry and larders. She decided they would set out crystal bowls of strawberries and raspberries, pots of butter and jam, along with bread and cake. Some asparagus salad and broiled bacon would also be nice, and Aline would also tell the housekeeper, Mrs. Faircloth, to serve the chilled lobster soufflé that had been intended as a supper course for later in the day. Something else could be substituted at dinner, perhaps some tiny salmon cutlets with egg sauce, or sweetbreads with celery stalks—

"Well," Livia said prosaically, interrupting her speculations, "Have a pleasant day. I shall proceed to skulk about as usual."

"There is no need for that," Aline said with an instant frown.

Livia had virtually gone into hiding after the scandalous consequences of her tragic love affair with Lord Amberley. Although she was generally regarded with sympathy, Livia was still considered "ruined," and therefore unfit company for those of delicate sensibilities. She was never invited to social events of any kind, and when a ball or soiree was held at Stony Cross Park, she stayed in her room to avoid the gathering. However, after two years of witnessing Livia's social exile, Marcus and Aline had both agreed that enough was enough. Perhaps Livia could never regain the status she had enjoyed before her scandal, but the siblings were determined that she should not be forced to live the rest of her life as a recluse. They would gently wedge her back into the fringes of good society, and eventually find her a husband of suitable fortune and respectability.

"You've done your penance, Livia," Aline said firmly. "Marcus says that anyone who does not wish to associate with you will simply have to leave the estate."

"I don't avoid people because I fear their disapproval," Livia protested. "The truth is that I'm not ready to get back into the swim of things just yet."

"You may not ever feel ready," Aline countered. "Sooner or later you will simply have to jump back in."

"Later, then."

"But I remember how much you used to love to dance, and play parlor games, and sing at the piano—"

"Aline," Livia interrupted gently, "I promise you, someday I will dance and play and sing again—but it will have to be at the time of my choosing, not yours."

Aline relented with an apologetic smile. "I don't mean to be over-bearing. I just want you to be happy."

Livia reached for her hand and squeezed it. "I wish, dearest, that you were as concerned for your own happiness as you are for everyone else's."

I am happy, Aline wanted to reply, but the words stuck in her throat.

Sighing, Livia left her standing in the hall. "I will see you later this evening."

Aline took hold of the painted porcelain doorknob, pushed into her bedroom, and tugged the bonnet from her head. The hair at the back of her neck was wet with perspiration. Pulling the crimped wire pins from her long chocolate-brown locks, she set them on her dressing table and picked up a silver-backed brush. She dragged it through her hair, relishing the soothing scratch of boar bristles on her scalp.

It had been an exceptionally warm August so far, and the county was swarming with fashionable families who would not be caught dead in London in the summer months. Marcus had said that Mr. Shaw and his business partner would be traveling back and forth between Hampshire and London, with the rest of their entourage remaining firmly entrenched at Stony Cross Park. It appeared that Mr. Shaw planned to establish a London office for his family's new enterprises, as well as secure the all-important docking rights that would allow his ships to unload their cargo at the docklands.

Although the Shaw family was already wealthy from real estate and Wall Street speculation, they had recently launched into the fast-growing business of locomotive production. It seemed their ambition was not only to supply American railways with engines, coaches, and parts, but also to export their products to Europe. According to Marcus, Shaw would have no shortage of investors for his new enterprise—and Aline sensed that her brother was interested in becoming one of them. With that goal in mind, Aline intended to see that Mr. Shaw and his partner had an extremely enjoyable stay at Stony Cross.

Her mind filled with plans, Aline changed into a light summer frock of white cotton printed with lavender flowers. She did not ring for a maid to help her. Unlike other ladies of her situation, she dressed herself most of the time, requesting help only from Mrs. Faircloth when necessary. The housekeeper was the only person who was ever allowed to see Aline bathing or dressing, except for Livia.

Closing the line of tiny pearl buttons up the front of her bodice, Aline stood before the looking glass. Expertly she braided and pinned her dark hair in a twist at the back of her neck. As she anchored the last pin in her coiffure, she saw in the reflection that something had been left on the bed . . . a stray glove or garter, perhaps . . . on the gleaming pink damask coverlet. Frowning curiously, Aline went to investigate.

She reached out to lift the object from the pillow. It was an old hand-kerchief, the silk embroidery faded to near-colorless hues, many of the threads worn away. Puzzled, Aline traced her fingertip over the pattern of rosebuds. Where had it come from? And why had it been left on her bed? The fluttery feeling came back to her stomach, and her fingertip stilled on the delicate web of embroidery.

She had made this herself, twelve years ago.

Her fingers closed around the bit of cloth, compressing it into her palm. Suddenly her pulse drummed in her temples, ears, throat, and chest. "McKenna," she whispered.

She remembered the day she had given it to him . . . or more accurately, the day he had taken it from her, in the carriage room of the stables. Only McKenna could have returned this fragment of the past to her. But that was not possible. McKenna had left England years ago, breaking his apprenticeship agreement with the Bristol shipbuilder. No one had ever seen or heard from him again.

Aline had spent her entire adult life trying not to think about him, entertaining the futile hope that time would soften the memories of aching love. Yet McKenna had remained with her like a phantom, filling her dreams with all the abandoned hopes she refused to acknowledge during the daytime hours. All this time she had not known if he was dead or alive. Either possibility was too painful to contemplate.

Still clutching the handkerchief, Aline walked from her room. She slipped through the east wing like a wounded animal, using the servants' entrance to leave the manor. There was no privacy in the house, and she had to steal a few minutes alone to gather her wits. One thought was foremost in her mind . . . *Don't come back, McKenna . . . It would kill me to see you now. Don't come back, don't . . .*

Marcus, Lord Westcliff, welcomed Gideon Shaw into his library. Marcus had met Shaw before, on a previous visit to England, and he had found much to recommend the man.

Admittedly, Marcus had been predisposed not to like Shaw, who was a well-known member of the so-called American aristocracy. Despite a lifetime of social indoctrination, Marcus did not believe in aristocracy of any kind. He would have disclaimed his own title, were it legally possible. It was not that he minded responsibility, nor did he have an aversion to inherited money. It was just that he had never been able to accept the concept of one man's innate superiority over another. The notion was inherently unfair, not to mention illogical, and Marcus had never been able to tolerate a breach of logic.

However, Gideon Shaw was nothing like the American aristocrats that Marcus had encountered. In fact, Shaw seemed to enjoy making his New York family cringe with his cheerful references to his great-grandfather, a crude and outspoken sea merchant who had amassed a staggering fortune. Subsequent generations of refined and well-mannered Shaws would have preferred to forget their vulgar ancestor . . . if only Gideon would let them.

Shaw entered the room with a loose, easy stride. He was an elegant man of about thirty-five years of age. His wheat-colored hair was cropped in short, gleaming layers, and his skin was tanned and close-shaven. His looks were quintessentially American . . . blue-eyed, blond, with an air of irreverence. But there was a darkness beneath his golden surface, a cynicism and dissatisfaction that had etched deep lines around his eyes and mouth. His reputation was that of a man who worked hard and played even harder, triggering rumors of drinking and debauchery that Marcus suspected were well deserved.

"My lord," Shaw murmured, exchanging a decisive handshake, "it is a pleasure to arrive at last."

A maid came bearing a silver coffee service, and Marcus gestured for her to place it on his desk.

"How was the crossing?" Marcus asked.

A smile crinkled the corners of Shaw's blue-gray eyes. "Uneventful, thank God. May I ask after the countess? She is well, I trust?"

"Quite well, thank you. My mother bid me to convey her regrets that she could not be here at this time, but she is visiting friends abroad." Standing over the refreshment tray, Marcus wondered why Aline had not yet appeared to greet the guests. No doubt she was busy adjusting plans to compensate for the party's early arrival. "Will you take some coffee?"

"Yes, please." Lowering his rangy form into the chair beside the desk, Shaw sat with his legs slightly spread.

"Cream or sugar?"

"Just sugar, please." As Shaw received his cup and saucer, Marcus noticed a distinct trembling of his hands, causing the china to rattle. They were the unmistakable tremors of a man who had not yet recovered from a previous night's drinking.

Without missing a beat, Shaw set the cup on the desk, withdrew a silver flask from the inside of his well-tailored coat, and poured a liberal quantity of spirits into the coffee. He drank from the cup without benefit of the saucer, closing his eyes as the hot alcohol-infused liquid poured down his throat. After downing the coffee, he extended the cup without comment, and Marcus obligingly refilled it. Again the ritual of the flask was performed.

"Your business partner is welcome to join us," Marcus said politely.

Settling back in his chair, Shaw drank the second cup of coffee more slowly than the first. "Thank you, but I believe that at the moment, he is busy giving instructions to our servants." An ironic smile touched his lips. "McKenna has an aversion to sitting down in the middle of the day. He is in constant motion."

Having taken his own seat behind the desk, Marcus paused in the act of lifting a cup to his own lips. "McKenna," he repeated quietly. It was a common name. Even so, it sounded a note of warning inside him.

Shaw smiled slightly. "They call him 'King' McKenna in Manhattan.

It's entirely because of his efforts that the Shaw foundries have begun to produce locomotive engines instead of agricultural machinery."

"That is seen by some as an unnecessary risk," Marcus commented. "You are already doing quite well with the production of agricultural machines . . . the mowers and grain drills, in particular. Why venture into locomotive manufacturing? The principal railway companies already build their own engines—and from all appearances, they supply their own needs quite efficiently."

"Not for long," Shaw said easily. "We're convinced that their production demands will soon exceed their capability—and they'll be forced to rely on outside builders to make up the difference. Besides, America is different from England. There, most of the railways rely on privately owned locomotive works—such as mine—to provide their engines and parts. Competition is fierce, and it makes for a better, more aggressively priced product."

"I would be interested to learn why you believe that the railway-owned foundries in England won't be able to maintain an acceptable pace of production."

"McKenna will provide all the figures you require." Shaw assured him.

"I look forward to meeting him."

"I believe you already have, my lord." Shaw's gaze did not stray from Marcus's as he continued with studied casualness. "It seems that McKenna was once employed here at Stony Cross Park. You may not remember him, as he was a stable boy at the time."

Marcus showed no reaction to the statement, but inwardly he thought, *Oh, bloody hell!* This McKenna was indeed the same one whom Aline had loved so long ago. Marcus felt an immediate urgency to reach Aline. He had to prepare her somehow for the news that McKenna had returned. "Footboy," he corrected softly. "As I recall, McKenna was made a house servant just before he left."

Shaw's blue eyes were deceptively guileless. "I hope it will cause you no discomfort to receive a former servant as a guest."

"On the contrary, I admire McKenna's achievements. And I will not hesitate to tell him so." That was half the truth. The problem was,

McKenna's presence at Stony Cross would certainly cause Aline discomfort. If so, Marcus would have to find a way to deal with the situation. His sisters meant more to him than anything else on earth, and he would never allow either of them to be hurt.

Shaw smiled at Marcus's reply. "I see that my judgment of you was correct, Lord Westcliff. You are as fair and open-minded as I suspected."

"Thank you." Marcus devoted himself to stirring a spoonful of sugar in his own coffee, wondering grimly where Aline was.

Aline found herself walking quickly, almost running, to her favorite place by the river, where a wildflower meadow sloped down to tall grasses alive with meadow-brown and marbled-white butterflies. She had never brought anyone here, not even Livia. It was the place she had shared only with McKenna. And after he had gone, it was where she had cried alone.

The prospect of seeing him again was the worst thing that could happen to her.

Still clutching the embroidered handkerchief, Aline lowered herself to a patch of grass and tried to calm herself. The sun struck off the water with brilliant glints, while tiny black beetles crawled along stalks of spiny gorse. The pungency of sun-warmed thistle and marsh marigold mingled with the fecund smell of the river. Numbly she stared at the water, tracking the progress of a crested grebe as it paddled by industriously with a slimy clump of weed clamped in its beak.

Voices from long ago whispered in her mind . . .

"I'll marry no man but you, McKenna. And if you ever leave me, I'll be alone for the rest of my life."

"Aline . . . I would never leave unless you told me to go . . ."

She shook her head sharply, willing the tormenting memories to go away. Wadding the handkerchief into a ball, she drew her arm back to throw it into the gentle river current. The movement was stayed by a quiet sound.

"Wait."

Six

Aline closed her eyes, while the word tugged gently at her shrinking soul. *His* voice . . . only deeper and richer now, the voice of a man, not a boy. Although she heard the sounds of his feet treading closer, crushing the moor grass, she refused to look at him. It took all her strength just to keep breathing. She was paralyzed by something that felt like fear, a kind of incapacitating heat that pumped into her with each frantic beat of her heart.

The sound of his voice seemed to open pathways of sensation inside her. "If you're going to throw that into the river, I want it back."

As Aline tried to loosen her clutch on the handkerchief, it dropped completely from her stiff fingers. Slowly she made herself turn to look at him as he approached. The black-haired man she had seen in the courtyard was indeed McKenna. He was even larger and more imposing than he had seemed at a distance. His features were blunt and strong, his bold, wide-bridged nose set with perfect symmetry between the distinct planes of his cheekbones. He was too masculine to be considered truly handsome—a sculptor would have tried to soften those uncompromising features. But somehow his hard face was the perfect setting for those lavish eyes, the clear blue-green brilliance shadowed by thick black lashes. No one else on earth had eyes like that.

"McKenna," she said huskily, searching for any resemblance he might bear to the lanky, love-struck boy she had known. There was none.

McKenna was a stranger now, a man with no trace of boyishness. He was sleek and elegant in well-tailored clothes, his glossy black hair cut in short layers that tamed its inherent tendency to curl. As he drew closer, she gathered more details . . . the shadow of bristle beneath his close-shaven skin, the glitter of a gold watch chain on his waistcoat, the brutal swell of muscle in his shoulders and thighs as he sat on a rock nearby.

"I didn't expect to find you here," he murmured, his gaze never leaving hers. "I wanted to have a look at the river . . . it's been so long since I've seen it."

His accent was strange, soft and drawn-out, with extra vowels added in places that weren't necessary.

"You sound like an American," Aline whispered, willing her tight throat to relax.

"I've lived in New York for a long time."

"You disappeared without a word to anyone. I . . ." She paused, scarcely able to breathe. "I worried for you."

"Did you?" McKenna smiled faintly, though his face was cold. "I had to leave Bristol rather suddenly. The shipbuilder I was apprenticed to, Mr. Ilbery, turned out to be a bit heavy-handed in his discipline. After a beating that left me with a few broken ribs and a cracked skull, I decided to leave and make a new start somewhere else."

"I'm sorry," Aline whispered, blanching. Fighting back a ripple of queasiness, she forced herself to ask, "How were you able to afford the passage to America? It must have been expensive."

"Five pounds. More than a year's pay." A touch of irony edged his voice, revealing that the sum, so desperately needed then, was nothing to him now. "I wrote to Mrs. Faircloth, and she sent it to me from her own savings."

Aline bent her head, her mouth trembling as she remembered the day his letter arrived . . . the day that her world had fallen apart and she had been forever changed.

"How is she?" she heard McKenna ask. "Is she still employed here?"

"Oh yes. She is still here, and quite well."

"Good."

Carefully McKenna leaned over and picked up the discarded handkerchief from the ground, seeming not to notice the way Aline stiffened at
his proximity. Straightening, he resumed his seat on the nearby rock, and
studied her. "How beautiful you are," he said dispassionately, as if he
were admiring a painting or a striking view. "Even more so than I remembered. You wear no ring, I see."

Her fingers curled into the loose folds of her skirts. "No. I never married."

That earned a strange glance from him. Brooding darkness filtered
through the vivid blue-green of his eyes, like a summer sky filling with
smoke. "Why not?"

She fought to conceal her upheaval with a calm, offhand smile. "It
wasn't my fate, I suppose. And you? Did you ever—"

"No."

The news should not have brought the pressure of a rapid heartbeat to
the base of her throat. But it did.

"And Livia?" McKenna asked softly. "What became of her?"

"Unmarried as well. She resides here with Marcus and me, and
she . . . well, you will probably see very little of her."

"Why?"

Aline searched for words that would explain her sister's situation in a
way that would not cause him to judge her harshly. "Livia does not often
go out into society, nor does she choose to mix with the guests here.
There was a scandal two years ago. Livia was betrothed to Lord Amberley, a young man with whom she was very much in love. Before they
could be married, he was killed in a hunting accident." She paused to
brush away a beetle that had landed on her skirt.

McKenna's expression was impassive. "What is the scandal in that?"

"Not long after that, Livia had a miscarriage, and so everyone knew
that she and Amberley had . . ." She paused helplessly. "Livia made the
mistake of confiding her sorrows to one of her friends, who couldn't keep
a secret to save her life. Although Marcus and I tried to stem the gossip,
soon the entire county was buzzing, and it spread to London." She shot
him a defiant glance. "In my opinion, Livia did nothing wrong. She and

Amberley were in love, and they were going to be married. But of course there are those who try to make her a pariah, and Livia refuses to come out of mourning. My mother is mortified by the situation, and has spent most of her time abroad ever since. And I am glad my father is no longer living, as he would undoubtedly have condemned Livia for her actions."

"But your brother doesn't?"

"No, Marcus is nothing like our father. He is every bit as honorable, but he is also very compassionate, and rather freethinking, too."

"A freethinking Marsden," McKenna mused, seeming to find it a contradictory phrase.

The glint of humor in his eyes somehow soothed her, eased her, and she was finally able to take a full breath. "You will agree, after you come to know Marcus better."

It was clear that the gulf between them was now even wider than it had been in childhood. Their worlds were, as always, so vastly different that there was no possibility of intimacy between them. Now they could interact as polite strangers, with no danger of heartbreak. The old McKenna no longer existed, just as the girl Aline had once been was also gone. She looked at the moss-carpeted earth, the torpid flow of the river, the diluted blue of the sky, before she was finally able to meet his gaze. And she was desperately grateful for the feeling of unreality that allowed her to face him without falling apart.

"I had better return to the house," she said, levering herself from the rock. "I have many responsibilities . . ."

McKenna stood immediately, the silhouette of his body dark and graceful against the flow of the river behind him.

Aline forced herself to break the excruciating silence. "You must tell me about how you have come to work for a man like Mr. Shaw."

"It's a long story."

"I am eager to hear it. What happened to the boy who didn't even care if he made it to first footman?"

"He got hungry."

Aline stared at him with a mixture of dread and fascination, sensing the complexity beneath the simple statement. She wanted to know every detail, to understand what had happened to McKenna, and to discover the facets of the man he had become.

McKenna seemed unable to take his gaze from hers. For some reason a band of color appeared high on his cheeks, as if he had spent too long in the sun. He came toward her with undue caution, as if her nearness presented some threat to him. As he stopped just a foot away from her, the paralyzing heat flooded her again. She inhaled quickly, the air feeling rich and heavy in her lungs.

"Will you take my arm?" he asked.

It was a commonplace courtesy that any gentleman would have offered . . . but Aline hesitated before touching him. Her fingers fluttered over his sleeve like the wings of a silver moth. "Thank you." She bit her lip and took hold of his arm, her hand conforming to the outline of heavy muscle beneath the soft layers of broadcloth and linen. The reality of touching him, after years of hopeless longing, made her sway slightly, and her grip tightened as she sought to steady herself. The rhythm of McKenna's breathing was abruptly fractured, as if something had caught him by the throat. However, he quickly recovered his self-possession as he escorted her up the gentle incline toward the house. Sensing the enormous power of his body, Aline wondered what he had done to acquire such physical strength.

"I worked as a boatman, ferrying passengers between Staten Island and the city," McKenna said, seeming to read her thoughts. "Twenty-five cents round-trip. That's how I met Shaw."

"He was one of your passengers?" Aline asked. At his nod, she sent him a quizzical glance. "How did a chance meeting turn into a business association?"

His expression became guarded. "One thing led to another."

She managed to smile at his evasiveness. "I see I'll have to use all my arts to bring out your talkative side."

"I don't have a talkative side."

"It is a guest's responsibility to be entertaining," she informed him.

"Oh, I'll entertain you," he murmured. "I just won't talk while I'm doing it."

As he must have intended, the remark dismantled her composure. Blushing, Aline gave a rueful laugh. "You haven't lost your knack for making wicked remarks, I see. Remember that you're in the company of a sheltered English lady."

He did not look at her as he replied. "Yes, I remember."

They approached the bachelor's quarters, a small residence set apart from the main house and reserved for the use of guests who wished for more privacy than the manor afforded. Marcus had told Aline that Mr. Shaw had specifically requested that he alone be given the bachelor's house, even though it could have accommodated three additional guests. Although there was no sign of Mr. Shaw yet, Aline saw a pair of servants entering the place with trunks and baggage.

McKenna stopped, his vivid eyes catching the sunlight as he glanced at the little house. "Shall we part company here? I will come to the manor soon—but first I want to have a look around."

"Yes, of course." Aline supposed that it must be overwhelming for him to return to Stony Cross, with memories lurking in every corner and path. "McKenna," she said unsteadily, "was it coincidence that Mr. Shaw decided to accept my brother's invitation for a visit? Or did you deliberately arrange things so that you could come back?"

McKenna turned to face her, his shoulders looming over hers. "What reason would I have to come back?"

Aline met his unfathomable gaze. There was nothing in his appearance or manner to suggest anger, but she sensed the tension coiled like a watch spring inside him.

And then she understood what he was concealing so carefully . . . what no one could have seen unless she had once loved him. Hatred. He had come back for revenge—and he would not leave until he had punished her a thousand ways for what she had done to him.

Oh, McKenna, she thought dazedly, feeling a curious sympathy for him even as her instincts screamed at her to flee from the imminent danger. *Does it still hurt that much?*

She glanced away, her brows drawing together as she reflected on how little it would take for him to annihilate her. Bringing herself to look up into his dark face, she spoke with great care. "How much you've accomplished, McKenna. You seem to have gotten everything you've ever wanted. More, even." Turning, she left him with measured strides, calling upon all her self-restraint to keep from running.

"Not everything," McKenna said beneath his breath, his gaze tracking her carefully until she disappeared.

McKenna wandered into the bachelor's house, disregarding the servants as they laid out Shaw's belongings. The furniture was heavy and authentically Jacobean, the shapes ponderous and stately. Lavish rosewood paneling covered the walls, and the windows were hung with fringed velvet that obliterated all traces of light. That was good. Much of the time, sunlight was anathema to Gideon Shaw.

McKenna knew exactly why Gideon needed the privacy of the bachelor's house. Ever a gentleman, Gideon scrupulously avoided making scenes or appearing out of control. McKenna had actually never even seen him drunk. Gideon would just quietly lock himself into a room with a bottle or two, and reappear two or three days later, pale and unsteady, but sharp-witted and perfectly groomed. Nothing in particular seemed to spur such episodes—it was simply the pattern of his life. His siblings had confided that the ritualistic drinking had begun not long before he and McKenna had met, when the oldest son, Frederick Shaw III, had died of a weak heart.

McKenna watched as Gideon's valet set out a japanned box of cigars on a blockfront desk with a multitude of drawers and pigeonholes. Although McKenna seldom smoked, and never at this time of day, he reached for the box. He extracted a cigar, its leaves oily and richly pungent. Immediately the well-trained valet produced a tiny pair of wickedly sharp scissors, and McKenna received them with a nod of thanks. He snipped off the end of the cigar, waited as the valet lit the end, then drew on it rhythmically until it produced a heavy draught of soothing smoke. Dispassionately he saw the trembling of his own fingers.

The shock of seeing Aline again was even greater than he had anticipated.

Detecting the evidence of his shattered nerves, the valet shot him an assessing glance. "Shall I fetch something else for you, sir?"

McKenna shook his head. "If Shaw comes, tell him I'm at the balcony in back."

"Yes, sir."

Like the main house, the bachelor's lodgings were set near a bluff overlooking the river. The land was heavily wooded with pine, the sounds of flowing water underlying the trill of nesting willow warblers. Shedding his coat, McKenna sat in one of the chairs on the covered balcony and smoked clumsily until he had regained a semblance of his self-control. He barely noticed when the valet brought out a crystal dish for the clumps of ash from his cigar. His mind was completely occupied with the image of Aline by the river, the rich mass of her pinned-up hair, the exquisite lines of her body and throat.

Time had only made Aline's beauty more eloquent. Her body was ripe and fully developed, the form of a woman in her prime. With maturity, her face had become more delicately sculpted, the nose thinner, the lips faded from deep rose to the pale shade of pink that tinted the inside of a seashell. And there was that damned, never-forgotten beauty mark, the festive dark fleck that lured his attention to the tender corner of her mouth. The sight of Aline had caused a remnant of humanity to stir inside McKenna, reminding him that he had once had the ability to experience joy—an ability that had vanished a long time ago. It had taken years to alter the obstinate course of his fate, and he had sacrificed most of his soul to do it.

Stubbing out his half-finished cigar, McKenna leaned forward with his forearms braced on his thighs. As he stared at a nearby hawthorn in full bloom, he wondered why Aline had remained unmarried. Perhaps like her father, she was essentially cold-natured, the passions of her youth having eventually been replaced by self-interest. Whatever the reason, it didn't matter. He was going to seduce Aline. His only regret was that old Lord Westcliff would not be around to find out that McKenna had finally taken his pleasure between his daughter's lily-white thighs.

Abruptly McKenna's attention was captured by the creak of the flooring and the liquid rattle of ice shards in a glass. Settling back in his chair, he glanced up as Gideon Shaw crossed the threshold of the covered balcony.

Turning to face McKenna, Gideon half sat on the railing and hung his free arm loosely around a support column. McKenna met his gaze steadily. Theirs was a complex friendship, supposed by outsiders to be founded purely on a shared desire for financial gain. Though that was an undeniable facet of their relationship, it was by no means the sole reason for it. As with most solid friendships, they each possessed characteristics that the other lacked. McKenna was of common origins, and rampantly ambitious, whereas Gideon was cultivated and subtle and complacent. McKenna had long ago acknowledged that he could not afford scruples. Gideon was a man of impeccable honor. McKenna had grimly enmeshed himself in the daily battles of life, while Gideon chose to remain detached.

The shadow of a smile crossed Gideon's mouth. "I encountered Lady Aline as she returned to the house. A beautiful woman, just as you described. Is she married?"

"No." McKenna stared moodily through the veil of smoke in the air.

"That makes things easier for you, then."

McKenna's broad shoulders twitched in the barest of shrugs. "It wouldn't matter one way or the other."

"You meant you wouldn't let a minor thing like a husband get in the way of what you wanted?" Gideon's smile broadened into an admiring grin. "Damn, you're a ruthless bastard, McKenna."

"That's why you need me as a partner."

"True. But the realization that there is such a poverty of morals between us . . . It makes me want a drink."

"What doesn't?" McKenna asked in a friendly gibe, taking the glass from him. Raising it to his lips, he drained it in a few efficient gulps, welcoming the velvety burn of iced bourbon.

Gideon's keen gaze didn't miss the residual unsteadiness of McKenna's hand, causing the ice to rattle in the glass. "Don't you think you're taking your revenge a bit too far? I have no doubt you'll succeed with Lady Aline. But I don't think it will bring you any peace."

"It's not revenge," McKenna muttered, setting aside the glass. His mouth twisted in a bitter smile. "It's an exorcism. And I don't expect to find any peace afterward. I just want . . ."

He trailed into silence. As always, he was in the grip of a hunger that had begun twelve years ago, when he had been cast into a life he had never envisioned for himself. In America, an opportunist's paradise, he had become successful beyond his wildest dreams. But it still wasn't enough. Nothing could satisfy the beast inside him.

Memories of Aline had tormented him forever. Certainly he did not love her—that illusion had faded long ago. He no longer believed in love, nor did he want to. But he needed to satisfy the raging need that had never allowed him to forget her. He had seen Aline's eyes, her mouth, the turn of her jaw, in the faces of a thousand strangers. The harder he had tried to ignore her memory, the more persistently she had haunted him.

"What if she gets hurt during this so-called exorcism?" Gideon asked. His tone was not shadowed by any form of judgment. It was one of Gideon's better qualities, his ability to look at things without filtering them through an ethical prism.

Reaching inside the glass, McKenna fished out a shard of ice and popped it into his mouth. He crunched it between his strong teeth. "Perhaps I want to hurt her."

That was an understatement. McKenna didn't intend to merely hurt Aline. He was going to make her suffer, weep, scream, beg. He was going to bring her to her knees. Break her. And that was just the beginning.

Gideon stared at him skeptically. "That's a rather strange attitude, coming from a man who once loved her."

"It wasn't love. It was a mixture of animal passion and youth and idiocy."

"What a glorious concoction," Gideon said with a reminiscent smile. "I haven't felt that way since I was sixteen and became infatuated with my sister's governess. An older woman, being all of twenty . . ." He paused, and his smile became brittle, his blue eyes darkening.

McKenna plucked another piece of bourbon-washed ice from the glass. "What happened to her?"

"We had an affair. And I seem to have gotten her with child, though she never told me about it. I believe it was mine, as there was no reason to think otherwise. She went to some fraud of a doctor who 'fixed' these things in his backroom. Bled to death. A pity, as my family would have compensated her for the child, had she told them about it. We Shaws always take care of our bastards."

Although his posture was relaxed as usual, Gideon could not hide the bleakness in his eyes.

"You've never mentioned her before," McKenna said, staring at him intently. They had known each other for more than ten years, and he had thought that he knew Gideon's every secret.

"Haven't I?" Seeming to recover himself, Gideon stood and brushed some imaginary dust from his hands. "Something about this place is making me maudlin. Too damned picturesque." He motioned to the door with a nod of his head. "I'm going to have another drink. Care to join me?"

McKenna shook his head, standing also. "I have some things to attend to."

"Yes, of course. You'll want to make the rounds—no doubt some of the servants here will remember you." A mocking smile touched Gideon's lips. "A lovely place, Stony Cross. One wonders how long it will take for its residents to realize they've let a serpent into paradise."

Seven

Without question, the best-smelling room in the manor house at Stony Cross Park was the storeroom, a chamber next to the kitchen where Mrs. Faircloth stored blocks of soap, candles, crystallized flowers, and fancy edibles such as bottled fruit. Today the housekeeper was unusually busy, with the household filled with guests and servants. She left the storeroom, her arms filled with heavy bricks of newly made soap. As soon as she carried the bricks to the stillroom, a pair of housemaids would use string to cut the soap into hand-sized cakes.

Preoccupied with the multitude of tasks yet to be done, Mrs. Faircloth became vaguely aware of the large bulk of a footman as he followed her along the narrow hall. "James," she said distractedly, "be a good lad and take these things to the stillroom. I have need of a strong pair of arms. And if Salter takes exception, you tell him that I bade you to help me."

"Yes, ma'am," came the obedient reply.

The voice did not belong to James.

As Mrs. Faircloth hesitated in confusion, the burden was taken from her, and she realized that she had just issued orders to one of the master's guests. His well-tailored clothes proclaimed him to be a man of privilege—and she had just ordered him to carry something for her. Servants, even upper ones, had been dismissed for less. "Sir, do forgive me . . ." she began in distress, but the dark-haired gentleman continued to the stillroom, hefting the weighty soap bricks with ease. He set the soap on the slate-topped table, turned from the openmouthed housemaids, and regarded Mrs. Faircloth with a rueful smile.

"I should have known you'd start giving commands before I had the chance to say hello."

Staring into his glowing blue-green eyes, Mrs. Faircloth pressed her hands to her heart as if to stave off the threat of apoplexy, and blinked with sudden tears of astonishment. "McKenna?" she exclaimed, impulsively holding out her arms. "Oh, good Lord . . ."

He reached her in two strides and caught her stout form against his, briefly lifting her off her feet as if she were a slight-framed girl. His gruff laugh was muffled in her silvery curls.

Dumbfounded by the emotional scene involving their normally stoic housekeeper, the maids in the stillroom drifted into the hallway. They were followed by a gaping scullery maid, a kitchen maid, and the cook, who had worked at the manor for only five years.

"I never thought to see you again," Mrs. Faircloth gasped.

McKenna tightened his arms around her, basking in the never-forgotten maternal comfort of her presence. He remembered the countless times that Mrs. Faircloth had saved extra food for him—the heels of the bread loaves, the leftover tea biscuits, the flavorful dregs from the stew pot. Mrs. Faircloth had been a source of necessary softness in his life . . . someone who had always believed the best of him.

She was much smaller than he remembered, and her hair was now pure white. But time had painted her gently, adding only a few softening wrinkles across her rosy cheeks, and a nearly imperceptible bow to the formerly straight lines of her shoulders and spine.

Drawing back her lace-capped head, Mrs. Faircloth regarded him with open disbelief. "My heavens, you've grown into a Goliath! I would scarcely have known you, were it not for your eyes." Becoming aware of their audience, the housekeeper released the large young man from her arms and gave the assembled servants a warning stare. "Busy yourselves at once, all of you. There's no need to stand there with your eyes bulging from your heads."

Mumbling obediently, the maids scattered and resumed their posts, throwing discreet glances at the visitor as they worked.

Mrs. Faircloth pressed McKenna's hand between her small, plump ones. "Come with me," she urged. They went in tacit agreement to the housekeeper's personal room. She unlocked the door and let him inside, and the familiar smell of clove pomanders and beeswax and tea-dyed linen mingled in a perfume of pure nostalgia.

Facing Mrs. Faircloth, McKenna saw that the housekeeper was becoming tearful once again, and he reached out to wrap his fingers around hers. "I'm sorry," he said gently. "I should have found a way to warn you before I appeared so suddenly."

Mrs. Faircloth managed to master her welling emotions. "What has happened to you?" she asked, staring at his elegant clothes, even noting the polished black shoes on his feet. "What has brought you back here, after so many years?"

"We'll talk later, when we both have more time," McKenna said, remembering the tumult of activity on days such as this, when dozens of visitors kept most of the servants at a dead run. "You have a house full of guests—and I haven't yet seen Lord Westcliff." He withdrew a packet of wax-sealed papers from his coat. "Before I go, I wanted to give you this."

"What is it?" the housekeeper asked in bewilderment.

"The money you gave me for my passage to America. I should have repaid you long before now, but—" McKenna paused uncomfortably. Words were inadequate to explain how, for the sake of his own sanity, he'd had to avoid anything or anyone in connection with Aline.

Shaking her head, Mrs. Faircloth tried to give the packet back to him. "No, McKenna, that was my gift to you. I was only sorry that I hadn't more to spare at the time."

"That five pounds saved my life." With great care, he straightened the cap on her head. "I'm returning your gift with interest. Those are shares in a brand-new locomotive foundry, all in your name. You can cash them immediately, if you wish. But I'd advise you to let them ripen a bit more. In the next year, they'll probably triple in value." McKenna couldn't restrain a rueful grin as he saw the perplexed way Mrs. Faircloth regarded the packet. She had little knowledge of stocks, equity, and future prospects.

"There's no actual money in here, then?" she asked.

"It's better than money," McKenna assured her, half suspecting that the stock certificates would soon be used to wrap fish. "Put that in a safe place, Mrs. Faircloth. What you're holding in your hands is worth about five thousand pounds."

Blanching, she nearly dropped the bundle. "Five thousand . . ."

Instead of demonstrating the elation McKenna had anticipated, the housekeeper seemed utterly dazed, as if she could not absorb the fact that she had just been made a wealthy woman. She swayed a little, and McKenna quickly reached out to steady her shoulders.

"I want you to retire," he said, "and buy a house for yourself, with your own servants, and a carriage. After all you've done for so many other people, I want you to enjoy the rest of your life."

"But I can't accept so much," she protested.

McKenna helped her to sit in the chair by the hearth, and sank to his haunches before her. He settled his hands on either arm of the chair. "That's only a drop in the bucket. I'd like to do more for you. To start with, I want you to consider coming back to New York with me, so that I can look after you."

"Ah, McKenna . . ." Her eyes glittered as she laid her work-roughened hand atop his. "I could never leave Stony Cross! I must stay with Lady Aline."

"Lady Aline?" he repeated, giving her an alert glance as he wondered why she had mentioned Aline in particular. "She can hire a new house-keeper." His senses sharpened as he saw her guarded expression.

"Have you seen her yet?" the housekeeper asked cautiously.

McKenna nodded. "We spoke briefly."

"Fate has not been kind to either of Lord Westcliff's daughters."

"Yes, I'm aware of that. Lady Aline told me about what happened to her sister."

"But nothing about herself?"

"No." McKenna did not miss the shadow of consternation that crossed her face. "What is there to tell?"

The housekeeper seemed to choose her words carefully. "Not long after you left Stony Cross, she was . . . quite ill." Two small, sharp indentations formed between the silvery arcs of her brows. "She was bedridden for at least three months. Although she recovered in time, she . . . has never been quite the same."

His eyes narrowed. "What happened to her?"

"I dare not tell you. The only reason I've mentioned it is that the illness has left her somewhat . . . fragile."

"In what way?"

She shook her head decisively. "I cannot say."

McKenna sat back on his heels, staring at her. Calculating the most effective way to elicit the information he wanted, he made his voice gentle and coaxing. "You know you can trust me. I won't tell anyone."

"Surely you wouldn't ask me to break a promise," Mrs. Faircloth chided.

"Of course I would," he said dryly. "I ask people to break promises all the time. And if they don't, I make them sorry for it." He rose to his feet in a fluid movement. "What do you mean, Lady Aline was 'never the same'? She damned well looks the same to me."

"Profanity!" The housekeeper clicked her tongue reprovingly.

Their gazes caught, and McKenna grinned suddenly as he thought of how many times he had received that same look from her in his boyhood. "Don't tell me, then. I'll get the truth from Lady Aline herself."

"I doubt that. And if I were you, I shouldn't push her too far." Mrs. Faircloth stood as well. "What a fine-looking man you have become," she exclaimed. "Is there a wife waiting for you back in America? A sweetheart?"

"No, thank God." His grin faded, however, at her next words.

"Ah . . ." Her tone was imbued with what could have been either pity or wonder. "It's always been her, hasn't it? That must be why you've come back."

McKenna scowled. "I've come back for business reasons, not the least of which is the likelihood that Westcliff will invest in the foundry. My presence here has nothing to do with Lady Aline—or a past that no one remembers."

"You remember it," she said. "And so does she."

"I must go," he said brusquely. "I have yet to find out if Westcliff will object to my presence here."

"I don't believe that will be the case," Mrs. Faircloth said at once. "Lord Westcliff is very much a gentleman. I expect he will offer you a gracious welcome, as he does to all his guests."

"Then he is remarkably *un*like his father," McKenna said sardonically.

"Yes. And I suspect you'll get on quite well with him, as long as you give him no cause to fear that you might harm Lady Aline. She has suffered quite enough, without you adding to it."

"Suffered?" McKenna couldn't restrain the contempt that curled through his tone. "I've seen real suffering, Mrs. Faircloth . . . people dying for lack of food and medicine . . . breaking their backs with hard labor . . . families wretched with poverty. Don't try to claim that Aline has ever had to lift a finger for her own survival."

"That is narrow-minded of you, McKenna," came her gentle rebuke. "It is true that the earl and his sisters suffer in different ways than we do, but their pain is still real. And it is not Lady Aline's fault if you've had a difficult life, McKenna."

"Nor is it mine," he said softly, while his blood boiled like a cauldron in hell.

"Good heavens, what a diabolical look," the housekeeper said softly. "What are you plotting, McKenna?"

He divested his face of all expression. "Nothing at all."

She regarded him with patent disbelief. "If you intend to maltreat Lady Aline in some way, I warn you—"

"No," he interrupted gently. "I would never cause her harm, Mrs. Faircloth—you know what she once meant to me."

The housekeeper seemed to relax. And, turning away, she missed the dark smile that crossed his hard features.

McKenna paused before reaching for the doorknob, and glanced back over his shoulder. "Mrs. Faircloth, tell me . . ."

"Yes?"

"Why is she still unmarried?"

"That is for Lady Aline to explain."

"There must be a man," McKenna murmured. A woman as stunningly beautiful as Aline would never lack for male companionship.

Mrs. Faircloth replied cautiously. "As a matter of fact, there is a gentleman with whom she keeps company. Lord Sandridge, who now owns the old Marshleigh estate. He took up residence there about five years ago. I suspect you may see him at the ball tomorrow night—he is often invited to Stony Cross Park."

"What kind of man is he?"

"Oh, Lord Sandridge is a very accomplished gentleman, and well liked by his neighbors. I daresay you'll find much to recommend him, when you meet."

"I look forward to it," McKenna said softly, and left the housekeeper's room.

Aline greeted the guests mechanically. After encountering Mr. Gideon Shaw on the way back to the manor house, she made the acquaintance of the Chamberlains—his sister and brother-in-law, and their wealthy New York friends, the Laroches, the Cuylers, and the Robinsons. As one might have predicted, they possessed the typical American awe of British nobility. The fact that Aline asked about their comfort during the Atlantic crossing elicited a torrent of gratitude. The mention of the refreshments that would soon be served was received with the volume of joy one would expect from a condemned man who had just received a pardon. Aline was strongly hopeful that after they had all lived beneath the manor roof for a few days, they would cease to be quite so dazzled by her.

Taking leave of the guests, Aline went to the kitchen in search of Mrs. Faircloth. Oddly, although the scene was completely normal, Aline knew without being told that McKenna had just been there. The air seemed alive with energy, as if a lightning bolt had just been hurled across the room. One look into Mrs. Faircloth's eyes confirmed her suspicion. Yes, McKenna had come immediately to find the housekeeper, after seeing Aline. Of everyone who had once known him, they were the two who had loved him best.

McKenna . . . Thoughts swarmed in her head like bees in an overturned hive . . . she couldn't seem to catch hold of one coherent notion, one clear image. It seemed impossible that McKenna could have returned to Stony Cross as if drawn by the polarity of some magical lodestone, needing a resolution to the past that had haunted them both. He wanted something from her . . . some ransom of pain, regret, or pleasure, that would finally bring him a measure of peace. And she had nothing to offer him, though she would have given her very soul as a willing sacrifice, were it possible.

She wanted another glance of him, just to make certain that he was real. She needed the sound of his voice, the feel of his arm beneath her hand, anything to confirm that she had not gone mad from her eternal craving. Struggling for self-mastery, Aline made her face blank as she moved toward the long wooden table. She glanced at the page of notes between the cook and Mrs. Faircloth, and quietly suggested a few changes to the menus. When the final decisions were agreed upon, Aline considered the prospect of joining the crowd of visitors for the midmorning meal, and felt a wave of exhaustion sweep over her. She did not want to eat and smile and make conversation with so many eager strangers. And to have to do so with McKenna there watching . . . impossible. Later tonight she would have set herself to rights, and she would be the consummate hostess. Right now, however, she wanted to go somewhere private, and think. *And hide,* a little mocking voice added. Yes, and hide. She did not want to see McKenna again until she had managed to compose herself.

"The earl will want to see you," Mrs. Faircloth said, drawing aside with her to the kitchen entrance. Her gaze was warm and concerned as she stared into Aline's bloodless face.

Of course. Marcus would want to make certain that she wasn't weeping or shaken, or otherwise dismantled by the appearance of a man whom she had once loved. "I will go find him," Aline said. "And I will also tell him that he will have to entertain the guests this morning without my help. I feel . . . rather fatigued."

"Yes," Mrs. Faircloth agreed, "you will want to be well rested for the ball tonight."

McKenna, attending a ball at Stony Cross Park—it was something Aline had never dared to imagine. "Life is strange, isn't it," she murmured. "How ironic it is that he should finally come back."

Naturally Mrs. Faircloth knew which "he" Aline was referring to. "He still wants you."

The words caused a quiver to run through her, as if her spine had been plucked like an archer's drawn bow. "Did he say so?"

"No . . . but I saw his face when I mentioned your name."

Aline took a strained breath before asking, "You didn't tell him—"

"I would never betray your secret," the housekeeper assured her.

Discreetly Aline took Mrs. Faircloth's warm, work-coarsened hand in her own soft, cold one. She was comforted by the housekeeper's touch as their fingers entwined tightly. "He must never know," she whispered. "I couldn't bear it."

Aline found Marcus and Livia together in the family receiving room, a private place where they occasionally met to discuss issues of particular urgency. This appeared to be one of them. Despite her inner havoc, Aline smiled as she glanced at her brother's dark, concerned face, and her sister's tense one. "There is no reason to look as if you expect me to hurl myself through the window," she told them. "I assure you, I am perfectly calm. I have seen McKenna, we spoke quite cordially, and we both agreed that the past is completely irrelevant."

Marcus came forward and took her shoulders in his broad, square hands. "The past is never irrelevant," he said in his distinctively gravelly voice. "And now, circumstances being what they are . . . I don't want you to be hurt again."

Aline tried to reassure him with a smile. "I won't be hurt. There is nothing left of the feelings I once had for him. I was just a muddle-headed girl. And I am convinced that McKenna feels nothing for me now either."

"Then why is he here?" Marcus asked, his gaze hard.

"To conduct business with Mr. Shaw, of course. And to discuss your investment in their foundries—"

"I suspect that is a subterfuge to conceal McKenna's true purpose."

"Which would be . . . what?"

"To finally make a conquest of you."

"Really, Marcus, do you know how ridiculous that sounds?"

"I'm a sportsman," he said flatly. "I've ridden to the hounds and shot game for most of my life—and I know a hunt when I see one."

Pulling back from her brother, Aline gave him a mocking glance. "I should have known you'd reduce it to that. Life is about more than pursuit and conquest, Marcus."

"For a woman, perhaps. Not for a man."

Aline sighed and gave Livia a meaningful glance, silently enlisting her support.

Her younger sister complied immediately. "If Aline says that she is not troubled by McKenna's presence, then I think we shouldn't take exception to it either."

Marcus's expression did not soften. "I'm still considering asking him to leave."

"Good Lord, do you know how much gossip that would cause?" Aline asked impatiently. "Why bother asking for my opinion, if you've already decided what to do? Just leave it be, will you? I want him to stay."

She was surprised by the way that her brother and sister both looked at her, as if she had spoken in a foreign language. "What is it?" she asked warily.

"Just now, I saw some of your old spirit," Marcus said. "It's a welcome change."

Aline responded with a wry laugh. "What are you implying, Marcus? That I've become timid and spineless?"

"Withdrawn is more like it," he retorted. "You refuse to accept the attentions of any man except Sandridge—and it's obvious that nothing will ever come of *that*." As Aline spluttered in protest, Marcus turned his attention to Livia. "And you're no better than Aline," he said flatly. "It's been two years since Amberley died, and you might as well have gone to the grave with him. Time to shed the widow's weeds, Livia, and start living again. Good God, you're the two prettiest women in Hampshire, and you both live like nuns. I fear I'm going to be saddled with the both of you until I'm bald and toothless."

Livia gave him an offended glare, while Aline suddenly snickered at the image of her virile brother as a hairless old codger. She went to kiss him affectionately. "We're exactly what you deserve, you arrogant meddler. Just be thankful that I'm not of a mind to lecture you on *your* faults, my dear, *unmarried* thirty-four-year-old brother, whose sole purpose in this life should be to produce an heir for the title—"

"Enough," he groaned. "I've heard that a thousand times from Mother. God knows I don't need it from you."

Aline glanced triumphantly at Livia, who had managed a wan smile. "Very well, I'll desist for now, *if* you'll promise to do and say nothing in regard to McKenna."

Marcus nodded and grumbled, taking his leave.

Holding Livia's gaze, Aline saw how Marcus's remarks had troubled her. She smiled reassuringly. "He's right about one thing," she said. "You should begin to mix in company again."

"In the company of men, you mean."

"Yes. You're going to fall in love again someday, Livia. You'll marry some wonderful man, and bear his children, and have the life that Amberley would wish for you."

"What about you?"

Aline's smile vanished. "You know why those dreams are no longer possible for me."

A sigh burst from Livia's lips. "It's not fair!"

"No," Aline agreed softly. "But there you have it—some things are just not meant to be."

Wrapping her arms tightly around herself, Livia frowned at the carpeted floor. "Aline, there is something I've never said to you—I've always been too ashamed. But now that McKenna has returned, and the past is so much in my thoughts, I can't ignore it any longer."

"No, Livia," Aline said gently, sensing what her younger sister was about to say.

A sudden tear slid to the delicate curve of Livia's chin. "I was the one who told Father about seeing you and McKenna together in the stables, all those years ago. You've suspected it, of course, but you've never asked. I wish I had kept silent. I'm so sorry that I didn't. I ruined everything for you."

"It wasn't your fault," Aline exclaimed, moving forward to hug her. "How could I blame you for that? You were just a child, and . . . no, don't cry! It doesn't matter that you told Father. Nothing could ever have come of my relationship with McKenna. There was no place that we could have gone, nothing that could have been done, that would have allowed us to be together."

"I'm still sorry."

Making a soothing noise, Aline patted her slender back. " 'Only a fool argues with his fate' . . . that's what Father always said, remember?"

"Yes, and it always made him sound like a complete idiot."

Laughter rose in Aline's throat. "Perhaps you're right. McKenna has certainly defied his own fate, hasn't he?"

Pulling a handkerchief from her sleeve, Livia drew back and blew her nose. "The servants are talking," she said, her voice muffled in the wad of crumpled cotton. "Apparently Mr. Chamberlain's butler told James the footman—who told one of the housemaids—that McKenna is called 'King' McKenna in New York, and he has a huge mansion on Fifth Avenue, and he is known by everyone on Wall Street."

Aline smiled crookedly. "From a stable boy to a king. I should have expected no less of him."

"Aline, what if McKenna falls in love with you again?"

The question caused her to shiver. "He won't. Believe me, once the flame of a past love affair has been extinguished, there is no way to revive it."

"What if it was never extinguished?"

"Livia, I assure you that McKenna has not been pining after me for twelve years."

"But haven't you—" Livia stopped abruptly.

Realizing what her sister had been about to ask, Aline flushed. She wandered to the window, staring out at a path of stone arches that led through the east garden. The arches had overgrown with roses, clematis, and honeysuckle, forming a fragrant tunnel that led to a stone-walled summerhouse with a wood-latticed ceiling. Memories of McKenna were everywhere in the garden . . . his hands moving carefully among the roses, pruning the dead blossoms . . . his tanned face dappled with the sunlight that broke through the leaves and lattices . . . the hair on the back of his neck glittering with sweat as he shoveled gravel onto the path, or weeded the raised flower beds.

"I don't know that one could call it pining," Aline said, stroking the windowpane with her fingertips. "McKenna will always be a part of me, no matter where he goes. They say that people who've lost a limb sometimes feel as if they still have it. How many times I've felt that McKenna was still here, and the empty space beside me was alive with his presence." She closed her eyes and leaned forward until her forehead and the tip of her nose touched the cool glass. "I love him beyond reason," she whispered. "He's a stranger to me now, and yet he is still so familiar. I can't imagine a sweeter agony, having him so close."

A long time passed before Livia was able to speak. "Aline . . . won't you tell McKenna the truth, now that he has come back?"

"For what purpose? It would only earn his pity, and I would sooner throw myself from the bluff." Pushing back from the window, Aline rubbed the side of her sleeve over the smudge her face had made on one of the gleaming panes. "Better to let him go on hating me."

"I don't know how you can endure it!" Livia exclaimed.

Aline smiled wryly. "Well, I find a strange comfort in the fact that he wouldn't feel this degree of animosity now, had he not loved me so much before."

Despite entreaties from both Marcus and Aline, Livia refused to attend the welcoming ball that would be attended by everyone of note in the county. "I need you there," Aline had insisted, trying to think of any way that would induce her sister to emerge from her self-imposed seclusion from society. "I am feeling unsettled tonight, Livia, and your presence at my side would be such a help—"

"No," Livia said placidly, settled in the family receiving room with a book in one hand and a glass of wine in the other. She wore her hair in a loose braid, and her feet were tucked into soft knit slippers. "I have no desire to mix with that mob of Americans. Besides, I know exactly why you're unsettled, and my company won't make a bit of difference to you."

"Have you no desire to see McKenna, after all these years?"

"God help me, no." Livia's bright hazel-green eyes surveyed her over the rim of the glass as she sipped her wine. "The thought of facing McKenna after the way I tattled on the two of you so long ago makes me want to sink through the floor."

"He doesn't know about that."

"Well, I do!"

Frowning, Aline decided to take another tack. "What about Mr. Shaw? Aren't you the least bit desirous of meeting him?"

"From what Marcus has told me about the infamous Mr. Shaw, I would do well to stay far away from him."

"I thought Marcus liked Shaw."

"He does, but not as a companion for either of his sisters."

"I should think that would make Mr. Shaw very entertaining," Aline said, making Livia laugh.

"Since he's staying here for a month, we'll probably find out. In the meantime, go downstairs and enjoy yourself. You look so beautiful in that gown . . . didn't you once tell me that blue was McKenna's favorite color?"

"I don't remember."

It had indeed been blue. Tonight Aline had not been able to prevent herself from reaching for a silk gown the color of Russian lapis. It was a simple gown with no flounces or overskirt, just a demi-train in the back and a low, square-cut bodice. A string of pearls was wrapped twice around her throat, with the lower loop hanging almost to her waist. Another strand had been artfully entwined in her pinned-up curls.

"You're a goddess," her sister proclaimed cheerfully, raising her wineglass in tribute. "Good luck, dear. Because once McKenna sees you in that gown, I predict that you'll have a difficult time keeping him at bay."

Once McKenna's business partnership with Gideon Shaw had been struck, Gideon had insisted on making him presentable for Knickerbocker society. This had entailed a long and rigorous period of training and instruction, which had given McKenna suitable polish to mingle with those in the Shaws' elevated circles. However, McKenna would never deceive himself into thinking that his cultivation was anything more than skin-deep. Being a member of the upper class consisted of far more than clothes and manners. It required an attitude of entitlement, an intrinsic confidence in one's own superiority, and an elegance of character that he knew he could never attain.

Luckily for McKenna, in America money was enough. As exclusive as the American upper class was, it still reluctantly made room for wealthy climbers. A man with new money, usually referred to as a "swell," found that most doors were open to him. Women were not so fortunate. If an heiress's family was not well established, no matter how financially well endowed, she would never be accepted by Old New York, and she was obliged to do her husband hunting in Paris or London rather than at home.

After the captious atmosphere of the New York balls, McKenna was pleasantly surprised by the relaxed quality of this gathering. When he said as much to Gideon, his friend laughed quietly.

"It's always like this in England," Gideon said. "English peers have nothing to prove. Since no one can ever take their titles away from them, they are free to do and say as they wish. Whereas in New York, one's social status is a rather precarious thing. The only way you can be certain of your standing is if you're included on one damned list or another. Committee lists, guest lists, members lists, visiting lists . . ."

"Are there any lists that you aren't on?" McKenna had asked.

"God, no," Gideon said with a self-mocking laugh. "I'm a Shaw. Everyone wants me."

They stood together at one end of the ballroom, which contained what seemed to be acres of parquet flooring. The air was dense with the fragrance of roses, irises, and lilies, cut from the estate gardens and expertly arranged in crystal vases. The niches set into the walls had been fitted with tiny velvet-upholstered benches, where dowagers and wall-flowers sat in tightly compacted groups. Music floated down from an upper-floor balcony, the small orchestra half concealed by bowers of lush greenery. Although this ball did not approach the extravagance of some of the Fifth Avenue affairs McKenna had attended, it put those opulent balls to shame. There was a difference between quality and mere showiness, he thought. That notion was reinforced immediately by the appearance of Lady Aline.

She was dazzling, with strands of white pearls in her lustrous dark hair, her voluptuous body wrapped in a blue dress that molded tightly over the swell of her breasts. A double circlet of fresh white rosebuds was wrapped around one of her gloved wrists. Extending her hands in welcome, she went to a group of guests near the door of the ballroom. Her smile was a flash of magic. As he watched her, McKenna noticed something about her that had not registered during their earlier meeting . . . she walked differently than he remembered. Instead of exhibiting the impetuous grace she had possessed as a girl, Aline now moved with the leisurely deliberateness of a swan gliding across a still pond.

Aline's entrance attracted many gazes, and it was obvious that McKenna was not the only man who appreciated her sparkling allure. No matter how tranquil her facade, there was no concealing the luminous sensuality beneath. McKenna could barely restrain himself from going over to her and dragging her away to some dark, secluded place. He wanted to tear the pearls from her hair, and press his lips to her breast, and breathe in the scent of her body until he was drunk from it.

"Lovely," Gideon commented, following his gaze. "But you could find someone almost as attractive—not to mention quite a bit younger—back in New York."

McKenna threw him a dismissive glance. "I know what's back in New York." His gaze returned compulsively to Aline.

Gideon smiled and rolled the stem of a wineglass between his long fingers. "Although I wouldn't claim that all women are alike, I can say with some authority that they do possess the same basic equipment. What makes this one so infinitely preferable to all the rest? The simple fact that you couldn't have her?"

McKenna did not bother replying to such inanity. It would be impossible to make Shaw—or anyone else—understand. The dark reality was that he and Aline had never been separate—they could live on opposite sides of the earth, and they would still be caught together in a hellish tangle. Not have her? He had never *stopped* having her . . . She had been a perpetual torment to him. She was going to suffer for that, as he had suffered for more than a decade.

His thoughts were interrupted as Lord Westcliff approached. Like the other men present, Westcliff was clad in a formal scheme of black and white, with fashionably wide, straight-cut coat lapels and loose, expertly tailored trousers. He had the powerful build of a sportsman, and his manner was straightforward rather than scheming. His resemblance to the old earl, however, caused a prickle of animosity that McKenna couldn't ignore. On the other hand, not many peers would receive a former servant as a valued guest—McKenna would give him that.

As Westcliff greeted them, his expression was pleasant, if not precisely friendly. "Good evening," he murmured. "Are you enjoying yourselves so far, gentlemen?"

"Quite," Shaw said cordially, lifting his glass in approbation. "A very fine Bordeaux, my lord."

"Excellent. I will see that some of that particular vintage is stocked in the bachelor's house for your convenience." Westcliff's gaze moved to McKenna. "And you, sir? What do you think of your first ball at Stony Cross Park?"

"It looks different from this side of the windows," McKenna said frankly.

That drew a reluctant smile from Westcliff. "It is a long distance from the stables to the ballroom," he acknowledged. "And not one that many men could have traversed."

McKenna barely heard the remark. His attention had returned to Aline, who had gone to greet a newcomer.

It appeared the guest had come alone. He was a handsome man of not more than thirty years of age, with blond good looks that were comparable to Gideon Shaw's. However, whereas Gideon was golden and weathered, this man was wintry-fair . . . his hair pale and gilded, his eyes piercing. The sight of him with Aline, light matched with dark, was strikingly attractive.

Following his gaze, Westcliff saw the pair. "Lord Sandridge," he murmured. "A friend of the family, and held in high regard by Lady Aline."

"Apparently so," McKenna said, not missing the air of intimacy between the two. Jealousy spread through him in a poisonous tide.

Westcliff continued casually. "They have been friends for at leave five years. My sister has an unusual affinity with Sandridge—which pleases me a great deal, as I desire her happiness above all else." He bowed to them both. "At your service, gentlemen."

Gideon smiled as he watched the earl leave. "A proficient strategist is our Westcliff," he murmured. "He seems to be warning you away from Lady Aline, McKenna."

McKenna gave him a damning glance, though he had long been accustomed to Gideon's perverse delight in jabbing at his self-possession. "Westcliff can go to hell," he growled. "Along with Sandridge."

"You're not afraid of competition, then?" Gideon murmured.

McKenna arched one brow and spoke scornfully. "After five years of knowing Lady Aline, Sandridge hasn't yet laid claim to her. That's not what I would call competition, in any sense of the word."

"Hasn't *publicly* laid claim to her," Gideon corrected.

McKenna shook his head with a faint smile. "To my knowledge, Shaw, that's the only way that counts."

Eight

There had been few people in Aline's life that she had trusted enough to love. However, loving Adam, Lord Sandridge had been one of the easiest things she had ever done. Theirs was a friendship in its purest form, uncompromised by any nuance of sexuality. Many rumors of an affair had circulated during the past five years, which served both their purposes. Aline liked the fact that fewer men dared to approach her because of her supposed romantic involvement with Adam. And Adam, for his part, was grateful that the gossip about them prevented other, more destructive rumors that might have arisen otherwise.

Aline had never pried into the subject of Adam's sexual preferences, as they had nothing to do with her. But she knew what very few people suspected—that his attraction was limited exclusively toward other men. Which would make some like-minded fellow very fortunate indeed. Adam's charm, his intelligence, and his finely honed wit would have made him desirable no matter what his physical appearance. But as it happened, he was also resplendently handsome, with thick hair the color of white gold, dark-lashed gray eyes, and a lean, well-exercised body.

When Aline was with Adam, she couldn't help but enjoy herself. He made her laugh, he made her think, and he understood what she was going to say before she even said it. Adam could lift her from her occasional depressions of the spirit as no one else could, and she had, on occasion, done the same for him. "Sometimes you make me wish that I were a man," she told him once, laughing. His answering smile was a dazzle of white in his lightly tanned face.

"No, you're too perfect as a woman."

"Far from perfect," she had murmured, conscious of the thick mass of scar tissue that covered her legs.

Being Adam, he had not resorted to platitudes or lies, but had only taken her hand in his and held it for a long time. She had already told him about her accident, and the damage it had done to her legs, not long after they had met. Odd, really, as she had kept it a secret from friends she had known for years . . . but there was no hiding anything from Adam. She had also told Adam every detail of her forbidden love for McKenna, and how she had sent him away. Adam had received her confidences with quiet understanding and just the right amount of sympathy.

Wearing a stiff social smile, Aline took his hands in a viselike grip, and spoke beneath her breath. "I need you, Adam."

He looked into her face with light, intent eyes. "What is it?"

"McKenna," she managed to say. "He's come back."

Adam shook his head incredulously. "To Stony Cross?" At her jerking nod, he shaped his lips in a soundless whistle. "Good God."

Aline smiled tremulously. "He's staying at the manor—he came with the Americans."

"Poor sweet," he said ruefully. "Your bad luck is holding true, it seems. Come with me to the garden, and we'll talk."

She longed to comply, but she held back uncertainly. "I must stay and receive the guests."

"This is more important," Adam informed her, pulling her hand to the crook of his arm. "Just a few minutes—I'll have you back before you are missed. Come."

They walked to the stone-flagged balcony overlooking the back terraces, where a row of French doors were open to admit any stray breeze from outdoors. Aline spoke rapidly, telling Adam everything while he listened in thoughtful silence. Pausing at the open doors, Adam glanced back at the milling throng. "Tell me which one he is," he murmured.

Aline barely needed to glance inside the ballroom, so attuned was she to McKenna's presence. "He's over there, near the gilded frieze. My brother is speaking to him."

After a discreet glance, Adam returned his gaze to hers and spoke dryly. "Quite nice, if one likes the dark, brooding sort."

As distraught she was, Aline couldn't suppress a wry laugh. "Is there anyone who doesn't like that sort?"

"I, for one. You're welcome to your Sturm und Drang, darling—I'll take someone who's a bit easier to manage."

"What is Sturm und Drang?"

"Ah . . . I see that I'll have to introduce you to the finer points of German literature. It means passionate turmoil—literally translated, 'storm and stress.' "

"Yes, well, there is nothing quite as exciting as a storm, is there?" Aline asked ruefully.

Adam grinned as he drew her to a nearby bench. "Only when one is viewing it from inside a nice, cozy house." As they sat, he took Aline's hand in his and pressed it lightly. "Tell me, sweet, what are we to do about this problem of yours?"

"I'm not yet certain."

"Has McKenna said yet what he wants from you?" Adam answered his own question before she was able. "Never mind—I know exactly what he wants. The question is, is there a possibility that he might force or coerce you in some way?"

"No," she said at once. "No matter how McKenna has changed, he would never resort to that."

Adam seemed to relax slightly. "That's good news."

"I'm afraid, Adam," Aline confessed in a whisper, laying her head on his shoulder. "Not of what will happen now, or during the next few weeks . . . I'm afraid of afterward, when McKenna leaves again. I survived it once, but I don't know if I can again."

He slid his arm around her and squeezed comfortingly. "Yes, you will—I'll be here to help you." A long pause ensued as he considered his next words. "Aline, what I'm about to say may seem rather ill-occasioned . . . but I've been considering an idea lately, and this may be as good a time as any to mention it."

"Yes?"

Adam looked down at her, their noses nearly touching. He smiled, his gray eyes gleaming as they reflected the gathering moonlight. "We're a good pair, sweet. In the five years that we've known each other, I've come to adore you as I have no other person on earth. I could spend the next hour enumerating your many virtues, but you're well aware of them already. My proposition is this—I think we should continue on as we have, with one minor alteration. I want to marry you."

"Have you been drinking?" Aline asked, and he laughed.

"Think about it—you would be mistress of Marshleigh. We would be that rarest of all combinations, a husband and wife who actually like each other."

She stared at him in confusion. "But you would never want to—"

"No. We would each find one kind of satisfaction in marriage, and another kind outside it. Friendship is a hell of a lot more durable than love, Aline. And I'm very much a traditionalist in one sense—I see the wisdom in keeping passion entirely separate from marriage. I won't blame you for seeking your pleasures where you can find them, and you won't blame me for doing the same."

"I won't be seeking those kinds of pleasures," she murmured. "Any man who saw my legs would find it impossible to make love to me."

"Then don't let him see them," Adam said casually.

She gave him a skeptical glance. "But how would I—"

"Use your imagination, darling."

The devilish glint in his eyes caused her to blush. "I've never considered the possibility before. It would be strange and awkward—"

"It amounts to a simple matter of logistics," Adam informed her sardonically. "But back to my proposal—will you give it some thought?"

She shook her head with a reluctant smile. "I may be a bit too conventional for such an arrangement."

"Conventions be damned." Adam kissed her hair. "Let me help to mend your heart when it's broken. Let me rub your legs at night, and hold you as a beloved friend would. Let me take you to beautiful places when you tire of English views."

Aline smiled against the fine weave of his coat. "May I have some time to consider your very tempting offer?"

"All the time in the world." Suddenly Adam shifted, though his arms remained around her, and he spoke quietly into her ear. "Mr. Sturm is coming this way, Miss Drang. What will you have me do—stay or leave?"

Aline eased away from him. "Leave," she whispered. "I can manage him."

"We'll make that your epigraph," Adam teased, and brushed his lips across her cheek. "Good luck, sweet. Give a shout if you need me."

"You don't want to meet him before you go?" she asked.

"God, no. Slay your own dragons, my lady," he said, and left her with a grin.

Aline looked up from her seated position at the bench as McKenna approached her, his dark presence falling over her like a shadow. Adam's reference to McKenna was not quite accurate—he looked far more like a devil than a dragon, needing only a pitchfork to complete the image. A tall, brooding, smoldering-eyed devil, in a formal scheme of black and white. He literally took her breath away. Aline was shocked by her own uncontrollable hunger to touch him. This was the feeling of her youth, the wild, dizzying excitement that she had never been able to forget. "McKenna," she said breathlessly. "Good evening."

He stopped before her and glanced intently at the doorway through which Adam had just departed. "Who was that?" he asked, although she suspected that he already knew.

"Lord Sandridge," she murmured. "A very dear friend."

"Only a friend?"

Ten minutes ago, Aline would have replied with an unhesitating yes. Now in light of Adam's marriage proposal, she considered the question thoughtfully. "He wants to marry me," she admitted.

McKenna's expression was perfectly bland, though there was an odd flicker in his eyes. "And will you?"

Aline stared at him as he stood before her, half in shadow, half in light, and she felt a change coming over her body, skin tingling beneath the covering of blue silk, the tips of her breasts turning hard. Warmth moved over the surface of her chest and stomach as if someone were breathing against her. "Probably," she heard herself whisper.

McKenna came to her, reaching a hand down in a silent gesture of command. She let him pull her up, and felt his long fingers encircle her gloved wrist just beneath the ring of entwined white rosebuds. Her wrist remained pliable and unresisting in his grasp. She felt her heart contract briefly as his thumb slipped into the cup of her palm. Their hands were sheathed in two thickness of gloves, and yet the mere pressure of his fingers against her was enough to send her pulse hurtling.

"McKenna," she asked quietly, "why did you give me no warning before you came back to Stony Cross so suddenly?"

"I didn't think it would matter to you if I came or not."

The obvious lie was delivered smoothly. Anyone would have believed him, except her. *Not matter?* she thought, suspended between anguish and miserable laughter. How many rain-swept days and lonely nights she had spent longing for him. In the fever-induced delirium that had brought her to the threshold of death, she had spoken his name, begged for him, dreamed that he held her while she slept. "Of course it matters," she said with forced lightness, pushing aside the memories. "We were friends once, after all."

"Friends," he repeated without inflection.

Cautiously Aline eased her wrist away from his hold. "Why, yes. Very good friends. And I so often wondered what became of you, after you left."

"Now you know." His face was hard and smooth. "I wondered as well . . . what happened to you after I was sent to Bristol? I've heard mention of an illness—"

"Let's not talk about my past," Aline interrupted with a quick, self-deprecating laugh. "It is quite dull, I assure you. I am far more interested in hearing about *you*. Tell me everything. Start with the moment you first set foot in New York."

The artful flattery of her gaze seemed to amuse McKenna, as if he understood somehow that she had decided to keep him at a distance by flirting with him, thereby averting the possibility of discussing anything meaningful. "It's not ballroom conversation."

"Ah. Then is it parlor conversation? Cardroom conversation? No? Heavens, it must be lurid indeed. Let's walk outside somewhere. To the stables. The horses will be quite entertained by your story, and they hardly ever gossip."

"Can you leave your guests?"

"Oh, Westcliff is an adept host—he'll make do."

"What about a chaperone?" he asked, though he was already guiding her to the side entrance of the ballroom.

Her smile turned wry. "Women my age don't require chaperones, McKenna."

He slid an unnervingly thorough glance over her. "You may need one yet."

They walked through the outside gardens to the back entrance of the stables. The estate manor had been laid out in the European fashion, with the stables forming one of the wings that enclosed the courtyard in front. It was jokingly remarked that Lord Westcliff's horses lived in a grander fashion than most people, and there was more than a little truth in it. The stone-flagged central court of the stables contained a large marble drinking fountain for the horses. Archways led to the harness room, rows of five dozen stalls, and a carriage room that smelled strongly of brass polish, leather, and wax. The stables had changed little in the years since McKenna had left Stony Cross Park. Aline wondered if he took pleasure in the familiarity of the place.

They stopped in the harness room, the walls hung with saddles, bridles, halters, breastplates, and leathers. Wooden boxes filled with grooming implements were aligned neatly on shelves. The smell of horses and leather made the air sweetly pungent.

McKenna wandered to a saddle and smoothed his fingertips over the well-worn surface. His dark head bent, and he suddenly seemed lost in memory.

Aline waited until his gaze returned to her. "How did you get your start in New York?" she asked. "I would have thought you'd find something to do with horses. Why on earth did you become a boatman?"

"Moving cargo at the docks was the first job I could find. When I wasn't loading boats, I learned how to hold my own in a fistfight. Most of the time the dockers had to brawl over who was going to get the work." He paused, and added frankly, "I learned in no time to bully my way into getting what I wanted. Eventually I was able to buy a small sailboat with a shallow draft, and I became the fastest ferryman going to and from Staten Island."

Aline listened carefully, trying to understand the gradual process by which the cavalier boy had become the hard-driven man standing before her. "Did someone act as a mentor to you?" she asked.

"No, I had no mentor." He ran his fingers over the line of a tightly braided crop. "I thought of myself as a servant for a long time—I never thought I would be more than I was right then. But after a while I realized that the other ferrymen had ambitions far beyond mine. They told me stories about men like John Jacob Astor—have you heard of him?"

"I'm afraid not. Is he a contemporary of the Shaws?"

The question made McKenna laugh suddenly, his teeth flashing white in his dark face. "He's richer than the Shaws, though even Gideon won't admit it. Astor was a butcher's son who started with nothing and made a fortune in the fur trade. Now he buys and sells New York real estate. He's worth at least fifteen million dollars by now. I've met Astor—he's a domineering little runt who can barely speak English—and he's made himself into one of the richest men in the world."

Aline's eyes widened. She had heard about the explosive growth of industry in America, and the fast-rising value of New York property. But it seemed nearly impossible for one man—especially one of low station—to have acquired such a fortune.

McKenna seemed to follow the train of her thoughts. "Everything's possible, over there. You can make a lot of money if you're willing to do what it takes. And money is all that matters, since Americans aren't distinguished by titles or noble blood."

"What do you mean, 'if you're willing to do what it takes'?" Aline asked. "What have you had to do?"

"I've had to advantage of others. I've learned to ignore my conscience, and put my own interests above anyone else's. Most of all, I've learned that I can't afford to care about anyone but myself."

"You're not really like that," she said.

His voice was very soft. "Don't doubt it for a minute, my lady. I'm nothing like the boy you knew. He may as well have died when he left Stony Cross."

Aline could not accept that. If there was nothing left of that boy, then a vital part of her heart would die too. Turning toward the tack on the wall nearest her, she concealed the unhappiness that had pulled her features taut. "Don't say that."

"It's the truth."

"You seem to be warning me away from yourself," she said thickly.

Aline was not aware of McKenna's approach, but suddenly he was right behind her. Their bodies were not touching, but she was acutely aware of the solidity and size of him. In the midst of her inner turmoil, pure physical hunger stirred. She went weak with the need to lean back against him and pull his hands to her body. It had been a bad idea for her to go somewhere with him alone, she thought, closing her eyes tightly.

"I *am* warning you," McKenna said gently. "You should tell me to leave Stony Cross. Tell your brother to get rid of me, that my presence here offends you. I'll go, Aline . . . but only if you make it happen."

His mouth was very close to her ear, his breath fanning over the tender outer rim.

"And if I don't?"

"Then I'm going to bed you."

Aline turned to face him with a bemused gaze. "What?"

"You heard me." McKenna leaned forward and braced his hands on either side of her, palms flattened on the ancient stable wood. "I'm going to take you," he said, his voice laced with soft menace. "And it will be nothing like the gentlemanly lovemaking that you're used to from Sandridge."

That was a shot in the dark. McKenna watched her intently, to see if she would contradict his assumption.

Aline held her silence as she realized that giving him any thread of truth would cause all her secrets to unravel. Better for him to think that she and Adam were lovers, than to wonder why she had remained alone for so many years.

"You . . . you don't waste time on subtlety, do you?" she managed, staring at him in wonder, while a warm, prickling sensation invaded the pit of her stomach.

"I thought it only fair to give you advance warning."

She was jarred by the strange familiarity of the moment, as she was held in thrall by those extraordinary blue-green eyes. Surely this could not really be happening. "You would never force yourself on a woman," she murmured. "No matter how much you may have changed."

McKenna answered steadily, while his gaze encompassed every degree of temperature between fire and ice. "If you don't send me away from Stony Cross by tomorrow morning, I'll take it as a personal invitation to your bed."

Aline was filled with the most bewildering mix of emotions imaginable . . . annoyance, amusement, consternation . . . not to mention admiration. The boy who had been born in service had become a splendidly arrogant man, and she loved his simmering self-confidence. If circumstances were different, how utterly willing she would have been to give him anything and everything he desired of her. If only—

Suddenly her mind went blank as McKenna took the double rope of pearls in his hand. He rested most of his weight on one leg, letting the other press gently into the mass of her skirts. In that moment of fully clothed proximity, Aline felt her self-control crumbling. The smell of his skin filled her nostrils—the hints of cologne and shaving soap, and the clean, sun-warmed, masculine essence that belonged to him alone. Breathing deeply of the fragrance, she felt an elemental jolt of response.

With a deliberateness that stunned her, McKenna used the front of his body to anchor her against the wall. She felt his free hand slide behind her neck, his gloved thumb and forefinger spread in a firm vise around the back of her skull. For some reason it did not occur to Aline that she should try to resist him. She could only hang there in his grasp, weak with excitement and desire and trepidation.

"Tell me to go," McKenna muttered, appearing to want her to struggle, almost willing her to. Her lack of opposition seemed to inflame him. The hot waft of his breath struck her lips, and she felt her body tightening inside. "Tell me," he urged, as his head bent over hers.

And the memories of who and what they had been, of past kisses, of agonizing longing, were consumed in a roar of desire. There was only now, her moan trapped in McKenna's hot mouth, the kiss beginning as a near-assault, transforming swiftly to a kind of greedy, ecstatic worship. His tongue plunged inside her, strong and sure, and she cried out at the pleasure of it, the sound smothered by his lips. McKenna had taught her how to kiss, and he still remembered all the tricks that aroused her. He paused to toy with her, using his lips, teeth, tongue, then settled back in, delving into her mouth with gloriously aggressive kisses. His hand slid from her nape to the bottom of her spine, bringing her more tightly against him. Arching in response, Aline whimpered as his palm reached the swell of her buttocks and urged her into his loins. Even with the thickness of her skirts between them, she could feel the hard ridge of his arousal.

The pleasure intensified to an almost frightening pitch. *Too much, too strong, too fast . . .*

Suddenly McKenna made a rough sound and jerked away from her.

Staring at him, Aline leaned back against the wall, her legs threatening to collapse beneath her. They both breathed with deep, wracking pulls of their lungs, while frustrated passion saturated the air like steam.

Finally McKenna managed to speak. "Go back to the house," he said hoarsely, "while I can still let you. And think about what I told you."

It took several minutes for Aline to compose herself sufficiently to return to the ball. She thought she had managed to paste a facade of deceptive poise over her inner tumult—no one seemed to notice that anything was amiss as she greeted guests and conversed and laughed with artificial cheer. Only Marcus, who gave her a narrowed, meditative stare from halfway across the ballroom, made her aware that narrow strips of heat were glowing at the crests of her cheeks. And Adam, of course, who appeared at her left elbow and gazed into her upturned face with discreet concern.

"Do I look all right?" she whispered to him.

"Aside from being your usual ravishingly beautiful self," Adam said, "you are a bit flushed. What happened between the two of you? Did you exchange words?"

Far more than words, she thought ruefully. That kiss . . . the annihilating pleasure like nothing she had ever felt before. Years of longing and fantasy distilled into pure physical sensation. It seemed impossible to layer detachment over the seething desire, to stand while her knees showed a dismaying inclination to fold. Impossible to pretend everything was as it should be . . . when nothing was.

That kiss, charged with their mutual hunger to discover the changes that had been wrought over a dozen years of living apart. McKenna presented a danger to Aline in every way, and yet she was somehow certain that she was going to make the wrong choices, take insane risks, all in the futile attempt to appease her need for him.

"Adam," she murmured without looking at him, "have you ever wanted something so much that you would do anything to have it—even knowing that it was bad for you?"

They walked slowly, taking a slow turn around the outskirts of the ballroom. "Of course," Adam replied. "All the truly enjoyable things in life are invariably bad for you—and they're even better when done to excess."

"You are not being helpful," Aline said severely, struggling to hold back a sudden smile.

"Would you like for someone to give me permission to do what you've already decided to do? Would that help to pacify your guilty conscience?"

"Yes, as a matter of fact. But no one can do that for me."

"I can."

She laughed suddenly. "Adam . . ."

"I hereby give you permission to do as you please. Now do you feel better?"

"No, just frightened. And as my friend, you should be doing your utmost to prevent me from making a mistake that will result in a great deal of pain."

"You've already had the pain," he pointed out. "Now you may as well have the pleasure of making the mistake."

"My God," Aline whispered, squeezing his arm tightly, "you are *such* a terrible influence, Adam."

"I try," he murmured, smiling down at her.

Gideon wandered to the terraced gardens behind the estate manor, following a flagstone path that curved around a row of artfully shaped yews. He had hoped that the outside air would distract him from temptation. The night was still young, and he had to slow the pace of his drinking a bit. Later, when the guests disbanded for the night, he could allow his thirst free rein, and he would pickle himself properly. Unfortunately, he still had to endure a few hours of relative sobriety until then.

A few strategically lit garden torches provided enough light to accommodate an evening stroll. In his aimless wandering, Gideon came to a small paved clearing with a splashing fountain embedded in the middle. To his surprise, he saw a girl moving about in the clearing. She seemed to be enjoying the distant music that floated from the open windows of the ballroom. Humming gently, she glided in a dreamy approximation of a waltz, pausing occasionally to sip from a glass of wine. Catching a glimpse of her profile, Gideon saw that she was not a girl but a young woman with pretty, if unremarkable features.

She must be a servant, he thought, noting that her gown was old, and her hair was braided loosely down her back. Perhaps she was a housemaid indulging in a stolen glass of wine.

The woman swirled back and forth like some misguided Cinderella whose ball gown had vanished before she had even reached the party. She made Gideon smile. Temporarily forgetting his desire for another drink,

Gideon drew closer, while the gurgle of the fountain obscured the sound of his footsteps.

In the midst of a slow twirl, the woman saw him and froze.

Gideon stood before her with his customary elegant slouch, dipping his head and regarding her with a teasing gaze.

Recovering quickly, the woman stared back at him. A rueful smile curved her lips, and her eyes sparkled in the soft glow of torchlight. Despite her lack of classic beauty, there was something irresistible about her . . . a kind of vibrant feminine cheerfulness that he had never encountered before.

"Well," she said, "this is *quite* mortifying, and if you have any mercy, you will forget what you have just seen."

"I have a memory like an elephant's," he told her with feigned regret.

"How disagreeable of you," she said, and laughed freely.

Gideon was instantly captivated. A hundred questions crowded in his mind. He wanted to know who she was, why she was there, if she liked sugar in her tea, had she climbed trees as a girl, and what her first kiss had been like . . .

The flood of curiosity puzzled him. He usually managed to avoid caring about anyone long enough to ask questions about him. Not quite trusting himself to speak, Gideon approached her cautiously. She stiffened slightly, as if she was unused to proximity with a stranger. As he drew closer, he saw that her features were even and her nose was a little too long, and her mouth was soft and sweetly shaped. Her eyes were some light color . . . green, perhaps . . . shining eyes that contained unexpected depths.

"Waltzing is somewhat easier with a partner," he commented. "Would you care to try it?"

The woman stared at him as if she had suddenly found herself in a strange land with a friendly foreigner. Music from the ballroom drifted through the air in a heady current. After a long moment, she shook her head with an apologetic smile, searching for an excuse to refuse him. "My wine isn't finished."

Slowly Gideon reached for the nearly empty glass in her hand. She surrendered it without a word, her gaze remaining locked with his. Raising the glass to his lips, Gideon downed the contents in one expert swallow, then set the fragile vessel on the edge of the fountain.

She laughed breathlessly and shook her finger at him in mock reproof.

As he stared at her, Gideon's chest felt very hot, the way it had once when he'd had croup and his nurse had made him breathe the reviving steam from a boiling pot of herbs. He remembered the relief of being able to breathe after hours of near-suffocation, the greedy movement of his lungs as they drew in the hot, precious air. Oddly, this felt rather like that . . . a sensation of relief, though from what he wasn't quite certain.

He offered her a bare hand, having removed his gloves and placed them in his pocket as soon as he had entered the garden. Turning his palm up, he silently willed her to take it.

Apparently the decision was not an easy one. She looked away from him, her expression suddenly contemplative, the edges of her teeth catching at the plush curve of her lower lip. Just as Gideon thought she was going to refuse him, she reached out impulsively, her warm fingers catching at his. He held her hand as if he cradled a fragile bird in his palm, and drew her close enough that he could smell the hint of rose water in her hair. Her body was slim, sweetly curved, her uncorseted waist soft beneath his fingers. Despite the undeniable romance of the moment, Gideon felt a most *un*romantic stirring of lust as his body reacted with typical male awareness to the nearness of a desirable female. He eased his partner into a slow waltz, guiding her expertly across the uneven flagstones.

"I've seen fairies dancing on the lawn before," he said, "when I got deep enough in a bottle of brandy. But I've never actually danced *with* one before." He held her more tightly as she tried to alter their direction. "No, let me lead."

"We were too close to the edge of the pavement," she protested, laughing as he compelled her back into his rhythm.

"We were not."

"Bossy American," she said, wrinkling her nose at him. "I'm sure I shouldn't dance with a man who admits to seeing fairies. And no doubt your wife would have a thing or two to say about this."

"I have no wife."

"Yes, you do." She gave him a chiding smile, as if he were a school-boy who had just been caught in a lie.

"Why are you so certain of that?"

"Because you're one of the Americans, and they're all married, except for Mr. McKenna. And you are *not* Mr. McKenna."

"There's one other unmarried American in the group," Gideon commented lazily, releasing her waist and turning her with one hand. At the completion of the turn, he caught her back against him and smiled down at her.

"Yes," she replied, "but that would be . . ."

"Mr. Shaw," Gideon said helpfully, as her voice trailed into silence.

"Oh . . ." She looked up at him with wide eyes. Were he not holding her so securely, she would have stumbled. "I'm supposed to stay away from you."

He grinned at that. "Says who?"

She ignored the question. "And while I'm certain that at least half the rumors about you couldn't possibly be true—"

"They are," Gideon said without a trace of shame.

"You're a rake, then."

"The worst kind."

She pulled away from him with a laugh. "At least you're honest about it. However, it is probably best if I go now. Thank you for the dance . . . it was lovely."

"Don't go," Gideon said, his voice soft and urgent. "Wait. Tell me who you are."

"You're allowed three guesses," she said.

"Are you a servant?"

"No."

"You can't be one of the Marsdens—you look nothing like them. Are you from the village?"

"No."

Gideon scowled at a sudden thought. "You're not the earl's mistress, are you?"

"No," she said sweetly, smiling. "That was your third guess. Good-bye, Mr. Shaw."

"Wait—"

"And no dancing with fairies on the lawn," she admonished. "It's wet, and you'll ruin your shoes."

She left him swiftly, leaving only the empty wineglass on the fountain, and the bemused smile on Gideon's lips, as evidence that she had been there.

"He said *what?*" Livia demanded, nearly toppling from her cross-legged seat on the edge of Aline's bed. As was their habit, she had come to Aline's room after the ball to hear the latest gossip.

Aline sunk deeper into the steaming, oily water of her bath in the center of the room. Hot as the water was, it was not entirely responsible for the flush that rose in her face. She looked from her younger sister's incredulous face to Mrs. Faircloth's openmouthed astonishment. Despite her own turmoil, Aline couldn't help but be amused. "He said that if he is allowed to stay at Stony Cross, he is going to bed me."

"Did McKenna also say that he still loves you?" Livia asked.

"Good Lord, no," Aline said wryly, stretching her sore legs and wiggling her toes beneath the water. "McKenna's intentions toward me have nothing to do with love—that is quite clear."

"But . . . but a man doesn't just come out and say he's going to . . . to . . ."

"Apparently McKenna does."

Livia shook her head in bemusement. "I've never heard of such arrogance!"

A wisp of a smile came to Aline's lips. "One could call it flattering, I suppose, if one chose to view it in that light." A stray lock of her hair fell from her topknot, and she reached up to reanchor it.

Livia laughed suddenly. "Even sporting, really, to warn you of his intentions."

"I call it grossly insolent," Mrs. Faircloth said, approaching the side of the tub with a folded towel, "and I will waste no opportunity in telling him so."

"No, no, don't mention it to him," Aline said hastily. "You mustn't. It's only a game. I want to enjoy it, just for a little while . . ."

The housekeeper stared at her in astonishment. "My lady, have you taken leave of your senses? This is very far from a game, in light of your history with McKenna. The emotions on both sides are too deep, and have been buried too long. Don't start on this path with him, my lady, if you aren't prepared to follow it to the end."

Remaining mutinously silent, Aline stood to be enfolded in the depths of the thick cotton towel that Mrs. Faircloth held up. She stepped from the tub and stood still as Mrs. Faircloth bent to dry her legs. Glancing at Livia, she saw that her younger sister had suddenly averted her gaze, staring into the hearth as if occupied in thought. She did not blame Livia for not wanting to look. Even after all these years, the sight of her own legs never failed to surprise even Aline.

Twelve years had passed since the accident, very little of which she remembered. She was well aware, however, that it was only because of Mrs. Faircloth that she had survived. When the doctors summoned from London had said that nothing could be done for Aline, the housekeeper had sent one of the footmen to fetch a healer from the neighboring county. A white witch, actually, who was regarded with both reverence and fear by the local villagers, who swore to the efficacy of her healing gifts.

Marcus, being a hard-bitten realist, had protested violently at the appearance of the witch, who turned out to be a middle-aged woman of unassuming appearance, carrying a small copper cauldron in one hand and a bulging sack filled with herbs in the other. Since Aline had been near death at the time, she had no memory of the witch, but she had been greatly entertained by Livia's account of the episode.

"I thought Marcus would drag her away bodily," Livia had told Aline with relish. "He planted himself in front of your bedroom door, having decided that he would protect you in your last hours. And this woman walked right up to him without any fear—she wasn't even half his weight—and demanded that she be allowed to see you. Mrs. Faircloth and I had begged Marcus all morning to let her do what she could for you, as we thought it could do no harm at that point. But he was being especially mulish, and he made some dreadfully obscene comment to her about broomsticks."

"And the witch wasn't frightened of him?" Aline had asked, knowing how intimidating their older brother could be.

"Not in the least. She told him that if he did not let her enter your room, she would cast a spell on him."

Aline had grinned at that. "Marcus doesn't believe in magic or witchcraft—he's far too practical."

"Yes, but he's a man, after all. And it seems the spell she threatened to use would have removed his . . . his . . ." Livia had begun to choke with laughter. "His manly potency," she managed to gasp out. "Well, the very idea was enough to turn Marcus pale, and after some fierce negotiating, he told the witch that she had exactly one hour to spend in your room, and he was going to watch her the entire time."

Livia had described the scene that had ensued, the blue candles . . . the circle that had been drawn around her bed with a sage smudge stick . . . the incense that had saturated the air with a pungent haze while the witch performed her rituals.

To everyone's amazement, Aline had lived through the night. When the herb-dressed sheets that covered her were removed in the morning, her wounds were no longer putrid, but clean and beginning to heal. Unfortunately, the witch's remarkable abilities had not been able to prevent the formation of thick, elevated red scars that went from Aline's ankles to the tops of her thighs. Her legs were hideous . . . there was no other word for it. Her feet, which had been encased in leather shoes at the time of her accident, had mercifully been spared much of the damage. However, in the areas where large expanses of skin had been destroyed, the scar tissue had pulled tightly at the edges of remaining skin, affecting the movement of muscles and joints beneath. Walking was occasionally difficult and even painful, on the days when she pushed herself too far. She took nightly baths in oily herbal water to soften the scars, and followed them with gentle stretching to keep herself as limber as possible.

"What if you told McKenna about your legs?" Mrs. Faircloth asked, settling a thin white nightgown over Aline's head. "What do you think his reaction might be?"

The garment settled over her, covering a body that encompassed the incongruous difference of pure white skin and a shapely torso melded to a pair of damaged legs.

"McKenna cannot abide weakness in any form," Aline said, padding to a chair and sitting heavily. "He would pity me, and that emotion is so close to contempt, it makes me ill to think of it."

"You can't be certain of that."

"Are you saying that McKenna wouldn't find these scars repellent?" Aline asked, wincing slightly as the housekeeper began to rub her legs with herbal salve that soothed the itching scar tissue. No one else, not even Livia, was ever permitted to touch her that way. "You know he would. Anyone would."

"Aline," came her younger sister's voice from the bed, "If someone loved you, he would be able to look beyond your appearance."

"That's all well and good, for a fairy tale," Aline said. "But I don't believe in those anymore."

In the uncomfortable silence that took hold of the room, Livia slipped from the bed and wandered to the vanity, sitting before the square Queen Anne looking glass. She picked up a brush and smoothed the ends of her braid, while making an effort to change the topic of conversation. "You'll never guess what happened to me tonight, either of you. I went to the garden for a breath of fresh air, and found myself at the mermaid fountain . . . you know the place, where you can hear the music from the ballroom."

"You should have been *inside* the ballroom, dancing," Aline said, but Livia waved her into silence.

"No, no, this was much better than anything that could have happened in there. I was drinking a glass of wine, and tottering about like a demented ballerina, when all of a sudden I saw someone standing nearby, watching me."

Aline laughed, diverted by the story. "I would have screamed."

"I nearly did."

"Was it a man or a woman?" Mrs. Faircloth asked.

"A man." Livia turned on the vanity stool to grin at them both. "Tall and ridiculously handsome, with the most wonderful head of golden hair. And before we even got around to introducing ourselves, he took me into his arms, and we danced."

"You didn't," Aline exclaimed in surprised delight.

Livia hugged herself in excitement. "Yes! And it turned out that my waltz partner was none other than that Mr. Shaw, who is the most debonair man I've ever met in my life. Oh, I'm certain that he is a terrible rake . . . but what a dance it was!"

"He drinks," Mrs. Faircloth said darkly, being privy to the servants' gossip.

"I don't doubt it." Livia shook her head in puzzlement. "There is such a look in his eyes, as if he has seen and done everything a thousand times, and takes no real pleasure or interest in anything."

"He sounds very different from Amberley," Aline remarked carefully, concerned by the realization that her sister was quite taken with the American.

"Different in every way," Livia agreed, setting aside the silver-backed brush. Her tone mellowed as she continued thoughtfully. "I do like him, though. Aline, you must find out everything you can about him, and tell me—"

"No." Aline tempered her refusal with a teasing smile, and winced as Mrs. Faircloth gently manipulated her ankle, flexing the stiff joint. "If you want to know more about Mr. Shaw, you'll have to come out of hiding and ask him yourself."

"Bother you," Livia rejoined without heat, and yawned. "Perhaps I will." Standing, she wandered to Aline and dropped a kiss on top of her head. "As for you, dearest, have a care in your dealings with McKenna. I suspect that he is a far better game player than you."

"We'll see about that," Aline replied, eliciting a laugh from Livia and a worried frown from Mrs. Faircloth.

Nine

After a night of dancing, none of the guests at Stony Cross Park was inclined to awaken before noon, except for a small group of men who wished to go shooting. As Aline sipped from a cup of tea and smiled at the early risers who were gathering at the back terrace, she was disconcerted to see McKenna in their midst.

It was daybreak. The air was cool and heavy as the weak English sun struggled ineffectually to burn through the haze. Sitting at an outside table with a silk shawl knotted over her thin morning dress, Aline tried not to stare at McKenna. However, it was difficult to conceal her fascination. McKenna possessed a dynamic presence, an inherent virility, that she had seen in no other man except perhaps her brother. And the sportsman's attire suited McKenna perfectly, the black coat defining the breadth of his shoulders, with dark forest-green breeches closely following his muscular legs, and black leather boots conforming to his long calves. Such garments were becoming to any man, but on someone as big as McKenna, the effect was awe-inspiring.

Sensing her discreet regard, McKenna glanced at her quickly. Their gazes held in a flash of raw interest, before he forced himself to turn and reply to a guest who had approached him.

Aline stared into the hot amber depths of her tea, her body filled with exquisite tension. She did not look up until her brother approached to ask about the day's schedule.

"Breakfast will be served at the pavilion by the lake," Aline replied. On extended visits such as this, the first meal of the day was never served before noon. It would be a prodigious repast, with a multitude of hearty dishes and just enough champagne to revive the mood of the previous evening. Aline reached out to touch her brother's broad brown hand. "Have a good morning," she said cheerfully, "and do try to keep your distance from guests with bad aim."

Marcus grinned and spoke in a low voice. "That's not usually a problem with Americans. Although few of them can ride worth a damn, they're fair shots." Continuing to lean over Aline, he waited until her gaze lifted to his. His black eyes narrowed. "You disappeared with McKenna for almost a half hour last evening. Where did you go, and what did you do with him?"

"Marcus," Aline said with a reproving smile, "on the occasions when you have disappeared with a female guest—and there have been many— I've never demanded to know where you went and what you did."

"It's different for you than it is for me."

Aline was both touched and amused by his protectiveness. "Why?"

Marcus's dark brows drew together in a frown, and his voice was infused with surliness. "Because you're my sister."

"I have nothing to fear from McKenna," she said. "I know him quite well, Marcus."

"You knew him when he was a boy," her brother countered. "But McKenna is a stranger now, and you have no idea of what he's capable of."

"Don't meddle, Marcus. I will do as I please with McKenna. And I hope that you won't try to manipulate things as Father did, all those years ago. His interference cost me dearly, and while I had no choice but to accept it then, things are different now."

Marcus settled a hand on the back of her chair. The tautness of his mouth betrayed his concern. "Aline," he asked carefully, "What do you think he wants from you?"

The answer was clear to both of them. However, Aline saw that her brother didn't yet understand what *she* desired. "The same thing that I want from him," she replied.

"What did you just say?" Marcus stared at her as if he didn't recognize her.

Sighing, Aline glanced across the terrace at McKenna, who was engaged in a conversation with two other men. "Haven't you ever wished that you could steal back just a few hours of your past?" she asked softly. "That's all I want . . . just a taste of what might have been."

"No, I never wish for that," came his brusque reply. "The words 'might have been' mean nothing to me. There's only now, and the future."

"That's because there are no limitations to your future," she said evenly. "But there are to mine."

Marcus's hand compressed into a hard fist. "Because of a few scars?"

The question made her eyes flash dangerously. "You've never seen my legs, Marcus. You don't know what you're talking about. And coming from a man who takes his pick of the most beautiful women in London as if he were sampling from a tin of bonbons—"

"Are you implying that I'm some shallow fool who values a woman only for her appearance?"

Aline was tempted to retract her charge in the interest of maintaining peace between them. But as she considered the last few women that Marcus had carried on with . . . "I'm sorry to say, Marcus, that each of your recent choice of companions—the last four or five, at least—displayed all the intelligence of a turnip. And yes, they were all quite beautiful, and I doubt that you were able to have a sensible conversation with any of them for longer than five minutes."

Marcus stood back and glared at her. "How does that pertain to what we were discussing?"

"It illustrates the point that even you, one of the finest and most honorable men I've ever known, place great importance on physical attractiveness. And if I ever see you consort with a woman who is less than stunningly perfect, then perhaps I'll listen to your lectures on how appearance doesn't matter."

"Aline—"

"Have a good shoot," she said. "And heed my warning—don't cross me in this, Marcus."

Heaving a sigh, her brother went to find his valet, who was laden with rifles and leather bags.

More of the shooting party came to Aline's table to exchange pleasantries, and she smiled and chatted pleasantly, always aware of McKenna's dark figure in the background. Only when the guests began to descend en masse down the terrace steps, led by Marcus, did McKenna come to her.

"Good morning," Aline said, while her heartbeat rapidly outpaced her ability to think. She offered him her hand, and her breath caught at the gentle clasp of his fingers. Somehow she managed to find a calm social voice. "Did you rest well last night?"

"No." His eyes glinted as he retained her hand a moment longer than was acceptable.

"I do hope that your room is not uncomfortable," Aline managed to say, tugging free of him.

"What would you do if I said it was?"

"Offer you another room, of course."

"Don't bother—unless it's yours."

His boldness nearly startled a laugh from her—she couldn't remember when, if ever, a man had spoken to her with such a stunning lack of respect. And it reminded her so much of the comfortable ease they had once shared that she actually found herself relaxing in his presence. *"That* obliging a hostess, I'm not," she informed him.

McKenna leaned over the table, resting his hands lightly on the glossy surface. His dark head hovered over hers, his stance reminding her of a cat poised to strike its prey. A flicker of predatory interest lightened the turquoise depths of his eyes. "What's the verdict, my lady?"

She pretended not to understand. "Verdict?"

"Am I to leave the estate, or shall I stay?"

Idly Aline drew an invisible circle on the table with a well-manicured fingertip, while her heart thumped in her chest. "Stay, if you wish."

His voice was very soft. "And you understand what will happen if I do?"

Aline had never thought that McKenna could be so arrogant—or that she would enjoy it so much. A sense of challenge, male against female, rippled between them. When she replied, her voice matched his for softness. "I don't wish to disappoint you, McKenna, but I have complete faith in my ability to resist your advances."

He seemed mesmerized by whatever he saw in her face. "Do you?"

"Yes. Yours wasn't the first proposition I've ever received. And at the risk of sounding rather conceited, it probably won't be the last." Aline finally let herself smile at him as she wanted to, full and provocative and gently mocking. "Therefore, you may stay and do your worst. I fully expect to enjoy your efforts. And you should know that I do appreciate a certain amount of finesse."

His gaze fell to her smiling lips. Although he showed no reaction to her impudence, Aline sensed how greatly she had astonished him. She felt a bit like a damned soul who had gone right up to Lucifer and chucked him playfully beneath the chin.

"Finesse," he repeated, looking back into her eyes.

"Well, yes. Serenades, and flowers, and poetry."

"What kind of poetry?"

"The kind that you write yourself, of course."

His sudden lazy smile caused soft prickles of pleasure to course through her. "Does Sandridge write poetry for you?"

"I daresay he would." Adam was clever with words—no doubt he would perform such a task with great style and wit.

"But you haven't asked him to," McKenna murmured.

She shook her head slowly.

"I've never given much thought to finesse," he told her.

Aline arched her brows. "Even when it comes to seduction?"

"The women I take to bed don't usually require seduction."

She rested her chin on her hand, staring at him intently. "They're simply yours for the taking, you mean?"

"That's right." He gave her an inscrutable glance. "And most of them are ladies of the upper class." With a perfunctory bow, he turned and left with the shooting party.

Aline worked to keep her breath even, and sat until her pulse had steadied.

It was now clear to both of them that the game had two fully committed players . . . a game with no rules and no clear outcome, and potentially heavy losses on both sides. And as much as Aline feared for herself, she feared even more for McKenna, whose knowledge of the past was riddled with significant and hazardous gaps. She must let him go on thinking the worst of her . . . to take what he wanted of her, and to eventually leave Stony Cross with his sense of vengeance appeased.

Now that she had seen the shooting party off, she had time to relax with a cup of tea in the breakfast room. Preoccupied with thoughts of McKenna, she nearly bumped into someone who was leaving the manor at the same time.

The man reached out to steady her, grasping her elbows until he was assured of her balance. "Forgive me. I was in a bit of a hurry to join the others."

"They've only just left," Aline said. "Good morning, Mr. Shaw."

With his sunstruck hair, lightly tanned complexion and sapphire eyes, Gideon Shaw was dazzling. He possessed an elegant insouciance that could only have come from being born to limitless wealth. The faint lines that cynicism had carved around his eyes and mouth only enhanced his looks, weathering his golden handsomeness agreeably. He was a tall and well-formed man, though his proportions did not approach McKenna's warriorlike build.

"If you descend the stairs on the left and follow the path to the forest, you will catch up to them," Aline told him.

Shaw's smile was like a ray of sunshine piercing a cloud bank. "Thank you, my lady. It is my particular torment to enjoy sports that can only take place early in the morning."

"I assume you also like to fish, then?"

"Oh yes."

"Some morning you must go with my brother to our trout stream."

"Perhaps I will—although I may not be up to the challenge. English trout are far more wily than American ones."

"Can the same be said for English businessmen?" Aline asked, her eyes twinkling.

"Much to my relief, no." Shaw made a slight bow in preparation to leave, then paused as a thought occurred to him. "My lady, I have a question . . ."

Somehow Aline knew exactly what he was going to ask. It took considerable acting ability to maintain an ingenuous expression. "Yes, Mr. Shaw?"

"Last night, as I took a stroll through the back gardens, I happened to make the acquaintance of a young woman . . ." He paused, obviously considering how much of the encounter he should describe.

"She did not give you her name?" Aline asked innocently.

"No."

"Was she one of the guests? No? Well, then, she was probably a servant."

"I don't believe so." His brow was hemmed with a slight frown of concentration as he continued. "She has light brown hair and green eyes . . . at least, I think they are green . . . and she is small of stature, perhaps only an inch taller than you."

Aline shrugged apologetically. Although she would have liked to oblige him by giving him her sister's name, she wasn't certain that Livia wanted him to know her identity yet. "At the moment, Mr. Shaw, I can think of no one on the estate who matches that description. Are you certain that she wasn't a figment of your imagination?"

He shook his head, his dark lashes lowering over rich blue eyes as he seemed to contemplate a problem of great magnitude. "She was real. And I need— that is, I would very much like—to find her."

"This woman seems to have made quite an impression on you."

A self-mocking smile deepened the corners of Shaw's lips, and he dragged a hand through the gleaming layers of his hair, carelessly disheveling the amber-shaded locks. "Meeting her was like taking a deep breath for the first time in years," he replied, not quite meeting her gaze.

"Yes, I understand."

The unmistakable sincerity in her voice seemed to snare his attention. He smiled suddenly, and murmured, "I see that you do."

Feeling a rush of liking for the man, Aline gestured in the direction of the departing sportsmen. "You can still catch the shooting party if you run."

Shaw laughed briefly. "My lady, there is nothing in this life I want badly enough to chase after it."

"Good," she said, pleased. "Then you may take an early breakfast with me instead. I'll have it served out here."

With her companion seeming more than agreeable at the prospect, Aline directed a servant to set out breakfast for two at the table. A steaming basket of scones and sweetened buns was brought to them quickly, along with plates of broiled eggs, baked mushrooms, and thin slices of roast partridge. Although Shaw seemed to enjoy the breakfast offering, he seemed far more interested in a carafe of strongly brewed coffee, drinking it as if it were the antidote to some recently ingested poison.

Settling back in her chair, Aline popped a morsel of buttered scone into her mouth, and slid him a glance of flirtatious inquiry—the look that never failed to elicit the information that she wanted from a man. "Mr. Shaw," she asked, following the scone with a sip of well-sugared tea, "how many years have you known McKenna?"

The question did not seem to surprise Shaw. After having downed two cups of coffee with barely a pause for breath, he now applied himself to drinking a third at a more leisurely pace. "About eight," he replied.

"McKenna told me that the two of you met while he was still a ferryman—that you were a passenger on his boat."

A peculiar smile curved his lips. "Is that what he told you?"

She tilted her head to the side as she regarded him closely. "Is it not the truth?"

"McKenna tends to shade certain details in the interest of shielding my reputation. In fact, he's far more concerned about my reputation than I am."

Carefully Aline stirred more sugar in her tea. "Why did you strike up a partnership with a mere ferryman?" she asked in a deliberately relaxed tone.

Gideon Shaw took a long time to answer. He set down his half-empty cup and stared at her steadily. "McKenna saved my life, to start with."

Aline did not move or speak as he continued.

"I was wandering along the waterfront, blind drunk. Even now I can't remember how I got there, or why. On occasion I have some memory loss while drinking, and I can't account for hours or even days." His bleak smile chilled her to the marrow. "I stumbled and fell into the water, far enough along the docks that no one saw me, especially as the weather was inclement. But McKenna happened to be ferrying back from Staten Island, and he jumped into that damned freezing ocean—in the midst of a brewing storm, no less—and fished me out."

"How fortunate for you." Aline's throat tightened at the thought of the risk that McKenna had taken for a complete stranger.

"Since McKenna had no means of identifying me," Shaw continued, "and I was out cold, he took me to the tenement room he rented. A day and a half later I found myself in a rat hole of a room, being slapped awake by a giant, irate ferryman." A reminiscent smile touched his lips. "As you can imagine, I was much the worse for wear. My head felt like it had been split open. After McKenna brought me some food and drink, I was lucid enough to tell him my name. As we talked, I became aware that despite his rough appearance, my rescuer was surprisingly well informed. He'd learned a great deal from all the passengers he'd ferried back and forth, much of it concerning Manhattan real estate. He even knew about a parcel of land that my family had bought on a long-term lease, and had never developed, and then he had the b—pardon me, the audacity . . . to propose a deal."

Aline smiled at that. "What was the deal, Mr. Shaw?"

"He wanted to subdivide the land into a series of lots and sell them as short-term leases. And of course he wanted ten percent of whatever he could get for them." Leaning back, Shaw rested his interlaced fingers on his midriff. "And I thought, *Why not?* No one in my fam-ily had bothered doing anything with the land—we third-generation Shaws are accurately known as a bunch of idle pleasure-seeking good-for-naughts. And here was this stranger, reeking of ambition and primal intensity, obviously willing to do anything to make a profit. So I gave him all the cash in my wallet—about fifty dollars—and told him to buy himself a new suit of clothes, cut his hair and shave his beard, and come to my offices the following day."

"And McKenna did well for you," Aline said rather than asked.

Shaw nodded. "Within six months he had leased every square inch of that land. Then, without asking permission, he used the profits to buy up acres of submerged shoreline property from the city, in the area below Canal Street. That made me rather nervous, especially when I began to hear the jokes circulating about the Shaw and McKenna 'underwater lots' for sale . . .". A gentle reminiscent laugh escaped his lips. "Naturally I questioned his sanity. But at that point, there was nothing I could do but stand aside as McKenna arranged for the submerged acreage to be filled in with rocks and soil. Then he built tenements and a string of warehouses, transforming it into valuable commercial property. Eventually McKenna turned an investment of one hundred and fifty thousand dollars into a development that yields approximately a million dollars annually."

The numbers, so casually spoken, stunned Aline.

Seeing her wide eyes, Shaw laughed softly. "Not surprisingly, McKenna has become a sought-after guest in New York, not to mention one of the city's most eligible bachelors."

"I suppose his attentions are encouraged by many women," Aline said, trying to keep her tone offhand.

"He has to beat them off," Shaw replied with a sly grin. "I would not claim, however, that McKenna is known as a ladies' man. There have been women—but to my knowledge, none that he has ever taken a serious interest in. Most of his energies have been directed toward his work."

"What about you, Mr. Shaw?" she asked. "Are your affections engaged by someone back home?"

He shook his head at once. "I'm afraid that I share McKenna's rather skeptical view of the benefits of marriage."

"I think you will fall in love someday."

"Doubtful. I'm afraid that particular emotion is unknown to me . . ." Suddenly his voice faded into silence. He set his cup down as he stared off into the distance with sudden alertness.

"Mr. Shaw?" As Aline followed his gaze, she realized what he had seen—Livia, wearing a pastel flower-printed walking dress as she headed to one of the forest trails leading away from the manner. A straw bonnet adorned with a sprig of fresh daisies swung from her fingers as she held it by the ribbons.

Gideon Shaw stood so quickly that his chair threatened to topple backward. "Pardon," he said to Aline, tossing his napkin to the table. "That figment of my imagination has reappeared—and I'm going to catch her."

"Of course," Aline said, struggling not to laugh. "Good luck, Mr. Shaw."

"Thanks." He was gone in a flash, descending one side of the U-shaped stone staircase with the ease of a cat. Once he reached the terraced gardens, he cut across the lawn with long, ground-eating strides, just short of breaking into a run.

Standing to better her view of his progress, Aline couldn't suppress a mocking grin. "Why, Mr. Shaw . . . I thought there was nothing in life you wanted badly enough to chase after it."

Ten

*E*very evening since Amberley had died, Livia had gone to sleep with images of him filtering through her mind. Until last night.

It felt strange to be preoccupied with some man other than Amberley, especially when he was so very different. Remembering Gideon Shaw's lean face and golden-blond hair, and the gentle expertise of his touch, Livia felt guilty and intrigued and unsettled. Yes, quite different from Amberley.

Her fiancé had not been a complicated man. There were no layers of darkness in him, nothing to prevent him from giving and accepting love with ease. He came from a family of pleasant people, who were well-off but never arrogant, and scrupulously mindful of their duty to those in less fortunate circumstances. Amberley had been exceedingly attractive, with dark brown eyes and shiny brown hair, and a becoming cowlick that made the locks fall in a tempting sweep across his brow. He had been slim and fit, loving sports and games and long walks.

It was hardly remarkable that they had fallen in love, for it was obvious to everyone how well suited they were. Amberley brought out a side of Livia's nature that she had never been fully aware of. In his arms, she had become uninhibited. She had reveled in his lovemaking, and she had been willing to do anything, anywhere, with passionate abandon.

Now that Amberley was gone, Livia had been without a man for a long time. Her mother had lectured that she should apply herself to catch-

ing a husband as soon as possible, before the last vestiges of youth had
left her. Livia did not disagree. She was lonely, and she missed the comfort and pleasure to be found in a man's arms. But somehow she could not
make herself take an interest in the prospect . . . she could only wait for
someone, something, to free her from the invisible chains that bound her.

She wandered through the oak and hazel forest, which was unusually
dark for morning time, as the sky was still covered with a silver-gray
haze. Coming to a bridle path, she followed it to a sunken lane, and
paused every once in a while to kick a stone with the toe of her leather
walking shoe. A breeze stirred the air, drawing a distant rustling from the
forest and causing a lone nuthatch to chirp indignantly.

Livia wasn't aware that someone else was following the sunken lane
until she heard a series of footfalls coming up hard behind her. Turning,
she saw the tall figure of a man approaching. He walked with a fluid ease
that made his sportsman's clothes seem as elegant as formal wear. Livia
drew in a quick breath as she realized that Gideon Shaw had found her.

As spectacular as he had been in the moonlight, Shaw was even more
breathtaking in the daytime, his close-cropped hair glowing like antique
gold, his face beautiful but completely masculine, the nose narrow and
long, the cheekbones high, the eyes astonishingly blue.

For some reason Shaw stopped as their gazes met, as if he had run
into an invisible wall. They stared at each other across a distance of perhaps five yards, while Lydia became aware of a low, warm ache inside.
There was a peculiar expression on his face . . . interest struggling
through disillusionment . . . the reluctant fascination of a man who was
trying very hard not to want her.

"Good morning, sir."

The sound of her voice seemed to draw him forward. He approached
slowly, as if he feared that a sudden move might startle her into fleeing. "I
dreamed about you last night," he said.

As a conversational gambit, the statement was somewhat alarming,
but Livia smiled nonetheless. "What was the dream about?" she asked,
tilting her head as she stared at him. "Or is that a dangerous question?"

The wind teased a lock of hair that had fallen on his forehead. "Most definitely a dangerous question."

Livia realized that she was flirting with him, but she couldn't seem to help it. "Have you come to walk with me, Mr. Shaw?"

"If you have no objection to my company."

"The only thing I would object to is your absence," she told him, enjoying the sight of his sudden easy grin. Motioning for him to join her, she turned and continued along the sunken lane, toward the gatehouse garden in the distance.

Shaw fell into step beside her, his brown leather boots crunching the stray twigs and leaves that had blown onto the lane. He tucked his hands into the pockets of his tweed coat, casting a sideways glance at Livia's profile as they walked. "You know," he said casually, "I'm not going to let you get away from me again without telling me who you are."

"I prefer to remain mysterious."

"Why?"

She told him the truth. "Because I did something scandalous in the past, and now it is horribly awkward for me to come out in society."

"What kind of scandal?" His sardonic tone made it clear that he expected her transgression to be a minor one. "You went somewhere unchaperoned, I suppose. Or you let someone steal a kiss from you in public."

She shook her head with a wry smile. "Clearly you have no idea of how badly behaved we young ladies can be."

"I would love for you to enlighten me."

At Livia's indecisive silence, Shaw abandoned the subject, and fastened his gaze on the tousled, heavily planted cottage garden ahead of them. Long banners of honeysuckle trailed over the garden fence, its fragrance making the air thick and sweet. Butterflies danced amid bright splotches of poppies and peonies. Beyond a plot of carrots, lettuce, and radishes, a rose-covered archway led to a tiny glasshouse that was shaded by a parasol-shaped sycamore.

"Very nice," Shaw remarked.

Swinging her bonnet, Livia led him to the glasshouse, a cozy nook that no more than two people could occupy at the same time. "When I was a little girl, I used to sit in this glasshouse with my books and dolls, and pretend that I was a princess in a tower."

"You grew up at Stony Cross Park, then," he said.

Livia opened the glasshouse door and looked inside. It was clean and well-kept, the wooden seat gleaming from a recent polishing. "Lord Westcliff is my brother," she finally admitted, her voice sounding hollow as it resounded inside the little glass-paned room. "I am Lady Olivia Marsden."

Shaw stood behind her, close but not touching. Her awareness of him was so electric that it compelled her to step forward into the glasshouse. Shaw remained in the doorway, filling it with his lean body and broad shoulders. When Livia turned to face him, she was struck by the differences between him and Amberley. Shaw was at least ten years older than Amberley had been. A powerful, worldly man, and so clearly a disenchanted one, with tiny lines of cynicism etched around his eyes. But when he smiled, it temporarily banished every sign of disillusionment, and made him so attractive that her heart nearly stopped.

"Lady Aline mentioned that she had a sister," Shaw said. "However, I had the impression that you lived away from the estate."

"No, I am definitely a resident of Stony Cross Park. But I keep to myself. The scandal, you understand."

"I'm afraid I don't." The corners of his mouth lifted in a relaxed smile. "Tell me, Princess Olivia . . . why do you have to stay in your tower?"

The soft entreaty made Livia feel as if she were melting inside. She laughed unsteadily, wishing for a moment that she dared to trust him. But the habit of independence was too strong. Shaking her head, Livia approached him, expecting him to back away from the doorway. He retreated a half step, his hands still grasping the edges of the doorway, so that she couldn't help but walk into an open-armed embrace. The bonnet ribbons slipped from her fingers.

"Mr. Shaw—" she began, making the mistake of looking up at him.

"Gideon," he whispered. "I want to know your secrets, Olivia."

A bitter half smile touched her lips. "You'll hear them sooner or later from other people."

"I want to hear them from you."

As Livia began to retreat into the glasshouse, Shaw deftly caught the little cloth belt of her walking dress. His long fingers hooked beneath the reinforced fabric.

Unable to back away from him, Livia clamped her hand over his, while a hectic blush flooded her face. She knew that he was toying with her, and that she once might have been able to manage this situation with relative ease. But not now.

When she spoke, her voice was husky. "I can't do this, Mr. Shaw."

To her amazement, he seemed to understand exactly what she meant. "You don't have to do anything," he said softly. "Just let me come closer . . . and stay right there . . ." His head bent, and he found her mouth easily.

The coaxing pressure of his lips made Livia sway dizzily, and he caught her firmly against him. She was being kissed by Gideon Shaw, the self-indulgent, debauched scoundrel her brother had warned her about. And oh, he was good at it. She had thought nothing would ever be as pleasurable as Amberley's kisses . . . but this man's mouth was warm and patient, and there was something wickedly erotic about his complete lack of urgency. He teased her gently, nudging her lips apart, the tip of his tongue barely brushing hers before it withdrew.

Wanting more of those silken strokes, Livia began to strain against him, her breath quickening. He nurtured her excitement with such subtle skill that she was utterly helpless to defend against it. To her astonishment, she found herself winding her arms around his neck and pressing her breasts against the hard plane of his chest. His hand slid behind her neck, tilting her head back to expose her throat more fully. Still gentle and controlled, he kissed the fragile skin, working his way down to the hollow at the base of her throat. She felt his tongue swirl in the warm depression, and a moan of pleasure escaped her.

Shaw lifted his head to nuzzle the side of her cheek, while his hand smoothed over her back. Their breaths mingled in swift puffs of heat, his hard chest moving against hers in an erratic rhythm. "My God," he finally said against her cheek, "you are trouble."

Livia smiled. "No, *you* are," she managed to accuse in return, just before he kissed her again.

The bag for the morning was respectable, consisting of at least twenty grouse and a half-dozen woodcocks. The women joined the sportsmen for a hearty breakfast by the lake, and they all chattered and laughed lazily while the servants kept their plates and glasses filled. Afterward the guests separated into groups, some of them going for carriage drives or walks through the grounds, others retreating to the manor house to write letters or play cards.

When Aline saw the considerable amount of uneaten food that had been brought back to the kitchen, she and two housemaids packed it into jars and baskets, to be distributed to villagers in Stony Cross. As lady of the manor in her mother's absence, Aline was mindful to call on the families who had need of extra food and household supplies. It was an obligation that she did not always enjoy, for these visits took up a full day or more of the week. She would enter cottage after cottage, sit by a multitude of hearths, listen diligently to complaints, and dispense advice when necessary. Aline feared that she was insufficiently equipped with both the wisdom and the stoicism that such calls required. On the other hand, the knowledge of how little the cottagers possessed, and how hard they toiled, never failed to humble her.

In the past few months Aline had often managed to persuade Livia to accompany her to the village, and her sister's presence always made the day go by much faster. Unfortunately Livia was nowhere to be found this afternoon. Perturbed, Aline wondered if her sister was still in the company of Mr. Shaw, as he was also absent. Surely not—Livia hadn't spent this much time with a man in years. On the other hand, it was just possible that Shaw had been able to draw Livia out of her shell.

But was that a good thing or a bad thing? Aline fretted silently. It would be just like Livia, the contrary imp, to focus her attention on a licentious rake rather than on some upright gentleman. Smiling ruefully, Aline hoisted a heavy basket in her arms and made her way out to the carriage. The dishes clinked in the basket, while the salty tang of ham and the rich fragrance of an egg casserole rose to her nostrils.

"Oh, milady," came a maid's voice from behind her, as they walked from the kitchens. "Let me take that from ye, please!"

Glancing over her shoulder, Aline smiled as she saw that the young maid was already burdened with two heavy baskets. "I can manage, Gwen," she replied, huffing slightly as she ascended a short flight of steps. An obstinate pull from a contracture scar made her right knee stiffen. Gritting her teeth, Aline forced her leg to stretch its full range of motion.

"Milady," Gwen persisted, "if ye'll just set it to the side, I'll come back for it—"

"No need for that. I want to load these into the carriage and be off, as I am already pressed for t—"

Aline broke off suddenly as she saw McKenna standing near the entrance to the servants' hall. He was talking with a giggling housemaid, casually leaning one shoulder against the wall. It seemed that his ability to charm women had not faded . . . he was smiling at the red-haired maid, reaching out to give a light, teasing tap beneath her chin.

Although Aline made no sound, something must have alerted McKenna to her presence. He glanced in her direction, his gaze turning wary.

Instantly the housemaid departed, while McKenna continued to stare at Aline.

She reminded herself that she had no right to feel possessive of him. After all, she was no longer a nineteen-year-old girl infatuated with a stable boy. Nevertheless, a burn of anger raced through her at the evidence that she was not the only woman that McKenna had targeted for seduction. Her face felt stiff as she continued toward the entrance hall. "Go on," she murmured to Gwen, and the girl obediently hurried ahead of her.

McKenna reached Aline in a few long strides. His dark face was unreadable as he reached for the basket. "Let me have that."

Aline jerked it away from him. "No, thank you."

"You're limping."

His observation caused tendrils of alarm to spread through her stomach.

"I turned my ankle on the stairs," she said shortly, resisting as he tugged the basket from her. "Let go. I don't need your help."

Ignoring her, McKenna carried the basket with ease, his brow creasing as he stared at her. "You should let Mrs. Faircloth bind that before it worsens."

"It's already feeling better," Aline said in exasperation. "Go find someone else to bother, McKenna. I'm certain there are many other women you wish to trifle with today."

"I wasn't trying to seduce her."

She responded with a speaking glance, and his dark brows lifted in mocking crescents. "You don't believe me?" he asked.

"No, actually. I think that she is your insurance, in case you don't succeed in bedding me."

"First, I have no intention of bedding one of the housemaids. I was trying to get some information from her. Second, I don't need insurance."

The arrogance of his statement was enough to make Aline speechless. She had never met a man so abominably sure of himself—and that was fortunate, as there was not sufficient room in the civilized world to accommodate more than a handful of men like him. When she thought she could speak without stuttering, she finally asked in a clipped voice, "What information would a housemaid have that could possibly interest you?"

"I found out that she was employed here at the time of that mysterious illness of yours. I was trying to make her tell me something about it."

Aline fixed her gaze on the knot of his cravat, her entire body tensing. "And what did she tell you?"

"Nothing. It seems that she and the rest of the servants are determined to keep your secrets."

His answer afforded Aline boundless relief. She relaxed slightly as she replied. "There are no secrets to discover. I had a fever. Sometimes it happens to people for no apparent reason, and sends them into decline. I recovered eventually, and that was that."

He gave her a hard stare as he replied. "I don't buy that."

The expression was unfamiliar, but its meaning was clear. "Obviously you will believe whatever you wish to," she said. "I can do no more than offer you the truth."

One of his eyebrows lifted at her tone of offended dignity. "As I learned in the past, my lady, you play fast with the truth when it suits you."

Aline scowled at her own inability to defend her past actions, without having to tell him far more than she would ever want him to know.

Before she could reply, McKenna stunned her by pulling her to the side of the narrow passageway. He set the basket down and straightened to face her. As they stood in the hallway with their bodies almost touching, erotic urgency sang through Aline's body. Shrinking away from him, she felt her shoulders come up against the wall.

McKenna stood close enough that she could see the grain of his close-shaven whiskers, a shadow that enhanced his swarthy masculine appeal. His lips were set in severe alignment, until brackets formed at the sides of his mouth. Aline wanted to kiss those lines of tension, soothe them away with her tongue, taste the corners of his lips . . . Desperately she shoved the thoughts away and lowered her face to avoid the sight of his mouth.

"It makes no sense that you should have stayed unmarried," came his low, aggravated voice. "I want to know what happened to you all those years ago, and why you're alone. What is the matter with the men of Hampshire, that none of them has taken you for himself? Or is the problem with you?"

That was so close to the truth that Aline felt a chill of unease. "Is this an example of your seductive skills, McKenna?" she asked crisply. "Seizing a lady in the servants' hallway and subjecting her to an inquisition?"

That provoked a sudden grin, his baffled frustration disappearing with startling quickness. "No," he admitted. "I can do better than this."

"One would hope so." She tried to move past him, but he stepped forward, his solid weight impelling her against the wall until there was no possibility of retreat. Aline gasped at the feel of his body, the thick-muscled wedge of his thigh between hers, the touch of his breath against her ear. He did not attempt to kiss her, only continued to hold her care-fully, as if his body were absorbing the details of hers.

"Let me pass," Aline said thickly.

He did not seem to have heard her. "The feel of you . . ." he muttered.

Awareness rippled through her as she was trapped between the cold, hard wall and the warm, hard man who held her. His body was different from how she remembered it, no longer loose-limbed and narrow, but big-ger, heavier, imbued with the strength of a male in his full-blooded prime. McKenna was no longer the winsome boy she remembered . . . he had become someone else entirely. A powerful, ruthless man, with a body to match. Fascinated by the differences in him, Aline could not stop herself from sliding her hands beneath his coat. Her fingers passed over the bur-geoning muscles of his chest, the sturdy vault of his ribs. McKenna went still, disciplining himself so sternly that a tremor of effort went through his limbs.

"Why are *you* still alone?" Aline whispered, swimming in the scent of him, a salty, sun-heated fragrance that made her heart pound in almost uncomfortably heavy beats. "You should have married by now."

"I've never met a woman I wanted that much," McKenna muttered. He stiffened as her hands coasted over the lean sides of his waist. "To be shackled by marriage vows would drive me—" He broke off and began to breathe like a winded racehorse as Aline let the backs of her fingers stroke his tense abdomen.

Relishing a sudden sense of power mingled with searing excitement, Aline prolonged the moment, letting him wonder if she would dare touch him the way he so obviously craved. His body was thoroughly excited, heat pouring from him in waves. She longed to feel the sleek masculine form beneath the layers of cotton and summer wool. Hardly able to be-lieve her own wild recklessness, she slid her fingers over the outside of his trousers, until they curved delicately over the jutting length of his erection. A shock of pleasure went through her, the nerves in her palms tingling at the contact with his hard, tensile flesh. Memories of physical rapture elicited thrills of response from her sensation-starved body, delicate tissues swelling with anticipation.

McKenna groaned faintly and rested his hands on her shoulders, fingers splayed as if he were afraid of clenching her too tightly. She caressed the swelling, twitching shaft . . . up . . . her thumb rubbing lightly at the top . . . then down . . . her fingers flexing tentatively until his breath hissed between his clenched teeth. Up and down . . . the thought of having him inside her, being impaled with such plentiful maleness, brought a surge of liquid warmth to her own loins.

McKenna lowered his head, his mouth brushing over her face with the softness of butterfly wings. His reverence astonished her. His lips coasted to the corners of her mouth, lingered, then quested across her jaw until his tongue touched the soft lobe of her ear. Blindly Aline turned her mouth to his, wanting the full pressure of his kiss. He gave it to her slowly, possessing her by agonizing degrees, causing her to moan when he finally settled his mouth fully upon hers. Sagging against him, Aline opened to the penetration of his tongue. He tasted her gently, stroking the satin interior of her mouth with an exquisite skill that demolished her ability to think. The rhythm of her breath turned desperate, while all her muscles tightened with delicious urgency. She wanted to wrap herself around him, welcome him deeper into her embrace until he had sunk fully inside her.

Trying to pull her even closer, McKenna hunched his shoulders over hers and clamped one hand over her buttocks, lifting her to the tips of her toes. His mouth drifted to her throat, then wandered back to her lips, and he kissed her over and over, as if he were trying to discover all the ways that their mouths could fit together. His lips caught hers at a particularly luscious angle, and a soft moan rose in her throat, and she squirmed with the need to feel the full length of him against her. The movement of her breasts against his chest drew a harsh sound from him. Suddenly he broke a kiss with a low curse.

Aline wrapped her arms around herself and stared at him dumbly, knowing that her trembling must have been visible to him . . . just as his was to her.

McKenna turned away from her and folded his arms across his chest, his head bent as he glared at the floor. "Only so much . . . self-control," he muttered, the words compressed by his stiff jaw.

The knowledge that he had been about to lose all ability to master himself—and the fact that he was willing to admit it—filled Aline with a mindless excitement that was slow to subside.

It seemed to take forever for both of them to regain their self-possession. Finally McKenna bent to pick up the discarded basket and gestured wordlessly for her to precede him.

Dazedly Aline led the way to the entrance hall, where she encountered the housemaid Gwen, who was heading back to fetch the last basket from her.

McKenna refused to yield the heavy parcel to the girl. "No need," he said easily. "I'll carry it for you—just show me where you want it."

"Yes, sir," Gwen said at once.

He turned to exchange a brief glance with Aline, his blue-green eyes narrowed and dark. A silent message passed between them . . . *later* . . . and then he left with long, easy strides.

Standing still as she tried to gather her wits, Aline was diverted by the unexpected appearance of her brother, who wore a perturbed frown as he came to the hall entrance. Marcus had changed from his shooting clothes into pearl-gray trousers, a dark blue waistcoat, and a blue patterned silk necktie.

"Where is Livia?" Marcus demanded without preamble. "She's gone missing all morning."

Aline hesitated before replying, keeping her voice low. "I suspect she may be in Mr. Shaw's company."

"What?"

"I believe he joined Livia for her morning walk," Aline said, striving to sound casual. "To my knowledge, neither of them has been seen since then."

"And you let him go with her?" Marcus whispered in outrage. "For God's sake, why didn't you do something to stop him?"

"Oh, don't carry on so," Aline said. "Believe me, Marcus, Livia is perfectly capable of telling a man to leave her alone. And if she wishes to spend some time in Mr. Shaw's company, I think she's earned the right to do so. Besides, he seems to be a gentleman, regardless of his reputation."

"He's not like the gentlemen that Livia is accustomed to. He's *American.*" The particular emphasis he placed on the last word made it sound like an insult.

"I thought you liked Americans!"

"Not when they're sniffing around one of my sisters." Marcus's gaze was taut with suspicion as he regarded her more closely. "And what have *you* been doing?"

"I . . ." Briefly taken aback, Aline put a hand to her throat, which had become the focus of his darkening scowl. "Why are you looking at me like that?"

"There is a whisker burn on your neck," he said grimly.

Deciding to play ignorant, Aline gave him a blank look. "Don't be silly. It is merely some chafing caused by my cameo ribbon."

"You're not wearing a cameo ribbon."

Aline smiled and stood on her toes to kiss his cheek, knowing that underneath his glowering exterior, he was terrified that one of his adored sisters might be hurt. "Livia and I are grown women," she said. "And there are certain things you can't protect us from, Marcus."

Her brother accepted her kiss and offered no further complaint, but as Aline walked away from him, she heard him murmur something that sounded suspiciously like "Oh yes, I can."

That night Aline found a single red rose on her pillow, its lush petals slightly unfurled, its long stem carefully stripped of thorns. Picking up the fragrant blossom, she drew it over her cheek and parted lips.

My lady,

Flowers, and a serenade to come forthwith. As for the poetry . . . you'll have to provide me with further inspiration.

Yours,

M.

Eleven

For the next two days McKenna could find no opportunity to get Aline alone. Playing the part of hostess with sparkling skill, she seemed to be everywhere at once, efficiently orchestrating suppers, games, amateur theatricals, and other entertainments for the horde of guests at Stony Cross Park. Short of stalking up to her, seizing her, and dragging her away in front of everyone, McKenna had no recourse but to wait for his chance. And as usual, he found it hard to be patient.

Everyone flocked around Aline whenever she appeared. Ironically, she possessed the ability that her mother, the countess, had always coveted—to draw others to herself. The difference was that the countess had wanted their attention for her own benefit, whereas Aline seemed to possess a sincere desire to make people happy in her presence. She flirted skillfully with old men, and sat and gossiped over glasses of cordial with old women. She played games with the children, listened sympathetically to the unmarried girls' tales of romantic woe, and deflected any young men's interest by acting like a kind older sister.

In this last endeavor Aline was not entirely successful. Regardless of her lack of interest, many men were obviously smitten with her . . . and the sight of their hopeful, barely suppressed ardor turned McKenna's entire being to gall. He wanted to dispatch them all, drive them away, bare his teeth at them like a snarling wolf. He owned her, by virtue of his need and the bitter-washed memories of their past together.

. . .

In the afternoon, as McKenna, Gideon, and Lord Westcliff relaxed in an outside conservatory, Aline appeared bearing a silver tray. A footman followed closely, carrying a small portable mahogany table. The day was humid, the summer breeze doing little to cool them as they sat in their shirtsleeves. Lazy quietness ruled the estate, most of the guests having elected to nap with the windows open until the cooler evening hours approached.

For once, no soiree, supper, or al fresco party had been scheduled for tonight, as the annual village fair had begun. There would be much drinking and reveling in Stony Cross while practically everyone in the county attended the fair. It had been held once a year since the mid-1300s, a week-long event at which all of Stony Cross was overtaken with happy chaos. High Street was virtually unrecognizable, the usually tidy succession of storefronts surmounted with booths run by jewelers, silk mercers, toymakers, cobblers, and a host of other craftsmen. McKenna still remembered the excitement he had felt as a boy at fair time. The first night always began with music, dancing, and a bonfire located at a short distance from the village. Together he and Aline had watched the conjurors, tumblers, and stilt walkers. Afterward they had always gone to the horse fair, to view dozens of gleaming Thoroughbreds and massive draught horses. He still remembered Aline's face in the light of the bonfire, her eyes shining with reflected flame, her lips sticky from the iced gingerbread she had bought from one of the merchant stalls.

The object of his thoughts entered the conservatory, and all three men began to stand. Aline smiled and quickly bade them to remain seated. Although Westcliff and Gideon obediently settled back in their chairs, McKenna stood anyway, taking the tray of iced lemonade from Aline while the footman unfolded the portable table. Aline smiled up at McKenna, her cheeks flushed from the heat, her brown eyes velvety. He wanted to taste her dewy pink skin, lick the salt of her perspiration, and strip away the gown of thin pastel-yellow muslin that clung to her body.

After setting the tray on the table, McKenna straightened and caught Aline staring at the hair-roughened surface of his forearms, where his sleeves had been rolled snugly over his tanned skin. Their gazes meshed, and suddenly it was difficult for him to remember that they were not alone. He could no more hide the fascination in his eyes than Aline could conceal her own helpless attraction.

Turning to the tray, Aline reached for the etched-glass pitcher and poured some lemonade, the brief rattle of ice shards betraying a momentary slip of composure. She gave him the glass, refusing to look into his face again. "Do be seated, kind sir," she said lightly. "And continue your conversation, gentlemen—I did not intend to interrupt you."

Gideon received his glass of lemonade with a grateful smile. "This kind of interruption is always welcome, my lady."

Westcliff motioned for Aline to join them, and she sat gracefully on the arm of his chair as she gave him a glass. The warm friendship the siblings shared was obvious. Interesting, McKenna thought, remembering that in the past, their relationship had been rather distant. Aline had been intimidated by her accomplished older brother, and Marcus had been isolated from the family during his years at school. Now, however, it seemed that Marcus and his sister had formed a close bond.

"We were discussing the question of why British firms don't sell their products abroad as effectively as the Americans and Germans do," Westcliff told his sister.

"Because Englishmen don't like to learn foreign languages?" she suggested cheerfully.

"That's a myth," Westcliff told her.

"Is it?" she responded. "Then tell me how many languages you know—aside from Latin, which doesn't count."

Westcliff gave his sister a challenging glance. "Why doesn't Latin count?"

"Because it's a dead language."

"It's still a language," Westcliff pointed out.

Before the siblings became detoured in an argument, McKenna steered them back on course. "The problem isn't language," he said, earning the attention of them both. "The difficulty with British trade abroad is that the manufacturers here have an aversion to mass producing their goods. You value individuality over conformity—and as a result, the average British manufacturer is too small, and their products are too varied. So few of them can afford to launch a strong selling effort in the world markets."

"But shouldn't a company please its patrons by offering a variety of products?" Aline asked, her brow puckered in a way that made McKenna want to kiss it smooth.

"Within certain limits," McKenna said.

"For example," Gideon broke in, "British locomotive foundries are so specialized that no two engines coming out of any one factory look alike."

"It's that way with other British-owned firms," McKenna continued. "A biscuit factory will make a hundred varieties of biscuits, when it would do far better to offer only twelve. Or a wallpaper printer will produce five thousand designs, even though it would be more profitable to offer one-fifth that amount. It's too expensive to offer so many different products, especially when one is trying to market them overseas. The numbers don't support it."

"But I *like* having a large assortment of things to choose from," Aline protested. "I don't want my walls to look like everyone else's."

She looked so adorably perturbed by the notion of having fewer choices of wallpaper that McKenna couldn't help grinning. Noticing his amusement, Aline raised her brows in a coquettish tilt. "What are you smiling at?"

"When you spoke just now, you sounded very British," he told her.

"Aren't you British too, McKenna?"

Still smiling, he shook his head. "Not any longer, my lady."

McKenna had become an American the very second his foot had touched Staten Island all those years ago. While he would always admit to a certain nostalgia for his birthplace, he had been reinvented and forged in a country where his common blood was not a hindrance. In America he had learned to stop thinking of himself as a servant. Never again would he bow and scrape before anyone. After years of backbreaking work, sacrifice, worry, and sheer mulishness, he was now sitting in Lord Westcliff's library as a guest, instead of working in the stables for five shillings a month.

McKenna quickly became aware of the way Marcus looked from him to Aline, his sharp black eyes missing nothing. The earl was no fool—and it was obvious that he would not suffer Aline to be taken advantage of.

"I suppose you're right," Aline said. "If a man looks, speaks, and thinks like an American, he probably *is* one." She leaned toward him slightly, her brown eyes sparkling. "However, McKenna, there is some small part of you that will always belong to Stony Cross—I refuse to let you disclaim us entirely."

"I wouldn't dare," he said softly.

Their gazes held, and this time neither of them could manage to look away, even when an uncomfortable silence gathered in the conservatory.

Westcliff broke the spell, clearing his throat and standing so abruptly that Aline's weight on the arm of the chair nearly caused it to topple sideways. She stood as well, giving her brother a little frown. As Westcliff spoke, he sounded so much like the old earl that the hairs prickled on the back of McKenna's neck. "Lady Aline, I want to discuss some of the arrangements you've made for the next few days, to ensure that our schedules do not conflict. Accompany me to the library, if you will."

"Certainly, my lord," Aline said, and smiled at McKenna and Gideon, who had both risen to their feet. "Do excuse me, gentlemen. I wish you a pleasant afternoon."

After the earl and his sister had departed, McKenna and Gideon resumed their seats and stretched out their legs.

"So," Gideon remarked in a casual tone, "it seems that your plans are well on the way."

"What plans?" McKenna asked, moodily surveying the watery remains of his lemonade.

"To seduce Lady Aline, of course." Lazily Gideon went to pour himself more lemonade.

McKenna responded with a noncommittal grunt.

They sat in companionable silence for a few moments, until McKenna asked, "Shaw . . . has a woman ever asked you to write a poem for her?"

"Good God, no," Gideon replied with a snicker. "Shaws don't write poetry. They pay others to write it for them and then they take the credit for it." He arched his brows. "Don't say that Lady Aline asked for such a thing?"

"Yes."

Gideon rolled his eyes. "One can't help but marvel at the variety of ways that women have devised to make us look like flaming idiots. You're not actually considering it, are you?"

"No."

"McKenna, how far do you plan to take this revenge notion of yours? I rather like Lady Aline, and I'm discovering an odd reluctance to see her hurt."

McKenna shot him a glance of cold warning. "If you try to interfere—"

"Easy," Gideon said defensively. "I don't intend to foul up your plans. I expect you'll foul them up quite well enough on your own."

McKenna lifted one brow sardonically. "Meaning?"

Gideon withdrew his flask and poured a liberal quantity of alcohol into his own lemonade. "Meaning that I've never seen you so spellbound by anyone or anything as you are by Lady Aline." He took a deep swallow of the potent mixture. "And now that I've had some liquid fortification, I'll venture to say that in my opinion, you still love her. And deep down, you'd rather die by slow inches than cause her one moment of pain."

McKenna stared at him stonily. "You're a drunken fool, Shaw," he muttered and rose to his feet.

"Was that ever in question?" Gideon asked, tossing back the rest of his drink with a practiced swallow as he watched McKenna's departing figure.

As evening approached and the temperature cooled, the guests at Stony Cross Park began to congregate in the entrance hall. Small groups drifted out to the graveled drive, where a line of carriages waited to convey them to the village. Among those who wished to amuse themselves at the fair were Gideon's sister, Mrs. Susan Chamberlain, and her husband, Paul. During the past few days Aline had found it easy enough to socialize with the Chamberlains, but she could not summon any real liking for them. Susan was golden-haired and tall like her brother Gideon, but she did not possess his easy humor or his gift of self-mockery. Rather, she seemed to take herself a bit too seriously—a quality that was shared by her husband, Paul.

Just as the first carriage left, Aline happened to glance at Gideon Shaw, and she saw that his attention was ensnared by someone coming from the house. A faint smile curved his lips, and his expression softened. Following his gaze, Aline saw with a jolt of glad surprise that Livia had finally ventured out of her self-imposed seclusion. It was the first time that Livia had gone on a public outing since Amberley's death. Dressed in a deep rose gown edged with pale pink piping, Livia looked very young, and more than a little nervous.

Aline went to her sister with a welcoming smile. "Darling," she said, sliding an arm around her sister's slender waist, "how nice that you've decided to join us. Now the evening will be perfect."

Susan Chamberlain turned to whisper to her husband, delicately cupping her hand over one side of her mouth to mask the gossip she was relating. Chamberlain's gaze flickered to Livia and then slid quickly away, as if he did not want to be caught staring at her.

Determined to shield her sister from any slights, Aline urged Livia to come forward. "You must meet some of our guests. Mr. and Mrs. Chamberlain, I should like to introduce you to my younger sister, Lady Olivia Marsden." Aline adhered exactly to the order of precedence, wishing there were some way she might emphasize that they were, socially speaking, of a lower rank than Livia—and therefore they had no right to slight her. After the Chamberlains had acknowledged Livia with shallow smiles, Aline introduced the Cuylers and Mr. Laroche, whose wife had already departed in the first carriage.

Suddenly McKenna appeared before them. "I doubt you'll remember me, my lady, after all the years that have passed."

Livia smiled at him, though she suddenly looked pale and guilty. "Of course I remember you, McKenna. Your return to Stony Cross is quite welcome, and long overdue."

They came to Gideon Shaw, who did a poor job of concealing his fascination with Livia.

"A pleasure to make your acquaintance, my lady," Shaw murmured, taking her hand and bowing over it, rather than simply nodding as the others had. When his head raised, he smiled at Livia, whose cheeks had turned several shades darker than her dress. The attraction between the pair was nearly tangible. "You will ride to the village in our carriage, I hope," Shaw said, releasing her hand with obvious reluctance.

Before Livia could reply, Shaw's sister Susan intervened. "I'm afraid that won't be possible," she told Shaw. "There simply won't be enough room in the carriage for someone else. We've already got you and Paul and I, and Mr. Laroche, not to mention McKenna—"

"McKenna isn't riding with us," Shaw interrupted. He glanced at McKenna meaningfully. "Isn't that right?"

"Indeed," McKenna confirmed, taking his cue. "Lady Aline has already arranged for me to ride in another carriage."

"Whose?" Susan asked peevishly. It was obvious that she was not pleased by the substitution.

Aline smiled brightly. "My own, actually," she lied. "McKenna and I have not finished an earlier conversation about, er . . ."

"Poetry," McKenna supplied gravely.

"Yes, poetry." Maintaining her smile, Aline resisted the temptation to step hard on his foot. "And I had hoped to continue our discussion on the way to the village."

Susan's blue eyes narrowed into suspicious slits. "Really. I doubt that McKenna has ever read a poem in his life."

"I've heard McKenna recite one before," Shaw said. "I believe it started with the line 'There once was a man from Bombay.' But as I recall, the rest of it would prove unsuitable for present company."

Mr. Chamberlain turned red and began to snicker, betraying his familiarity with the rest of the so-called poem.

McKenna grinned. "Obviously it falls to Lady Aline to improve my literary tastes."

"I doubt that can be accomplished during one carriage ride," Aline replied demurely.

"That depends on how long the ride lasts," McKenna rejoined.

The remark could hardly be construed as a suggestive one, but something in his tone and the way he looked at her brought a blush to Aline's face.

"I suggest you don't stop until you reach Siberia, then," Shaw said, breaking the sudden tension between them, and a chuckle rumbled through the group. Gallantly he presented his arm to Livia. "My lady, please allow me . . ."

As Shaw guided her sister to the waiting carriage, Aline stared after them in wonder. It was a bit odd, really, to see Livia with another man. And yet Gideon Shaw seemed to be good for her. Perhaps Livia needed a man with his easy confidence and worldliness. And he seemed to be a gentleman, in spite of his cynicism.

However, there seemed to be no real possibility of a match between Shaw and Livia. His drinking was a problem that worried Aline greatly, not to mention his wicked reputation, and the fact that he came from an entirely different world from Livia's. Sighing with a thoughtful frown, Aline looked up at McKenna.

"He's a good man," McKenna said, reading her thoughts with an ease that amazed her.

"I believe that," Aline said quietly. "But if Livia were your sister, McKenna . . . would you want her to be involved with him?" The question was asked without prejudice, only concern.

McKenna hesitated for a long moment, then shook his head.

"I was afraid of that," Aline murmured. She took his arm. "Well, since you've availed yourself of my carriage, we may as well depart."

"Is your brother coming with us?" he asked, escorting her along the drive.

"No, Westcliff has no interest in the fair. He's staying at the manor this evening."

"Good," McKenna said with such obvious satisfaction that Aline laughed.

It was clear that McKenna would have preferred to ride alone with her in the carriage, but they were joined by the Cuylers, who turned the conversation to the subject of local cheeses. As Aline answered their questions in detail, she found it difficult to hide a grin at the sight of McKenna's disgruntlement.

By the time the entire party had arrived in the heart of Stony Cross, the village was blazing with lamps and torches. Music floated over the oval-shaped village green, which was crowded with exuberant dancers. Tidy rows of thatched black and white cottages were nearly obscured by a proliferation of booths. The flimsy wooden structures were all similar, with a stall in front for selling and a tiny room in back where the owner took shelter at night. There were stalls featuring jewelry, cutlery, toys, shoes, fans, glassware, furniture, and specialty foods. Bursts of laughter issued from the crowds around the theatrical booths, where actors and comedians entertained as coins were scattered at their feet.

Allowing McKenna to escort her along the rows, Aline glanced at him curiously. "This must bring back many memories."

McKenna nodded, his gaze turning distant. "It seems as if it was a lifetime ago."

"Yes," Aline agreed with a touch of melancholy. How different they both had been. The innocence of those days, the exquisite simplicity, the sense of life and youth that had imbued every moment with a golden aura . . . remembering, she was suddenly invaded by a warm impatience that seemed to have no particular aim or outlet. The feeling coalesced inside her until her blood was pumping and she felt radiantly aware of every sight and sound and sensation. Walking through the village with McKenna by her side . . . it was a lovely echo of the past, like listening to a beautiful melody she had not heard since childhood.

Staring into his eyes, she saw that he too was becoming enmeshed in the feeling. He was relaxing, smiling more easily, losing the harsh look about his eyes and mouth. They pushed through a tightly packed section of High Street, where a pair of conjurors was eliciting cries of delight from the gathering onlookers. Sliding an arm around Aline to protect her from being jostled, McKenna continued to shoulder his way through the crowd. In the excitement of the fair, no one took notice of the gesture, but Aline was stunned by the naturalness of it, and by the response he evoked from her. It felt completely right to be held close against his side, to let him guide her where he would, to surrender to the coaxing pressure of his hand at her back.

As they emerged from the densely gathered fairgoers, McKenna's hand found hers, and he pulled it back to the crook of his arm. Aline's fingers conformed to the hard swell of muscle, while the side of her breast brushed against his elbow. "Where are we going?" she asked, vaguely perturbed by the languid, almost dreamlike quality of her own voice.

McKenna didn't answer, only led her past more stalls until they reached the one he wanted. The pungent fragrance of gingerbread rose in a warm draught to her nostrils, and Aline laughed in delight. "You remembered!" As a girl, the first thing she had always done at the fair was to gorge on iced gingerbread—and although McKenna had never shared her fondness for the treat, he had always gone with her.

"Of course," McKenna said, extracting a coin from his pocket and purchasing a thick slice for her. "To this day, I've never seen anyone devour an entire loaf the way you used to."

"I did not," Aline protested with a frown, sinking her teeth into the heavy, sticky bread.

"I was in awe," McKenna continued. He drew her away from the stall. "To watch you eat something the size of your head in less than a quarter hour—"

"I would never be that gluttonous," she informed him, deliberately taking another huge bite.

He grinned. "I must be thinking of someone else, then."

As they browsed leisurely among the stalls, McKenna bought some sweet wine for Aline to wash down her gingerbread with, and she drank thirstily. "Slowly," McKenna admonished, his gaze caressing. "You'll make yourself dizzy."

"Who cares?" Aline asked blithely, drinking again. "If I stumble, you'll be here to catch me, won't you?"

"With both arms," he murmured. Coming from anyone else, the statement would have had the ring of gallantry. From McKenna, however, it contained a deliciously threatening edge.

They made their way toward the village green, but before they reached it, Aline saw a familiar face. It was Adam, his blond hair glittering in the torchlight. He was accompanied by friends, both male and female, and he parted from the group with a brief comment, eliciting a few knowing laughs as they saw that he was heading to Aline.

She went to him eagerly, while McKenna followed like a grim specter. Reaching Adam, Aline took his hands and smiled up at him. "I behold a handsome stranger," she teased. "No, wait—were you not once a frequent visitor to Stony Cross Park? It has been so long since I've seen you, my memory fails me."

Adam's mouth quirked with amusement as he replied. "My absence has been deliberate, sweet—and you know why."

She felt a glow of fondness, comprehending that he had stayed away to allow her to deal with McKenna in any way she desired. "That doesn't prevent me from missing you, however."

Adam's smooth, strong fingers squeezed hers before he released her hand. "I'll come to call soon," he promised. "Now, introduce me to your companion."

Obediently Aline made the introduction between her dearest friend and her past love . . . the former, who would never cause her unhappiness, and the latter, who almost certainly would again. It was strange to see McKenna and Adam shaking hands. She had never imagined the two of them meeting, and she could not help but mark the contrasts between them, the angel and the devil.

"Mr. McKenna," Adam said easily, "your return to Stony Cross has afforded Lady Aline such delight that I can't help but share it, as I am appreciative of all things that bring her pleasure."

"Thank you." McKenna subjected him to a coldly hostile stare. "You have been friends for some time, I gather."

"Well nigh five years," Adam replied.

A stilted silence ensued, until it was broken by a cry from several yards away. "McKenna? . . ."

Glancing in the direction of the voice, Aline realized that some of McKenna's old friends had seen him . . . Dick Burlison, once a carrot-headed, gangly-legged boy, who was now a stocky married man in his mid-thirties . . . Tom Haydon, the baker's son, who now ran his father's business . . . and Tom's wife, Mary, the buxom butcher's daughter whom McKenna had so often flirted with in his youth.

Smiling, Aline nudged McKenna gently. "Go on."

He needed no further urging. As he strode to the group with a grin, they all let out jubilant laughs and shook hands enthusiastically. Mary, a mother of five, wore a look of astonishment on her round face as McKenna bent to kiss her cheek.

"I perceive that you have not been intimate with him yet," Adam said to Aline sotto voce.

She replied softly as she continued to watch McKenna. "I may not be brave enough to take such a risk."

"As your friend, I should probably advise you not to do something that you may regret later." Adam smiled as he added, "Of course, one tends to miss out on a great deal of fun that way."

"Adam," she chided, "are you encouraging me to do the wrong thing?"

"Only if you promise to tell me all about it afterward."

Aline shook her head with a laugh. Hearing the sound, McKenna turned and looked at her, a scowl working between his dark brows.

"There, I've just made it easier for you," Adam murmured. "The flames of jealousy have been fanned. Now he won't rest until he claims his territory. My God, you do like them primitive, don't you?"

Sure enough, McKenna returned to her in less than a minute, his fingers clasping Aline's elbow in a clear display of ownership. "We were heading to the village green," he reminded her curtly.

"So we were," Aline murmured. "Lord Sandridge, will you join us?"

"Regretfully, no." Adam lifted Aline's free hand to kiss the points of her knuckles. "I must rejoin my companions. Good evening to you both."

"Goodbye," McKenna said, making no effort to hide his animosity as the handsome viscount took his leave.

"Do be civil to him, please," Aline said. "Lord Sandridge is quite dear to me, and I wouldn't have his feelings hurt for the world."

"I was being civil," McKenna muttered.

She laughed, relishing his obvious jealousy. "You barely said one word to him, except to bid him goodbye. And the way you glowered reminded me of a stuck boar, ready to charge—"

"What kind of a man is he," McKenna interrupted, "that he makes no objection when he sees you being escorted through the village by someone like me?"

"A trusting one. Lord Sandridge and I have a certain understanding— we allow each other as much freedom as is needed. It's a very enlightened arrangement."

"Enlightened," he repeated with ill-concealed contempt. "Sandridge is a fool. And if I were in his place, you wouldn't even be here."

"Where would I be, then?" she asked pertly. "At home, I suppose, mending your shirt cuffs?"

"No, in my bed. Under me."

Her amusement dissolved at once. Reaction to the soft-voiced words skittered through her body, making her feel light and shivery. She kept silent, her face turning pink as she walked with him to the village green. More than a few people glanced at them speculatively as they passed. After McKenna had spent so many years away, his return was reason enough for the villagers' interest, but the fact that he was in Aline's company caused tongues to wag even more eagerly.

The music was accompanied by clapping hands and stomping feet as men and women skipped and spun to a spirited folk tune. Enjoying the infectious melody, Aline let McKenna draw her closer to the musicians.

As soon as the song finished, McKenna gestured to their leader, a fiddle player, who approached him at once. McKenna spoke close to the man's ear and crossed his palm with a few coins, while Aline observed him with sudden suspicion.

Grinning broadly, the fiddle player hastened back to his companions, held a quick conference, and the group of eight musicians walked en masse to Aline. She regarded McKenna with growing suspicion. "What have you done?"

Bringing her with them to the center of the crowd, the musicians stood her in front where she was visible to everyone. Their leader gestured with his bow to McKenna. "My merry friends," he called, "this gentleman has requested a song to honor the charms of the lady who stands before us. I beg your kind assistance in singing 'The Rose of Tralee' to Lady Aline."

The audience applauded heartily, for the tune was a wildly popular one that had just been published that year. Turning scarlet, Aline gave McKenna a glance that openly threatened murder, causing most of the assemblage to laugh. He returned her gaze with an innocent smile, lifting his brows mockingly to remind her that *she* had been the one to request a serenade.

The musicians gazed at Aline with exaggerated soulful gazes, and she shook her head with a grin as they began to play, accompanied by at least two hundred voices. Even some of the shopkeepers and traveling merchants gathered near to join in, substituting her name for that of the heroine in the song:

The pale moon was rising
above the green mountain;
the sun was declining
beneath the blue sea
when I strayed with my love
to the pure crystal fountain
that stands in the beautiful
vale of Tralee.

She was
lovely and fair
as the rose of the summer
yet 'twas not her beauty

alone the won me
Oh, no! 'twas the truth
in her eye ever dawning
that made me love Aline,
the Rose of Tralee

The cool shades of evening
their mantle was spreading,
and Aline, all smiling,
was listening to me,
The moon through the valley,
her pale rays was shedding
when I won the heart
of the rose of Tra-leeeeee!

At the conclusion of the song, Aline curtsied deeply in acknowledgment. She gave the lead fiddle player her hand, and after bending to kiss it, he pretended to fall backward in a swoon, eliciting a round of applause and friendly laughter from the gathering.

Returning to McKenna, Aline regarded him with a mock glare. "You're going to pay for this," she warned.

He grinned. "You wanted a serenade."

Laughter rustled up from her chest. "From *you*," she exclaimed, taking his arm once again. "Not from the entire population of Stony Cross!"

"Trust me—that was far better than hearing me sing alone."

"As I recall, you had a very nice voice."

"I'm out of practice."

They stared at each other, smiling, while delight hummed through Aline's veins. "I also asked for a poem," she said.

The flirtatious sparkle of her eyes seemed to affect McKenna, causing his voice to deepen as he replied. "And I told you I needed more inspiration."

"I'm afraid you'll have to be more precise. What kind of inspiration are you referring to?"

His wide mouth curled up at the corners. "Use your imagination."

Aline was struck by the words. Unknowingly, McKenna had used the same phrase that Adam had once spoken, when they had discussed the scars on her legs.

The feeling of impatience returned, and she could hardly draw breath around the billowing excitement and confusion in her chest. If she was clever, if she was bold, she might be able to have what she wanted most in the world. One night with McKenna . . . no, just a few minutes stolen from the grasp of an uncharitable Fate . . . Dear God, was that too much to ask for?

No.

No matter what it cost her, she would have a few precious moments of intimacy with the man she had never stopped loving. And she would find a way to do it without letting him know her secrets. *Tonight,* she thought in passionate rebellion, and damn anyone or anything that tried to stop her. Damn Fate itself . . . she and McKenna were finally going to have their reckoning.

Twelve

It was long past midnight, and the torches were burning down. Villagers and visitors swarmed through the darkened streets, many of them intoxicated. Some sang, some scuffled and disputed, while others took advantage of the shadows to indulge in brazen kisses. Those of more genteel sensibilities had prudently left for home, while those who remained could not help but be aware that the crowd's inhibitions were fading as fast as the torchlight. Musicians played near the bonfire, while dancers perspired freely as they moved in and out of the pool of flickering light.

Staring into the glow of the bonfire, Aline leaned back against McKenna. He supported her automatically, one hand settling at the nipped-in curve of her waist, the other cupping gently around her elbow. On any other night, in any other circumstances, the way they stood would have caused a scandal. However, the usual standards of propriety were relaxed, if not outright ignored, at fair time. And in the milling crowd, no one seemed to notice or care that Aline and McKenna had materialized like a pair of shades from a time long past.

Aline's eyes half closed as the heat of the firelight limned her face. "You're taller," she murmured absently, thinking of how he used to stand with his chin resting on the top of her head. Now he couldn't do the same without hunching over.

He bent his head, his voice warm and soft in her ear. "No, I'm not."

"Yes, you are." Wine had loosened her tongue. "We don't fit the way we used to."

His chest, so solid behind her, moved in a huff of amusement. "The fit may be better than before. Let's try it, and see."

Aline smiled and almost let herself melt back against him . . . oh, how she wanted, needed, to lean her head on his shoulder and feel his mouth brush over the fragile arch of her neck. Instead she stood in absolute stillness, staring blindly at the bonfire. McKenna's skin and clothes carried the scents of midnight air and summer meadows and smoke . . . and the far subtler aura of a healthy, aroused male. Desire was thick between them, intoxicating them, blurring the edges of reality. The sounds of the bonfire, the crackling and smoldering and breaking wood, seemed a perfect expression of her own inner dismantling. She was not the heedless girl of the past, nor was she the resigned Aline with so many empty places inside, but some other, temporary self . . . an eager insurgent, rebellious with love.

"Not at the house," she heard herself whisper.

McKenna did not move, but she sensed the shock of response that went through him. A full minute passed before he murmured, "Where, then?"

"Let's walk through the woods," she said recklessly, "along the path that goes by the wishing well."

McKenna knew the path she referred to—a dark and unfrequented route that they had traversed a thousand times in their youth. There could be no doubt in his mind as to why she suggested it.

A rueful little smile rose to Aline's lips as she reflected that coupling in the forest was hardly the stuff of great romance. Furtive, inelegant, hasty, and almost certainly uncomfortable. But she would never have the luxury of candlelight and white linen and leisurely lovemaking. If she were to keep McKenna from seeing her scars, she needed darkness and expedience, so that he wouldn't have the opportunity to notice her legs. The fact that she was actually contemplating such a thing—an act so utterly devoid of grace and tenderness—was astonishing. But this was all she could have of McKenna. And whom would it hurt? Clearly McKenna wanted the opportunity to take what he'd been denied in the past. For her part, she wanted something to remember, for all the long years she had yet to live without him. They desired each other for what were probably selfish reasons—and in Aline's current mood, that was just fine.

"The wishing well . . ." McKenna murmured. "Do you still visit it?"

She remembered how, as a girl, she had often gone to cast a pin into the well and wish for the one thing she couldn't have. "No," she said, and turned to face him with a faint smile. "That well ran out of magic a long time ago. It never made any of my wishes come true."

His face was shadowed as he stood with his back to the firelight. "Maybe you wished for the wrong things."

"Always," she admitted, her smile holding a bittersweet curve.

McKenna stared at her intently, then led her away from the bonfire, toward the forest that surrounded Stony Cross Park. They were soon swallowed in the night, their way illuminated by the cloud-crossed moon. After a while Aline's eyes adjusted to the thickening darkness, but she was less surefooted than McKenna as they walked through the coppices of hazel and elm. He caught her hand in his. Remembering how he had once caressed her, the tender places those fingers had ventured so long ago, Aline felt her breathing turn choppy. She tugged free of him with a low, nervous laugh.

"Am I walking too fast for you?" McKenna asked.

"Just a bit." She had walked too much that evening—her right knee was threatening to stiffen beneath the tightening scar tissue.

"Then we'll stop for a moment." He drew her to the side of the path, where a massive oak tree spread, and they stood in a cleft of its roots. The forest seemed to sigh as it enfolded them in rustling, mossy dampness. As Aline leaned back against the tree trunk, McKenna loomed over her, his breath stirring the wisps of hair that fell on her forehead.

"McKenna . . ." she said, trying to sound casual, "I want to ask you something . . ."

His fingertips touched the side of her neck, brushing against the sensitive nerves. "Yes?"

"Tell me about the women you've known. The ones you . . ." Aline paused as she considered the appropriate word.

McKenna drew back a few inches. "What do you want to know?"

"If you loved any of them."

At McKenna's silence, Aline looked up to find him staring at her with an intensity that sent hot and cold chills through her body.

"I don't believe in love," he said. "It's a sugar-coated pill—the first taste is tolerable enough, but you quickly reach the bitter layers beneath."

She had been the only one, then. Aline knew that she should regret the fact that after her, his interactions with women had been purely physical. But as always, she was selfish where McKenna was concerned. She couldn't help but be glad that his words of long-ago had proven true . . . *"You'll have my heart always . . . you've ruined me for life . . ."*

"What about Sandridge?" McKenna asked. "Do you love him?"

"Yes," Aline whispered. She loved Adam dearly—just not in the way he meant.

"And yet you're here with me," he murmured.

"Adam—" She stopped and cleared her throat. "Whatever I choose to do . . . he doesn't mind. This has nothing to do with him . . . you and I . . ."

"No, it doesn't," he said with sudden anger. "My God, he should be trying to tear my throat out, instead of letting you go somewhere alone with me. He should be willing to do anything short of murder—hell, I wouldn't even stop at that—to keep other men away from you." Disgust thickened his voice. "You're lying to yourself, if you think that you'll ever be satisfied with the kind of bloodless arrangement your parents had. You need a man who will match your will, own you, occupy every part of your body and every corner of your soul. In the eyes of the world, Sandridge is your equal—but you and I know better. He's as different from you as ice from fire." He leaned over her, his body forming a hard, living cage around her. "*I'm* your equal," he said harshly, "though my blood is red instead of blue, though I was condemned by my very birth never to have you . . . inside, we're the same. And I would break every law of God and man if—"

McKenna stopped suddenly, biting back the words as he realized that he was revealing too much, allowing his rampaging emotions to get the better of him.

Aline longed to tell him that she had never thought of him as anything but an equal. Instead she reached for the buttons of his waistcoat and began to unfasten them. "Let me," she whispered. Even through the layers of fabric, she could feel the hardness of his stomach, the rigid layers of muscle.

McKenna was unmoving, the knuckles of his clenched fists digging into the oak bark. She worked carefully at the row of buttons, then began on his shirt. He did not try to help her, only stood still beneath her ministrations. Trembling with excitement, she finally unbuttoned his shirt and pulled it free of his trousers. The garment was crumpled and hot where it had been tucked in at his waist. Slipping her hands inside McKenna's open clothes, Aline inhaled swiftly. His skin was fever-hot, salt-scented, tantalizing. Her palms traveled slowly across his hair-covered chest. She was fascinated by the textures of his body, so much more varied than her own. Determined and ardent, Aline found his nipple with her fingertip. She leaned forward to touch the satiny circle with her tongue, while the crisp curls of his chest brushed against her cheek.

McKenna drew in a quick breath and shoved his hands behind her, tugging at the fastenings behind her gown. His mouth came to her throat, nuzzling and kissing, while he pulled hard at the back of her bodice. Her dress fell around her waist, revealing a corset that pushed her breasts high beneath a thin cotton chemise. Suddenly a sense of unreality made Aline fearless. Sliding the straps of her chemise down her shoulders, she pulled her arms free and peeled the garment down over the top of her corset. Her breasts spilled out, the shadowy tips contracting in the open air.

McKenna's fingers slid beneath the pale curve of one breast, and his head bent over her chest. She jumped a little as the wet warmth of his mouth closed over her. His tongue traced the edge of the taut aureole, then stroked over the tip, tickling the sensitive flesh. She squirmed and gasped, while desire thumped through every part of her body. Releasing the nipple, McKenna drew back to caress her aching flesh with the humid waft of his breath. His tongue flicked her, the feathery laps causing her to twist and moan.

He took the throbbing peak between his teeth, nibbling with a delicate pressure that caused darts of sensation all the way down to her toes. Aline was so mesmerized by the pleasure of his mouth that she didn't notice him pulling her dress down until it fell to the ground in a heap, leaving her in her underclothes. Dismayed, she bent automatically to retrieve her gown, but McKenna pushed her back against the tree and seized her mouth in a pillaging kiss. His fingers went to the tapes of her drawers, loosening them until they dropped to her knees.

Awkwardly she reached for the tops of her stockings, checking to make certain that her garters hadn't slipped. Her heart gave a sickening jerk as she felt one of his hands cover hers.

"I'll do it," McKenna muttered, evidently thinking that she wanted to untie the garter.

"No." Hastily she seized his hand and tugged it to her breast.

To her relief, McKenna was instantly distracted by the maneuver, his thumb brushing over the bud of her nipple. Aline lifted her face for his kiss, her lips parting eagerly beneath his. She felt the shape of arousal against her thigh, the hardness straining behind a row of trouser buttons. Hungrily Aline reached for him, working at the buttons, the backs of her knuckles dipping behind the skin-warmed fabric. They both gasped as she finally freed him, his stiff flesh springing from the confines of thick broadcloth. Shivering in anticipation, Aline curved her fingers around him in a delicate, hot grip.

Growling quietly, McKenna pulled her wrists up over her head and anchored them to the tree. He kissed her mouth, his tongue searching her while his free hand drifted over her stomach. He sifted through the dark curls between her thighs, while one of his feet pushed at her instep, forcing her stance to widen. Aline experienced a thrill of primal pleasure at being so utterly mastered. Having unleashed McKenna's passion, she now had to accept the consequences . . . and she was more than ready to give him what they had both wanted for so long.

His fingers traced the swollen folds of her cleft, then parted her with utter gentleness. Pulling helplessly at her imprisoned wrists, Aline stiffened at the feel of his fingertip sliding against the opening of her body. McKenna's fingertip played in the moisture, skimming over the tender threshold of her sex until beseeching hums rose in her throat. Releasing her hands, McKenna slid a supportive arm around her corseted back. His mouth fed on hers, while he found the aroused peak hidden beneath the soft hood of her sex. The kiss was barbaric, wet, violent, contrasting sharply with the skillful delicacy of his fingers. He tormented the little peak with soft, slippery nudges, tickling and prodding until she canted her hips tightly. Closer . . . closer . . . her flesh throbbing, sizzling with sensation. She writhed on his fingers, hovering at the precipice of a release so acute that she couldn't think or breathe. Then he brought her over the edge, and she was suspended in wrenching pleasure, her body spasming, her throat dilating with a deep gasp of air. After what seemed an eternity, the pleasure eased into exquisite ripples, and she whimpered against his lips.

McKenna bent to lift the twisted hem of her chemise. The rough silk of his tongue stroked the place on her abdomen where the structure of her corset compressed her pale flesh. Leaning weakly against the tree, Aline stared at the top of his dark head. "McKenna," she said, flooded with riotous heat as he knelt to inhale the scent of her body. Remembering the scars, she reached down to tug her garters upward, then pushed at him helplessly. "Wait . . ." But his mouth was already on her, nuzzling into the wet cleft, his tongue sliding past the thick curls.

Aline's legs trembled violently. If not for the support of the oak behind her, she would have melted to the ground. Her shaking hands went to his head, her fingers tangling in the close-cropped locks. "McKenna," she moaned, unable to believe what he was doing to her.

He licked deeper into the furrow of her sex, his tongue invading the melting tenderness until she fell silent, her labored breaths puncturing the air. Tension gathered once more, coiling with every tug of his mouth.

"I can't bear it," she gasped. "Please, McKenna . . . please . . ."

Apparently those words were what he had been waiting for. Standing, he gathered her against his body and lifted her with incredible ease. One of his arms shielded her back from the scrape of the tree trunk, while the other hooked neatly beneath her buttocks. She was completely helpless, unable to move or even squirm. Her scars pulled, and she shifted her knee upward to ease the tension.

McKenna kissed her, his hot breath filling her mouth. She felt the blunt pressure of his sex, the hardness pushing into the vulnerable cove of her body. Her flesh resisted, tightening against the threat of pain. The tip of his shaft entered her, and as McKenna felt the hot, snug clasp of her, his urgency seemed to magnify a hundred times. He pushed upward, while at the same time allowing Aline's own weight to impel her onto his engorged length. A broken gasp came from Aline's throat as her body gave way to the unrelenting invasion. Suddenly he was inside her, rending and filling and stretching the soft tissues. Aline arched in shock, her hands fisted against his back.

McKenna froze as the signs of her pain registered in his lust-clouded brain. Realizing what the peculiar resistance of her body had meant, he let out an astonished breath. "My God. You're not a virgin. You can't be."

"It doesn't matter," she gasped. "Don't stop. It's all right. Don't stop."

But he remained still, staring at her in the secret darkness, his arms clamping around her until she could barely breathe. He was part of her, finally, in this ultimate and necessary act that her entire life had led to. She held on to him with every part of herself, drawing him deep, binding him in the light, secure grasp of her arms. Feeling the rhythmic squeeze of her inner muscles, McKenna bent to kiss her fiercely, his tongue stroking the edge of her teeth and probing the dark sweetness beyond. Aline clenched her stockinged legs around his waist, while he began to thrust in slow, tireless movements. The stinging eased, though it did not fade completely—and Aline didn't care. All that mattered was possessing him, containing his rising flesh, her body and soul changed forever by his passionate invasion.

Groaning between his clenched teeth, McKenna braced his feet and pumped harder, burrowed deeper, sweating with pleasure and exertion. He spurted inside her, his climax primitive, fierce, endless. Aline wrapped herself around him, dragging her open mouth over his face and neck, licking greedily at the trails of sweat.

McKenna panted and shivered and held himself inside her for a long time. Slowly the tension drained from Aline's body, leaving her exhausted. As McKenna withdrew from her, she felt hot liquid seeping between her thighs. Realizing that her stockings had slipped, she wriggled in sudden anxiety. "Please let me down."

Lowering her carefully to the ground, McKenna steadied her with his hands, while she fumbled to yank her stockings upward, and pull the straps of her chemise back over her shoulders. When she was safely covered, she reached for the bedraggled heap of her gown. Oh, how she wanted to lie with him somewhere, and sleep nestled against his body, and awaken to the sight of him in the morning sunlight. If only that were possible.

Clumsily jerking on the rest of her clothes, Aline stood with her face averted, and let McKenna fasten the back of her gown. Something had happened to one of her shoes . . . she had kicked it off during their encounter, and it took a minute of dedicated searching before McKenna finally located it behind a tree root.

Aline's lips twitched with reluctant humor as he brought the shoe to her. "Thank you."

McKenna did not smile, however. His features were as hard as stone, his eyes gleaming dangerously. "How the hell is it possible," he asked in controlled fury, "that you were a virgin?"

"It's not important," she muttered.

"It is to me." His fingers grasped her chin none too gently, forcing her to stare at him. "Why have you never let any man bed you before tonight?"

Aline licked her dry lips as she tried to come up with a satisfactory explanation. "I . . . I decided to wait until I married."

"And in the five years of knowing Sandridge, you've never let him touch you?"

"You needn't sound as if that's a crime," she said defensively. "It was a matter of respect, and mutual choice, and—"

"It is a crime!" he exploded. "It's unnatural, damn you, and you're going to tell me why! And then you're going to explain why you let *me* take your virginity!"

Aline fumbled for a lie to divert him . . . anything to conceal the truth. "I . . . suppose I felt I owed it to you, after the way I sent you from Stony Cross all those years ago."

McKenna seized her shoulders. "And you think the debt has been paid now?" he asked incredulously. "Oh no, my lady. Let us be clear on that point . . . you haven't begun to make amends for that. You're going to reimburse me in more ways than you can imagine—with interest."

Aline turned cold with alarm. "I'm afraid this is all I can offer, McKenna," she said. "One night, with no promises and no regrets. I'm sorry if you want more than that. It just isn't possible."

"The hell it isn't," he muttered. "My lady, you're about to receive an education in how to conduct an affair. Because for the duration of my stay at Stony Cross, you're going to work off your debt to me . . . on your back, your knees, or any other position I desire you in." He pulled her away from the huge oak, her gown bedraggled, and her hair mussed and littered with flecks of bark. Jerking her forward, he covered her mouth with his, kissing her not with the intent to please, but to demonstrate his ownership. Although Aline knew it would be to her advantage to keep from responding, his kiss was too compelling for her to resist. She did not have the strength to break free of his inexorable grasp, nor could she avoid his compelling mouth, and before long she melted against him with a shaken moan, her lips feverishly answering his.

Only when her response was obvious to both of them did McKenna lift his head. His rapid breath mingled with hers as he spoke. "I'm going to come to your room tonight."

Aline wrenched herself away from him, stumbling back to the forest path. "I'll lock the door."

"I'll break it down, then."

"Don't be an ass," she said with a touch of exasperation, hastening her stride despite the protests of her much-abused legs.

The rest of the walk back to the manor was silent, except for the sound of their feet crunching leaves and twigs and gravel. Aline was increasingly uncomfortable, becoming aware of a multitude of twinges and aches, not to mention the cold stickiness between her thighs. Her scars had begun to itch and burn. She had never wanted a hot bath so badly in her life. She only prayed that McKenna was too preoccupied to notice the pained hobble of her gait.

The manor was dark and quiet, only a few lights burning as a concession to guests who had decided to prolong their revels. McKenna walked Aline to a servants' entrance at the side of the house, where there was far less likelihood of either of them being seen. Anyone who witnessed Aline's disheveled condition would easily guess what she had been doing.

"Tomorrow, then," McKenna warned her, standing in the entrance . . . watching as she made her slow, painstaking way upstairs.

Thirteen

McKenna wandered to the back terrace in a kind of stupor, feeling drugged and floundering . . . no doubt similar to the way Gideon Shaw had felt while he was drunk and drowning in a storm-swept ocean. In all of McKenna's imaginings of this night, he had always pictured himself as completely in control. He was experienced with women, cognizant of his own sexual needs and the responses of his partners. He had known exactly what he was going to do with Aline, and how the scene would be played out. And then Aline had changed everything.

Sitting at an outside table in the shadows, McKenna clasped his head in his hands and closed his eyes. The faint mingled scents of oak and sap and female arousal clung to his hands . . . he inhaled the fragrance greedily and felt heat stirring in his groin. He remembered the feeling of sliding inside her, the lush flesh that had surrounded him so tightly. The gasps that had come from her throat. The taste of her mouth, spiced with wine and ginger. She had satisfied him more than anyone ever had, and yet he already desired her again.

A virgin . . . *damn her*. Damn her for the feelings she roused in him, the confusion and suspicion and protectiveness and sexual hunger. He would have bet every last cent that she had taken dozens of lovers by now.

And he would have lost.

McKenna tightened his palms on his head as though he could crush out the traitorous thoughts. She was not the girl he had once loved, he reminded himself grimly. That girl had never really existed. And yet it didn't seem to matter. Aline was his curse, his fate, his consuming desire. He would never stop wanting her, no matter what she did, no matter how many oceans and continents he managed to put between them.

God . . . the sweetness of her body, so tight and warm around him . . . the salty-fresh scent of her skin, the perfumed softness of her hair. He had felt his sanity dissolve as he took possession of her, and he had lost all thought of withdrawing at the moment of climax. It was possible that he had made her pregnant. The thought filled him with primitive satisfaction. To see her big and helpless with his child, overtaken with his seed, dependent in every way on him . . . yes, he thought grimly. He wanted to occupy her with his own flesh, and chain her to him with a bond she could never break. Aline didn't realize it yet, but she would never be free of him—or the demands he would make of her.

"What a deadly dull evening," Susan Chamberlain, Gideon Shaw's sister, remarked sourly. They had just returned from the village fair, having left the festivities just as things began to get interesting. Apparently the provincial pleasures of having one's palm read, or watching tumblers and fire eaters, or drinking local elder wine, was lost on people as urbane as the Shaws and their kin.

"Yes," her husband, Mr. Chamberlain, chimed in, "the novelty of mingling with rustics wears off rather quickly, I'm afraid. It is better to spend time in one's own company than to consort with people who have no more intelligence than the sheep and goats they herd."

Annoyed by his snobbery, Livia could not resist making a retort. "You are fortunate, then, Mr. Chamberlain. With that attitude, it seems likely that you will indeed be spending a great deal of time in your own company."

While both the Chamberlains glared at her, Gideon Shaw laughed freely at her impudence. "I enjoyed the fair," he said, his blue eyes twinkling. He glanced at Susan. "And you seem to have forgotten, dear sis, that most of those so-called rustics have better bloodlines than the Shaws."

"How could I forget?" Susan Chamberlain asked sharply. "You are always so eager to remind me."

Livia bit the insides of her lips to keep from laughing. "I suppose I shall retire for the evening. I bid you all a good night."

"Not yet," Shaw said softly. "The night is still young, my lady. Shall we play a hand of cards, or have a turn at the chessboard?"

She smiled and asked ingenuously, "Do you like to play games, Mr. Shaw?"

His gaze was subtly seductive, but his tone matched hers for innocence. "Of every kind."

Livia's teeth caught at her lower lip in the way that had always inspired Amberley to say that she was adorable. How strange—she hadn't consciously done that in so very long. Which made her realize how very much she wanted to attract Gideon Shaw.

"I never play when I don't think I can win," she told him. "Therefore, I suggest that we take a turn through the portrait gallery, and you can view *my* ancestors. You may be interested to know that our family tree boasts of a pirate. Quite a ruthless fellow, I've been told."

"So was my grandfather," Shaw remarked. "Although we politely refer to him as a sea captain, he did things that would make a pirate blush for shame."

His sister Susan made a strangled sound. "I will not join you, Lady Olivia, as it is obvious that my brother is determined to denigrate his antecedents at every opportunity. Heaven knows for what purpose."

Livia tried to suppress a rush of pleasure at the prospect of being alone with Shaw again, but a betraying tide of color burnished her cheeks. "Certainly, Mrs. Chamberlain. Again, I wish you good night."

The Chamberlains' replies, if they made any, were inaudible. And Livia wouldn't have been able to hear them in any case: her ears were filled with the pounding of her own heartbeat. She wondered what they thought of her going somewhere unchaperoned with Shaw, and then decided in a rush of happy self-indulgence that it did not matter. The night *was* young, and for the first time in a long while, she felt young too.

Leading Shaw to the portrait gallery, Livia gave him an arch glance. "You are wicked, to tease your sister so," she said severely.

"It is a brother's duty to torment his older sister."

"You perform your duty with awe-inspiring thoroughness," she said, and his grin broadened.

They entered the long, narrow portrait gallery, where paintings had been hung in six rows up to the ceiling, clearly intended not as a display of art but rather a display of aristocratic heritage. At the far end of the gallery stood a pair of immense gothic thrones. The backs of the chairs were eight feet tall, and the seats were surfaced by cushions that managed to be harder than a wooden plank. To the Marsdens, bodily comfort was of far less importance than the fact that the thrones dated back to the 1500s and represented a lineage far less corrupted by foreign influences than that of the current monarch.

As they walked back and forth along the gallery, the conversation quickly detoured from the subject of ancestry into far more personal channels, and somehow Shaw managed to guide Livia into the subject of her love affair with Amberley. There were countless reasons why Livia should not have confided in him. She ignored them all. Somehow Livia did not want to keep anything hidden from Gideon Shaw, no matter how shocking or unflattering. She even told him about her miscarriage . . . and as they talked, Livia found herself being pulled to one of the enormous chairs, and suddenly she was sitting on his lap.

"I can't," she whispered anxiously, staring at the empty doorway of the gallery. "If someone should catch us like this—"

"I'll watch the doorway," Shaw assured her, his arm tightening around her waist. "It's more comfortable to sit like this, isn't it?"

"Yes, but—"

"Stop wiggling, darling, or you're going to embarrass us both. Now . . . you were telling me . . ."

Livia went still in his lap, blushing wildly. The endearment, commonplace as it was, and the prolonged contact with his body, and the friendly sympathy in his gaze, made her weak all over. She struggled to remember what they had been talking about. Ah . . . the miscarriage. "The worst part was that everyone thought I was fortunate to have lost the baby," she said. "No one said it in those exact words, but it was obvious."

"I imagine that it wouldn't have been easy, to be unmarried with a fatherless child," Shaw said gently.

"Yes. I knew that at the time. But I still grieved. I even felt as if I had failed Amberley, by not managing to keep that last little part of him alive. And now there are even times when I find it difficult to remember exactly what Amberley looked like, or what his voice sounded like."

"Do you think he would have wanted you to commit suttee?"

"What is that?"

"A Hindu practice in which a widow is expected to throw herself on her husband's burning funeral pyre. Her suicide is considered as proof of her devotion to him."

"What if the wife dies first? Does the husband do the same thing?"

Shaw threw her a mildly taunting grin. "No, he remarries."

"I should have known," Livia said. "Men always manage to arrange things for their own benefit."

He tsked in mock reproof. "You're too young to be so disillusioned."

"What about you?"

"I was born disillusioned."

"No, you weren't," she said decisively. "Something made you that way. And you should tell me what it was."

Subtle amusement flickered in his eyes. "Why should I do that?"

"It's only fair, after I told you about Amberley and my scandal."

"It would take the rest of the night to tell you about *my* scandals, my lady."

"You owe it to me," she said. "Surely you are too much of a gentleman to renege on a debt to a lady."

"Oh, I'm quite the gentleman," Shaw said sardonically. Reaching into his breast pocket, he withdrew the small silver flask. He tucked her deeper into the crook of his arm and brought his hands together to uncap the flask. Livia gasped a little as she was lightly squeezed amid taut bands of muscle. When the task was accomplished, Shaw's arms relaxed, and he brought the flask to his lips. The smell of expensive liquor drifted to Livia's nostrils, and she watched him warily.

Shaw let out a measured sigh, welcoming the calming effect of the bourbon. "Very well, Princess Olivia . . . how do you like your scandal . . . *au tartare*, or well done?"

"Something in-between, perhaps?"

Shaw smiled and took another pull on the flask. For a long minute they sat together in silence, with Livia piled on his lap in a heap of skirts and stays and confined female flesh. She saw the careful consideration in his eyes as he weighed how much to tell her, which words would most efficiently convey his meaning . . . and then his mouth quirked with moody resignation, and his shoulders tensed in the bare promise of a shrug. "Before I tell you anything, you have to understand the Shaws' perception—no, conviction—that no one is quite good enough for them."

"Which Shaws are you referring to?"

"Most of them—my parents in particular. I have three sisters and two brothers, and believe me, the ones who are married had the very devil of a time getting my father to approve of their prospective spouses. It was infinitely more important to my parents that their offspring should marry people of the right backgrounds, with the appropriate bloodlines and financial endowments, rather than marry someone whom we may have actually liked."

"Or loved," Livia said perceptively.

"Yes." Shaw regarded the worn silver flask and drew his thumb across the warm, scuffed metal. Livia had to avert her gaze from the sight, astonished by the sudden intense wish that his hand was on her body instead. Fortunately Shaw seemed too lost in his thoughts to notice the way she had tensed in his lap. "I am . . . was . . . the second oldest son," he said. "While my brother Frederick struggled beneath the weight of expectation, I became the black sheep of the family. When I reached a marriageable age, the woman I fell in love with was nowhere near the standards that the Shaws had established. Naturally that only made her more attractive."

Livia listened carefully, her gaze on Shaw's face as he smiled with self-derision. "I warned her what to expect," he continued. "I told her they would likely disown me, they would be cruel, they would never approve of someone they had not chosen themselves. But she said that her love for me would never waver. We would always be together. I knew that I would be disinherited, and it didn't matter. I had found someone who loved me, and for the first time in my life I would have the chance to prove to myself and everyone else that I didn't need the Shaw fortune. Unfortunately, when I took her to meet my father, the relationship was immediately exposed for the sham that it was."

"She crumbled beneath your father's disapproval," Livia guessed.

Shaw laughed darkly, recapping the flask and replacing it in his coat pocket. " 'Crumbled' is not the word I would use. They struck a deal, the two of them. My father offered her money to simply forget my proposal and go away, and she responded with a counteroffer. The two of them bargained like a pair of bookies in a listmaker's office, while I stood by and listened, slack-jawed. When they reached an acceptable sum, my beloved left the house without once looking back. Apparently the prospect of marrying a disinherited Shaw wasn't nearly as attractive as a nice big payoff. For a while I couldn't decide whom I hated more—her or my father. Not long after, my brother Frederick died unexpectedly, and I became the heir apparent. My father made his disappointment in me clear from then until the day he died."

Livia was careful not to reveal her sympathy, fearing that he would misread it. A dozen platitudes occurred to her, about how Shaw would certainly find a woman worthy of his love someday, and perhaps his father had only wanted the best for him . . . but in the stark honesty of the moment, she couldn't say anything so banal. Instead she sat in silence with him, eventually glancing into his face to find that instead of looking bitter or disillusioned, he was staring at her with a quizzical smile.

"What are you thinking?" he asked.

"I was just reflecting on how fortunate I am. Even though I only had Amberley for a short time, at least I know that once I was truly loved."

His fingers touched the edge of her jaw, stroking delicately. The gentle caress made Livia's heart throb violently. He held her gaze deliberately, his fingertips playing on her skin until he found the tender hollow behind her earlobe. "Anyone would love you."

Livia could not seem to look away from him. He was a dangerous man, offering sensation in lieu of safety, passion instead of protection. Once she never would have believed that she would consider having an affair with a man whom she didn't love. But there was something tantalizing about him, a promise of wicked enjoyment, of fun, that she found impossible to resist.

Impulsively she leaned forward and touched her mouth to his. The texture of his lips was smooth and silken, cool at first, then warming rapidly. As before, his kisses were playful, expressive, nipping with gentle curiosity, then pressing with more purposeful intent. After coaxing her lips apart, he settled in for a long, open kiss, his tongue delving in soft exploration.

As Livia squirmed closer to him, she felt the tension of his body, the taut muscle of his chest and abdomen . . . and lower down, a rising pressure that made her flush in sudden awareness. His hand moved over her back in a lazy circle, influencing her to lean harder against him, until one of her hands encountered the edge of the silver flask. The metal object interfered with her explorations, giving her an unwelcome jolt of reality.

Livia pulled back, smiling and trembling.

"Don't go yet," Shaw murmured, feeling the way she tensed in preparation to climb off his lap.

His hand was at her waist, and she reluctantly pushed it away. "I can't do this with my entire family watching, Mr. Shaw." She gestured at the rows of solemn-faced ancestors lining the walls.

Shaw responded with a slow smile. "Why not? Don't they approve of me?"

Livia pretended to consider the question seriously, contemplating the countless austere Marsden faces. "They don't seem to. Perhaps they should get to know you better."

"No," he replied without hesitation. "I don't improve on closer acquaintance."

She arched her brows, wondering if the statement had been made out of sincerity, or manipulation, or merely a dark sense of humor. Unable to decide, she shook her head with a reluctant smile. "Actually, the closer you are, the more I like you."

Instead of replying, Shaw took her small head in both his hands and pulled her close, and crushed a kiss on her mouth. The smacking imprint of his lips was hardly romantic—it was too hard, too fast, though gratifyingly enthusiastic. Yet it affected Livia even more intensely than the languid, soft searching of a few minutes earlier.

Releasing her, Shaw watched as Livia slid from his lap. The floor seemed to slant beneath her feet before she finally regained her balance. Shaw settled back in the throne, staring at her in a way that drew a quiver from deep in her abdomen.

"What are you thinking?" Livia whispered, echoing his earlier question.

He answered with a startling lack of pretense. "I'm wondering how much I can take from you without hurting you."

It was then that Livia was certain of something: before Gideon Shaw returned to America, she and he were going to be lovers. She saw from the expression in his eyes that he knew it too. The knowledge filled her with a shivery kind of anticipation. Blushing, she backed away from him a step or two, and murmured good night. Turning to walk away from him, she could not resist throwing a glance over her shoulder.

"I'm not afraid of being hurt," she murmured.

He smiled faintly. "All the same . . . you're the last person in the world I want to cause any harm."

Aline discovered that the door to her room was half open, with golden lamplight spilling invitingly into the hallway. Desperately self-conscious, she went inside and hesitated as she saw Mrs. Faircloth waiting at a chair near the grate. Her usual bath had been placed in the center of the room, with a kettle of scalding water on the hearth.

Naturally Mrs. Faircloth understood everything in one incisive glance.

Aline closed the door, not looking at the housekeeper. "Good evening, Mrs. Faircloth. If you will unfasten the back of my gown, I will manage everything else by myself. I don't need any help tonight."

"Yes, you do," Mrs. Faircloth said, coming to her.

Wry amusement broke through Aline's misery. There was no possible chance that the housekeeper would ignore this turn of events without having her say. After helping Aline off with her gown, Mrs. Faircloth fetched the kettle from the hearth and warmed the bath with a new infusion of boiling water. "I expect you're sore," the housekeeper said. "The hot water will help."

Turning crimson all over, Aline unhooked her corset and dropped it to the floor. The sudden inrush of oxygen made her dizzy, and she waited until she felt steadier before removing the rest of her clothes. The tight cinch of her garters had left dark red rings around her thighs, and she sighed in relief as she untied them and removed her stockings. Filled with the uncomfortable suspicion that the things that she had done with McKenna were probably visible on her body, Aline hurriedly entered the bath. She sank down into the water with a hiss of comfort.

Mrs. Faircloth went to straighten various articles around the room, while a pair of notches appeared in the space between her silvery brows. "Did he see the scars?" she asked quietly.

Aline let the top of her right knee break through the steaming surface of the water. "No. I managed things so that he didn't notice them." She narrowed her eyes against the sudden sting of tears, willing them not to fall. "Oh, Mrs. Faircloth, it was such a mistake. And so appallingly wonderful. Like finding a part of my soul that had been ripped away." She grimaced in self-mockery at the melodrama of the words.

"I understand," the housekeeper said.

"You do?"

An unexpected glint of humor appeared in Mrs. Faircloth's eyes. "I was a young woman once, difficult as that may be to believe."

"Who did you—"

"It is not something I ever discuss," the housekeeper said firmly. "And it has no relevance to your predicament with McKenna."

A more accurate word could not have been chosen. It was not a difficulty, or a problem, or even a dilemma. It was indeed a predicament.

Morosely Aline swirled her hands in the water, while Mrs. Faircloth came to pour some herb-infused oil into the bath. "I've behaved like a greedy child," Aline said ruefully. "I reached out for what I wanted without giving a thought to the consequences."

"McKenna's behavior has been no better." The housekeeper retreated to the chair near the fire. "Now you've both gotten what you wanted, and it seems that you're both the worse off for it."

"The worst is yet to come," Aline said. "Now I've got to drive him away without ever explaining why." She paused, rubbed her wet hands over her face, and added bleakly, "Again."

"It needn't be that way," Mrs. Faircloth countered.

"Are you suggesting that I tell him the truth? You know what his reaction would be."

"You can never know someone else's heart completely, my lady. Why, I've known you since the day you were born, and yet you still have the ability to surprise me."

"What I did with McKenna tonight . . . did that surprise you?"

"No." For some reason the promptness of Mrs. Faircloth's reply caused them both to laugh.

Leaning her head against the rim of the tub, Aline flexed her knees, willing the heat of the bath to soften her scars. "Has my sister returned from the fair yet?"

"Yes, she came back in the company of Mr. Shaw and the Chamberlains, at least three hours ago."

"How was she? Did she seem happy?"

"Rather too much so."

Aline smiled faintly. "Is it possible for someone to be too happy?"

The housekeeper frowned. "I only hope that Lady Livia understands what kind of gentleman Mr. Shaw is. No doubt he has dallied with a hundred women before her, and will continue doing so long after he's left Stony Cross."

The words caused Aline's smile to fade. "I will talk to her tomorrow, and perhaps together we can settle our heads."

"That's not what needs settling," Mrs. Faircloth said, and Aline made a face at her.

Fourteen

To Livia's disappointment, Gideon Shaw did not surface at all the next day. His absence at breakfast and lunch were not remarked on by any of the American entourage, who seemed to take Shaw's disappearance as a matter of course. After bidding Mrs. Faircloth to make discreet inquiries as to his whereabouts, Livia learned that Shaw had simply closed himself away in the bachelor's house and left word that he was not to be bothered for any reason. "Is he ill?" Livia asked, imagining him helpless and feverish in a sickbed. "Should he be left alone at such a time?"

"Ill with liquor, one would surmise," Mrs. Faircloth said in disapproval. "In which case, Mr. Shaw should most definitely be left alone. There are few sights more unpleasant than that of a gentleman in his cups."

"What reason would he have to do this?" Livia fretted, standing at the huge oak worktable in the kitchen, where the maids had just finished rolling out and cutting pastry dough. She used her fingertip to make a pattern in the heavy dusting of flour, leaving a succession of tight little circles. "What could have set him off? He seemed perfectly fine last evening."

Mrs. Faircloth waited to reply until the maids had taken the rounds of pastry to the next room. "Drunkards need nothing in particular to set them off."

Livia disliked the images that the word conjured, of nasty, sloppy, ridiculous men who said disagreeable things and tripped over invisible furniture, and ended up florid and fat. Although it was well known that practically all men drank to excess now and then, one wasn't considered a drunkard until it became obvious that his thirst was perpetual, and that he had no ability to hold his liquor. Livia had known very few such men. In fact, she had never seen Marcus intoxicated, as he had always maintained a rigorous grip on his self-control.

"Shaw isn't a drunkard," Livia countered in a half whisper, mindful of the servants' sharp ears. "He's only, well . . ." Pausing, she furrowed her forehead until it resembled a window shutter. "You're right, he's a drunkard," she admitted. "How I wish that he were not! If only someone or something might inspire him to change . . ."

"That kind of man does not change," Mrs. Faircloth murmured with dismaying certainty.

Livia stepped back from the table as one of the maids came to clean it with a damp cloth. She dusted the traces of flour from her hands and folded her arms across her chest. "Someone should go and make certain that he is all right."

The housekeeper regarded her with disapproval. "If I were you, my lady, I should leave the matter alone."

Livia knew that Mrs. Faircloth was right, as always. However, as the minutes and hours crawled by, and suppertime approached, she went in search of Aline. Who, now that Livia thought of it, had seemed rather distracted today. For the first time all day, Livia tore herself away from her absorption with Gideon Shaw long enough to wonder how her sister was faring with McKenna. Livia had seen the two of them walking together at the fair, and of course she had heard about the "Rose of Tralee" serenade. She had found it interesting that McKenna, whom she had thought of as very private and self-contained, would have resorted to making a public demonstration of his interest in Aline.

It was likely that no one had been surprised, however, as it was clear that Aline and McKenna belonged together. There was something invisible and yet irrefutable that made them a couple. Perhaps it was the way both of them stole quick glances at each other when one thought the other wasn't looking . . . glances of wonder and hunger. Or the way McKenna's voice changed subtly when he spoke to Aline, his tone deepening, softening. No matter how circumspectly they behaved, anyone could tell that Aline and McKenna were drawn together by a force more powerful than either of them. They seemed to want to breathe the same air. Their need for each other was painfully obvious. And Livia was convinced that McKenna worshipped her sister. Perhaps it was wrong, but Livia couldn't help but wish that Aline could find the courage to trust McKenna with the truth about her accident.

Absorbed in her thoughts, Livia managed to find Aline in Marcus's private study, the one their father had always used. Like their father, it was all hard angles. The walls were covered with polished rosewood paneling, ornamented only by a row of rectangular stained-glass windows. Although Aline often visited Marcus there to discuss household matters, they appeared to be discussing something far more personal at the moment. They seemed to be arguing, actually.

". . . don't see why you should have taken it upon yourself . . ." Aline was saying sharply, just as Livia entered the room with a cursory knock at the door.

Neither sibling looked particularly thrilled to see her. "What do you want?" Marcus growled.

Unruffled by his rudeness, Livia focused her attention on her sister. "I wanted to talk with you before supper, Aline. It's about . . . well, I'll tell you later." Pausing, she regarded them both with raised brows. "What are you arguing about?"

"I'll let Marcus explain," Aline said shortly. She sat on the corner of the large desk, leaning back to brace her hand on the glossy oiled surface.

Livia stared suspiciously at Marcus. "What has happened? What have you done?"

"The right thing," he said.

Aline gave a scornful huff.

"What do you mean?" Livia asked. "Marcus, must we play twenty questions, or will you just tell me?"

Marcus went to stand by the empty hearth. Had he been a tall man, he might have been able to rest his elbow on the mantel in a nicely casual pose. As it was, he got nearly the same effect by leaning his broad shoulders back against it. "I merely took it upon myself to send word to a few of Shaw's potential investors—all of whom are acquaintances of mine—to be cautious about investing in the Shaw foundries. I informed them of some potential problems in the deal that Shaw and McKenna have proposed. I warned them that in the Americans' drive to expand their business, we have no guarantee against falling production quality, debasement of design, defective service, even fraud—"

"That is nonsense," Aline interrupted. "You are just playing on the typical Englishman's fear of large-scale production. You have no evidence that it will be a problem for the Shaw foundries."

"I have no proof that they won't," Marcus said.

Folding her arms across her chest, Aline gave him a challenging glance. "I predict that your efforts will come to nothing, Marcus—Shaw and McKenna will prove themselves more than capable of settling any concerns their investors might have."

"That remains to be seen. I also put a few words in Lord Elham's ear—he sits on the board of the Somerset Shipping Company—and now he's going to think twice about selling his docking rights to Shaw. And those rights are an essential part of Shaw's plans."

Livia followed the conversation with complete bewilderment, understanding only that her brother had deliberately undertaken to make Shaw's and McKenna's forthcoming business negotiations difficult. "Why would you do that?" she asked.

"Simple," Aline said, before Marcus could reply. "By throwing obstacles in Mr. Shaw's path, Marcus has ensured that he—and McKenna—will have to go to London at once, to deal with all the mischief he has wrought."

Livia stared at her brother with dawning fury. "How could you do that?"

"Because I intend to keep those two bastards as far away from my sisters as I can," Marcus said. "I've acted in your best interests—both of you—and someday you'll see the wisdom in what I've done."

Livia glanced wildly around the room, searching for something to throw at him. "You are just like our father, you self-important, interfering *clod!*"

"At this very moment," Marcus told her grimly, "Shaw is drowning himself in a bottle of something-or-other, after spending all day holed up in a dark room. What a fine character for you to associate with, Livia. How happy Amberley would be."

Livia turned white at his sarcasm. Incoherent with hurt and anger, she strode from the room, not bothering to close the door.

Aline stared at her brother with narrowed eyes. "That was going too far," she warned gently. "Don't ever forget, Marcus, that some things can never be taken back once they are said."

"Livia would do well to remember the same," he retorted. "You heard what *she* just said."

"Yes, that you are just like Father. And you disagree?"

"Categorically."

"Marcus, in the last few minutes you have never sounded or behaved or looked more like him."

"I'm not!" he said in outrage.

Aline held up her hands as if in self-defense, and spoke in sudden weariness. "I won't waste time arguing the point. But you might use that clever brain to consider something, my dear . . . how many other ways might you have handled the situation? You took the shortest and most efficient route to accomplish your goal, without pausing to consider anyone else's feelings. And if that wasn't like Father . . ." Her voice trailed away, and she shook her head with a sigh. "I'm going to find Livia now."

Leaving her unrepentant brother in the study, Aline hurried after her sister. The effort of walking so fast caused her scars to pull, and she sighed impatiently. "Livia, where are you going? For heaven's sake, stop for a moment and let me come even with you!"

She found Livia standing in a hallway, her cheeks streaked red with wrath. Suddenly Aline remembered when Livia had been a small child and had once frustrated herself by building a tower of blocks that was too tall to stand. Over and over, Livia had painstakingly constructed the same wobbly tower, crying angrily when it fell . . . never accepting that she should have just settled for building a less ambitious structure.

"He had no right," Livia said, shaking from the violence of her feelings.

Aline regarded her sympathetically. "Marcus has been high-handed and arrogant," she agreed, "and obviously he has done the wrong thing. But we must both keep in mind that he did it out of love."

"I don't care about his motivation—it doesn't change the result."

"Which is?"

Livia looked at her with annoyance, as if she was being willfully obtuse. "That I won't see Mr. Shaw, of course!"

"Marcus is assuming that you won't leave Stony Cross. You haven't traveled out of the county since Amberley passed away. But what doesn't seem to have occurred to either you or Marcus is that you can go to London." Aline smiled as she saw the dawning surprise on Livia's face.

"I-I could, I suppose," Livia said distractedly.

"Then why don't you? There's no one to stop you."

"But Marcus—"

"What could he possibly do?" Aline pointed out. "Lock you in your room? Tie you to a chair? Go to London if you wish, and stay at Marsden Terrace. I will manage Marcus."

"It seems rather brazen, doesn't it? Chasing after Mr. Shaw . . ."

"You won't be chasing after him," Aline assured her immediately. "You're going shopping in town—and a long overdue trip it is, I might add. You need to visit the dressmaker, as everything you own is sadly out of fashion. And whose concern is it if you happen to be shopping in London at the same time that Mr. Shaw is there?"

Livia smiled suddenly. "Will you go with me, Aline?"

"No, I must stay at Stony Cross with our guests. And . . ." She hesitated for a long moment. "I think it would be best to effect a separation between McKenna and myself."

"How are things between you and him?" Livia asked. "At the fair, the two of you seemed—"

"We had a lovely time," Aline said lightly. "Nothing happened—and

I expect that nothing ever will." She felt a sharp twinge of discomfort at lying to her sister. However, the experience with McKenna last night had been too intensely personal—she was not up to the challenge of putting it into words.

"But don't you think that McKenna—"

"You had better go make plans," Aline advised. "You'll need a chaperone. I have no doubt that Great-Aunt Clara would stay at the terrace with you, or perhaps—"

"I'll invite old Mrs. Smedley from the village," Livia said. "She's from a respectable family, and she would enjoy a trip to London."

Aline frowned. "Dearest, Mrs. Smedley is hard of hearing, and as blind as a bat. A less effective chaperone I couldn't imagine."

"Precisely," Livia said, with such satisfaction that Aline couldn't help laughing.

"All right, then, take Mrs. Smedley. But if I were you, I should keep everything quite discreet, until you have actually departed."

"Yes, you're right." With furtive excitement, Livia turned and hastened through the hallway.

Deciding that it was only fair to let McKenna know about her brother's machinations, Aline decided to approach him after supper. However, she had the opportunity to speak to McKenna sooner than expected, as the meal ended in a precipitate and distinctly awkward manner. Gideon Shaw was conspicuously absent, and his sister Susan Chamberlain seemed to be in an ill humor.

Seeing that Susan was consuming her wine a bit too freely, Aline exchanged a subtle glance with the first footman, communicating that the wine should be more heavily watered. Within a minute, the footman had circumspectly handed a carafe of wine to a subordinate, who secreted it to the serving room and then quickly returned with it. The entire process was unnoticeable to any of the guests except McKenna, who regarded Aline with a quick smile.

As the first course of asparagus soup and salmon with lobster sauce was removed, the conversation veered to the subject of the business negotiations that would take place in London. Mr. Cuyler innocently undertook to ask Marcus's opinion about how the negotiations would turn out, and Marcus replied coolly, "I doubt this subject can be adequately discussed in Mr. Shaw's absence, as the outcome will depend strongly upon his performance. Perhaps we should wait until he is no longer indisposed."

"Indisposed," Susan Chamberlain said with a mocking laugh. "Are you referring to my brother's habit of swilling rotgut from sunup to sundown? Quite the family figurehead, isn't he?"

All conversation stopped. Inwardly startled by Susan's flash of hostility toward her brother, Aline tried to ease the tension in the room. "It seems to me, Mrs. Chamberlain," she said, "that your family has prospered under Mr. Shaw's leadership."

"That has nothing to do with him," Susan said scornfully, resisting her husband's attempts to shush her. "No, I will have my say! Why must I pay homage to Gideon merely because he had the fool's luck to be next in line when poor Frederick died?" Her mouth twisted bitterly. "The reason the Shaws have prospered, Lady Aline, is because my brother decided to place his family's welfare at the mercy of an uneducated immigrant who happened to make a few lucky choices." She began to laugh. "A drunkard and a docker—what a distinguished pair. And my future lies completely in their hands. So very amusing, don't you think?"

No one else seemed to share her amusement. A long moment of silence ensued. McKenna's expression was implacable. He seemed completely unaffected, as if he had long ago been inured to poisonous words. Aline wondered how many insults and affronts he had endured over the years, merely because he had committed the unpardonable sin of laboring for his keep.

Standing, McKenna bowed to the company at large, his gaze catching briefly with Aline's. "Excuse me," he murmured. "My appetite fails me this evening."

Everyone wished him a pleasant evening, except for Susan Chamberlain, who proceeded to bury her resentment in another glass of wine.

Aline knew that she should have stayed to ease the atmosphere with light conversation. But as she stared at McKenna's empty chair, the urge to follow him became unbearable. *Stay where you are, and do what you should,* she disciplined herself, but with every second that passed, the sense of exigency became sharper, until her heart pounded and sweat trickled beneath her dress. Aline found herself rising from the table, obliging the gentlemen to stand. "I beg your pardon . . ." she murmured, trying to come up with some reason for her sudden departure. "I . . ." However, she couldn't seem to think of anything. "Do excuse me," she said lamely, and left the room. Ignoring the whispers that followed her departure, she hurried after McKenna. When she reached the top of the staircase, she found him waiting for her. He must have heard her footsteps behind him.

Waves of cold and heat winnowed through her as they faced each other. McKenna's eyes were bright in his dark face, his piercing gaze invoking the memory of the two of them clutching greedily at each other in the forest . . . her body impaled and writhing on his.

Discomfited, Aline closed her eyes, while pinpoints of heat seemed to cover her face. When she finally managed to look at him once more, his eyes still held a disquieting gleam.

"Are all the Shaws like that?" Aline asked, referring to Susan Chamberlain.

"No, she's the nice one," McKenna said dryly, startling a laugh from her.

Twisting her fingers into a little knot, she asked, "May I speak with you for a minute? I have something rather important to tell you."

He stared at her alertly. "Where shall we go?"

"The family receiving room," Aline suggested. It was the most appropriate second-floor room to hold such a conversation.

"We'll run the risk of being interrupted if we talk in there," McKenna said.

"We'll close the door."

"No." He took her hand, pulling her along with him. Bemused by his authoritative manner, Aline went without resistance. Her heart kicked in an unruly pattern as she realized where he was taking her. "We can't go to my room," she said warily, glancing up and down the long hallway. "Is that where you . . . no, *really,* we can't . . ."

Ignoring her protests, McKenna went to the door of the room she had slept in all her life, and pushed his way in. A brief contemplation of his large, broad-shouldered form convinced Aline that it was useless to argue. She could hardly throw him out, after all. With a sigh that conveyed exasperation, she entered the room and closed the door.

A lamp reposed on a table near the entrance. Aline paused to light it deftly, the flame casting long shadows across the bedchamber and dressing room beyond. Picking up the lamp by its painted porcelain handle, she followed McKenna into the cabinet—the private space he had never dared to trespass in their childhood.

A daybed—the only piece of furniture in the room—was littered with embroidered cushions. Nearby, a strand of pearls hung from a gold hook, beside a collection of tiny beaded reticules and purses. Out of the corner of her eye, Aline saw McKenna reach out to touch one of the delicate reticules, which looked absurdly small beside his hand.

She went to the cabinet's ancient window. The age-rippled glass panels made the view of the outside grounds pleasantly blurred, as if one were looking through water. The other three sides of the cabinet were lined with squares of silvered glass, creating a myriad of reflections that multiplied one another. As McKenna stood behind her, Aline saw his face, and her own, reproduced infinitely in the glow of lamplight.

Exploring, McKenna went to the window and picked up an object from the painted sill. It was a child's toy, a little metal horse with the figure of a man riding it. Aline saw at once that he recognized the object . . . it had been his favorite toy, so well loved that most of the brightly colored paint had worn off. Mercifully McKenna set it down without making a comment.

"What do you want to tell me?" he asked quietly. Aline was fascinated by the perfect juxtaposition of hardness and softness in his face . . . the bold angle of his nose, the lush curve of his bottom lip, the way the feathery silk of his eyelashes cast shadows over his cheekbones.

"I'm afraid that my brother has made your negotiations a bit more difficult than you may expect," she said.

His gaze sharpened. "In what way?"

As she proceeded to explain what Marcus had done, McKenna listened with a reassuring lack of alarm.

"It will be all right," he said when she had finished. "I can ease the investors' concerns. And I'll find a way to convince Elham that it's in his best interests to sell us those docking rights. Failing that, we'll build our own damned dock."

Aline smiled at his self-confidence. "That wouldn't be easy."

"Nothing worthwhile ever is."

"I'm certain that you must be furious with Marcus. But he only did it out of a mistaken desire to . . ."

"Protect you and your sister," McKenna finished for her, as she hesitated. "I can hardly blame him for that." His voice was very gentle. "Someone should keep you safe from men like me."

Turning away, Aline confronted the panels of mirror glass, the mosaic of her own flushed face . . . and the way the lamplight slid over McKenna's gleaming black hair as he came to stand behind her. Their gazes met in the midst of the fragmented images.

"You will have to go to London right away, won't you?" she asked, flustered at being in such close quarters with him.

"Yes. Tomorrow."

"Wh-what will you do about Mr. Shaw?"

His head bent over hers until she felt his breath at her temple. One of his hands came to the exposed top of her shoulder, his fingertips brushing over the pale skin with the lightness of a butterfly's wing. "I'll have to sober him up, I suppose."

"I think it is so unfortunate that he chooses to—"

"I don't want to talk about Shaw." McKenna turned her to face him, and his hand drifted up her neck until his sun-browned fingers were cupping her cheek.

"What are you doing?" Aline asked, tensing as she felt his other hand slide to the back of her gown.

"Exactly what you knew I would do, if you let me in here." McKenna kissed her as he began to unfasten her gown, the bristle of his cheek making her skin tingle.

"You left me no choice," Aline protested. "You just barged in and—"

His mouth sealed over hers, while his fingers worked until he had exposed the laces of her corset. He wound the thin cords around his knuckles and tugged, until the web of stays expanded, and her compressed flesh was released. The corset dropped to the floor, beneath the dress she still wore. Her unbound flesh felt tender and swollen, aching for the clasp of his hands.

The rush of her heartbeat filled her ears as his mouth possessed hers with sweet, foraging kisses. The warm male incense of his skin, spiced with cologne, edged with starch and a pungent whiff of tobacco, filled her with drugging pleasure. She felt wildly excited at the prospect of having him inside her again, but at the same time an inner voice warned that he must not be allowed to explore her at his leisure.

"Hurry," she urged unsteadily. "Just . . . hurry, please—" The words were crushed by his mouth, more steamy, delicious kisses, more dizzying closeness with his aroused body. His hands slipped inside her open dress, skimming the soft line of her back, down to the full swell of her buttocks. She felt a twinge of response between her thighs, the concealed flesh becoming supple and hot, and she strained hungrily into the wickedly gentle courtship of his fingers.

Tearing his mouth from hers, McKenna turned her to face away from him, his hands coming to her shoulders.

"Get on your knees," he whispered.

At first she didn't understand. But the pressure of his palms guided her, and she found herself sinking before the daybed. She knelt amid the shimmering billows of her dress. The pattern of an embroidered cushion blurred before her eyes as she heard the sound of McKenna shedding his coat. The garment landed on the daybed before her. More rustling, the sound of fabric being unfastened, and then McKenna knelt behind her.

Efficiently he reached beneath her skirts, smoothing up yards of layered material to find the vulnerable body beneath. She felt him grasp her hips, his thumbs digging into the plumpness of her buttocks. One of his hands slid between her legs, searching for the opening of her linen drawers. He seemed to measure the length of the lace-edged slit with his fingers, and Aline quivered as his knuckles brushed against the curling hair beneath the fabric. He used both hands to rend the slit another few inches, until the drawers gaped open. Gently McKenna adjusted her position, pushing her forward to lean harder on the daybed, kneeing her thighs open until she was spread wide before him.

McKenna moved closer behind her, covering her, his shoulders slightly hunched. "Easy," he murmured, as she shivered beneath him. "Easy. I won't hurt you this time."

Aline couldn't answer. She could only tremble, and wait, her eyes closing as she lowered her face to his forearm. She felt his hips shift, and something brushed between her legs . . . his male part, nudging the delicate tissues that he had exposed. His free hand moved beneath her skirts, over her front and down her stomach, until his fingers slid through the matted curls. He parted the soft furrow of her sex, following as her hips jerked backward against his solid body. She moaned at his gentle teasing, the tiny circles he made around the sensitive nub.

McKenna's hand left her, and he touched her face, using the tip of his middle finger to stroke her lower lip. Opening her mouth obediently, she let his finger slip inside the warm dampness. His hand dipped beneath her skirts once more, and this time his finger was slippery when he stroked her. He aroused her softly, massaging the wetness all around until she clawed the upholstery of the daybed and dug her sweating forehead into the cushions. A shuddering sound escaped her as she felt his finger enter her, gliding farther and farther until her swollen flesh had enveloped every joint. Her buttocks rose to fit as closely against his body as possible, and she waited in brimming hunger while he stretched her in gentle circling thrusts, preparing her for the invasion yet to come.

Again, that maddeningly light nudge of his organ, a teasing brush of stiff, silken tension. Her breath caught, and she remained utterly passive, her thighs spread in helpless offering. McKenna entered her in a slow thrust . . . again, she experienced that startling sense of fullness, but this time there was only a brief flicker of pain. He went deep, encountering no resistance as the throbbing depths of her body welcomed him. Each time he pulled back to tunnel inside her again, Aline writhed to press closer to him. His fingers played in the wet curls of her sex, tenderly rubbing the source of her craving, stroking sweetly in counterpoint to the rhythm of his thrusts. The sensation multiplied rapidly, building on itself with each delicious lunge, the hardness advancing ever deeper into the slick channel of her body. The pleasure sharpened to a harrowing pitch, gathering in the part of her that he possessed so consummately, until she could bear it no longer. Arching against his fingers, she convulsed uncontrollably, muffling her groans in the upholstery of the daybed. McKenna contained her with a growl, driving hard into her center until a raw sound was torn from his throat and he pulsed violently inside her.

They remained locked together for a long, breathless minute, their bodies joined and clinging, while McKenna's weight nearly smothered her. Aline never wanted to move again. Her eyes remained closed, her damp lashes sticking to her cheeks. When she felt him ease away from her, she bit her lip to keep from moaning a protest. Instead, she continued to lean against the cushions in a heap of silk and torn linen, her limbs weak in the aftermath of their lovemaking.

McKenna restored his clothing and fumbled for his discarded coat. He had to clear his throat before speaking, his voice sounding scratchy. "No promises, no regrets—just as you wanted."

Aline did not move as he left the cabinet. She waited until he had left her suite of rooms, listening for the sound of the door clicking shut, before she let the tears slide from her eyes.

The long, hellish supper was over. Although Livia knew that almost everyone at Stony Cross Park suspected that she had gone to visit the bachelor's house, she felt that it was only decent to try to be discreet. She used a path at the side of the manor and kept to the side of a tall yew hedge before slipping over to the quiet residence. No doubt it would be wise to leave well enough alone, but her concern for Gideon Shaw compelled her to go see him. After she had made certain that he was all right, she would go back to the manor and find some nice long novel to occupy herself with.

Knocking on the door, Livia waited tensely for some response. Nothing. Frowning, Livia knocked again. "Hullo?" she called. "Hullo? Can anyone hear me?"

Just as Livia began to consider the option of going to fetch a key from Mrs. Faircloth, the door vibrated and clanked as it was unlocked. It opened a cautious crack, revealing Shaw's valet. "Yes, milady?"

"I've come to see Mr. Shaw."

"Mr. Shaw is not receiving visitors at this time, milady."

The door began to close. Livia wedged her foot in it. "I won't leave until I've seen him," she said.

The valet's gaze conveyed infinite exasperation, though his tone remained courteous. "Mr. Shaw is not in a suitable condition, milady."

Livia decided to be blunt. "Is he drunk?"

"As David's sow," the valet confirmed sourly.

"Then I'll send for some tea and sandwiches."

"Mr. Shaw has asked for more brandy."

Livia's jaw firmed, and she pushed her way past him. Being a servant, he could not stop her—no one in service would ever dare to lay a hand on a lady of the manor. Ignoring the valet's protests, she surveyed the darkened receiving room. The air was tainted with the smells of liquor and tobacco. "No brandy," she said in a tone that allowed no room for argument. "Go to the manor, and bring back a pot of tea and a plate of sandwiches."

"He won't take that well, milady. No one stands between Mr. Shaw and what he wants."

"It's time someone did," Livia said, motioning him away. The valet left reluctantly, and Livia ventured farther into the darkened bachelor's house. The glow of a lamp filled the main bedroom with quiet amber light. The unmistakable rattle of ice in a glass floated to her ears. Assuming that Shaw was in a drunken stupor, Livia went to the doorway.

The sight that greeted her eyes caused her to gasp.

Gideon Shaw was reclining in a slipper tub that had been set near the fire, his head leaning back against the mahogany rim, one long leg dangling carelessly over the side. He held an ice-filled glass in his hand, his gaze arrowing to hers as he took a swallow. Steam rose in veils from the bathwater, condensing on the golden curvature of his shoulders. Droplets glistened on the amber curls of his chest and the small circles of his nipples.

Good Lord in heaven, Livia thought dazedly. Gentlemen suffering the aftereffects of an excess of strong spirits usually looked terrible. "Death's head on a mop stick" was how Marcus liked to describe them. However, Livia had never seen anything as magnificent as an unshaven and unkempt Gideon Shaw in his bath.

Scowling, Shaw levered himself upward, causing water to slosh gently against the rim of the tub. Glittering rivulets slid over the muscular surface of his chest. "What are you doing here?" he asked curtly.

Livia was so mesmerized that she could barely manage a reply. Tearing her gaze away from him, she moistened her dry lips with the tip of her tongue. "I came to see if you were all right."

"Now you've seen me," he said coldly. "I'm fine. Get out."

"You're not fine," she countered. "You're intoxicated, and you probably haven't eaten anything all day."

"I'll eat when I'm hungry."

"You need something more nourishing than the contents of that glass, Mr. Shaw."

His hard gaze met hers. "I know what I need, you presumptuous wench. Now leave, or you're going to get a big eyeful of Gideon Shaw."

Livia had never been called a wench before. She supposed she should be offended, but instead she felt a little smile push up from her chest. "I've always thought it so pompous for someone to refer to himself in the third person."

"I'm a Shaw," he replied, as if that was a perfectly acceptable exemption for pomposity.

"Do you know what is going to happen to you if you keep drinking this way? You're going to turn into an ugly wreck of a man, with a big red nose and an overhanging belly."

"Is that so," he said stonily, tossing back the rest of his liquor in a deliberate swallow.

"Yes, and your brain will rot away."

"I can hardly wait." He leaned over the edge of the tub, setting the glass of ice on the carpet.

"*And* you'll be impotent," Livia finished triumphantly. "Sooner or later, alcohol robs a man of his virility. When was the last time you made love to a woman, Mr. Shaw?"

Evidently the challenge was too much for him to withstand. Shaw clambered out of the tub with a sneer. "Are you asking for proof of my potency? By all means—come and get it."

As Livia's gaze swept over his rampantly aroused body, she felt herself turn crimson. "I-I should probably go now. I'll leave you to consider what I've said—" She whirled to escape, but before she could take a step, he reached her, and caught her from behind. Livia stopped, her eyes closing at the feel of the wet masculine body pressing against her back. His dripping forearm locked just beneath her breasts.

"Oh, I'm considering it, my lady," he said near her ear. "And I've just come to the conclusion that there's only one truly effective rebuttal for your argument."

"No need," she gasped, while his arm shifted and his hand cupped over her left breast. Heat and water soaked through the fabric, causing her nipple to tighten against his palm. *"Oh—"*

"You shouldn't cast aspersions on my virility. It's a subject we men are rather touchy on."

Livia began to tremble, her head falling back against his shoulder. His warm hand left her breast, swept over the exposed skin of her neck, then slipped beneath the edge of her bodice. She jolted as she felt him touch the hard tip of her nipple. "I'll have to remember that," she whispered.

"See that you do." Turning her in his arms, he covered her mouth with his. The softness of his lips, surrounded by the wiry scratch of unshaven bristle, was wildly exciting. Livia arched up to him fervently, her hands sliding over his gleaming body. Realizing dimly that she was about to take her first lover after Amberley, Livia tried to gather her wits . . . but it was impossible to think, with Gideon kissing her over and over, until they both sank to their knees on the water-splotched carpet.

Pushing Livia to her back, Gideon settled into the billowing heap of her skirts. He unfastened the first few buttons of her bodice and pulled the top of her chemise downward, revealing the shallow curves of her breasts. She wanted him to kiss them. She wanted his mouth on her, his tongue . . . the thought of it drew a moan from her throat.

Breathing fast, Gideon levered his body farther over hers, reaching for something just beyond her head. She heard the rattle of melting ice, and for a moment of confusion, Livia wondered if he was going to take a drink, now of all times. But he fished a shard of ice from the glass and popped it into his mouth, and then, to her bewilderment, he bent his head over her. He engulfed the tip of her breast in an icy kiss, his tongue sweeping across the nipple with chilling, supple strokes. Livia wriggled beneath him with an astonished cry, but Gideon held her down and persisted, until the ice dissolved and his mouth warmed. The heavy length of his arousal pressed against the inside of her thigh, while each caress of his tongue tightened a coil of pleasure in Livia's belly. Sliding her hands into his thick, damp golden hair, she held his head against her, while her hips strained upward.

But Gideon pulled away suddenly, rolling off her with a groan. "No," he said raggedly. "The first time can't be like this. I'm too damned drunk to do it properly, and I won't insult you that way."

Livia stared at him blankly, too filled with desire to think clearly. Her breast tingled and throbbed. "I wouldn't feel insulted. You weren't doing badly at all, actually—"

"And on the floor, no less," he muttered. "My God. Forgive me, Livia. You don't deserve to be treated this way."

"You're forgiven," she said quickly. "I wasn't at all uncomfortable. I *like* this carpet. So let's just go back to—"

But her companion had already risen to his feet. Livia was later to learn that Gideon had a genuine horror of being ungentlemanly. Finding a robe, he jerked it over himself and tied it at his waist. He returned to Livia and pulled her up from the floor. "I am sorry," he said as he straightened her clothes and clumsily refastened her gown.

"It's all right, *really—*"

"You have to leave, Livia. Now, before I have you on your back again."

Only pride kept her from telling him how very amenable she was to the idea, when he was obviously so determined to get rid of her. Sighing in defeat, she allowed him to push and prod her from the bedroom.

"I sent your valet for sandwiches," she said, preceding him along the hallway.

"Did you?"

"Yes, and I expect you to eat them, and there will be no more brandy for you tonight."

"I'm not hungry."

Livia made her voice as stern as possible. "You will eat, however, as it is part of your penance for trying to ravish me on the floor—"

"All right," Gideon said hastily. "I'll eat."

Biting back a smile, Livia allowed him to open the door for her, and she crossed the threshold. Only when the door closed behind her did she let out a shaky sigh and finish her sentence. ". . . And how I wish you had finished!"

Fifteen

$\mathcal{I}$t would have been an exaggeration to claim that Gideon was completely sober when McKenna loaded him into the carriage the next day. However, he was at least clean and shaven, his face pale beneath the gleaming cap of expertly clipped blond hair. They were bound for the Rutledge, a London hotel comprising four luxurious homes that were let to well-to-do gentlemen or families from abroad. McKenna hoped that the investment negotiations would keep him so busy that he would stop thinking about Aline. At least for a few minutes at a time.

A faint groan came from Gideon's side of the carriage. Wreathed in a queasiness that was nearly palpable, Gideon had said virtually nothing so far that morning. "Goddamn," Gideon said in bleary realization, "I'm riding backward. Change seats with me, will you?"

Recalling Gideon's aversion to facing the rear of the carriage while traveling, McKenna complied. When they had both settled, Gideon propped one foot on the opposite cushion, heedless of the fine velvet upholstery. "What are you brooding about?" He braced his head on his hand as if to prevent it from toppling off his shoulders. "Haven't you managed to tumble Lady Aline yet?"

McKenna gave him a narrow-eyed stare.

Gideon sighed and rubbed his aching temples. "I'll say this—there is something about those Marsden women and their aristocratic little notches that is impossible to resist."

The remark so perfectly expressed McKenna's own sentiments that he smiled grimly. "You've taken an interest in Livia, it seems."

"Yes," came the none-too-happy reply. "An interest that has earned me the worst case of blue balls I've had in years."

McKenna was perturbed by the realization that his friend was strongly attracted to Aline's sister. It seemed an inappropriate match in every regard. "Aren't you too old for her?"

Fumbling for the ever-dependable silver flask, Gideon registered extreme annoyance at the realization that he'd forgotten to fill it. Tossing the empty container to the floor, he glared at it blearily. "I'm too *everything* for her. Too old, too damned jaded, too thirsty . . . the list is endless."

"You'd better take care, or Westcliff will slaughter and dress you like a yuletide goose."

"If he'll do it quickly, he has my blessing," Gideon replied morosely. "Damn you, McKenna, I wish I hadn't let you talk me into visiting Stony Cross. We should have gone directly to London, conducted our business, and returned to New York as soon as possible."

"You didn't have to come with me," McKenna pointed out.

"I had some misguided notion of keeping you out of trouble. And I wanted to see what kind of woman could turn you into such a mooncalf."

Stewing, McKenna gazed out the window, watching the quiet green countryside that rolled beside them. Only Lady Aline Marsden, he thought balefully. A woman of such discriminating taste that she had remained unwed rather than accept a suitor who was below her standards.

"I want to take her back to New York with me," he said.

Gideon was silent for a long time. "Has Lady Aline indicated that she might consider such a proposition?"

"No. In fact, she's made it clear that anything other than a five-minute hump in the closet is out of the question. Because I'm not of her class."

Gideon did not seem at all surprised. "Naturally. You're a professional man in a culture that values indolence and has contempt for ambition."

"*You* work."

"Yes, but not regularly, and everyone knows that I don't have to. And my money is old, if only by New York standards." Gideon paused for a thoughtful moment before continuing. "Don't mistake me, McKenna— you're the best man I've ever known, and I'd give my life for you if necessary. But the fact is, socially speaking, you're not just a step down for Lady Aline. You're a long tumble from the mountaintop."

The words hardly did anything to improve McKenna's mood. However, Gideon could always be counted on to speak to him honestly—and McKenna appreciated that far more than countless well-meant lies. Receiving the observation with a nod, he frowned at the tops of his shiny black shoes.

"I wouldn't say that your situation is completely hopeless," Gideon continued. "You've got some advantages that would inspire many women, even Lady Aline, to overlook the fact that you're an oversized mongrel. The ladies seem to find you attractive enough, and the devil knows you don't lack for money. And you're damned persuasive when you want to be. Don't tell me that you can't manage to convince a thirty-one-year-old spinster from Hampshire to marry you. Especially if she's already demonstrated her willingness to, er . . . favor you, as she apparently has."

McKenna threw him a sharp glance. "Who said anything about marriage?"

The question seemed to catch Gideon off-guard. "You just said you want her to come to New York with you."

"Not as my wife."

"As a mistress?" Gideon asked incredulously. "You can't really believe that she would lower herself to accept such an arrangement."

"I'll make her accept it—by any means necessary."

"What about her relationship with Lord Sandridge?"

"I'll put an end to that."

Gideon stared at him, seeming confounded. "My God. Have I misunderstood, McKenna, or do you really intend to ruin Lady Aline's hopes of marriage, blacken her name on two continents, break all ties to her family and friends, and destroy all hope of her ever participating in decent society? And probably foist a bastard child on her in the bargain?"

The thought caused McKenna to smile coldly. "A Marsden giving birth to the bastard of a bastard . . . yes, that would suit me quite well."

Gideon's eyes narrowed. "Holy hell—I never would have thought you capable of such malice."

"You don't know me, then."

"Apparently not," Gideon murmured with a wondering shake of his head. Though it was clear that he would have liked to continue, a particularly bumpy stretch of road caused him to subside back in his seat and clutch his head with a groan.

McKenna returned his gaze to the window, while the remnant of a cool smile remained on his lips.

Marcus's pleasure at Shaw and McKenna's departure lasted for precisely one day . . . until he discovered that Livia had left for London on the following morning. It had been no mean feat to accomplish the necessary packing and make the travel arrangements, all in secret. Aline had been certain that one of the servants might let something slip before Livia was actually off. Thanks to Mrs. Faircloth, however, lips were buttoned everywhere from the scullery to the stables, as no one dared to incur the housekeeper's wrath by betraying Livia's plans.

When Livia's carriage finally rolled away, the sun had just begun to shed its first feeble rays on the drive leading from Stony Cross. Heaving a sigh of relief, Aline stood in the entrance hall, wearing a soft blue morning gown and worn felt slippers. She smiled at Mrs. Faircloth, whose obvious ambivalence about Livia's actions had not prevented her from doing whatever was necessary to help her.

"Mrs. Faircloth," Aline said, slipping her hand into the housekeeper's. Their fingers clung briefly. "How many years have you stood by and watched Marsdens doing things you haven't approved of?"

The housekeeper smiled at the rhetorical question, and they stood together in silent affection, watching the carriage disappear at the end of the drive.

A voice startled the two of them, and Aline turned to meet her brother's suspicious gaze. Marcus was dressed in his hunting clothes, his eyes cold and black amid the hard angles of his face. "Would you care to tell me what is going on?" he asked brusquely.

"Certainly, dear." Aline glanced at Mrs. Faircloth. "Thank you, Mrs. Faircloth—I am certain that you have things to do now."

"Yes, my lady," came the immediate and distinctly grateful reply, as the housekeeper had no wish to be present during one of Marcus's rare but volcanic rages. She sped away, her black skirts fluttering behind her.

"Who was in that carriage?" Marcus demanded.

"Shall we go to the parlor?" Aline suggested. "I'll ring for some tea, and—"

"Don't tell me that it was Livia."

"All right, I won't." She paused before adding sheepishly. "But it was. And before you work yourself into a lather about it—"

"By all that's holy, my sister has *not* raced off to London to pursue that damned libertine!" Marcus said in murderous fury.

"Livia will be perfectly fine," Aline said hastily. "She's going to stay at Marsden Terrace, and she has a chaperone, and—"

"I'm going to fetch her at once." Squaring the muscled bulk of his shoulders, Marcus started for the door.

"No!" Well intentioned he might be, but her brother's high-handedness had just reached its limits. "You will not, Marcus." Although she did not raise her voice, her tone stopped him in his tracks. "If you dare try to follow her, I will shoot your horse out from under you."

Marcus swiveled around to stare at her incredulously. "Good God, Aline, I don't have to tell you what she's risking—"

"I know perfectly well what Livia is risking. And so does she." Sailing past him, Aline went to the parlor that adjoined the entrance hall, while he followed at her heels.

Marcus closed the door with a perfectly executed swipe of his foot. "Give me one good reason why I should stand by and do nothing!"

"Because Livia will resent you forever if you interfere."

Their gazes locked for a long time. Gradually the fury seemed to drain from Marcus, and he went to sit heavily in the nearest chair. Aline could not help but feel a flicker of sympathy for him, knowing that for a man like her brother, this enforced helplessness was the worst sort of torture. "Why does it have to be him?" he grumbled. "Why couldn't she pick some decent young man from a solid English family?"

"Mr. Shaw is not so terrible," Aline said, unable to repress a smile.

He gave her a dark look. "You refuse to see anything past that blond hair and all that empty charm, and that damned American insolence that women seem to find so alluring."

"You forgot to mention all that nice American money," Aline teased.

Marcus lifted his gaze heavenward, clearly wondering what he had done to deserve such infernal aggravation. "He's going to use her, and then break her heart," he said flatly. Only someone who knew him well could hear the edge of fearful worry in his voice.

"Oh, Marcus," Aline said gently, "Livia and I are both stronger than you seem to believe. And everyone must risk heartbreak, at one time or another." Coming to stand by his chair, she smoothed a hand over his crisp black hair. "Even you."

He shrugged irritably and ducked away from her hand. "I don't take unnecessary risks."

"Not even for love?"

"Especially not for that."

Smiling fondly, Aline shook her head. "Poor Marcus . . . how I look forward to the day when you fall under some woman's spell."

Marcus stood from the chair. "You'll have to wait a long time for that," he said, and left the parlor with his usual impatient stride.

The Rutledge Hotel was currently approaching a remarkable metamorphosis, at the conclusion of which it would undoubtedly be the most elegant and modern hotel in Europe. In the past five years, the owner, Harry Rutledge—a gentleman of somewhat mysterious origins—had quietly and ruthlessly acquired every lot on the street between the Capitol Theater and the Embankment, in the heart of the London theater district. It was said that in his ambitions to create the ultimate hotel, Rutledge had visited America to observe the latest in hotel design and service, which was developing much faster there than anywhere else. Currently the Rutledge consisted of a row of private homes, but these structures would soon be razed in preparation for a monumental building the likes of which London had never seen.

Although Lord Westcliff had offered McKenna and Gideon the use of Marsden Terrace, they had opted for the more convenient location of the Rutledge. Not unexpectedly, Harry Rutledge had identified himself as a close friend of Westcliff's, leading Gideon to observe sourly that the earl certainly had a healthy proliferation of acquaintances.

Taking up residence in an elegantly appointed suite filled with brass-bound mahogany furniture, Gideon soon discovered that the hotel's reputation for quality was well deserved. After a night of sound sleep and a breakfast of crepes and out-of-season plovers' eggs, Gideon had decided to amend his opinion of London. He had to admit that a city with so many coffeehouses, gardens, and theaters couldn't be all bad. Moreover, it was the birthplace of the sandwich and the modern umbrella, surely two of man's greatest inventions.

A day of meetings and a long supper at a local tavern should have left Gideon exhausted, but he found it difficult to fall asleep that night. There was no mystery as to why he was so restless—his usual talent for self-deception was failing him. He very much feared that he was falling in love with Livia Marsden. He wanted her, adored her, craved her, every waking moment. However, whenever Gideon tried to think of what to do about Livia, he was helpless to arrive at a solution. He was not the marrying kind, and even if he were, he cared for her too much to expose her to the pack of sharks that was his family. Most of all, he was far too closely wed to the bottle to consider taking a bride—and that was something he doubted that he could change, even if he wanted to.

It began to storm outside, thunder growling and clapping while rain fell in intermittent bursts. Gideon opened a window an inch or two to admit the smell of summer rain into the room. Resting fitfully between freshly ironed linen sheets, he tried—and failed—to stop thinking about Livia. Sometime in the middle of the night, however, he was rescued by a rap on his bedroom door and his valet's quiet murmur.

"Mr. Shaw? Pardon, Mr. Shaw . . . someone is waiting for you in the entrance hall. I requested that she return at a more suitable hour, but she will not go."

Gideon struggled to a sitting position and yawned, scratching his chest. "She?"

"Lady Olivia, sir."

"Livia?" Gideon was stupefied. "She can't be here. She's in Stony Cross."

"She is indeed here, Mr. Shaw."

"Jesus." Gideon leaped from the bed as if electrified, searching hastily for a robe to cover his nakedness. "Is something wrong?" he demanded. "How does she look?"

"Wet, sir."

It was still raining, Gideon realized in growing concern, wondering why in the hell Livia would have come here in the midst of a storm. "What time is it?"

The valet, who showed signs of having tugged on his rumpled clothes in a great hurry, gave a beleaguered sigh. "Two o'clock in the morning."

Too worried to bother with finding his slippers or combing his hair, Gideon strode from his bedroom, following the valet to the entrance hall.

And there was Livia, standing in a little puddle of water. She smiled at him, though her hazel-green eyes were wary beneath the brim of a sodden hat. Right at that moment, staring at her across the entrance hall, Gideon Shaw, cynic, hedonist, drunkard, libertine, fell hopelessly in love. He had never been so completely in the thrall of another human being. So enchanted, and foolishly hopeful. A thousand endearments crowded his mind, and he realized ruefully that he was every bit the mooncalf that he had accused McKenna of being the previous day.

"Livia," he said softly, approaching her. His gaze raked over her flushed, rain-spattered face, while he thought that she looked like a bedraggled angel. "Is everything all right?"

"Perfectly all right." Her gaze chased down the front of his silk robe to his bare feet, and she reddened at the realization that he was naked beneath.

Unable to keep from touching her, Gideon reached out and took her coat, letting a shower of droplets cascade to the floor. He handed it to the valet, who went to hang the garment on a nearby rack. The sopping wet hat followed, and then Livia stood shivering before him, the hem of her skirts drenched and muddy.

"Why have you come to town?" Gideon asked gently.

Livia gave an impudent shrug, her teeth chattering from the damp. "I had some sh-shopping to do. I'm staying at Marsden Terrace. And since our r-respective lodgings are s-so close, I thought that I would pay a call."

"In the middle of the night?"

"The shops don't open till nine," she said reasonably. "That gives us some time to ch-chat."

He gave her an ironic look. "Yes, about seven hours. Shall we chat in the parlor?"

"No—in your room." She hugged herself in an effort to stay her shivering.

Gideon searched Livia's eyes, looking for uncertainty, finding only a need for connection, for closeness, that paralleled his own. She held his gaze as she continued to tremble. She was cold, he thought. He could warm her.

Suddenly Gideon found himself acting before he gave himself a chance to think sensibly. He gestured to the valet and murmured a few directions to him, about sending away the footman and carriage outside, and that Lady Olivia would need to be conveyed back to her residence at a discreet hour in the morning.

Taking Livia's hand, Gideon slid his arm behind her back and guided her to his room. "My bed isn't made. I wasn't expecting company at this hour."

"I should hope not," she remarked primly, as if she weren't about to launch herself into a clandestine affair with him.

After closing the bedroom door behind them, Gideon lit a small fire in the hearth. Livia stood before him docilely, bathed in a flickering yellow-orange glow as he began to undress her. She was silent and passive, raising her arms when necessary, stepping out of her gown as it dropped in a wet heap. One by one Gideon draped her damp garments over the back of a chair, carefully removing layers of muslin and cotton and silk from her body. When she was finally naked, the firelight gilding her slender body and her long, light brown hair, Gideon did not pause to look at her. Instead he removed his own robe and covered her with it, swaddling her in silk that had been heated by his own skin. Livia gasped a little as he picked her up and carried her to bed, laying her amid the rumpled bedclothes. He straightened the covers around her and joined her beneath them, gathering her in his arms. Holding her spoon-fashion, he laid his cheek against a swath of her hair.

"Is this all right?" he whispered.

She sighed deeply. "Oh yes."

They lay together for a long time, until Livia's tension eased, and her silk-draped body was warm and pliant. One of her feet moved, her toes exploring the hairy surface of his leg. Gideon drew in his breath sharply as he felt her hips inch backward until they were cradled against his. With only a thin layer of fabric between them, she could not help but be aware of the turgid length of his erection.

"Are you sober?" she asked, nestling closer.

Gideon was acutely aroused by the voluptuous brush of her body against his hard, sensitive flesh. "I occasionally am, despite my best efforts to prevent it," he said huskily. "Why do you ask?"

She took his hand and pulled it to her breast. "Now you can seduce me without being able to claim afterward that you didn't know what you were doing."

The sweet little hill beneath his fingers was too insanely tantalizing for Gideon to resist. He caressed her lightly over the silk, then slipped his hand beneath the robe. "Livia, darling, the unfortunate fact is, I nearly always know what I'm doing."

She gasped a little at the velvety stroke of his thumb and forefinger against her nipple. "Why is that unfortunate?"

"Because at times like this, my conscience is screaming at me to leave you alone."

Turning in his arms, Livia slid one of her thighs over his hip. "Tell your conscience *this,*" she said, and fastened her mouth to his.

Requiring no further encouragement, Gideon took her lips in slow, drifting, gently inquiring kisses. He opened the silk robe as if he were peeling a fragile, exotic fruit, laying her bare before him. His head lowered, and his mouth traveled tenderly over her downy skin. Finding the vulnerable places where her pulse beat most strongly, he stroked her with his lips and tongue, and caught at her lightly with his teeth until she made shivering sounds of delight. He had never known such an overwhelming need to penetrate, to enter, to possess another human being. Whispering her name, he touched the place between her thighs, where the flesh was silken and very wet, and he slipped his fingers inside her. Livia went rigid at his touch, delicate splotches of passion marking her skin, her hands opening and closing frantically against his shoulders.

Gideon teased her languidly, loving her faraway expression, the sensual helplessness of a woman being fondled and stroked into climax. Livia's eyes closed as she gave herself over to his gentle skill, gasping and arching in mounting pleasure. She reached the peak, going stiff against him, her toes curling tightly. "Yes," he whispered, his thumb swirling over her clitoris, "yes, sweet lady, sweet darling . . ." He brought her down slowly, tracing erotic patterns in the damp thatch of curls between her thighs, kissing her breasts until she was calm and still beneath him. Then he drew his lips over her midriff, and the soft skin of her stomach, and he pressed her thighs open with his hands.

Livia moaned as his tongue found her, while his thumb pushed inside the swollen entrance of her body. Gideon nibbled and teased her, loving the sounds she made, the rhythmic undulation of her hips as they rose against his demanding mouth. Feeling the delicate clench of her muscles around his thumb, he realized that she was at the edge of another orgasm, and he withdrew his hand slowly. With a little protesting cry, she stretched her entire body toward him. He levered himself over her, spread her trembling limbs, and thrust inside her warm, pulsing softness.

"Oh God," he whispered, suddenly unable to move, so intense was his pleasure.

Purring, Livia wrapped her slim arms around his back and rocked her hips upward to engulf his stiff length and pull him deeper. He answered her movements compulsively, nudging, pushing, then plunging, until the sweet impact of flesh into flesh was too much to bear. She held her breath and shuddered, her body tightening around him in a rippling inner caress. Gideon withdrew from her with a harsh cry, his cock throbbing in frenzied release against her stomach.

Groaning, he collapsed beside her dizzily, his pulse thudding in his chest and loins and ears.

A long time passed before either of them could speak. Livia lifted her face from his shoulder and smiled drowsily. "Amberley never did that, at the end," she told him, her fingers playing in the hair on his chest.

Gideon grinned suddenly at the reference to his last-second withdrawal. "It's the coffeehouse method of contraception."

"Coffeehouse?"

"You go in and out without ever spending anything," he explained, and she pushed against him with a muffled laugh. He caught her wrists easily. "Livia . . . I have to protect you from the consequences of what we're doing, until—"

"I know," she interrupted, pulling away from him. Clearly she did not want to discuss anything of importance right now. Slipping out of bed, she gave him a provocative smile. "We'll talk about that later. But for now . . ."

"Yes?"

"Come and bathe me," she said . . . and he obliged without hesitation.

Sixteen

The first morning of waking in Gideon Shaw's arms made Livia feel as if the world had been transformed while she had slept. She had never expected to feel this intimate connection with a man again. Perhaps only those who had loved and lost could truly appreciate this magic, she thought, nestling against the soft, springy fur that covered his chest. As Gideon slept, his face robbed of its usual expressiveness, he had the countenance of a stern angel. Smiling, Livia let her gaze trace over the severe beauty of his features, the long straight nose, the lushness of his lips, the widow's peak that caused a stray lock of amber-gold hair to fall over his forehead.

"You're too handsome for words," she informed him, when he yawned and stretched. "It's a wonder that you can get anyone to listen to you seriously, when they probably just want to sit and stare at you for hours."

His voice was sleep-scratchy. "I don't want anyone to listen to me seriously. That would be dangerous."

Smiling, Livia smoothed his hair back from his forehead. "I must return to Marsden Terrace before Mrs. Smedley awakens."

"Who is Mrs. Smedley?" Gideon rolled to pin her beneath him, nuzzling into the warm curve of her neck.

"My chaperone. She's old, hard of hearing, and dreadfully nearsighted as well."

"Perfect," Gideon commented with a swift grin. He moved lower on her body, cupping her breasts in his hands and kissing them softly. "I have meetings this morning. But I would like to escort you and Mrs. Smedley somewhere this afternoon . . . out for fruit ices?"

"Yes, and perhaps a panorama show." Her skin became flushed beneath his ministrations, her nipples contracting as he painted them with the moisture of his mouth. "Gideon . . ."

"Although," he murmured, "the view at the panorama won't begin to compare with this one."

"It's nearly sunrise," she protested, wriggling beneath him. "I must leave."

"You'd better pray that Mrs. Smedley sleeps late this morning," he said, ignoring her protests.

Much later in the day, Gideon proved to be the most entertaining companion imaginable, especially to Mrs. Smedley, who resembled an imperious hen in her brown silk gown and her feathered headdress. Peering at Gideon through the inch-thick lenses of her spectacles, Mrs. Smedley could not see him well enough to be impressed by his dazzling handsomeness. And the fact that he was an American was not in his favor, as the chaperone was deeply suspicious of foreigners.

However, Gideon eventually won her over with sheer persistence. After he had purchased the best seats at the panorama, which featured views of Naples and Constantinople, he sat beside Mrs. Smedley and patiently shouted descriptions into the massive ear horn clasped against the side of her head. During intermission, he went back and forth numerous times to procure refreshments for her. After the panorama, as they rode through Hyde Park, Gideon listened humbly to Mrs. Smedley's booming lecture on the evils of tobacco use. His meek admission that he did at times enjoy an occasional cigar sent Mrs. Smedley into an ecstasy of disapproval, allowing her to continue with new vigor. How disagreeable, how corruptive tobacco was . . . and sitting in smoking rooms would expose him to vulgarity and obscene language, a fact that did not seem to perturb him nearly as much as it should have.

Seeing what a splendid time Mrs. Smedley was having in admonishing Gideon, Livia found an irrepressible grin breaking out, time and time again. Every now and then his gaze would meet with hers, and his smiling blue eyes held an expression that made her breath catch.

Finally the lecture on tobacco was diverted to the subject of etiquette, and then into the more sensitive area of courtship, which had Livia wincing even as Gideon seemed to be highly entertained by Mrs. Smedley's pronouncements.

". . . one should never marry someone who is similar in form, temperament and appearance to himself," the chaperone counseled them both. "A dark-haired gentleman, for example, should not marry a brunette, nor should a corpulent man marry an overendowed girl. The warm-hearted should unite with the cold-blooded, the nervous should be paired with the stoic, and the passionate should marry the cerebral."

"Then it is not advisable for two passionate individuals to wed?" Although Gideon was not looking at Livia, he somehow managed to avoid the kick she aimed at the front of his shin. Her foot connected harmlessly with a lacquered panel.

"No, indeed," was the emphatic reply. "Just think of the excitable natures of the children!"

"Terrifying," Gideon said, raising his brows mockingly at Livia.

"And societal position is most significant," Mrs. Smedley said. "Only those of equal situation should marry . . . or if there be inequity, the husband should be superior to his bride. It is impossible for a woman to esteem a man who is below her station."

Livia tensed suddenly, while Gideon fell silent. She did not have to look at him to know that he was thinking of McKenna and Aline.

"Will I have an opportunity to see McKenna in London?" she asked Gideon, while Mrs. Smedley kept on orating, oblivious to the fact that she wasn't being listened to.

Gideon nodded. "Tomorrow night, if you will do me the honor of accompanying me to the theater."

"Yes, I would like that." She paused before asking in a low tone, "Has McKenna mentioned my sister to you of late?"

He hesitated, and gave her a wary glance. "Yes."

"Has he given you any indication of the nature of his feelings for her?"

"One could say that," Gideon replied dryly. "He's quite bitter—and keenly desirous of revenge. The wounds she dealt him long ago were so deep as to be nearly lethal."

Livia felt a rush of hope followed closely by despair. "None of that was her fault," she said. "But she'll never bring herself to explain what happened, or why she behaved as she did."

Gideon stared at her intently. "Tell me."

"I can't," Livia said unhappily. "I promised my sister that I would never reveal her secrets. Once such a promise was made to me by a friend, and then she broke her word, and it caused me a great deal of pain. I could never betray Aline that way." Unable to read his expression, she frowned apologetically. "I know that you must fault me for remaining silent, but—"

"That's not what I'm thinking."

"Then what *are* you thinking?"

"That everything I learn about you makes me love you more."

Livia stopped breathing for a second, stunned by the admission. It took a long time for her to speak. "Gideon . . ."

"You don't have to say it back," he murmured. "For once, I want to have the pleasure of loving someone without asking for anything in return."

There were two kinds of theatergoers—those who actually went to enjoy the play, and then the great majority who went for purely social reasons. The theater was a place to be seen, exchange gossip, and carry on flirtations. Seated in a box along with Gideon Shaw, McKenna, Mrs. Smedley, and two other couples, Livia soon gave up all attempts to hear what was taking place onstage, as most of the audience had elected to talk through the entire performance. Instead she sat back and watched the parade of men and women who came by their box. It was remarkable, the amount of attention that two wealthy American industrialists could attract.

Gideon was an expert at social banter, appearing relaxed and smiling as he chatted with the visitors. McKenna, on the other hand, was far more reserved, making few remarks, and choosing his words with care. Dressed in a formal scheme of black and white, he was the perfect dark foil for Gideon's golden elegance. Livia was more than a little intimidated by McKenna, and awed that Aline held a man like this in her thrall.

As Gideon went to fetch her a glass of lemonade for her, and a cordial for Mrs. Smedley, Livia had the opportunity to speak with McKenna more or less privately, as her chaperone was deaf as a post. McKenna was polite and a bit distant, certainly seeming far from needing anyone's sympathy, and yet Livia couldn't help feeling sorry for him. Despite McKenna's invulnerable facade, she saw signs of fatigue in his swarthy face, and shadows beneath his eyes that bespoke many sleepless nights. She knew how terrible it was to love someone that you couldn't have—and it was even worse for McKenna, because he would never know why Aline had rejected him. As Livia's guilty conscience reminded her of the part she had played in causing McKenna to be sent away from Stony Cross all those years ago, she felt herself turn red. To her consternation, McKenna noticed the telltale blush.

"My lady," he murmured, "does my company disturb you for some reason?"

"No," she said swiftly.

McKenna held her gaze as he replied gently. "I think it does. I will find another place from which to view the play, if it would ease your discomfort."

As Livia stared into his weary blue-green eyes, she remembered the dashing boy he had once been, and she thought of the apology she had wanted to make for a dozen years. Agitation filled her as she considered the promise she had made to Aline—but that promise had been never to talk about the scars. She hadn't promised not to talk about their father's manipulations.

"McKenna," she said hesitantly, "my distress arises from the memory of something I did a long time ago. An injustice that I did to you, actually."

"Are you referring to the time I was in service at Stony Cross Park?" he asked with a slight frown. "You were only a little girl."

Livia fidgeted as she replied in a low voice. "I fear that little girls are quite adept at mischief making—and I was no exception. I was the reason that you were bundled off to Bristol so suddenly."

McKenna stared at her with sudden intensity, remaining silent as she continued.

"You know how I used to follow Aline around, watching everything she did. I worshipped her. And of course I knew about the attachment between the two of you. I suppose I was a bit jealous, wanting all of Aline's love and attention, as she was like a second mother to me. So when I happened to see you in the carriage room one day, while the two of you were—" Livia stopped and blushed even harder. "I did the worst possible thing—I didn't realize what the consequences would be. I went to my father and told him what I had seen. And that is why you were dismissed and sent to Bristol. Afterward, when I comprehended the results of my actions, and saw how Aline was suffering, I felt the worst kind of remorse. I've always regretted what I did, and although I do not expect you to forgive me, I do want to tell you how sorry I am."

"Suffering?" McKenna repeated tonelessly. "Lady Aline had me sent to Bristol because she regretted having feelings for a servant. She knew I would soon become an embarrassment to her—"

"No," Livia interrupted earnestly. "It was our father—you can't know what a vindictive man he was. He told my sister that if she ever saw you again, he would destroy you. He vowed that he wouldn't rest until you were left without a home or any means of supporting yourself—you would have ended up dead or in prison. And Aline believed him, because she knew what he was capable of. She never wanted you to leave Stony Cross—but she did what was necessary to protect you. To save you. In fact, the only reason Father secured your apprenticeship in Bristol, rather than cast you into the streets, was because Aline demanded it."

McKenna gave her a derisive glance. "Then why didn't she tell me so at the time?"

"My sister believed that if she had given you any reason to hope, you would have risked everything to come back to her." Livia looked down into her lap, smoothing the silk of her gown as she murmured, "Was she wrong about that?"

An endless silence passed. "No," he finally whispered.

Lifting her gaze, Livia saw that McKenna was staring blindly at the action onstage. He seemed composed . . . until one noticed the mist of sweat on his forehead, and the blanched surface of his knuckles as his fist rested on his thigh. Livia reflected uneasily that she had revealed too much, but now that she had started, she found it difficult to stop. She had to set things right, if only to make McKenna understand the truth about this one facet of the past. "After you left," she said, "Aline was never the same. She loved you, McKenna . . . enough that she chose to make you hate her, rather than see you harmed in any way."

His voice was thick with condensed hostility. "If that was true, she would have told me about it by now. Your father is dead, devil take his soul—and there is nothing to stop Aline from setting the record straight."

"Perhaps," Livia said carefully, "she does not want you to feel obligated to her in any way. Or perhaps she is afraid, for some reason that you have yet to learn. If you would only—"

She fell silent as McKenna unclenched his hand suddenly and gestured for her to stop, while his unseeing gaze remained locked on the stage. Noticing the slight tremor of his hand, Livia realized that the information had upset him, when she had thought he would receive it with gratitude, or even relief. Chewing the inside of her lip, Livia sat in abashed silence, while McKenna lowered his hand and continued to focus on some distant object.

It was with relief that Livia saw Gideon return to the box with her lemonade. He glanced alertly from her face to McKenna's, sensitive to the brittle tension in the air. Resuming his place beside Livia, Gideon engaged her with his easy charm until her uncomfortable flush faded, and she was able to smile naturally.

McKenna, on the other hand, looked as if he were staring into the bowels of hell. The perspiration on his face accumulated until the mist had transformed into heavy streaks, and every line of his body was tense and tightly marshaled. He seemed unaware of what was going on around him, or even where he was. When it seemed that he could stand it no longer, he rose from his seat with a murmur, and left the box swiftly.

Gideon turned to Livia with an astonished gaze. "What in God's name was said between you while I was gone?"

McKenna made his way outside the theater, where street vendors walked back and forth from Covent Garden. Passing the massive columns that braced the pedimented entrance, McKenna stopped in the lee of the farthest one, where he could stand in shadow. His mind and body were in chaos. The echo of Livia's words buzzed in his ears, eroding his self-possession, making him wonder angrily what the hell he should believe. The idea that everything he had thought for twelve years might not be true . . . It jarred him to the core. It terrified him.

Suddenly he remembered his own long-ago words. *"Aline . . . I would never leave unless you told me to go . . ."*

That hadn't been entirely true. The fact was, it would have required far more than that. Had McKenna retained any hope that Aline had loved him, he would have kept coming back to her, compelled by a need that far outweighed any sense of self-preservation.

Aline had known that.

McKenna dragged the sleeve of his fine broadcloth coat over his face. If it was true, if Aline had driven him away to protect him from the old earl's vengeance . . . then she had loved him. Perhaps there was nothing of it left by now, but she had loved him once. He struggled to keep from believing it, while at the same time he was filled with an agony of emotion that seemed impossible for mere human flesh to contain. He needed to go to her, and ask if it was true. But he already knew the answer, which was confirmed by a sudden certainty that emanated from the very marrow of his bones.

Aline had loved him . . . the knowledge sent him reeling.

A few passers-by glanced curiously at the dark figure that leaned against the massive column, his head bowed like that of a battered colossus. However, no one dared to stop or ask after his welfare. They sensed a coiled threat in his stillness, as if he were possibly a madman who might be provoked into some desperate action. Easier, and far safer, to walk away and pretend they had not seen him.

Gideon came to Livia later that night, slipping into the house and up to her bedroom. He undressed her carefully and made love to her for a long time, moving inside her with deep, languid glides, lifting her gently to change positions. Her moans were smothered by silken, questioning kisses, while her shivering body welcomed his anchoring weight.

It occurred to Livia that she was doing things with him that she had never even done with Amberley. There were no illusions in this bed, nothing but a terrible, wonderful honesty that left no corner of her soul to hide in. She wanted Gideon to know her completely, even her defects. Something about him—his intense physicality, perhaps, seemed to melt the reserve she had worn like a hair shirt, leaving her free to respond to him without inhibition. Whatever he wanted, she did with shameless delight, and in turn he loved her in ways that she would never have thought to ask for.

They lay peaceful and winded and sated in the aftermath, with Livia half lying on top of Gideon's body, her leg thrown heedlessly across his. She felt his fingers moving in her hair, finding the hot curve of her scalp beneath the fine locks, stroking his way down to the nape of her neck. As her leg shifted higher, she felt the pressure of his sex against her thigh, still half-turgid even after climax. Lazily she reached down to fondle him.

"You're insatiable," she accused with a tremor of laughter in her voice.

Smiling, Gideon hooked his hands beneath her arms and shifted her fully over him. "No more so than you."

She leaned down until their noses were touching. "I will confess, Mr. Shaw, that I am becoming rather enamored of you."

"Enamored?" he scoffed. "You're madly in love with me."

Livia felt her heart skip a beat, but she kept her tone light. "Now, why would I be so silly as to fall in love with you?"

"There are a multitude of reasons," he informed her. "Not only do I

satisfy you in bed, I also happen to be one of the richest men in the civilized world—"

"I don't care about your money."

"I know that, damn it." Now he began to sound disgruntled. "It's one
of the reasons I've got to have you."

"Have?"

"Marry."

Frowning, Livia began to slide off him, but Gideon grasped her hips
and made her stay. "It's worth considering, isn't it?" he asked.

"Not when we've known each other for little more than a fortnight!"

"Then tell me how long a courtship you want. I can wait."

"You have to go back to New York."

"I can wait," he repeated stubbornly.

Sighing, Livia lowered her face to his chest and rested her cheek
against the crisp, curling hair. She forced herself to be honest. "Nothing
would induce me to marry you, my darling."

Gideon's arms went around her then. He held her a little too tightly,
and ran his hands over her back in a long, supplicating stroke. "Why
not?"

"Because I care for you too much to watch you destroy yourself."

She felt the sudden tension in the long body beneath hers. Again she
moved to roll away from him, expecting that this time he would let her
go. But his arm tightened around her slender back, and one hand came to
press her head more firmly against his chest. Resignation flattened his
tone. "You want me to stop drinking."

"No—I want no part of that decision."

"But you would consider marrying me if I didn't drink?" At her long
hesitation, he urged her to raise her head and look at him.

"Yes," she said reluctantly. "In that case, I would probably consider it."

Gideon's expression was shuttered, his mouth twisting as if he were
looking inside himself and was dissatisfied with what he saw. "I don't
know if I can stop," he muttered with a frankness that she admired, even
if the words were unwelcome. "I don't even know if I want to. I'd rather
just keep drinking, and have you as well."

"You can't," she said flatly. "Even if you are a Shaw."

Gideon turned to his side, holding her head in the crook of his arm as he looked down at her. "I would give you everything you've ever wanted. I would take you anywhere in the world. Anything you asked for—"

"It would come between us, eventually." Livia began to wonder if she weren't insane, turning down a proposal from him when most women would have fallen to their knees in gratitude. A tremulous smile came to her lips as she saw his expression. Clearly he was not a man accustomed to being refused for any reason. "Let's just enjoy the time that we have together now. I'll be returning to Stony Cross in a few days, but until then—"

"A few days? No, stay longer, and go back with me."

She shook her head. "It wouldn't do for us to travel together—people would talk."

"I don't give a damn." Desperation threaded through his voice. "Just take me as I am, Livia."

"Perhaps I could, if I cared less," she returned, keeping her eyes closed as he brushed his lips over her delicate lids, her lashes, her hot cheeks, the tip of her nose. "But I won't subject myself to the process of losing you little by little, until you've either killed yourself or become someone that I don't recognize."

Gideon drew back and gave her a sullen stare. "At least tell me one thing—do you love me?"

Livia remained silent, uncertain whether the admission would make things better or worse.

"I have to know," Gideon said, his mouth twisting with self-derision as he heard the plea in his own voice. "If I'm to change my life for you, I've got to have some hope."

"I don't want you to change your life for me. You'll have to make the same decision every day, over and over—it must be for yourself alone. Otherwise you will come to resent me."

She saw how much he wanted to argue with her. Instead he settled beside her, loosely wrapping his arm around her waist. "I don't want to lose you," he whispered.

Stroking the back of his hand, Livia sighed. "I've been adrift for so long, ever since Amberley's death, and now I'm finally ready to start living again. You came along just at the time I needed you, and for that I will always remember you with fondness and gratitude."

"Fondness?" he repeated, his mouth twisting. "Gratitude?"

"I'm not going to admit that I feel anything more than that. It would be a form of coercion."

Grumbling beneath his breath, Gideon rose above her. "Maybe I should test your resolve."

"You're welcome to try," Livia said, but instead of sounding flirtatious, her voice was melancholy, and she found herself wrapping him in her arms and legs as if she could somehow protect him from the demons within himself.

Aline sighed as she extracted yet another sheet of cream paper from the drawer of her writing desk and wiped the quill of her pen with a square of black felt. Nearly a dozen letters were piled in front of her, from friends and relatives who were doubtless peeved at her lateness in replying. However, one could not simply dash off a conveniently quick reply. Letter writing was an art that demanded close attention to detail. One had to convey the latest news with style and verve . . . and if there had been a lack of noteworthy events to write about, one had to be creatively amusing, or philosophical.

Aline frowned at the three letters that she had already finished. So far she had described minor household complaints, related some choice bits of gossip, and even given commentary on the recent weather. "How skillful I've become at talking about everything but the truth," she commented to herself with a mocking smile. But she doubted that her real news would be music to the ears of her relatives . . . *I have recently taken a lover, and have participated in two decidedly torrid encounters, in the forest and in my bedroom cabinet. My sister Livia is enjoying good health, and is currently on a visit to London, where at this moment she is probably rolling in bed with a perpetually inebriated American . . .*

Picturing how such a missive would be received by her starchy cousin Georgina, or Great-Aunt Maude, Aline stifled a grin.

Her brother's voice came from the doorway, providing a welcome interruption. "Good God. You must be at a complete loss for something to do, if you've resorted to writing letters."

She glanced up at Marcus with a teasing smile. "Spoken by the one person on earth who is more abominable at correspondence than I."

"I despise every aspect of it," Marcus admitted. "In fact, the only thing worse than writing a letter is receiving one—God knows why anyone would think I would be interested in the minutiae of his or her life."

Continuing to smile, Aline set down her pen and glanced at a tiny smudge of ink on the tip of her finger. "Is there something you want, dear? I beg you, do something to rescue me from this unbearable tedium."

"No need to beg. Rescue is at hand . . . or at least a convenient distraction." He showed her the sealed letter in his hand, while an odd expression crossed his face. "A delivery has arrived from London. This came with it."

"All the way from London? If it's the oysters we sent for, they're two days early—"

"It's not oysters." Marcus strode to the doorway and gestured to her. "The delivery is for you. Come to the entrance hall."

"Very well." Methodically Aline stoppered the cut-glass bottle of glue that she used to seal the envelopes, and closed a box of red wax wafers. When all was in order, she rose from the desk and followed Marcus to the entrance hall. The air was steeped with the heady fragrance of roses, as if the entire hall had been rinsed with expensive perfume.

"Good Lord!" she exclaimed, stopping short at the sight of massive bunches of flowers being brought in from a cart outside. Mountains of white roses, some of them tightly furled buds, some in glorious full bloom. Two footmen had been recruited to assist the driver of the cart, and the three of them kept going outside to fetch bouquet after bouquet wrapped in stiff white lace paper.

"Fifteen dozen of them," Marcus said brusquely. "I doubt there's a single white rose left in London."

Aline could not believe how fast her heart was beating. Slowly she moved forward and drew a single rose from one of the bouquets. Cupping the delicate bowl of the blossom with her fingers, she bent her head to inhale its lavish perfume. Its petals were a cool brush of silk against her cheek.

"There's something else," Marcus said.

Following his gaze, Aline saw the butler directing yet another footman to pry open a huge wooden crate filled with brick-sized parcels wrapped in brown paper. "What are they, Salter?"

"With your permission, my lady, I will find out." The elderly butler unwrapped one of the parcels with great care. He spread the waxed brown paper open to reveal a damply fragrant loaf of gingerbread, its spice adding a pungent note to the smell of the roses.

Aline put her hand over her mouth to contain a bubbling laugh, while some unidentifiable emotion caused her entire body to tremble. The offering worried her terribly, and at the same time, she was insanely pleased by the extravagance of it.

"Gingerbread?" Marcus asked incredulously. "Why the hell would McKenna send you an entire crate of *gingerbread?*"

"Because I like it," came Aline's breathless reply. "How do you know this is from McKenna?"

Marcus gave her a speaking look, as if only an imbecile would suppose otherwise.

Fumbling a little with the envelope, Aline extracted a folded sheet of paper. It was covered in a bold scrawl, the penmanship serviceable and without flourishes:

No miles of level desert, no jagged mountain heights,
  no sea of endless blue
Neither words nor tears, nor silent fears
will keep me from coming back to you.

There was no signature . . . none was necessary. Aline closed her eyes, while her nose stung and hot tears squeezed from beneath her lashes. She pressed her lips briefly to the letter, not caring what Marcus thought.

"It's a poem," she said unsteadily. "A terrible one." It was the loveliest thing she had ever read. She held it to her cheek, then used her sleeve to blot her eyes.

"Let me see it."

Immediately Aline tucked the poem into her bodice. "No, it's private." She swallowed against the tightness of her throat, willing the surge of unruly emotion to recede. "McKenna," she whispered, "how you devastate me."

Sighing tautly, Marcus gave her a handkerchief. "What can I do?" he muttered, unraveled by the sight of a woman's tears.

The only reply that Aline could make was the one he most hated to hear. "There's nothing you can do."

She thought that he was about to put his arms around her in a comforting hug, but they were both distracted by the appearance of a visitor who entered the hall in the wake of the busy footmen. Strolling in with his hands thrust in his jacket pockets, Adam, Lord Sandridge, gazed at the proliferation of white roses with a bemused expression.

"I presume those are for you," he said to Aline, removing his hands from his pockets as he approached.

"Good afternoon, Sandridge," Marcus said, his manner turning businesslike as they shook hands. "Your arrival is well timed, as I believe Lady Aline is in need of some pleasant distraction."

"Then I shall endeavor to be both pleasant and distracting," Adam replied with a casual grin. He bowed gracefully over Aline's hand.

"Come walk with me in the garden," she urged, her fingers tightening on his.

"What an excellent idea." Adam reached out to one of the bouquets heaped on the entrance table, broke off a perfect ivory blossom, and tucked it into his lapel. Extending his arm to Aline, he walked with her through the hall to the French doors at the back of the house.

The gardens were brilliant with summer magic, with plump cushions of forget-me-nots, lemon balm, and vibrant yellow daylilies, surrounding plots of roses shot through with garnet clematis. Long rows of silvery lamb's-ear stretched between large stone urns filled with rainbows of Oriental poppies. Descending the terrace steps, Adam and Aline began on a winding gravel path that led past neatly clipped yews. Adam was one of those rare people who was comfortable with silence, waiting patiently for her to speak.

Feeling soothed by the serenity of the garden and Adam's reassuring presence, Aline let out a long sigh. "The roses were from McKenna," she finally said.

"I gathered that," Adam replied dryly.

"There was a poem too." She extracted it from her bodice and gave it to him. Adam was the only person on earth whom she would allow to read something so intimate. Pausing in the center of the path, Adam unfolded the slip of paper and scanned the few lines.

When he glanced at her, he seemed to read the exquisite mingling of pain and pleasure in her eyes. "Very touching," he said sincerely, returning the poem to her. "What are you going to do about it?"

"Nothing. I'm going to send him away, as I originally planned."

Considering the words carefully, Adam seemed inclined to venture an opinion, then appeared to think better of it. He shrugged. "If that's what you think best, so be it."

No one else of her acquaintance would have made such an answer. Aline took his hand and held on tightly as they continued to walk. "Adam, one of the things I adore most about you is that you never try to advise me what to do."

"I despise advice—it never works." They skirted the edge of the mermaid fountain, which splashed lethargically amid heavy beds of delphiniums.

"I've considered telling McKenna everything," Aline confided, "but it would turn out badly, no matter how he responded."

"How so, sweet?"

"The moment that I show McKenna my scars, he would either find them too horrible to accept, or worse, he'll pity me, and feel duty-bound to propose out of obligation or honor . . . and then he'll eventually come to regret his decision, and wish to be rid of me. I couldn't live like that, looking into his eyes every morning and wondering if that was the day he would leave me for good."

Adam made a soft, sympathetic sound.

"Am I doing the wrong thing?" she asked.

"I never define these matters in terms of right and wrong," Adam replied. "One should make the best choice possible given the circumstances, and then avoid second-guessing for the sake of one's own sanity."

Aline couldn't help contrasting him with Marcus, who believed so strongly in absolutes—right and wrong, good and bad—and her mouth curved with a bittersweet smile. "Adam, dear, I've considered your proposal over the past few days . . ."

"Yes?" They stopped once again, facing each other with their hands linked.

"I can't accept," she said. "It would be unfair to both of us. I suppose that if I can't have a real marriage, I should be happy with an imitation of it. But all the same, I'd rather share a genuine friendship with you than a counterfeit marriage."

Seeing the glitter of unhappiness in her eyes, Adam reached out to clasp her in a strong, warm hug. "Darling girl," he murmured, "my offer stands indefinitely. I'll be your genuine friend until my dying day. And if you ever change your mind about marriage, you have only to snap your fingers." He smiled wryly. "I've found that imitations can sometimes become damned attractive, when one can't afford the real thing."

Seventeen

Livia had spent approximately seven nights in London, returning with sufficient parcels and boxes to lend credence to the claim that she had gone to town for a shopping expedition. The female guests took great enjoyment in viewing some of Livia's purchases . . . a small, high-crowned hat trimmed with dyed feathers . . . gloves that had been embroidered and beaded at the wrists . . . shawls of lace, cashmere, and silk, . . . a sheaf of sketches and fabric samples from the London modiste who was making gowns for her.

Naturally, Susan Chamberlain asked if Livia had seen Mr. Shaw and McKenna while she was in London, and Livia replied with breezy offhandedness. "Oh yes, my chaperone Mrs. Smedley and I spent a most delightful evening with them at the Capitol Theater. Box seats, and an excellent view of the stage—we were positively transported!"

However, no matter how casual Livia's manner was, her statements were greeted by arched brows and pointedly exchanged gazes. Everyone, it seemed, suspected that there was far more to the story than what was being told.

Aline had heard the details of the London visit as soon as Livia had returned. She went to Livia's bedroom after her sister had changed into her nightclothes, and the two of them sat on the bed with glasses of wine. Aline leaned against one of the massive carved bedposts, while Livia settled back into the pillows. "I was with him every evening," she told Aline, her cheeks flushed. "Seven nights of absolute heaven."

"He's a good lover, then?" Aline asked with a smile, not above a little prurient curiosity.

"The most wonderful, the most exciting, the most . . ." Unable to think of the precise superlative she wanted, Livia sighed and sipped her wine. Regarding Aline over the delicate rim of the glass, she shook her head in wonder. "How strange it is that he could be so different from Amberley, and yet suit me just as well. Perhaps even better in some ways."

"Are you going to marry him?" Aline asked with a queer pang in her chest, happy for her sister, and yet at the same time thinking how far away America was. And if she was being honest with herself, she would have to admit that an envious voice inside was demanding to know why she too couldn't have what she most wanted.

"He proposed to me, actually," Livia said. Then she astonished Aline further by adding bleakly, "I turned him down."

"Why?"

"You know why."

Aline nodded, her gaze locking with Livia's as an entire silent conversation seemed to pass between them. Letting out a long breath, she looked down and traced the edge of her wineglass with her fingertip. "I'm certain that was the right decision, dear, though not an easy one to make."

"No, it wasn't." They sat in silence for a minute, until Livia asked, "Aren't you going to ask about McKenna?"

Aline stared into her glass. "How is he?"

"Quiet. Somewhat distracted. We . . . spoke of you."

A clang of warning sounded in Aline's mind as she heard the edge of guilt in Livia's cautious admission. She looked up quickly, her face stiffening. "What do you mean, you spoke of me?"

Livia took a large swallow of wine. "It turned out quite well, actually," she said guardedly. "At least, it didn't turn out *badly,* although one can't be certain how he reacted to—"

"Livia, *out with it!*" Aline demanded, turning cold with anxiety. "What did you tell him?"

"Nothing very much." Livia gave her a defensive glance. "I finally brought myself to apologize to him about what I did to both of you, so long ago. You know, when I told Father about—"

"Livia, you shouldn't have," Aline said, too furious and fearful to shout, her throat constricting to one thin channel. Her hands quivered so violently that her wine was in danger of spilling.

"There's no reason to be upset," Livia said, infuriating her further. "I didn't break my promise to you—I said nothing about your accident, or the scars. I just told him about my part in the matter, and about how our father manipulated everyone, and . . . well, I did happen to mention that you sent him away to protect him, because Father had threatened to harm him—"

"*What?* I never wanted him to know that. My God, Livia, what have you done?"

"I only told him a little part of the truth." It seemed that Livia was torn between defiance and repentance, her face flushing brightly. "I'm sorry if I've upset you. But as they say, honesty is the best policy, and in this case—"

"*I've* never said that!" Aline exploded. "That is the most overused, self-serving maxim in existence, and it is most definitely not the best policy in this situation. Oh, Livia, don't you realize how difficult you've made everything for me? How infinitely harder it's going to be to part from him again, now that he knows—" She broke off suddenly. "*When* did you tell him?"

"The second night I was in London."

Aline closed her eyes sickly. The flowers had arrived two days after that. So that was why McKenna had sent the gifts, and the poem. "Livia, I could kill you," she whispered.

Evidently deciding to go on the offensive, her younger sister spoke decisively. "I don't see what is so terrible about removing one of the obstacles between you and McKenna. The only thing left to do now is for you to tell him about your legs."

Aline responded with an icy glare. "That will never happen."

"You have nothing to lose by telling him. You've always been the bravest person I've ever known until now, when you finally have a chance at happiness, and you're throwing it away because you're too stubborn and afraid—"

"I've never been brave," Aline shot back. "Bravery isn't tolerating something merely because there is no other choice. The only reason that I haven't thrown myself to the ground and kicked my heels and screamed every day for the past twelve years is the knowledge that when I get up from the floor, nothing will have changed. My legs will always be repulsive. *You* can barely bring yourself to look at them—how dare you suggest that I'm being cowardly in not wanting to expose them to McKenna?" She left the bed and set her wineglass aside. "You're a bloody hypocrite, Livia—you seem to expect that McKenna should accept me no matter what my flaws are, when you refuse to do the same for Mr. Shaw."

"That's not fair," Livia protested indignantly. "The two situations are entirely different. Your scars aren't remotely comparable to his drinking—and how dare you imply that I'm being small-minded in refusing him?"

Steaming with fury, Aline strode to the door. "Just leave me in peace. And don't you dare say another word to McKenna about *anything*." She barely restrained herself from slamming the door as she left.

Aline and Livia had always lived in relative harmony. Perhaps it was because of the seven-year difference in their ages, which had caused Aline to assume a motherly role toward her younger sister. On the rare occasions in the past when they had argued, it had been their way to avoid each other afterward, letting their tempers cool as they sought to pretend that nothing had happened. If a quarrel had been particularly bitter, they each went separately to Mrs. Faircloth, who had always reminded them that nothing was more important than their sisterly bonds. This time, however, Aline did not confide in the housekeeper, nor did she think that Livia would. The issues were too explosively personal. Instead Aline tried to go on as usual, treating Livia with a stiff politeness that was all she could manage. She supposed that she should unbend enough to offer an apology . . . but apologies had never come easily to her, and she would most likely choke on it. Nor did it seem that Livia was inclined to offer the olive branch, though she was most definitely the one at fault. After three days, Aline and Livia managed to achieve a state of normalcy, although a residual frostiness lingered between them.

On Saturday evening Marcus gave an al fresco party that was soon threatened by clouds gathering overhead. The sky turned the color of black plums, while a few preliminary droplets of rain fell onto the crowd and caused the garden torches to sputter in protest. The crowd began to drift indoors, while Aline hurried back and forth giving directions to the servants as they labored to bring refreshments, glasses, and chairs into the drawing room. In the midst of the flurry, she saw something that caused her to stop in her tracks. Livia was talking with Gideon Shaw, who must have just returned from London. They stood near the doorway, while Livia rested back against the wall. Livia was laughing at some quip he had made, her face glowing, her hands clasped behind her back as if she had to restrain herself from reaching for him.

If there had been any doubt in Aline's mind that Livia loved Gideon Shaw, it was removed at once. She had seen her sister look at only one other man that way. And although Shaw's expression was not visible from this angle, the protective inclination of his posture spoke volumes. What a pity, Aline thought. It was clear that no matter what their differences were, they had each found something necessary in the other.

She was distracted from her thoughts as she felt an odd warmth spreading over every inch of her skin, all the way up to the roots of her hair. Transfixed, she stood still while people brushed by her, heading for refuge as the storm continued to gather. The air felt damp and alive with energy, causing thrills to chase over her skin.

"Aline."

A deep voice came from behind her. She looked down for a moment, concentrating fiercely on the ground as the world seemed to tilt off its axis. When she was able to move, she turned to find McKenna just a few feet away.

It was difficult to believe that she could need another human being this much, that longing could send one into near-delirium. It required scrupulous effort to breathe, while her heart tripped clumsily behind her lungs. They stood at the edge of the garden like a pair of cold marble statues, while the rest of the party swarmed away from them.

He knows, she thought, her nerves stretched to the breaking point. There had been a change in him, some inner transformation that seemed to have released him from all constraint. He stared at her the way he used to in the days of their youth, his eyes lit with open yearning. It produced the feeling in her that only he could engender, a sort of dreamlike excitement that seemed to open all her senses.

As Aline remained mute and unmoving, a cold drop of rain struck her cheek and slid down to the corner of her mouth. McKenna came to her slowly. His hand lifted, and he captured the raindrop with the pad of his thumb, and rubbed the dampness between his fingers as if it were a precious elixir. She back-stepped instinctively, away from him, from her own insatiable longing, and he caught her easily with one hand at her back. Slowly he drew her with him into the concealment of the yew hedge.

Unable to look at him, Aline bent her head, even as McKenna pulled her close. He moved with great care, bringing her against his body until her face rested near his collar. The delicious smell of his skin drew a catch of pain from beneath her ribs, a sting that quickly eased into fluid warmth. It went far beyond sexual pleasure, standing there with his hands on her, one at her back, one at her nape. It was bliss. Completeness. The heat of his touch sank through her skin and leaked down into the marrow of her bones. His thigh pressed between her legs, nudging so gently, as if he knew of the urgent fullness that was gathering in her tender flesh. And he held her, just held her, with his mouth against her temple and his hot breath blowing over her skin. Their bodies were so close, and yet not close enough. She would gladly give away the rest of her life in exchange for one night of pure intimacy, to feel the naked length of his body, skin to skin, heart to heart.

"Thank you," Aline whispered after a long time.

"For what?" His lips moved softly against her forehead.

"The gifts," she managed. "They were lovely."

McKenna remained silent, breathing in the scent of her hair. In a desperate attempt at self-preservation, Aline attempted conversation. "Did it go well for you, in London?"

To her relief, McKenna answered. "Yes." He eased her head back, with his hand still cradling the back of her neck. "We secured the docking rights from Somerset Shipping, and all the potential investors have made firm commitments."

"Including my brother?"

That drew a quick smile from him. "He's indicated that he will throw his lot in with theirs."

She sighed with relief. "That's good."

"Now that everything has been settled, I have to leave for New York. There is much to be done, and many decisions to make."

"Yes, I . . ." Her voice faded as she looked up at him anxiously. "When are you leaving?"

"Tuesday."

"So soon?" she whispered.

"Shaw and I will return to New York. The Chamberlains, the Cuylers, and the rest of them want to tour abroad. They'll go to Paris first, and then to Rome."

Aline absorbed the information quietly. If the ship sailed on Tuesday, then McKenna and Shaw would probably depart from Stony Cross the day after tomorrow. She couldn't believe that she would lose him so quickly.

The rain fell harder, until sparkling water beaded on the dense black locks of McKenna's hair and ran off as if it were a seal's pelt. "We should go in," Aline said, reaching up to brush a few droplets from the inky locks. He caught at her hand and wrapped his fingers around hers, and pressed the points of her knuckles against his lips.

"When can I talk to you?" he asked.

"We're talking right now."

"You know what I want," came his low murmur.

Aline fastened her gaze to the hedge beyond his broad shoulder. Yes, she knew exactly what he intended to discuss with her, and she would have given anything to avoid it. "Early in the morning, before the guests awaken," she suggested. "We'll meet at the stables, and walk somewhere . . ."

"All right."

"Tomorrow, then," she said, ducking her head as she began to walk around him.

McKenna caught her easily, bringing her close again. He gripped the back of her braided coiffure and tugged her head back, his mouth covering hers. Aline began to sigh repeatedly as he explored her with his tongue, filling her mouth the way he wanted to fill her body.

Sensing her rising need, McKenna gripped the sides of her hips and slid his knee between her legs. He urged her against him, over and over, until her heart was pounding madly and her skin was burning everywhere, even as the coolness of rain drenched her skin and clothing. Groping for balance, she held on to his shoulders while he pressed kisses and indistinct words against her parted lips. He pulled her forward until she rode him more fully, his hands moving her in a delicious rhythm. That steady friction, right where her body had become swollen and hot . . . the pleasure built too quickly, and she struggled against him with a moan of denial.

McKenna eased her away, breathing raggedly. They faced each other, standing in the rain like a pair of besotted half-wits. Shrugging out of his coat, McKenna held it over Aline as a makeshift umbrella and urged her to come with him. "Inside," he murmured. "We'll get struck by lightning, standing out here." A crooked smile crossed his face as he added wryly, "Not that I would notice."

Eighteen

Just after two o'clock in the morning, Livia sneaked into the darkened bachelor's house and was immediately accosted in the entranceway. Repressing a shriek of surprise, she found herself being jerked against a tall male body. It was Gideon, clad in a silk robe. Livia relaxed in his arms and returned his kisses eagerly, her tongue curling around his. He kissed her as if their separation had been a matter of months rather than days.

"What took you so long?" he demanded, giving her a bone-warping squeeze before hauling her toward the bedroom.

"This lurking-and-prowling-about business isn't easy, with the manor full of guests," Livia protested. "I had to wait until I was certain that no one could see me slipping off to the bachelor's house. Especially as we're already under suspicion."

"We are?" He stopped at the bedside and began to unfasten the back of her gown.

"Well, *naturally*, after I traipsed off to London while you just happened to be there. And then there's the way you look at me, which practically announces that we've been in bed together. For a man who is supposedly a sophisticate, you're terribly obvious."

"Terribly," he agreed, pulling her hand to his aroused body.

Drawing away with a giggle, Livia shed her gown, beneath which she was completely naked. Taken by surprise, Gideon drew his breath in sharply, his gaze riveted on her. "I came prepared," Livia told him smugly.

Shaking his head as if to clear it, Gideon dropped his robe and approached her. His hands skimmed the curves of her hips as if she were a priceless sculpture. "So did I, actually. I brought something from London." His hands drifted upward to her breasts, his thumbs lightly grazing the tips of her breasts. "Though you may not like it."

Intrigued, Livia looped her arms around his neck as he picked her up and carried her to the bed. He dropped her to the mattress, bent to kiss the smooth skin between her breasts, then reached for something at the bedside table. She was surprised when he gave her a little packet made of thin paper, which enclosed an unfamiliar object. It was an elastic sort of ring, covered with a thin, transparent skin. Regarding the object closely, Livia felt herself blush as comprehension dawned. "Oh . . . it's a . . ."

"Exactly." He shrugged and looked vaguely sheepish. "At the risk of seeming presumptuous, I thought there was a chance that we might have another night together."

"Presumptuous indeed," Livia told him with mock sternness, holding the sheath in the palm of her hand.

"Have you ever seen one before?"

"No, although I've heard of them." Her blush heightened. "It seems like an odd idea . . . and not especially romantic."

"Neither is an unwanted pregnancy," Gideon said frankly, pulling back the covers as he joined her on the bed. "I wouldn't mind getting you with child, but not if you're unwilling."

The thought of carrying his baby . . . Livia looked away from him, unable to keep from wishing for things that seemed likely never to happen. Gideon brought her beneath the bed linens with him and kissed her gently. "Do you want to try it this way?"

"I suppose so," Livia said doubtfully, holding the rolled-up sheath up to the lamplight and staring through the near-transparent membrane.

She felt Gideon shake with suppressed laughter. "It won't hurt," he said. "And you may appreciate the fact that when a man wears one of these, it takes much longer for him to climax."

"Does it? Why? Because you can't feel as much?"

"That's right." He smiled wryly. "Rather like trying to eat supper through a table napkin."

Livia gave him the sheath. "Don't wear this, then, and we'll do it the usual way."

Gideon shook his head decisively. "I don't trust myself to do that anymore. It's becoming impossible to withdraw at the moment that I most want to stay inside you. Here . . . help me put it on. You should try everything at least once, I always say."

Bashfully Livia followed his murmured instructions and unrolled it along the taut length of his erection, adjusting it to form a shallow pocket at the head. "It seems rather tight," she said.

"It's supposed to fit this way, or it will slide off."

Letting go of him, she lay back on the mattress. "Now what?"

"Now," he said, his body covering hers, "I'm going to make love to you the way I've imagined doing for five nights."

Livia's eyes half-closed as his head lowered to her breasts, his tongue swirling in intricate patterns over her skin. He took her nipple into his mouth and worried it gently with his teeth and licked until it was engorged and darkened. Then he moved to her other breast, treating it in a similar fashion until she was moaning and writhing beneath him. He made love to her with tender skill, attentive to every twitch and shiver of response. Pausing briefly, Gideon reached for something at the bedside. She heard him fumble with the lid of a jar, and then his hand slid between her thighs to distribute a satiny film of cream. His gentle fingertip slid through the soft folds, then circled the entrance of her body.

"Gideon," she said in agitation, "I'm ready now."

He smiled as he continued to play idly with her. "You're too impatient."

"I'm impatient because I'm *ready* . . . oh, why do you always have to take so much time?"

"Because I love to torment you." He bent to kiss her throat, while his fingertips combed through the wet thatch of curls. Willing herself to endure the teasing exploration, Livia reached upward to the spindles of the headboard and gripped the hard, slender cylinders of wood. Gideon knelt between her thighs and applied more of the slippery unguent, his fingers reaching deep inside her.

Livia was finally reduced to begging. "Gideon, please do it now, *please* . . ."

Her words were cut off as he entered her carefully, filling her until she groaned in relief. "Is it all right?" Gideon asked, bracing his forearms on either side of his head. "It's not uncomfortable, is it?"

Livia pushed up at him for answer, her body teeming with pleasure. Smiling down at her passion-taut features, Gideon rested his thumb lightly on the sensitive bud of her sex, and stroked her as he began to move in deep, rocking thrusts, and she was lost in a tide of bliss . . .

"Livia," he said a long time later, cuddling her against his chest while he played with the fine locks of her hair. "What if I decide not to return to New York?"

Her mind went blank. Wondering if he had just said what she thought he had said, she got up from bed and lit a lamp. Gideon remained on his side, the sheet draped loosely over his hips.

Returning to bed, Livia rolled to face him and pulled the sheet up beneath her arms. "You're thinking of staying in London?" she asked. "For how long?"

"At least a year. I would run the London office and develop business for us on the continental market. I would be as useful here as I would be in New York, if not more so."

"But your entire family is in New York."

"Another good reason to stay here," Gideon said dryly. "It has become clear that a period of separation will be to their benefit as well as mine. I'm tired of acting as the family patriarch—they can damned well learn to muddle through things on their own."

"What about the foundries, and your business properties—"

"I'm giving McKenna the authority to make any and all decisions in my absence. He's proven that he's ready for the responsibility—and I trust him more than I do my own brothers."

"I thought you didn't like London."

"I love it."

Amused by his change of tune, when she had heard him say just the opposite last week, Livia had to bite back a smile. "Why have you fallen in love with London so suddenly?"

Gideon reached out to stroke her hair, tucking a silken wisp neatly behind her ear. His eyes stared into her, the lamplight striking golden glints amid the depths of lambent blue. "Because it's close to you."

Livia closed her eyes, while the words riddled her with uncertainty and unwanted hope. The force of her longing seemed to fill the entire room. "Gideon," she said, "we've already discussed—"

"I'm not asking to see you, or court you," he said swiftly. "In fact, I insist on *not* seeing you for at least six months, until I can figure out if I'm able to stop drinking for good. It's not a pleasant process, I've heard . . . for a while I'm hardly going to be fit company. So for that and other reasons, it would be better for us to stay apart."

Livia was dumbstruck by the realization of what he was trying to do, the magnitude of effort it would require. "What do you want from me?" she managed to ask.

"To wait for me."

More self-imposed isolation, Livia thought, and shook her head reluctantly. "I can't remain secluded in Hampshire any longer, or I'll go raving mad. I need to take part in society, and talk and laugh and go places—"

"Of course. I don't want you to stay buried in Stony Cross. But don't let other men . . . that is, don't promise to marry anyone, or fall in love with some damned viscount . . ." Gideon scowled at the thought. "Just stay unmarried for six months. That's not too much to ask, is it?"

She considered the request with a thoughtful frown. "No, of course not. But if you are doing this for me . . ."

"I'd be lying if I said it wasn't partly for you," he said frankly. "However, it's for me as well. I'm weary of staggering through life in a fog."

Livia ran her palm along the strong line of his forearm. "It's possible that when you emerge from the fog, you won't want me anymore," she said. "Your perceptions may be different . . . your needs may change . . ."

He caught her hand in his, interlacing their fingers. "I'll never stop needing you."

She stared down at their joined hands. "When are you planning to start?"

"You're referring to the fiendish condition of sobriety? I'm sorry to say that I've already started. I haven't had a drink in twelve hours. By tomorrow morning I'm going to be a stinking, shivering, foul-tempered mess, and by the next day I'll probably have murdered someone." He grinned. "So it's a good thing that I'm leaving Stony Cross."

Undeceived by his flippant manner, Livia snuggled against his chest and pressed her lips to his heart. "I wish I could help you," she said softly, rubbing her cheek against the dark golden fur. "I wish I could suffer through some of it for you."

"Livia . . ." His voice thickened with emotion, and his hand passed gently over her hair. "No one can help me with this. It's my cross to bear—one I've fashioned entirely by myself. And that is why I don't want you to be any part of this. But there is one thing you could do to make it a bit easier . . . something to get me through the worst moments . . ."

She drew back to look up at him. "What is it?"

Gideon paused, and let out a taut sigh. "I know that you're not going to admit that you love me—and I understand why. But in light of the fact that I'm facing six months of hell, can't you give me just a little something?"

"Such as?"

He looked at her speculatively. "A blink."

"A what?" she asked in confusion.

"If you love me . . . just blink at me. One time. A *meaningful* blink. You don't have to say the words, just . . ." His voice trailed away as their gazes locked, and he stared at her with the ardent determination of a lost soul who had caught sight of his home far off on the horizon. "Just blink at me," he whispered. "Please, Livia . . ."

She would not have believed it was possible to love this way again. Perhaps some people would consider it a disloyalty to Amberley, but Livia did not. Amberley had wanted her to be happy, to have a full life.

She even thought that he might have approved of Gideon Shaw, who was struggling so hard to overcome his flaws . . . a warm, human, approachable man.

Gideon was still waiting. Livia held his gaze and smiled. Very deliberately, she closed her eyes and opened them again, and looked at him through the warm, blurry brightness of hope.

Aline was exhausted after a sleepless night, and filled with cold dread as she went to the stables, where she had promised to meet McKenna. She had rehearsed a list of objections over and over, arguments and counter-arguments . . . although when she practiced the words, she sounded unconvincing even to herself.

The household was slumbering except for the indoor servants who were busy with coal and ewers of hot water, and those who worked in the stables and gardens. Aline passed a footboy who had been assigned the task of pushing the mower machine back and forth across the velvety green lawn, while another lad followed to collect the cut grass with a rake and a small tip cart. In the stables, grooms were busy cleaning the stable gutters, distributing hay, and mucking out the stalls. The familiar scents of hay and horses saturated the air with a pleasantly earthy smell.

McKenna was already there, waiting near the tack room. Aline was tempted to run to him, equally as much as she wanted to flee in the opposite direction. McKenna smiled faintly, but Aline sensed that he was fully as nervous as she. They were both aware that this was one of the rare occasions when a single conversation might alter the entire course of one's future.

"Good morning," Aline managed to say.

McKenna looked at her in a way that suspended them both in silent tension. He offered an arm to her. "Let's go to the river."

Aline knew at once where he would take her . . . the spot that had always been theirs alone. The perfect place to say goodbye, she thought bleakly, taking his arm. They walked in silence, while the lavender tones of early dawn turned pale yellow, and long, light shadows crossed the lawn. Aline's knee joints felt stiff, as they always did in the morning before her scars were stretched by mild activity. She concentrated on walking smoothly, while McKenna matched his pace to her slower one.

They finally reached the clearing near the water, where a pied wagtail circled the glittering reeds several times before suddenly dropping in to roost. Aline sat on a large, flat rock and arranged her skirts carefully, while McKenna went to stand a few feet away from her. He bent to pick up a few small stones. One by one, he sent them skimming across the water with deft flicks of his wrist. She watched him, drinking in the sight of his tall form, the strong lines of his profile, the easy grace of his movements. When he turned to glance at her over his shoulder, his turquoise eyes were so vivid in his bronzed face that the color seemed almost unnatural.

"You know what I'm going to ask," he said quietly.

"Yes," Aline replied in mounting anxiety, "but before you say anything, I must tell you that I will never—"

"Hear me out," he murmured, "and then you can answer. There are things that I want to say to you. Difficult as this is, I'm going to talk to you honestly, or I'll regret it for the rest of my life."

Black misery swamped her. Honesty—the one thing she couldn't give him in return. "I'm going to refuse you, no matter what you say." Her breath felt caustic in her throat, as if she had swallowed acid. "Please spare us both the unnecessary discomfort—"

"I'm not going to spare either of us," he said gruffly. "It's now or never, Aline. After I leave tomorrow, I'm not coming back."

"To England?"

"To you." McKenna found a rock near hers and sat on the edge of it, leaning forward to brace his forearms on his thighs. His dark head lowered for a moment, the sunlight moving over his black hair in a bright gleam. He looked up with a penetrating gaze. "It was the curse of my life to be sent to this estate. From the moment I first saw you, I felt the connection between us—a connection that should never have existed, and never should have lasted. I tried to admire you from a distance . . . just as I saw the stars in the sky and knew I could never touch them. But we were too young, and I was with you too often, to preserve that distance. You were my friend, my companion . . . and later I came to love you as deeply as any man has ever loved a woman. That never changed for me, although I've lied to myself for years." He paused and took a long breath. "No matter how I want to deny it, I will always love you. And no matter how I wish I could be something other than what I am, I'm a commoner, and a bastard, and you're a daughter of the peerage."

"McKenna," she began miserably, "please don't—"

"My entire purpose in coming back to Stony Cross was to find you. That was fairly obvious, I think, as there was no practical reason to avail ourselves of your brother's hospitality. For that matter, there was no need for me to come to England at all, as Shaw could have managed well enough on his own while I remained in New York. But I needed to prove that what I felt for you wasn't real. I had convinced myself that I had never loved you . . . rather, it was that you represented all the things I could never have. I thought that an affair with you would dispel those illusions, and you would turn out to be like every other woman." He fell silent for a moment, while the jangling song of a reed warbler pierced the air. "Then I planned to return to New York and take a wife. A man of my position, even without a name and family, can marry well there. Finding a willing bride is easy enough. But now after finding you again, I've finally realized that you were never an illusion. Loving you has been the most real thing in my life."

"Don't," Aline whispered, her eyes stinging.

"I am asking you, with all the humility I possess, if you will marry me, and come to America. Once Westcliff takes a wife, he'll no longer need you as a hostess. You'll have no real place at Stony Cross Park. But as my wife, you would be the queen of New York society. I have a fortune, Aline, with the prospect of tripling it in the next few years. If you come with me, I'll do everything in my power to make you happy." His voice was so quiet, so careful, the voice of a man who was taking the most dangerous gamble of his life. "Obviously it would be a sacrifice for you to leave your family and friends, and the place where you've lived since you were born. But you could come back to visit—the crossing only takes twelve days. You could begin a whole new life with me. Name your price, Aline—it's yours for the asking."

With every word he had spoken, Aline felt despair twist inside her. She could hardly draw breath around the huge choking knot in her chest. "You must believe me when I say that it would impossible for us to be happy together. I care for you, McKenna, but I . . ." She hesitated and took a pained gasp before forcing herself to continue. "I don't love you in that way. I cannot marry you."

"You don't have to love me. I'll accept whatever you can give."

"No, McKenna."

He came to her, dropped to his haunches, and took one of her cold, perspiring hands in his own. The heat of his flesh was startling. "Aline," he said with difficulty, "I love you enough for the both of us. And there must be something about me worth loving. If you would just try . . ."

The need to tell him the truth was enough to drive Aline insane. As she considered it wildly, her heart beat so hard that it hurt, and there was an icy prickling all over her skin. She tried to envision it, showing him the disfiguring scars right here and now. No. *No.*

She felt like a creature caught in a net, struggling in vain to break free of the filaments of the past, which tightened around her with every movement. "It's not possible." Her hands clenched into the soft silk of her dress.

"Why?" The word was harshly spoken, but there was a vulnerability behind it that made her want to weep. Aline knew what McKenna wanted, and needed—a partner who would gladly yield herself to him, in and out of bed. A woman who had the wisdom to take pride in all the things he was, and never mind about the things he could never be. Once Aline might have been that for him. But now that could never happen.

"You're not of my class," she said. "We both know that."

It was the one thing she could say that would convince him. An American he might be, but McKenna had been born in England, and he would never be able to completely rid himself of the class awareness that had permeated every aspect of his existence for eighteen years. For such a comment to come from her was the ultimate betrayal. She looked away, not wanting to see his expression. She was dying inside, her heart turning to ash.

"Christ, Aline," came his ragged whisper.

She turned away from him. They stood like that for a long time, both struggling with unexpressed emotion, fury feeding on hopelessness. "I don't belong with you," she said hoarsely. "My place is here, with . . . with Lord Sandridge."

"You can't make me believe that you would choose him over me— not after what's happened between us, damn it! You let me touch you, hold you, in a way you never let him."

"I've gotten what I wanted," she forced herself to say. "And so have you. After you leave, you'll see that it was for the best."

McKenna nearly crushed her hand as his grip tightened. Turning her hand up, he laid his cheek against the soft cushion of her palm. "Aline," he whispered, mercilessly divesting himself of all pride, "I'm afraid of what I'll become if you won't have me."

Aline's throat and head ached, and she finally began to cry, tears sliding down her cheeks. She jerked her hand from his, when all she wanted to do was pull his head to her breasts. "You'll be fine," she said shakily, dragging a sleeve across her streaming face as she walked away without looking back. "You'll be fine, McKenna—just go back to New York. I don't want you."

Mrs. Faircloth arranged a row of rare crystal glasses on the shelves in her private room, where the most fragile household valuables were kept under lock and key. Her door had been left half open, and she heard someone approach the threshold in a slow, almost reluctant tread. Leaning out from the shelf, she glanced at the doorway to behold McKenna's large outline, his face shadowed. Poignant regret filled her as she realized that he must have come for a last private talk.

Recalling McKenna's offer to take her back to America with him, Mrs. Faircloth was conscious of a small, unheeded wish that she could accept the invitation. Foolish old hen, she scolded herself, knowing that it was too late for a woman her age to consider uprooting herself. All the same, the prospect of going to live in another country had kindled her blood with an unexpected sense of adventure. It might have been wonderful, she thought wistfully, to experience something new as she approached her sunset years.

However, she would never leave Lady Aline, whom she had loved too dearly and for too long. She had watched over Aline from infancy to adulthood, sharing in every joy and tragedy of her life. Although Mrs. Faircloth cared for Livia and Marcus as well, she had to admit privately that Aline had always been her favorite. In the hours when Aline had hovered closest to death, Mrs. Faircloth had felt the despair of a mother losing her own child . . . and in the years afterward, watching Aline grapple with fearful secrets and broken dreams, the bond between them had strengthened even more. As long as Aline needed her, there was no thought in the housekeeper's mind of leaving her.

"McKenna," Mrs. Faircloth said, welcoming him into her room. As he stepped into the quiet lamplight, the expression on his face troubled her, reminding her of the first time she had seen him, a poor motherless bastard with cold blue-green eyes. Despite his lack of expression, fury and grief clung to him in an invisible mantle, too profound, too absolute, for him to give voice to. He could only stand there and stare at her, not knowing what he needed, having come to her only because there seemed to be no other place to go.

Mrs. Faircloth knew that there could be only one reason that McKenna would look that way. Swiftly she went to shut the door. The servants at Stony Cross Park knew never to bother the housekeeper when her door was closed, unless the situation was near-catastrophic. Turning, she held her arms out to him in a maternal gesture. McKenna went to her at once, his black head lowering to her soft, round shoulder as he wept.

Aline never fully remembered the rest of that day, only that she had managed to play the part of hostess mechanically, talking and even smiling, without really taking notice of whom she was with or what she was saying. Livia gallantly sought to cover for her, diverting all attention with a show of effervescent charm. When it was noticed that McKenna was not present at the group's final supper, Gideon Shaw lightly excused his absence. "Oh, McKenna is putting things in order before his departure on the morrow—and making long lists for me, I'm afraid." Before more questions could surface, Shaw stunned them all with the information that instead of returning to New York with McKenna, he was going to stay on in London to manage the newly established office.

Even in her numbness, Aline grasped the import of the news. She threw a quick glance at Livia, who was devoting a great deal of concentration to slicing a bit of potato into minuscule portions. Livia's pretended disinterest, however, was belied by the tide of color that rose in her cheeks. Shaw was staying because of Livia, Aline realized, and wondered what sort of arrangement he and her sister had come to. Flicking a glance at Marcus at the head of the table, Aline saw that he was wondering the same thing.

"London is fortunate to be favored by your continued presence, Mr. Shaw," Marcus commented. "May I ask where you will reside?"

Shaw replied with the whimsical smile of a man who had recently discovered something unexpected about himself. "I'll remain at the Rutledge until the new construction begins, after which I will find some appropriate place to lease."

"Allow me to offer some assistance toward that end," Marcus said politely, his gaze calculating. Clearly he was planning to exert as much control over the developing situation as possible. "I can put a few words in the right ears to secure a suitable situation for you."

"Of that I have no doubt," Shaw replied, with a jaunty twinkle in his gaze that showed he was perfectly aware of Marcus's true intent.

"But you *have* to go back to New York!" Susan Chamberlain cried, glaring at her brother. "My God, Gideon, even you can't simply cast off your responsibilities in this cavalier manner! Who will look after the family business, and make decisions, and—" She stopped, suddenly aghast as the realization hit her. "*No.* You are not appointing that *docker* as a de facto head of the Shaw family, you sodden lunatic!"

"I'm perfectly sober," Shaw informed her blandly. "And the papers have already been drawn up and signed. I'm afraid there's not much you can do about it, sis. McKenna has well-established relationships with all our business associates, and he alone possesses the full information regarding our accounts, trusts, and contracts. You may as well settle back and give him free rein."

Seething with outrage, Susan Chamberlain seized her wine and drank angrily, while her husband tried to pacify her with low-voiced murmurs.

Gideon Shaw continued to eat calmly, as if oblivious to the upheaval he had caused. As he reached for a goblet of water, however, he shot a quick glance at Livia, whose lips twitched with a smile.

"I hope we will have the pleasure of seeing you from time to time, Mr. Shaw," Aline murmured.

The handsome American turned his attention to her, his expression becoming enigmatic. "It would be my pleasure as well, my lady. However, I fear that I will be completely occupied with work for a long while."

"I see," Aline said softly, while understanding dawned. She deliberately picked up her own water glass and lifted it in a silently encouraging toast, and he responded with a nod of thanks.

Aline was not such a coward that she could hide in her room to avoid McKenna . . . although the idea was not without its appeal. His quiet words of yesterday had annihilated her. She knew how inexplicable her rejection had been, leaving him no choice but to believe that she had no feeling for him. The thought of facing him this morning was unbearable . . . but she felt that she should at least have the courage to tell him goodbye.

The entrance hall and the courtyard outside were filled with servants and departing guests. A row of carriages lined the drive, being loaded with bags and boxes and trunks. Aline and Marcus moved among the throng, exchanging farewells and walking with guests to their carriages. Livia was nowhere in sight, leading Aline to suspect that she was making her goodbyes to Gideon Shaw in private.

From what little Livia had revealed to her during a brief conversation this morning, Aline gathered that the pair had decided not to see each other for a period of several months, to allow Shaw the time and privacy he needed to conquer his drinking habit. They had, however, agreed to correspond during their separation, which meant that their courtship would continue by means of ink and paper. Aline had smiled with sympathetic amusement when Livia told her that. "I think the two of you have got it backward," she said. "Usually a romantic involvement begins with exchanging letters, and then eventually leads to greater intimacy . . . whereas you and Mr. Shaw . . ."

"Began in bed and ended with correspondence," Livia finished dryly. "Well, none of us Marsdens seem to do things the usual way, do we?"

"No, indeed." Aline was glad that she and her younger sister seemed to be back on good terms. "It will be interesting to see what becomes of your relationship, limiting it to letter writing for such a long period."

"I'm looking forward to it, in a way," Livia reflected. "It will be easier to discern my true feelings for Mr. Shaw when the communication is entirely between our minds and hearts, with all the physical aspects removed." She grinned and blushed as she admitted self-consciously, "Although I will miss those physical aspects."

Aline had gazed at a distant point outside a nearby window while daylight stole over the grounds. Her smile turned wistful as she thought of how much she too would miss the joys to be found in a man's arms. "It will turn out all right," she said. "I have high hopes for you and Mr. Shaw."

"What about you and McKenna? Is there any reason to hope for the both of you?" As Livia saw Aline's expression, she frowned. "Never mind—I shouldn't have asked. I have promised myself to say nothing more on the subject, and from now on I will hold my silence even if it kills me . . ."

Aline's thoughts were brought back to the present as she stepped outside and noticed that one of the footmen, Peter, was having difficulty hefting a massive trunk onto the back of a carriage. Despite his brawny build, the weight of the brass-bound trunk was getting the better of him. The object slid from its precarious position, threatening to topple Peter backward.

Two of the guests, Mr. Cuyler and Mr. Chamberlain, noticed the footman's dilemma, but it did not seem to occur to either of them to offer assistance. They moved away from the vehicle in tandem, continuing their conversation while they observed Peter's struggles. Aline glanced quickly around the scene, looking for another servant to help the footman. Before she could say a word to anyone, McKenna seemed to appear from nowhere, striding to the back of the carriage and wedging his shoulder against the trunk. The muscles of his arms and back bulged against the seams of his coat as he shoved the trunk into its proper place, holding it steady while Peter clambered up to fasten a leather strap around it.

Cuyler and Chamberlain turned away from the sight, as if it embarrassed them to see one of their group assisting a servant with a menial task. The very fact of McKenna's superior physical strength seemed a mark against him, betraying that he had once labored at tasks that no gentleman should ever have done. Finally the trunk was secured, and McKenna stepped back, acknowledging the footman's thanks with a brief nod. Watching him, Aline could not help but reflect that had McKenna never left Stony Cross, he almost certainly would have been in Peter's place, serving as a footman. And that wouldn't have mattered to her in the least. She would have loved him no matter where he went, or what he did, and it tormented her that he would never know that.

Sensing her gaze, McKenna glanced up, then immediately averted his gaze. His jaw hardened, and he stood there in silent contemplation before finally looking at her once more. His expression sent a chill through her . . . so wintry and withdrawn . . . and she realized that his feelings for her were transforming into a hostility that was proportionate to how much he loved her.

He was going to hate her soon, she thought bleakly, if he didn't already.

McKenna squared his shoulders and came to her, stopping an arm's reach away. They stood together in brittle silence, while small clusters of people chatted and shifted around them. One of the most difficult things Aline had ever done in her life was to lift her chin and stare into his eyes. The exotic blue-green irises were nearly obliterated by the dark black of his pupils. He looked pale beneath his healthy tan, and his usual vitality had been crushed beneath an air of absolute grimness.

Aline lowered her gaze. "I wish you well, McKenna," she finally whispered.

He was very still. "I wish the same for you."

More silence, pressing down on her until she nearly swayed beneath its weight. "I hope you will have a safe and pleasant crossing."

"Thank you."

Clumsily Aline offered her hand to him. McKenna didn't move to take it. She felt her fingers tremble. Just as she began to withdraw her hand, he caught it and brought her fingers to his lips. The touch of his mouth was cool and dry against her skin. "Goodbye," he murmured.

Aline's throat closed, and she stood silent and shivering, her hand suspended in the air after he released it. Closing her fingers slowly, she brought her fist against her midriff and turned away blindly. She felt his gaze on her as she left. As she began to ascend the short flight of steps that led to the entrance hall, the thick scar tissue pulled at the back of her knee, a persistent, annoying burn that brought tears of rage to her eyes.

Nineteen

fter the last guest had departed, Aline changed into a comfortable
at-home gown and went to the family receiving room. Curling up
in the corner of a deeply upholstered settee, she sat and stared at nothing
for what seemed to be hours. Despite the warmth of the day, she shivered
beneath a lap blanket, her fingers and toes icy. At her request, a maid
came to light a fire in the hearth and brought a steaming pot of tea, but
nothing could take the chill away.

She heard the sounds of rooms being cleaned; servants' footsteps on
the stairs, the manor being restored to order now that the house was finally cleared of visitors. There were things that she should be doing; taking household inventory, consulting with Mrs. Faircloth about which
rooms should be closed and what items were needed from market. However, Aline could not seem to rouse herself from the stupor that had settled over her. She felt like a clock with a damaged mechanism, frozen and
useless.

She dozed on the settee until the fire burned low and the shafts of
sunlight that came through the half-closed curtains were replaced by the
glow of sunset. A quiet sound awakened her, and she stirred reluctantly.
Opening her bleary eyes, she saw that Marcus had come into the room.
He stood near the hearth, staring at her as if she were a puzzle that he was
uncertain how to solve.

"What do you want?" she asked with a frown. Struggling to a sitting position, she rubbed her eyes.

Marcus lit a lamp and approached the settee. "Mrs. Faircloth tells me that you haven't eaten all day."

Aline shook her head. "I'm just tired. I'll have something later."

Her brother stood over her with a frown. "You look like hell."

"Thank you," she said dryly. "As I said, I am tired. I need to sleep, that is all—"

"You seem to have slept most of the day—and it hasn't done you a damned bit of good."

"What do you want, Marcus?" she asked with a spark of annoyance.

He took his time about answering, shoving his hands into the pockets of his coat as he appeared to be thinking something over. Eventually he glanced at the shape of her knees, hidden beneath the folds of her blue muslin skirts. "I've come to ask something of you," he said gruffly.

"What?"

He gestured stiffly toward her feet. "May I see them?"

Aline gave him a blank stare. "My legs?"

"Yes." Marcus sat on the other side of the settee, his face expressionless.

He had never made such a request before. Why would he want to see her legs now, after all these years? Aline could not fathom his motive, and she felt too exhausted to sort through the many tiers of emotion she felt. Certainly it would do no harm to show him, she thought. Before she allowed herself to think twice, she kicked off her slippers. Her legs were bare beneath the gown. Lifting them to the settee cushions, she hesitated before tugging the hem of her skirts and drawers up to her knees.

Other than a nearly undetectable hitch to his breathing, Marcus showed no reaction to the sight of her legs. His dark gaze moved over the ropy pattern of scars, the patches of rough, ravaged skin, down to the incongruous whiteness of her feet. Watching his impassive face, Aline didn't realize that she was holding her breath, until she felt the taut burn of her lungs. She let out a slow sigh, rather amazed that she was able to trust Marcus to this extent.

"They're not pretty," he finally said. "But they're not quite as bad as I expected." Carefully he reached over to pull the skirt back over her legs. "I suppose things that are unseen are often worse in one's imagination than they are in reality."

Aline stared curiously at the overprotective, strong-willed, often annoying brother she had come to love so dearly. As children, they had been little more than strangers to each other, but in the years since their father's death, Marcus had proved himself to be an honorable and caring man. Like her, he was independent to a fault, outwardly social and yet fiercely private. Unlike her, he was always scrupulously honest, even when the truth was painful.

"Why did you want to see them now?" she asked.

He surprised her with a self-derisive smile. "I've never been certain how to contend with your accident, other than wish to hell that it had never happened. I can't help but feel that I failed you in some way. Seeing your legs, and knowing there is nothing I can do to make them better, is damned difficult for me."

She shook her head in bafflement. "Good Lord, Marcus, how on earth could you have prevented an accident from happening? That's taking your sense of responsibility rather too far, don't you think?"

"I've chosen to love very few people in this world," he murmured, "but you and Livia are among them—and I would give my life to spare either of you a single moment's pain."

Aline smiled at him, feeling a welcome crack in the numbness that surrounded her. Despite all better judgment, she couldn't prevent herself from asking a critical question, even as she struggled to crush the feeble stirring of hope within herself. "Marcus," she asked hesitantly, "if you loved a woman, would scars like this stop you from—"

"No," he interrupted firmly. "No, I wouldn't let them stop me."

Aline wondered if it was really true. It was possible that once again he was trying to protect her, by sparing her feelings. But Marcus was not a man to lie out of kindness.

"Don't you believe me?" he asked.

She looked at him uncertainly. "I want to."

"You are wrong to assume that I insist upon perfection in a woman. I enjoy physical beauty like any other man, but it's hardly a requirement. That would be hypocritical, coming from a man who is far from handsome himself."

Aline paused in surprise, regarding his broad, even features, his strong jaw, the shrewd black eyes set beneath the straight lines of his brows. "You are attractive," she said earnestly. "Perhaps not in the way that someone like Mr. Shaw is . . . but few men are."

Her brother shrugged. "Believe me, it doesn't matter, since I've never found my looks—or lack thereof—to be an impediment in any way. Which has given me a very balanced perspective on the subject of physical beauty—a perspective that someone with your looks rarely attains."

Aline frowned, wondering if she was being criticized.

"It must be extraordinarily difficult," Marcus continued, "for a woman as beautiful as you to feel that there is a part of you that is shameful and must be concealed. You've never made peace with it, have you?"

Leaning her head against the side of the settee, Aline shook her head. "I hate these scars. I'll never stop wishing that I didn't have them. And there's nothing I can do to change them."

"Just as McKenna can never change his origins."

"If you're trying to draw a parallel, Marcus, it won't do any good. McKenna's origins have never mattered to me. There is nothing that would make me stop loving him or wanting him—" She stopped abruptly as she understood the point he had been leading to.

"Don't you think he would feel the same way about your legs?"

"I don't know."

"For God's sake, go tell him the truth. This isn't the time for you to let your pride get the better of you."

His words kindled sudden outrage. "This has nothing to do with pride!"

"Oh?" Marcus gave her a sardonic look. "You can't bear to let McKenna know that you're less than perfect. What is that if not pride?"

"It's not that simple," she protested.

His mouth twisted impatiently. "Perhaps the problem isn't simple—

but the solution is. Start behaving like the mature woman you are, and acknowledge the fact that you have flaws. And give the poor devil a chance to prove that he can love you regardless."

"You insufferable know-all," she choked, yearning to slap him.

Marcus smiled grimly. "Go to him, Aline. Or I promise you that I'll go tell him myself."

"You wouldn't!"

"I've already had a carriage readied," he informed her. "I'm leaving for London in five minutes, with or without you."

"For God's sake," she exploded, "don't you ever get tired of telling everyone else what to do?"

"Actually, no."

Aline was torn between laughter and exasperation at his reply. "Until today you've done your best to discourage my relationship with McKenna. Why have you changed your mind now?"

"Because you're thirty-one and unmarried, and I've realized that this may be my only opportunity to be rid of you." Marcus grinned and ducked to avoid the halfhearted swipe of her fist, then reached out to fold her tightly in his arms. "And because I want you to be happy," he murmured against her hair.

Pressing her face against his shoulder, Aline felt tears well in her eyes.

"I feared that McKenna was going to hurt you," Marcus continued. "I believe that was his intent in the beginning. But he couldn't carry out his plans, after all was said and done. Even thinking that you had betrayed him, he couldn't help but love you. When he left today, he looked somehow . . . diminished. And I finally realized that he had always been in far more danger from you than you ever were from him. I actually pitied the bastard, because every man has a mortal terror of being hurt that way." Marcus fumbled for a handkerchief. "Here, take this before you ruin my coat."

Blowing her nose gustily, Aline pulled away from him. She felt horribly vulnerable, as if he were prodding her to jump off a cliff. "Remember when you once told me that you didn't like to take risks? Well, I don't either."

"As I recall, I said *unnecessary* risks," he replied gently. "But this seems to be a necessary one, doesn't it?"

Aline stared at him without blinking. Try as she might, she was unable to disavow the overwhelming need that would rule the rest of her life, no matter what she chose to do now. Nothing would end when McKenna left England. She would find no more peace in the future than she had during the past twelve years. The realization made her feel sick, scared, and yet oddly elated. A necessary risk . . .

"I'll go to London," she said, her voice shaking only a little. "I'll only need a few minutes to change into my traveling clothes."

"No time for that."

"But I'm not dressed to go out in public—"

"As it is, we may not reach the steamer before it departs."

Galvanized by the words, Aline jammed her feet into her discarded slippers. "Marcus, you have to get me there in time!"

Despite Marcus's advice that she should try to sleep during the journey to London, Aline was awake for most of the night. Her insides seemed to knot and twist as she stared through the darkened interior of the carriage, wondering if she was going to reach McKenna before his ship, the *Britannia,* left for America. From time to time the silence was broken by the rasp of her brother's snore as he dozed on the opposite seat.

Sometime before dawn, exhaustion overcame her. She fell asleep sitting up, with her cheek crushed against the velvet curtain that draped the interior wall. Floating in a dreamless void, she awakened with difficulty as she felt Marcus's hand on her shoulder.

"What . . . ?" she mumbled, blinking and groaning as he shook her lightly.

"Open your eyes. We're at the docks."

Aline sat up clumsily as Marcus rapped on the carriage door. The footman, Peter, who looked somewhat the worse for wear himself, opened the portal from outside. Immediately a curious mixture of odors filled the carriage. It was a malty, fishy smell, heavily tainted with coal and tobacco. The screeching of seagulls mingled with human voices . . . there were cries of "Rowse-in, and bend the cable," and "Break bulk," and other equally incomprehensible phrases. Marcus swung out of the carriage, and Aline pushed back a straggling lock of hair as she leaned forward to watch him.

The scene at the docks was a swarm of activity, with an endless forest of masts extending on both sides of the channel. There were coal barges, steamboats, and too many merchantmen to count. Crowds of burly, sweat-soaked dockers used hand-held hooks to move bales, boxes, barrels, and parcels of every kind to the nearby warehouses. A row of towering iron cranes were in constant motion, each long metal arm operated by a pair of men as they discharged cargo from the hold of a ship to the quay. It was brutal work, not to mention dangerous. She could hardly believe that McKenna had once earned his living this way.

On the far end of the dock, a kiln next to the warehouses was being used to burn off the damaged tobacco, its long chimney sending a thick stream of blue smoke into the sky.

"They call that the queen's pipe," Marcus said dryly, following the direction of her gaze.

Staring along the row of warehouses to the other end of the quay, Aline saw a massive wooden paddle steamer, easily over two hundred feet in length. "Is that the *Britannia?*"

Marcus nodded. "I'll go find a clerk to fetch McKenna from the ship."

Aline closed her eyes tightly, trying to picture McKenna's face as he received the news. In his current disposition, he wasn't likely to take it well. "Perhaps I should go aboard," she suggested.

"No," came her brother's immediate reply. "They're going to weigh anchor soon—I'm not going to take the chance of having you sail off across the Atlantic as an accidental passenger."

"I'll cause McKenna to miss his departure," she said. "And then he'll kill me."

Marcus gave an impatient snort. "The ship is likely to launch while I stand here arguing with you. Do you want to talk to McKenna or not?"

"Yes!"

"Then stay in the carriage. Peter and the driver will look after you. I'll be back soon."

"He may refuse to disembark," she said. "I hurt him very badly, Marcus."

"He'll come," her brother replied with calm conviction. "One way or another."

A hesitant smile worked its way past Aline's distress as she watched Marcus stride away, prepared to do physical battle, if necessary, with an adversary who was nearly a head taller than he.

Settling back in the carriage, Aline pushed the curtain open and stared through the window, watching a marine policeman wander back and forth past rows of valuable sugar hogsheads piled six and eight high. As she waited, it occurred to her that she must look as if she had been pulled backward through a hedge, with her clothes rumpled and her hair a disheveled mess. She wasn't even wearing proper shoes. Hardly the image of a fine lady visiting town, she thought ruefully, regarding her toes as she wiggled them inside the knit slippers.

Minutes passed, and it became warm and stuffy in the carriage. Deciding that the smell of the docks was better than the prospect of sitting in an enclosed vehicle with no breeze, Aline began to rap on the door to summon Peter. Just as her knuckles touched the paneling, the door was wrenched open with a violence that startled her. She froze, her hand stopped in mid-motion. McKenna appeared in the doorway of the carriage, his shoulders blocking the sunlight.

He reached out to grip her arm as if he were saving her from an unexpected fall. The urgent clamp of his fingers hurt. Wincing, Aline reflected that McKenna seemed like an utter stranger. She found it impossible to believe that this harsh-featured man had held and kissed her so tenderly. "What is the matter?" he demanded, his voice grating. "Have you seen a doctor?"

"What?" She stared at him in utter bewilderment. "Why would I need a doctor?"

McKenna's eyes narrowed, and his hand dropped from her abruptly. "You're not ill?"

"No . . . why would you think I . . ." As comprehension dawned,

Aline glared at her brother, who stood just beyond him. "Marcus! You shouldn't have told him that!"

"He wouldn't have come otherwise," Marcus said without a trace of remorse.

Aline gave him a damning glance. As if matters hadn't been difficult enough, Marcus had now succeeded in making McKenna even more hostile. Unrepentant, Marcus stepped back from the carriage to allow the two of them a marginal amount of privacy.

"I'm sorry," Aline said to McKenna. "My brother misled you—I'm not ill. The reason I am here is that I desperately need to talk to you."

McKenna regarded her stonily. "There's nothing left to be said."

"There is," she insisted. "You told me the day before yesterday that you were going to talk to me honestly, or you would regret it for the rest of your life. I should have done the same, and I am so sorry that I didn't. But I've traveled all night to reach you before you left England. I am asking—no, begging you to give me a chance to explain my behavior."

He shook his head. "They're about to pull the gangway. If I don't reboard within five minutes, I'm going to be separated from all my trunks and personal papers—everything but the clothes on my back."

Aline gnawed at the insides of her cheeks, trying to contain her rising desperation. "Then I'll come aboard with you."

"And sail across the Atlantic without so much as a toothbrush?" he jeered.

"Yes."

McKenna gave her a long, hard stare. He gave no indication of what he was feeling, or even if he was considering her plea. Wondering if he was going to refuse her, Aline cast about recklessly for the right words, the key to unlock his frozen self-control . . . and then she noticed the vein throbbing violently at his temple. Hope unfurled inside her. He wasn't indifferent to her, no matter that he tried to pretend otherwise.

Perhaps the only salve to McKenna's battered pride was the sacrifice of her own. Reluctantly letting her guard down, she spoke more humbly than she ever had in her life. "Please. If you still feel anything at all for me, don't go back on that ship. I swear that I will never ask anything else of you. Please let me tell you the truth, McKenna."

As another untenable silence spun out, McKenna's jaw tightened until a muscle in his cheek twitched. "Damn you," he said softly.

Aline realized with dizzying relief that he was not going to refuse her. "Shall we go to Marsden Terrace?" she dared to whisper.

"No—I'll be damned if I'll have your brother hovering over us. He can go to Marsden Terrace, while you and I talk in Shaw's rooms at the Rutledge."

Aline was afraid to say another word, on the chance that she might cause him to change his mind. She nodded and settled back in the carriage, while her heart slammed repeatedly against her ribs.

McKenna gave instructions to the driver and then climbed into the vehicle. He was immediately followed by Marcus, who did not seem terribly pleased by the plan, as he wanted the situation to remain under his immediate control. Nevertheless, he offered no protest, only sat beside Aline and folded his arms across his chest.

The silence was thick and heavy as the vehicle rolled away from the docks. Aline was wretchedly uncomfortable, her legs stiff and itching, her emotions in turmoil, her head aching. It didn't help that McKenna looked about as warm and understanding as a block of granite. Aline wasn't even certain about what she would say to him, how she could tell him the truth without engendering his pity or disgust.

As if sensing her worry, Marcus reached down and took her fingers in his, giving them a small, encouraging squeeze. Looking up, Aline saw that McKenna had noticed the subtle gesture. His suspicious gaze flickered from Marcus's face to hers. "You may as well start explaining now," he said.

Aline gave him an apologetic glance. "I would rather wait, if you don't mind."

"Fine," McKenna said derisively. "It's not as if I don't have the time."

Marcus stiffened at the other man's tone. "Look here, McKenna—"

"It's all right," Aline interrupted, digging her elbow into her brother's side. "You've helped quite enough, Marcus. I can manage on my own now."

Her brother frowned. "Be that as it may, I don't approve of you going to a hotel with no family member or servant to accompany you. There will be gossip, and you don't—"

"Gossip is the least of my worries," Aline interrupted, increasing the pressure of her elbow against his ribs, until Marcus grunted and fell silent.

After what seemed to be hours, they reached the Rutledge Hotel. The carriage stopped in the small street behind one of the four private accommodations. Aline was in an agony of anticipation as McKenna descended from the carriage and helped her down. Turning, she glanced back at Marcus. Seeing the raw helplessness in her eyes, Marcus gave her a reassuring nod, just before he spoke to McKenna in a hard voice.

"Wait. I want a word with you."

Arching one black brow, McKenna stepped aside with him. He met the earl's gaze with a look of icy inquiry. "What now?"

Marcus turned his back on Aline, and spoke too quietly for her to overhear. "I hope to hell that I haven't underestimated you, McKenna. Whatever comes of your conversation with my sister, I want to assure you of one thing—if you harm her in any way, you'll pay with your life. And I mean that literally."

Aggravated beyond bearing, McKenna shook his head and muttered some choice words beneath his breath. He strode to Aline and guided her forcibly to the back entrance, where the footman had already rapped at the door. Gideon Shaw's valet appeared at the doorway with an expression of open astonishment. "Mr. McKenna," he exclaimed, "I would have thought your ship had sailed by now—"

"It has," McKenna said curtly.

The valet blinked and strove to regain composure. "If you are searching for Mr. Shaw, sir, he is at the company offices—"

"I want the use of his rooms for a few minutes," McKenna said. "See that we're not disturbed."

With an admirable display of tact, the valet did not even glance in Aline's direction. "Yes, sir."

Brusquely McKenna ushered Aline into the residence, which was handsomely furnished in dark woods, the walls covered in rich plum-colored embossed paper. They went to the sitting room, with the bedroom visible just beyond. Heavy velvet drapes had been pulled back to reveal curtains of tea-dyed lace that softened the sunlight as it streamed into the room.

Aline could not control her nervousness. It erupted in a violent trembling that made her teeth click. Clenching her jaw, she went to sit in a large leather chair. After a long pause, McKenna did the same, settling back in a nearby chair and regarding her coldly. An antique French carriage clock ticked busily on the mantel, underscoring the tension that fractured the air.

Aline's mind went blank. In the carriage she had managed to think of a fairly well-structured explanation, but all her carefully considered phrases had suddenly vanished. Nervously she dampened her lips with the tip of her tongue.

McKenna's gaze flickered to her mouth, and his dark brows drew together. "Get on with it, will you?"

Aline inhaled and exhaled slowly, and rubbed her forehead. "Yes. I'm sorry. I'm just not quite certain how to begin. I'm glad of the chance to finally tell you the truth, except . . . this is the hardest thing I've ever done." Looking away from him into the empty hearth, Aline gripped the upholstered arms of the chair. "I must be a better actress than I thought, if I've managed to convince you that your social standing matters to me. Nothing could be further from the truth. I've never cared one whit about the circumstances of your birth . . . where you came from, or who you are . . . you could be a rag man, and it wouldn't matter to me. I would do anything, go anywhere, to be with you." Her nails dug deep crescents into the worn leather. She closed her eyes. "I love you, McKenna. I've always loved you."

There was no sound in the room, only the crisp tick of the mantel clock. As Aline continued, she had an odd sense of listening to herself as if from a distance. "My relationship with Lord Sandridge is not what it appears. Any appearance of romantic interest between the two of us is a deception—one that has served both Lord Sandridge and myself. He does not desire me physically, and he could never entertain that kind of feeling for me because he . . ." She paused awkwardly. "His inclinations are limited exclusively toward other men. He proposed marriage to me as a practical arrangement—a union between friends. I won't say that I didn't find the offer attractive, but I turned him down just before you returned from London."

Opening her eyes, Aline stared down at her lap, while the blessed feeling of numbness left her. She felt raw and exposed and terrified. This was the hardest part, making herself vulnerable to a man who had the power to demolish her with a single word. A man who was justifiably furious at the way she had treated him. "The illness that I had so long ago . . ." she said raspily, ". . . you were right to suspect that I was lying about that. It wasn't a fever. I was injured in a fire—I was burned quite badly. I was in the kitchen with Mrs. Faircloth, when a pan of oil started a fire in the basket grate on the stove. I don't remember anything else. I was told that my clothes caught fire, and I was instantly covered in flames. I tried to run . . . a footman knocked me to the ground and beat out the flames. He saved my life. You may remember him—William—I think he was second footman when you were still at Stony Cross." She paused to take a long breath. Her trembling had eased a little, and she was finally able to steady her voice. "My legs were completely charred."

Risking a glance at McKenna, she saw that he was no longer leaning back in his chair. His body was canted slightly forward, his large frame overloaded with sudden tension, his eyes a blaze of blue-green in his skull-white face.

Aline averted her gaze once more. If she looked at him, she wouldn't be able to finish. "I was in a nightmare that I couldn't awaken from," she said. "When I wasn't in agony from the burns, I was out of my head with morphine. The wounds festered and poisoned my blood, and the doctor said that I wouldn't last a week. But Mrs. Faircloth found a woman who was said to have special healing abilities. I didn't want to get better. I wanted to die. Then Mrs. Faircloth showed me the letter . . ." Remembering, she trailed into silence. That moment had been permanently engraved in her mind, when a few scrawled words on paper had eased her away from the brink of death.

"What letter?" she heard McKenna ask in a suffocated voice.

"The one you had sent to her . . . asking for money, because you needed to break your apprenticeship and flee from Mr. Ilbery. Mrs. Faircloth read the letter to me . . . and hearing the words you had written made me realize . . . that as long as there was a chance that you were in this world, I wanted to go on living in it." Aline stopped suddenly as her eyes blurred, and she blinked furiously to clear them.

McKenna made a hoarse sound. He came to the chair and sank to his haunches before her, breathing as if someone had delivered a crushing blow to the center of his chest.

"I never thought you'd come back," Aline said. "I never wanted you to find out about my accident. But when you returned to Stony Cross, I decided that being close to you—even for one night—was worth any risk. That is why I . . ." She hesitated, blushing wildly. "The night of the village fair . . ."

Breathing heavily, McKenna reached for the hem of her gown. Swiftly Aline bent to stop him, gripping his wrist in a convulsive movement. "Wait!"

McKenna went still, the muscles of his shoulders tightly bunched.

"Burn scars are so ugly," Aline whispered. "They're all over my legs. The right one is especially bad, where much of the skin was destroyed. The scars tighten and shrink until it's difficult to straighten my knee sometimes."

He absorbed that for a moment, and then proceeded to pry her fingers from his wrist and remove her slippers, one after the other. Aline fought a wave of nausea, knowing exactly what he was about to see. She swallowed repeatedly, while salty tears burned the back of her throat. He reached beneath her skirt and slid his hands along her tense thighs, his palms skimming the fabric of her drawers until he found the tapes at her waist. Aline turned chalk-white, followed by brilliant scarlet, as she felt him tugging at the undergarment.

"Let me," he murmured.

She obeyed clumsily, raising her hips while he pulled the drawers over her buttocks and stripped the garment from her legs. The hem of her skirt was pushed to the tops of her thighs, the cool air washing over her exposed skin. A profuse sweat of anxiety broke out on her face and neck, and she used her sleeve to blot her cheeks and upper lip.

Kneeling before her, McKenna took hold of one of her icy feet in his warm hand. He brushed his thumb over the pink tips of her toes. "You were wearing shoes when it happened," he said, staring at the pale, smooth skin of her feet, the delicate tracing of blue veins near the arch.

Perspiration stung her eyes as she opened them to look at the top of his dark head. "Yes." Her entire body jerked as his hands slid to her ankles.

McKenna's fingers stilled. "Does it hurt when I touch you?"

"N-no." Aline blotted her face again, gasping as the slow, easy exploration continued. "It's just . . . Mrs. Faircloth is the only one I've ever allowed to touch my legs. In some places I can't feel anything . . . and in others, the skin is too sensitive." The sight of his hands sliding along her ravaged calves was almost more than she could bear. Transfixed and miserable, she watched his fingertips pass over the rough, reddened scars.

"I wish I had known," he murmured. "I should have been with you."

That made Aline want to weep, but she set her jaw hard to keep it from quivering. "I wanted you," she admitted stiffly. "I kept asking for you. Sometimes I thought you were there, holding me . . . but Mrs. Faircloth said they were fever dreams."

The motion of his hands stopped. The words seemed to send a tremor across his wide shoulders, as if he had taken a chill. Eventually his palms resumed their progress along her thighs, pressing them apart, his thumbs skimming the insides. "So this is what has kept us apart," he said unsteadily. "This is why you wouldn't let me come to your bed, and why you refused my proposal. And why I had to hear the truth from Livia about what your father did, instead of hearing it from you."

"Yes."

McKenna rose on his knees, gripping the chair arms on either side of her, his face just inches from her own.

Aline had been prepared for sorrow, sympathy, repulsion . . . but she had never anticipated rage. She had not expected the gleam of primitive fury in his eyes, and the grimace of a man who had nearly been pushed beyond the limits of sanity. "What did you think I meant when I said that I loved you? Did you think I would give a damn about your scars?"

Stunned by his reaction, Aline responded with a single nod.

"My God." The blood rose higher in his face. "What if the situation were reversed, and I was the one who had been hurt? Would you have left me?"

"No!"

"Then why did you expect anything less of me?"

The explosive outburst caused her to shrink back in the chair. McKenna leaned forward, following her, his fury now edged with anguish. "*Damn* you, Aline!" He took her face between his shaking hands, his long fingers cradling her cheeks, his eyes liquid and glittering. "You're the other half of me," he said hoarsely. "How could you think that I wouldn't want you? You've put us both through hell for no reason!"

Clearly he did not understand the source of her fear. Taking hold of his broad, hard wrists, Aline gripped them tightly, her throat working.

McKenna glared at her with ardent, angry concern. "What is it?" He kept one hand at the side of her face, while using the other to smooth the hair back from her forehead.

"It was one thing to make love to me when you didn't know about my legs. But now that you know . . . you will find it difficult, perhaps even impossible . . ."

McKenna's eyes gleamed in a way that alarmed her. "You doubt my ability to make love to you?"

Hurriedly Aline pulled the gown back over her legs, infinitely relieved when they were covered once more. "My legs are horrible, McKenna."

He uttered a curse that startled her with its foulness, and gripped her head between his hands, forcing her to stare at him. His voice was savage. "For twelve years I have been in constant torment, wanting you in my arms and believing it would never be possible. I want you for a thousand reasons other than your legs, and . . . *no,* damn it, I want you for no reason at all, other than the fact that you're you. I want to shove myself deep inside you and stay for hours . . . days . . . weeks. I want morning and noon and nightfall with you. I want your tears, your smiles, your kisses . . . the smell of your hair, the taste of your skin, the touch of your breath on my face. I want to see you in the final hour of my life . . . to lie in your arms as I take my last breath." He shook his head, staring at her like a condemned man who beheld the face of his executioner. "Aline," he whispered, "do you know what hell is?"

"Yes." Her eyes overflowed. "Trying to exist with your heart living somewhere outside your body."

"No. It's knowing that you have so little faith in my love, you would have condemned me to a lifetime of agony." His face contorted suddenly. "To something worse than death."

"I'm sorry." Her voice cracked. "McKenna—"

"Not sorry enough." He pressed his wet face to hers, his mouth rubbing over her cheeks and chin in feverish, rough half kisses, as if he wanted to devour her. "Not nearly enough. You say you've had to live without your heart . . . how would you like to lose your soul as well? I've cursed every day I've had to live without you, and every night that I spent with another woman, wishing that it was you in my arms—"

"No—" she moaned.

"Wishing," he continued fiercely, "for some way to stop the memories of you from eating away at me until there was nothing left inside. I've found no peace anywhere, not even in sleep. Not even in dreams . . ." He broke off and assaulted her with hungry, shuddering kisses. The taste of his tears, his mouth, made Aline disoriented and hot, her head reeling from shocks of pleasure. McKenna seemed possessed by a passion that bordered on violence, his lungs wracked with hard breaths, his hands tightening with a force that threatened to leave bruises on her tender flesh. "By God," he said with the vehemence of a man to whom entirely too much had happened, "In the past few days I've suffered the torments of the damned, and I've had enough!"

Suddenly Aline felt herself being plucked out of her chair and lifted against his chest as if she weighed nothing. "What are you doing?" she gasped.

"Taking you to bed."

Aline squirmed and struggled in his arms. Wildly she wondered how to explain to him that this would require slow degrees of acclimation, rather than full and immediate submersion. "No, McKenna, I'm not ready for that yet! Please. I want to talk first—"

"I'm tired of talking."

"I can't," she said desperately. "I need some time. And I'm *exhausted* . . . I haven't slept properly in days, and—"

"Aline," he interrupted tersely, "the forces of heaven and hell combined couldn't stop me from making love to you right now."

That hardly left room for ambiguity. Quaking, Aline felt a renewed sweat break out on her face.

McKenna pressed his mouth to her shimmering cheek. "Don't be afraid," he whispered. "Not with me."

She couldn't help it. The habits of privacy and isolation had been established over twelve long years. And the knowledge that he would allow her no retreat, no refuge, made her heart thrash violently as McKenna carried her into the next room with purposeful strides. Reaching the bed, he lowered her to her feet, and leaned over to pull back the brocaded counterpane. As Aline stared at the smooth expanse of freshly laundered white linen, her stomach plummeted.

McKenna reached for the buttons of her gown, his fingers moving along the front placket to unfasten her bodice. After letting the loosened gown drop to the floor, McKenna grasped Aline's chemise and pulled it over her head. Goose bumps rose over her skin as she stood naked and trembling before him. It took all her will to keep from trying to cover herself, to hide the disparate parts of her body.

McKenna brushed the backs of his fingers against the slope of her breast, trailing them down to the quivering tautness of her midriff. He massaged the cool skin, then slid his arms around her with extreme care, whispering something soft and indecipherable into her tumbled hair. She took hold of the lapels of his coat, resting her face against his shirtfront. He was infinitely tender as he pulled the pins from her hair, dropping them to the carpeted floor. Soon the long locks hung loose and free, tickling her back with heavy silkiness.

Sliding his hand beneath her jaw, McKenna turned her face upward and fitted his lips to hers in a long, incendiary kiss that made her knees buckle. She was caught firmly against his body, the tips of her breasts softly abraded by the broadcloth of his coat. Her lips parted helplessly beneath his, and McKenna demanded more, creating a seal of moisture and heat and erotic suction as he drove his tongue into the warm depths of her mouth.

His hand ran possessively down her back and over the swell of her buttocks. Finding the vulnerable spot just below her spine, he brought her closer against his front until she felt the thick shape of his arousal mounded tightly behind his trousers. He nudged against her deliberately, as if to demonstrate the scalding eagerness of his flesh to join with hers. She gave a little sob against his mouth. Allowing her no time to think, McKenna reached over her buttocks and between her thighs, while one of his legs expertly nudged hers apart. He kept her locked securely against his body, while his fingers parted her intimate flesh, stroking, spreading the secret softness to leave her open and vulnerable.

Poised on his hand, Aline arched her back slightly as he slid two fingers inside her. *More,* her body demanded, undulating to take him deeper. She wanted McKenna all over her, against her, inside her, filling every empty space. More of him, and more, leaving no cruel modicum of distance between them.

McKenna adjusted her body until his shaft fit snugly against the notch between her thighs, providing a delectable friction that corresponded perfectly with the slow wriggle of his fingers. He urged her against himself, dragging her repeatedly over the rock-hard swell of his loins, caressing her outside and inside in a lazy but unfaltering rhythm. He smoothed his cheek over her hair, and rubbed his lips into the dark filaments until he had reached the sweat-dampened roots. Aline felt her body tightening, throbbing, the pleasure intensifying until she had almost reached the bright flashpoint of release. His mouth took hers again, his tongue penetrating her gently, a soul kiss that flooded her with aching bliss. Oh, yes . . . *oh yes* . . .

To her frustration, McKenna lifted his mouth from hers and withdrew his fingers just as the rocketing sensation began to crest. "Not yet," he whispered, while she shuddered wildly.

"I need you," she said, barely able to speak.

His damp fingers traced the taut line of her throat. "Yes, I know. And when I finally let you leave this bed, you're going to understand exactly how much I need *you*. You're going to know all the ways that I want you . . . and how completely you belong to me." McKenna picked her up and laid her on the bed, setting her on the pressed linen sheets. Still fully clothed, he leaned over her naked body. His dark head lowered, and she felt his lips touch her knee.

It was the last place she wanted to feel his mouth, against the ugliest of her scars. Turning cold, Aline protested and tried to roll away from him. McKenna caught her easily, grasping her hips in his hands. He pinned her to the mattress, while his mouth wandered back to her knee. "You don't have to do that," Aline said, cringing. "I would rather you didn't . . . *really*, there's no need to prove—"

"Shut up," McKenna said tenderly, continuing to kiss her legs, accepting her scars as she had never been able to do for herself. He touched her everywhere, his hands stroking and caressing her shrinking flesh. "It's all right," he murmured, reaching up to rub her taut stomach in soothing circles. "I love you. All of you." His thumb traced the small circle of her navel, and he nibbled at the delicate skin high inside her thigh. "Open for me," he whispered, and she colored violently. "Open," he urged, the velvety kisses venturing higher.

Moaning, she parted her legs, feeling the desire rise again. McKenna's mouth delved into the exposed cleft, his tongue tracing the swelling bud of her sex, then slipping lower to probe the salt-scented entrance of her body. Aline felt her body turning heavy, her senses unlocking, all awareness focused on the delicate, excruciatingly light stroking between her legs. McKenna drew back to blow lightly on her wet flesh, then worried the peak of her sex with the tip of his tongue. She clenched her fists and dug her head back, pressing herself upward, making pleading sounds in her throat. Just as she thought she could take no more of the artful torture, he slid three fingers inside her, the hard knobs of his knuckles plunging into the slick channel. She couldn't think, couldn't move, her body immersed with pleasure. His mouth tugged at her, while his entwined fingers twisted and thrust until she cried out sharply, convulsing in ecstasy.

While she lay gasping on the bed, McKenna stood and shrugged out of his coat, his gaze locked on her supine form. He undressed before her, dropping his shirt to reveal a tautly muscled torso and a chest covered with black hair. His big-framed body was clearly built for power rather than elegance. Yet there was something innately graceful about the long lines of muscle and sinew, and the heavy breadth of his shoulders. He was a man who made a woman feel safe, and at the same time, deliciously overpowered.

Joining her on the bed, McKenna slid a large hand behind her neck and settled over her, nudging her legs apart. Aline's breath caught as she absorbed the sensation of his naked body pressed all along hers . . . the hard, hair-roughened limbs, the stunning breadth of his chest, and the places where satin skin stretched over rippling muscle. McKenna grasped her right thigh, carefully adjusting her knee to keep the contracture scar from pulling.

Wonderingly she lifted a hand to the side of his face, caressing the close-shaven surface of his cheek. The moment was so tender, so sweet, that tears spilled from her eyes. "McKenna . . . I never dared to dream about this."

His thick lashes swept downward, and he pressed his forehead against hers. "I did," he said gruffly. "For thousands of nights I dreamed of making love to you. No man on earth has ever hated sunrise as much as I do." He bent to kiss her lips, her throat, the rosy tips of her breasts. Drawing on her lightly, he stroked her nipple with his tongue, and as she quivered in response, he reached down to guide himself inside her. He entered her, filling her until they were matched hip to hip. They both gasped at the moment of joining, hard flesh immersed in softness, the deep, unbearably sweet fusion of their bodies.

Aline drew her hands over McKenna's flexing back, while he slid his hands beneath her bottom, pulling her neatly into his savoring thrusts. "Don't ever doubt my love," he said raggedly.

She shuddered hungrily with each wet, hard lunge, and whispered obediently through kiss-swollen lips. "Never."

McKenna's features gleamed from mingled exertion and emotion. "Nothing in my life has ever compared to what I feel for you. You're all I want . . . all I need . . . and that will never change." He groaned harshly as the headlong rush of release began. "God . . . tell me that you know that . . . tell me . . ."

"I do," Aline whispered. "I love you." The ultimate pleasure rippled through her once more, silencing her with its power and acuity, causing her flesh to enclose his with pulsing heat.

Afterward, Aline was barely conscious as McKenna tenderly used a corner of the sheet to wipe the film of sweat and tears from her face. Cuddling against his bare shoulder, she closed her eyes. She was replete, and exhausted, and filled with wholesale relief. "I'm so tired, McKenna . . ."

"Sleep, my love," he whispered, smoothing her long hair, lifting the damp locks away from the back of her neck. "I'll be here to watch over you."

"You sleep too," she said groggily, her hand creeping to the center of his chest.

"No." McKenna smiled and pressed a soft kiss against her temple. His voice was husky with wonder. "Not when staying awake is better than anything I could find in a dream."

It was late afternoon by the time Gideon returned to his rooms at the Rutledge. He was tired, gray-faced, and irritable, wanting a drink so badly that he could hardly see straight. Instead he had downed enough coffee to float a timber barge. He had smoked too, until the smell of a cigar had started to make him nauseated. It was a novel experience, this pairing of exhaustion and overstimulation. Considering the alternative, however, he supposed he had better get used to the feeling.

Entering the residence, Gideon was immediately met by his valet, who had some rather surprising news to convey. "Sir . . . it seems that Mr. McKenna did not depart for New York as scheduled. He came *here,* as a matter of fact. Accompanied by a woman."

Gideon gave the valet a blank look. Considering the information for a long moment, he frowned inquiringly and rubbed his jaw. "Dare I ask— was it Lady Aline?"

The valet nodded at once.

"I'll be damned," Gideon said softly, his surliness replaced by a slow smile. "Are they still here?"

"Yes, Mr. Shaw."

Gideon's smile broadened into a grin as he speculated on the unexpected turn of events. "So he finally got what he wanted," he murmured. "Well, all I can say is, McKenna had better get his hindquarters back to New York soon. *Someone's* got to build the damned foundry."

"Yes, sir."

Wondering how long McKenna was going to make use of his rooms, Gideon headed to the bedroom and paused at the door, discerning that no noise came from within. Just as he turned to leave, he heard a brusque summons.

"Shaw?"

Cautiously Gideon opened the door a crack and ducked his head inside. He saw McKenna propped up on his elbow, his tanned chest and shoulders contrasting with the gleaming white linens. Little was visible of Lady Aline, save for a few locks of dark brown hair that draped over the edge of the mattress. She was snuggled in the crook of his arm, sleeping soundly as McKenna drew the bedclothes protectively over her bare shoulder.

"Missed your ship, did you?" Gideon asked mildly.

"Had to," McKenna replied. "It turns out that I was about to leave something important behind."

Gideon stared at his friend intently, struck by the difference in him. McKenna looked younger and happier than Gideon had ever seen him. Carefree, in fact, with a relaxed smile on his lips and a lock of hair tumbling over his forehead. As Lady Aline stirred against him, her sleep disrupted by the sound of their voices, McKenna bent to soothe her with a soft murmur.

In the past Gideon had seen McKenna with women in far more licentious circumstances than this. But for some reason the brilliant, unguarded tenderness of McKenna's expression seemed unspeakably intimate, and Gideon felt an unfamiliar heat creeping up his face. Damnation—he hadn't blushed since the age of twelve.

"Well," Gideon said flatly, "since you've helped yourself to the use of my rooms, it seems I'll have to find other accommodations for the night. Of course, I wouldn't think twice about putting *you* out . . . but for Lady Aline, I'll make an exception."

"Go to Marsden Terrace," McKenna suggested with a sudden gleam of mischief in his eyes. His gaze returned compulsively to Lady Aline's sleeping face, as if he found it impossible to look away from her for more than a few seconds. "Westcliff is there alone—he might welcome the company."

"Oh, splendid," Gideon replied sourly. "He and I can have a lengthy discussion about why I should stay the hell away from his youngest sister. Not that it matters, since Livia will have forgotten all about me in six months."

"I doubt it," McKenna said, and grinned. "Don't give up hope. Nothing's impossible—God knows I'm proof of that."

Épilogoue

The blustery February wind whistled against the parlor window, diverting Livia's attention from the letter in her hand. Curled in the corner of a settee with a cashmere blanket over her lap, she shivered pleasantly at the contrast of the damp, bitter winter day outside, and the cheerful warmth of the parlor. A mahogany letter box sat open beside her, one side of it filled with a neat stack of letters, and the other side stuffed with a far more ungainly pile tied with a blue ribbon. The smaller stack was from her sister Aline, whose letters from New York had been surprisingly regular, considering her notorious laxness in matters of correspondence.

The other mass of letters was from an entirely different source, all written in the same masculine scrawl. By turns playful, touching, informative and searingly intimate, these letters told the story of a man's struggle to change himself for the better. They also spoke of a love that had deepened and matured during the past months. It seemed to Livia that she had come to know a different man than the one she had met at Stony Cross, and while her attraction to the original Gideon had been impossible to resist, the former rake was turning into a man that she could trust and depend on. Reaching down to the blue ribbon, she stroked the satiny surface with her fingertip, before turning her attention back to the letter from Aline.

. . . they say the population of New York City will reach a half-million in the next two years, and I can well believe it, with for-

*eigners such as myself pouring in every day. This blend of na-
tionalities gives the city a wonderfully cosmopolitan aspect.
Everyone here seems to take a large, liberal view of matters,
and at times I have actually felt a bit provincial in my opinions.
I have finally begun to adjust to the pace of things here, and
have caught the New York mania for improving oneself. I am
learning a great many new things, and have acquired the art of
making decisions and purchases with a rapidity that will no
doubt amuse you when we meet again. As you can imagine, Mrs.
Faircloth has a firm command of the household staff, and
seems quite enamored of the markets west of Manhattanville,
where every conceivable variety of produce is available. It is
remarkable, really, that two miles away from towering eight-
story buildings, one can find rural country with an abundance
of miniature farms. I have barely begun to explore this handsomely built city, and I am pleased to say that I generally accomplish more in a week here than I did in a month back at
Stony Cross.*

*Lest I mislead you, however, I will confess that McKenna and
I do have our lazy days now and then. Yesterday we went sleigh-
ing through Washington Square, with silver bells jangling on the
horses's harnesses, and then we spent the rest of the day snuggled by the hearth. I forbade McKenna to do any work at all, and
naturally he obeyed me, as an American wife is ruler of the home
(though we cleverly give all outward appearance of authority to
the husband). I am a benevolent dictator, of course, and
McKenna seems to be quite content with the arrangement . . .*

Smiling, Livia looked up from the letter as she heard the sounds of a
carriage outside. As the parlor was conveniently situated at the front of
the manor, she had the advantage of seeing all the comings and goings at
the entrance drive. The sight of a black carriage and a team of four was
hardly unusual at Stony Cross Park. However, as Livia stared at the

horses, whose breath was blowing white from their nostrils, she felt a tug of curiosity. Marcus had said nothing about visitors arriving today—and it was too early in the day for anyone to make calls.

Standing from the settee, Livia wrapped the blanket around her shoulders and peered through the window. A footman headed for the front door, while another opened the vehicle and stood back. A tall, lean form emerged from the carriage, eschewing the use of a step and descending easily to the ground. The man was clad in a black coat and an elegant hat, beneath which a gleam of blond hair was visible.

A thrill of sudden, intense excitement stole Livia's breath away. She watched him without blinking, rapidly calculating . . . yes, it had been six months, almost to the day. But Gideon had made it clear that he wouldn't come for her unless he was certain that he could be the kind of man he felt she deserved. *And I'll come armed with honorable intentions,* he had written—*more's the pity for you.*

Now Gideon was more handsome than before, if that was possible. The lines of strain and cynicism had been smoothed away, and the dark smudges had disappeared from beneath his eyes, and he looked so vibrant and vigorous that her heart thudded wildly in response.

Although Livia didn't move or make a sound, something drew Gideon's attention to the window. He stared at her through the glass panes, seemingly riveted by the sight of her. Livia stared back at him, wrenched with exquisite longing. Oh, to be in his arms again, she thought, touching the window, her fingertips leaving watery circles in the thin glaze of frost.

A slow smile began on Gideon's face, and his blue eyes sparkled. With a shake of his head, he put his hand on his chest, as if the sight of her was more than his heart could bear.

Smiling brilliantly, Livia tilted her head to the side, gesturing to the front entrance. *Hurry!* she mouthed.

Gideon nodded at once, throwing her a glance rife with promise as he strode away from the window.

As soon as he was gone from sight, Livia tossed the blanket to the settee and found that her sister's letter was still half crumpled in the clutch of her fingers. She smoothed the sheet of paper and pressed a kiss to it. The rest of the letter could wait. "Later, Aline," she whispered. "I've got to see about my own happy ending." And laughing breathlessly, she dropped the letter into the mahogany box as she rushed from the room.